Mermicide
(An Illyria Novel)

by Mina Rose

Mermicide

Copyright © 2020 Amelia Rose Alderson

All rights reserved.

Edition 1 (B&W) – June 2020
ISBN: 9798651616145

DEDICATION

To my incredibly vivid dreams, because if they didn't show me such an HD Illyria in February 2015, I wouldn't have been inspired to write something about the place.

Mermicide

ACKNOWLEDGMENTS

I would like to extend my warmest thanks to my parents, Roger and Alison Alderson, for their time, guidance, and work to bring this book to life (but not in a necromancy way); to my favourite person – and illustrator – Daria Cohen, for her unconditional support of my creative endeavors; to my beautiful sister, Isabelle Alderson, for supporting me through my mental illness so I had the stability to create; to Amber Oakley, a past love who, despite being absent from my life for some years now, was one of the reasons I wrote Mermicide in the first place.

Oh, and special thanks that one song in the Carrie musical "I Remember How Those Boys Could Dance" – timestamp 3:00 in particular (I sure hope that's relevant in the future because who knows what will become of the future of music) – because it seriously inspired Elvira's character and backstory. Also, it's just a cool song.

.

Mermicide

Chapter One

*T*hirteen.

Elvira Tourneau frowns, her burgundy lips curling as she adjusts herself on the least broken chair in her dining room. According to the island's ever-popular (and only) newspaper, The Weekly Illyrian, thirteen citizens have lost their dreary lives over the past seven days. As usual, speculation of what happened to each person is heavily weighted in the mermaids' disfavour. She isn't surprised in the slightest.

"I swear," she begins, "there's more deaths every day. The whole damn paper will be an obituary soon." Her index finger rubs over her lower lip, a point of habit when she is bored or deep in thought and her eyes dart over each name, cataloguing them in her mind. Markus Beltran. Francis Goresky. Sabrina Serrano. Names and names of the deceased, none of which she recognises. "Somebody needs to sort out those damn mermaids. They're a plague."

Silence.

She looks up from the cheaply printed lettering and excessively grainy photographs – for the newspaper's budget is meagre, like most things in

Illyria – and casts her gaze upon her niece, Piper. She's a small and fragile little thing, shorter than average for a girl her age and very, very thin. You'd have thought she simply didn't eat. Nevertheless, she's admittedly quite pretty; Elvira is somewhat jealous of her unusually bright green eyes in particular. She's *not* jealous of her pale and perhaps even sickly-looking complexion, though. Both her face and shoulders are freckled with small brown splotches the colour of wet earth, especially over her nose, and littered with badly disguised bruises that bloom purple and black like petunias. She looks more like her father than her mother. Elvira can't be gladder of that.

"Well? Say something! Am I going to have to talk to myself? And sit up straight."

Piper clears her throat, a demure, quiet sound. She straightens up in her chair obediently with her knees pressed together, and tiredly responds, "Sorry. Yes. A plague."

"Eat your breakfast."

"I finished it."

"Fine."

There was a time when both Piper and Elvira slouched in their chairs. There was a time when they smiled and laughed and, in some instances, even sung. There was a time when mealtime conversations were entertaining and fun, when silence – let alone such *uncomfortable* silence – would have been unusual. That time, however, has long passed. Elvira knows very well that it won't be returning and doesn't want it to anyway. After all, there's no reason to be positive now. Not when people are *dead*. The world is cheerless and uninviting and in her opinion the sooner that fact is accepted the better – there's absolutely no use feigning otherwise. "You're pathetic. Where's your cousin?"

"Out…I think. At the bar."

"Idiot. You're both idiots."

"I'm sorry."

"Shut up."

Elvira diverts her attention back to the now-closed paper, staring down at the front page and its featured headline: 'Royal Surprise!'.

According to the text, a royal yacht from the far-off kingdom of Caldisa docked at Illyria's main pier on Tuesday morning. It's rumoured to contain Crown Prince Holt Davori, the only child of the nation's highly respected leaders, King Nicolai II and Queen Delilah. According to the paper he's running from an arranged marriage to Princess Isadora Petrova of Paliron. Of course, this is nothing Elvira is particularly interested in since the boy's love life (or lack thereof) is not really any of her business. She never was interested in such gossip-fuelled 'news' anyway.

"She's pulling our leg, this reporter," she states bitterly. "Oh, of course, *Valentina Victory* – embarrassingly fake name by the way – there's definitely a *prince* in Illyria. Ha! Likely story. Hey! Go 'head and look outside – tell me if you see some royal yacht."

Her eyes fall upon Piper again who gets the immediate and distinct feeling that she is about to be yelled at. She cowers involuntarily in preparation, yet no angered scorn comes her way. Instead her aunt merely takes a sip from her glass of water and nods her head in the direction of the window. "Well?" she asks. "Go look."

"Y-yes. Yes. Sorry."

The first step Piper takes towards the dining room window is hesitant, as though she doesn't particularly want to move at all. Glancing back at her aunt's callous expression speeds her up significantly; she hurries towards the glass panes and peers outside. A pronounced silence follows. Although favoured by Illyrians for its 'ideal location' within the city, the cul-de-sac of Dreracile Decks lives up to its name well. The area is indeed dreary and lacklustre at best. Unlike her childhood home located further north however, it has a particular redeeming quality – water all around. She likes the water. She loves watching the waves dance their wild ballet, highlighted by the dull yet steady sunlight shooting through the grey clouds.

As always, there's nothing but water.

"I can't see anything from here...but the main pier isn't that close to us so you'd have to go there to look and-"

"Then go look. Oh, and make yourself useful for once. Get some groceries while you're there."

Elvira rises to her feet. She is taller than Piper, significantly so, and unlike her niece – and her sister, for that matter – has far darker hair. Normally, she wears it in a bun, but today it hangs loose to just past her collarbones, thin and wispy in its straightness. There is something fiercely assertive in the firm glare of her dark, wide-set eyes and the tilt of her head, yet the suspicion of a smile plays about her mouth. It's unsettling; when she approaches Piper, the girl instinctively raises her hands and presses her palms into her soft brown hair. So afraid, so *very* afraid.

"Oh, and Piper?" she begins smoothly, placing a hand upon the girl's shoulder, "keep an eye out for Falké. If he ends up making a scene because of his drunkenness, you're to blame. You don't want to be an irresponsible cousin, do you?"

Piper isn't sure she likes being addressed by her name. It feels both too familiar *and* too condescending. Usually her aunt – her cousin too actually – refer to her as 'bait,' a derogatory nickname they came up with about three years ago. She's never really had it in her to argue against it, knowing very well that doing so would most likely result in her being hurt.

"No," she replies, stiffening under the woman's touch, "I – I don't want to be an irresponsible cousin. I'll keep an eye out for him. And I'll look for the yacht."

The words feel thin.

"Groceries," Elvira adds in reminder, almost humming in her patronising tone.

"Yes. Sorry. Yes. Groceries too. Is there a list? A shopping list you want me to take?"

"Mmmm," the woman thrums, "good girl. Smart of you. I'll write one now."

"Okay."

"Don't talk back."

"I wasn't, was I? I was just-"

"Don't talk back."

The woman removes a ripped piece of paper from the left pocket of her apron and searches through numerous drawers and cabinets for a working pen. Once she has finally found one (which takes three attempts and some cursing,) a list is created and thrust at Piper. The almost illegible scribblings are written on the back of a fishmonger's receipt for three tuna fillets. Piper studies it for a moment before moving away. "I'll, er, I'll go do this then…be back soon."

"Oh, you will be. The dishes don't do themselves you know. Besides, whether or not you find your idiotic excuse for a cousin he's going to have to come home sooner or later. I don't doubt he's going to be hungry when he does. You'll make him food, won't you?"

Piper nods in confirmation, starting towards the door. Honestly, she's glad to have a reason to leave the house, even if it's only for a short while. She can't be hurt by Elvira if she's not around her, that's for sure.

Outside, the dawn is as grey and dismal as usual. Light rain splashes against the small windowpane above the front door, and when she opens it the cool air rushes in with a few spots of precipitation. In her hurry to leave the house she doesn't bother properly tying her only pair of shoes, opting instead to pull them on half-laced. She stumbles slightly, and she can hear Elvira snigger behind her.

Chapter Two

*R*ain, rain, rain.

Piper's sure that it didn't rain so much when her father was around. She can recall the bright, sunny days spent walking down this very line of decking with him; the water moving like broken glass and the blue sky punctuated only by fluffy white clouds. Perhaps in hindsight, those days were only a dream. It's hard to dream in Illyria now.

Her father's name was Zachary and he was a marine biologist specialising in the Illyrian mermaids. He would spend countless hours studying their habits and behavioural patterns and she remembers waiting for him impatiently to return home every day just so she could hear his stories and all about what he'd found. He was, to her mother Elisa's dissatisfaction, close with the mermaids.

Very close. Maybe even too close.

One of them in particular he spoke about often, a beautiful creature with hair like 'moonbeams on a splashing spring'. It was his favourite and the one he spent the most time with, speaking of its exquisiteness on numerous occasions. But no matter how hard Piper tries, she can't recall what colour he said it was.

All mermaids have greyish skin as a base; not a dull, boring grey by any means but like shimmering stone combined with one palette from a certain range of colours. Their upper body tends to be sprinkled with light to dark spots that often overlap and their bellies, necks, chests and tails are lighter in colour and sprayed with darker spots. Often, they have a stripe on each side of their body. They are regularly compared to spotted dolphins, but more colourful – and colour is important when it comes to mermaids as it's a primary indicator of how they're likely to behave. Now, that she *does* remember.

Those with a red or orange colour palette, for example (the most common), are generally thought of as powerful group attackers who rarely stray from their fellow mermaids. Blue or violet ones on the other hand are considered to be the most intelligent and cunning, but prefer to live rather solitary existences. The other kinds – yellow and green – are unusual; unlike other mermaids they are driven by complicated emotions similar to those of a human. They tend to be seen in pairs and are the only branch of the species that her father believed could experience and understand platonic and romantic love.

She doesn't *entirely* believe that they killed him. Everybody else thinks so though, and it's what's written on his death certificate: 'Mermicide', plain and simple in black ink. It could have been anything really. Illyria is built on a rocky volcanic outcrop in a lonely, wild sea. The water is notoriously dangerous and, considering the local infrastructure's state of disrepair, with rotten decking stretching out over the water, he could have easily fallen into the waves and drowned because of a broken bridge. But oh, how the newspaper (and Valentina Victory of course, its head writer and journalist) loves to blame the ever-mysterious mermaids.

It probably is a fake name, Piper thinks. *But it's cool.*

She makes her way to the main pier in thoughtful silence, wondering what she, if she were a writer too, would choose as *her* name. The first ones that pops into her head she speaks aloud just to see how well they work with her. Simple names at first, with two syllables – Amber, Sarah, Lily. Then longer and more exotic sounding names like Valentina's – Cordelia, Genevieve, Anastasia. It's entertaining, but none of them fits.

Oh well. Piper I shall stay, she decides.

Predictably, the paths leading to the main pier are bustling with Illyrian citizens seeking a good deal. Sundays – market day – are always like this; the general shops on the pier open and close rather unpredictably and it's much more likely you'd get whatever you were looking for from a stall instead. Due to Illyria's thriving fishing community the majority of things sold there tend to be seafood and ocean-derived products. If you're looking for vegetables, it would be wiser to visit the small agricultural sector to the west. Today, there's no need for Piper to make that journey.

She glances back over her shoulder, scanning her surroundings.

The mayor's house is visible from where she is. It's by far the largest building in Illyria and despite being quite a way in the distance, looms over the others like a dark cloud.

It's odd. She recalls thinking in the past that it was

a magnificent castle-like structure, a lot less menacing and perhaps even pretty. But now, there seems to be a dark and gloomy air of austerity about it. Despite the mayor's riches – which Piper doesn't doubt he has since Illyria is a mining nation and trades in precious gemstones from kimberlite seams – it's exterior cracks with neglect and the once glossy and rich blue paint decorating the door and window shutters is peeling. Even the flag outside of the house is falling apart – it's ripped and tattered and the design in the centre (that, of course, being a mermaid surrounded by curls of water) is now faded and off-colour.

At one point there was a petition to eradicate the mermaid from the flag and replace it with a simple herring, the most common species of fish in Illyrian waters. It wasn't successful. The mermaids make Illyria what it is and the prospect of removing their image was declined by the mayor himself in consequence. And when it all comes down to it, the mayor can do as he likes. He controls everything and has for as long as Piper can remember: health, trade, law and order, defence, education, justice, aquaculture... anything. It's all managed by him.

It's difficult to like him when it's so clear that the island nation is in a sad state of decline. But then again, nobody's ever risen up to take his place. Of the three elections Piper has witnessed, there have been no candidates aside from him. The lack of opposition means he wins every time without fail, and that's just the way things are. And the way that she assumes they will continue to be;

even if the people do, quietly but desperately, want change.

In spite of the weather, there are significantly more

people at the market than usual. And much to Piper's surprise they're bundled together at the end of the pier, jostling around each other to get the best view of a very attractive boat. It *does* look royal from what she can see - glimpses of gleaming oak and gold in the gaps between bustling people.   Perhaps Miss Valentina Victory was right. Perhaps there *is* a prince in Illyria after all. But he mustn't enjoy publicity very much or surely he'd be out revelling in all this adulation.

The entire situation puzzles Piper; it makes no sense that of all people, a *prince* would visit Illyria. The area isn't really suited to relaxing getaways of any kind; it's a long way from anywhere else, the weather is dreadful, and the tourist industry isn't exactly burgeoning. Then again, nobody would think to look for a prince in such a dismal little location. If he is running away from something, perhaps that's why he's docked here. To hide.

After a moment, she moves away from the jostling crowd and continues on her way. It's all well and good standing around to stare at the boat, but her aunt would be unhappy if she didn't return soon with the shopping. The several stalls lining her path are predominantly selling fish, and fish alone. The nearest stall, covered in bloody slabs of what she *thinks* is tuna, has a smell so strong that she finds herself gagging.

She digs in her pocket for the shopping list but upon grasping it, collides with a middle-aged woman carrying a seeded baguette in one hand and a dead lobster in the other. The list is knocked from her now splayed fingers, whisked into the rainy breeze, and skips through the air before being caught by a shimmering hand amongst the crowd. With a distressed whine Piper attempts to locate the scrap of paper as the woman sighs dramatically and throws her arms in the air which causes the baguette to break in half.

"Oh for cryin' out loud!" she cries in exasperation as one half of it falls onto the grubby, soggy decking beneath her feet. "Would ya watch where you're going?! Shouldn't even be 'ere if ya can't walk without bumping into people! You're just as bad as those bleedin' mermaids, ya know. Move! Move!"

Piper doesn't move. Instead, she stares forward with wide eyes and allows the woman to simply shove her to the side and pass with a string of insults and grumbles.

There, in amongst the crowd, is one of *them*.

Like all mermaids, it is slender, exceptionally tall, and astoundingly beautiful, so much so that it seems alien. Long, starlight hair hangs in wet strands down its face, the silvery hue fading and culminating in a muted, soft periwinkle colour at the ends as though its tresses are made of the universe itself. It curls like seaweed around the fin-like protrusions from the side of its head, reminiscent of some sort of fish. Of course, Piper is well aware that mermaids are far from fish – they are aquatic mammals, sharing features similar to that of a dolphin. But a dolphin's eyes are far less menacing; this mermaid's are entirely black, sparkling like jewels and slanted in a most scheming fashion.

Piper wonders what it's thinking; if it's scheming like it appears to be. Well, perhaps – this one has pale grey-blue skin. An array of what seems to be barnacles adorns its wrists, sucking onto the skin like some sort of aquatic decoration. As Piper looks at it, she notices it is holding something in its right hand.

The list.

"They don't exactly blend in, do they?" an Illyrian mumbles as they walk past, and Piper can't help but nod in agreement. The question is clearly rhetorical, and not even directed at her, but holds a truth within it that she can't ignore. They *don't* blend in. And it's not a bad thing, not in Piper's eyes. Not a bad thing at all.

It's a shame that being seen around them is so frowned upon. It was never *really* encouraged, but in the past interspecies friendships and in some cases even relationships were (admittedly reluctantly) tolerated. But now, even making eye contact with a mermaid for too long is actively discouraged. The mayor's generally vicious police force are quick to swoop in should anybody appear to be consolidating or consorting with them. Not only that, but the mermaids themselves are generally viewed with distrust and fear by the public. They're undeniably beautiful and graceful, but they're powerful too, and the truce between them and the humans is rather uneasy.

"Ya gonna get somethin' or just stand there like yer stupid?!"

The deep voice of a fishmonger breaks into her thoughts. Standing at the stall covered in bloody tuna he watches her grumpily with a pair of sardines under one of his hands and a small, sharp knife in the other. "Buy somethin' or move on!"

"Y-yes. Yes, sorry. Erm…yeah. This please -" She reaches into her coat pocket for the list and pauses, clearing her throat awkwardly before allowing a small set of embarrassed giggles to escape her. "It's erm…it's not here, is it?" she asks, watching his eyebrows raise, "I mean…erm…in a minute. I'll – I'll be back in a minute."

He grumbles something incomprehensible which Piper deciphers as a string of curses, and then resumes filleting the sardines. She steps backwards, palms raised and facing outwards, and turns her head to look for the mermaid once again. Thankfully, it's still there. Its dark, coal-black eyes reach for hers and hold them like a vice, one in which she

finds herself instantly and entirely trapped. And then, as she stares in awe of its perfection, it begins to move. It's a small action, but speaks volumes; slowly, it raises its right hand, the other clutching the list, and gives a wide and disturbing smile as it beckons her over.

For a minute Piper isn't sure how to react to this. Her first thought is that approaching a sinister-looking mermaid isn't the best idea. After all, she isn't immune to the general sentiment that mermaids are unpredictable and dangerous creatures. But there *are* a lot of people around. Surely this one wouldn't try anything surrounded by so many humans. Right?

Plus, it has her list.

Without warning, the mermaid begins walking away and Piper's breath hitches in her throat. "Wait! I-I'm coming!" she calls into the bitter wind, and follows.

Chapter Three

The shredded silver waves fold and turn over each other in the rain. Foam as white as the crown of the mermaid's head lines each peak of liquid as it stretches upwards to the sky. Climbing, climbing, climbing to the heavens…and then dropping back down in failure. It's watching them with lips pursed and brows buckled when Piper approaches. It's as if they never did catch eyes, as if they never shared that moment of silent conversation. It's as if it's been here this whole time looking at the water and never did beckon Piper to follow.

The girl clears her throat awkwardly to gain the mermaid's attention. It works. The mermaid looks over its shoulder, and then turns around entirely to face her. Stoic and silent. Piper dons a lopsided, anxious little smile and speaks. "I - I'm Piper. You're," she stammers, her voice wavering a little, "a mermaid…right?"

She mentally berates herself the moment the words leave her lips. What an absolutely stupid question. She doesn't doubt the mermaid thinks so too, judging by the amused glint in its pitch-black eyes.

"How *observant*," it answers, the corner of its lips turning upwards into an amused – yet sinister-looking grin. "I am. And you are a human…" It moves with a slow, deliberate calmness when it leans towards Piper and tilts its hip sharply. It could slice Piper's throat on the angle of its hip. "…Right?"

"R-right. Right. Yes. Sorry that was…a dumb question."

It chuckles. Even *that* sounds like some kind of mystical, dreamlike choir.

"Mmmh…you were just nervous, don't punish yourself over it."

"Just nervous…"

"Just nervous."

"What's er – what's *your* name?"

There's a moment's silence before the mermaid proceeds to snake her arm around Piper's and starts walking. Expectedly, the girl follows quickly alongside, not wanting to break this physical link. "Wh-where are we going?" she asks once they move away from the main pier and towards the back alleys, "Just – I gotta – erm, I gotta shop for stuff. Actually, haha, speaking of that – can I have that list back?"

There's a small stairway leading down to the water. The mermaid lets go of Piper's arm once they reach it, sitting down on one of the steps. "Mmhm." It traces its fingers over the words on the list for a moment, sharp fingernails almost cutting the paper, and then raises it as if Piper will simply take it. This doesn't happen. After a few seconds of no movement, it raises its eyebrows and presses the list into the girl's warm hand.

"Astrid."

"W-what?"

"You asked my name. It's Astrid."

"Oh. So is that a girl's name, or...?"

Intrigue flickers in Astrid's expression and is dismissed just as quickly in favour of a daring, devil-may-care grin. "What makes a name a girl's name, or a boy's name?"

Piper falters. This interaction just happened – is happening now – and yet she's already replaying the minutiae of it over and over again in her head, mortified by her foolish behaviour in front of this magnificent being. Astrid is a different breed, a creature of perfection and mystery. Otherworldly, with arcane motivations and carefree immediacy. An elegantly simple yet entirely unsolvable riddle. A riddle that must think she is so stupid and ... *human* in comparison. "I – I don't know, actually. It just – well – no, I don't know. You just know that sort of thing, right? You just know. Except sometimes there's unisex names, aren't there? Boys' and girls' names, and unisex names, and – no, I don't know. I was just -"

Thankfully, the mermaid interrupts her anxious babbling and saves her from further embarrassment. "In my case, Piper, it is a girl's name," she answers with unparalleled calmness. She idly lifts her face to the sky and watches the sagging, grey clouds as they pass, rain rolling down the flawless angles of her face like glistening teardrops. And then after a moment she adds, "Although I am not sure why that is really so important."

"Me neither," Piper breathes, the sound of her voice almost lost in the constant drumming of the rain. She clears her throat, in awe of this seemingly faultless specimen. "It's a – er – it's a cool name. I'm sorry. Just I know you mermaids – you all look the same so I just didn't *know*. What you were, that is. I just didn't know. Never mind. Wh-what were you doing on land...Astrid?"

"Observing."

"Oh? Observing the people, or...?"

The mermaid curls her hands over the neat tuck of her waist and tilts her head to the side, focusing on Piper once again.

"There are three new humans in Illyria, I believe," she explains, "they have such interesting, charming little habits; thus, I felt the desire to observe them. The most fascinating one is a boy with golden curls, who that bothersome writer for The Weekly Illyrian – what's her name again? Valentina? Yes. Valentina Victory – has suggested is royalty."

Piper gulps. "A-ah! Yes, yes. I heard about that too. Have you – have you seen him, then? The boy? Do you think he's really a prince?"

"I am entertaining Valentina's suggestions. It *would* make things exciting if there was a prince in Illyria, that's for certain."

"It would...it really would. My er – my aunt thinks it's just made up, though."

"There's no doubt that the yacht belongs to somebody of high financial – and very likely social - standing. And to answer your question, yes I have seen him but not up close. Just glimpses through the porthole windows...he seems handsome enough. I shall keep watching and inform you if he exits the safety of his pretty little boat if you're interested. You seem to be."

The girl nods eagerly, impressed with how fluent of a conversation this is. Honestly, she was under the impression that mermaids barely spoke, let alone chose to partake in fluid, effortless discussion. "Y-yes! Yes, I am. I'm interested. You're – you're really good at…talking. That sounds stupid. Sorry. I just mean…er…you're not like I expected you to be."

"Hm. I'll take that as a compliment. Care to explain why you chose this outfit today?"

"What?"

"Your clothes."

"Ah, yes I know b– but it was such a sudden change of topic and- oh never mind."

Piper looks down at her thin brown overcoat and the navy-blue dress underneath, pocketing the small paper and taking a seat beside Astrid on the step. "Er…well…this dress used to be my aunt's when she was younger. She wanted me to wear it, so I did. I mean, she chose most of this 'outfit' honestly…does that make me weird? For letting her pick what I wear?"

Astrid stares. "Yes."

"Ah…well…yeah. I know most people choose what to wear by themselves…but my aunt gets *angry* if I don't let her."

"Hm."

"Sorry, I'm er…too much information. I'm giving too much information, aren't I?"

"No. What about your footwear?"

"H-huh?"

The mermaid points to the worn boots on her feet. "Did your aunt choose these too?"

"Ah, n-no, these boots are mine. I got them a while back because they were on sale…"

"I see."

"They're sorta old though. Sorta worn. But they

do the job, and I like them."

"I see."

A beat passes between them before Piper has the confidence to speak again. "I erm…like your hair," she says, "and…your…barnacles?"

Astrid follows her gaze, staring down at the crustaceans decorating her wrists. "I like them too; if I did not like them, I wouldn't have them on my skin. I would take them off."

"Ah…yes…of course. Silly me, I'm er…I'm sorry."

"Why are you sorry?"

"For er…being…annoying?"

"You are a strange human. Tell me about yourself."

"Ah! Yes! Well, er…I already said my name…er, I -"

She doesn't manage to finish her sentence before a rough voice interrupts her: "Bloody 'ell, look who it is," it starts, "Fish Bait. Illyria's lil' problem child. What ya doin' sittin' down 'ere in the back alleys, ey? Hidin' from ya auntie? I oughta tell Falké. I oughta tell ya auntie too."

Piper turns her head quickly to look at the boy from whom the question came. He stands smugly above her, on the top step with his arms crossed and feet shoulder-width apart, a pose clearly designed to display dominance. Behind him are three others, varied in height but clearly in the same age bracket. She recognises them instantly as his 'friends': Dante, Quinn, and Carmen. She knows none of their last names but *does* know they're particularly infamous in Illyria for their bad behaviour. Even when they were younger and still in school (although in a class older than Piper) they were all considered bullies and were forced to speak to the principal on several occasions after physically assaulting students. They never picked on her back then though; only recently have they taken a liking to humiliating her, Kyran in particular. She's not entirely sure why, but suspects her cousin has something to do with it. He was in their class after all, and she *thinks* Carmen is his best friend.

Piper shifts uncomfortably beside Astrid, who still hasn't turned to look at Kyran *or* his friends. She seems far more preoccupied with getting some grit out from underneath one of her nails and even when she's lightly nudged by Piper makes no comment on the situation. After a moment or so, the girl is dismayed to see her calmly slip into the water and vanish without another word. So much for moral support. Her face falls entirely. She's never really wanted to believe it, but her aunt has on numerous occasions called mermaids "empty, heartless beings" that have "no value for human lives whatsoever." Her mother also disliked them, commenting more than once on their incapacity for affection. And now, in this moment, it all seems a little more likely to be true.

"K-Kyran," she mutters, "I was just – I – er, I was just…please don't tell."

The boy lowers his voice intimidatingly. "Ya didn't answer me, kiddo. What ya doin' here? And what was that, huh? A mermaid? Whatcha' doin' hangin' with mermaids, huh?"

"I-I was…"

"You were what, Bait? Spit it out, I ain't got all day."

"I w-was just talking…to it…"

"Oooh, naughty lil girlie. Do mermaids make ya wet?"

"…What?"

The group snigger at the joke Piper doesn't quite understand.

"Why are you laughing? It-it's not funny," she comments shakily, trying desperately to appear confident and clearly failing. "It's not funny at all. L-leave me alone!"

This comment drives Kyran over the edge. "'Scuse me?!" he shouts, "ya think ya can boss me 'round, girlie? Ya ain't got no power o'er me! Not 'tall!" He approaches then, lacing his hand in Piper's wind-tousled hair, and drags her to her feet. "Ya wanna say that 'gain, Bait? I'll tell ya cousin and ya auntie how damn rude ya are!"

She groans uncomfortably, struggling weakly within his grip.

"Leave 'er be, Kyran!" Carmen exclaims from her place within the group. "Don't want no trouble with 'er aunt. She's one of them therapists, or whate'r." Dante nods in agreement, and Quinn throws his head back and groans: "I already got them on my case! Drop it, Ky."

"D'ya think I care?" Kyran retorts, "I don't give a crap 'bout Elvira. She's a fam'ly friend o' my folks. And if ya'll suddenly care 'bout ya reps, ya can beat it."

Quiet.

He shakes his head, clicking his tongue. "Ya been a bad girl," he whispers in Piper's ear, "ya gon' get in so much trouble. Ya gon' have to get treatment for this. Ya own auntie gon' beat ya."

As he rolls up the sleeves of her overcoat, he is surprised to see fresh bruises against her pale skin. Slowly, he pushes his index finger into one of the marks with a patronising grin: "Looks like she already do."

"Stop it -"

"Shame," he shrugs, "ya a pretty thing, Bait."

"Please -"

"Whats about ya give me somethin' I want, and I won't tell Elvira or Falké."

"I…don't have anything to give yo-" she begins, her voice cut off as his fist makes contact with her cheek and the hand on her arm is quickly withdrawn. The force of the punch sends her tumbling down the few steps beneath her like a rag doll. She hits the bottom one with significant force; her left arm dangles weakly in the salty water after impact, throbbing. She wonders if it's broken. Hopefully just twisted.

Kyran smiles triumphantly. He hops down the steps like an amused child, kneels beside a softly groaning Piper, and proceeds to raise his fist again. He doesn't manage to do anything further; a slender, glistening hand emerges from the water and takes hold of the girl's weak frame, dragging her into the waves. He jumps back in startled surprise, shouting "'Oly 'ell!" and earning a 'Pfff,' from Quinn.

"Wha' 'appened?!" Carmen cries, sprinting towards him. He presses his hands against the small of her back and pushes her lightly forward, down three of the steps.

"It's attackin' 'er! Do somethin', I ain't getting in no trouble for this!"

"I thought you didn't *care* about anything like

that," says Dante, now chewing idly on some bubblegum. "The kid's probably gon' die. Just leave 'er. Ain't nothin' I gon' do 'bout it, that's for sure. Them mermaids are totally deadly. Says so in the paper."

Astrid turns in the water and flexes her powerful tail. Holding the girl tightly against her shimmering body, with an ominously wide grin aimed towards Kyran, she makes a drama of bringing her hands to Piper's neck and holding them there like a collar. "What a silly boy," she remarks smoothly, leaning her cheek into Piper's wet hair, "how quickly the facade drops when you are frightened. How pathetic you look."

She raises one arm behind the brunette's trembling shoulders, secures her by the waist with the other, and sighs. "Sometimes, you humans disgust me. Poor girl. If anybody must be subjected to therapy, it is you."

"I ain't gettin' this pinned on me!" Carmen cries as the mermaid glides away with Piper.

Kyran grasps Carmen's upper arms and shakes her. "Stop acting like a bleedin' baby, Car!" he shouts angrily, hissing as if he has been stabbed. "We didn't do nothin', ya hear?! T'was all the mermaid's fault!"

"Kyran, people might 'ave seen us 'urt 'er! What if they be thinkin' we chucked 'er in the water?!"

"They won't! Shut ya damn trap!"

"I ain't goin' to no therapy with 'er aunt!"

"You ain't gonna! Nobody 'ere's gonna say a damn word to anybody 'bout what 'appened! Right, Quinn?!"

Quinn nods.

"Dante?!"

Dante nods.

Chapter Four

The moment Piper hits the water she strains to escape its cold, grasping hands, her face tilted upwards to the sky. Her struggles are futile; Astrid, her angel of death, clutches onto her with hands like anchors and forces her to remain in what she now assumes will soon be her grave. She can feel the mermaid's strong, powerful tail beneath her. Every time it slides past her legs, smooth yet somehow still like sandpaper, something frenetic and broken bounces around behind her eyes like she has trapped part of herself there and refuses to let it out again.

Astrid adjusts the girl's position in her arms. Firm. Protective. She hisses as two other mermaids, both green-coloured, approach and then leave. She moves through what feels like an entire forest of unusually tall seaweed, the wild tangle of slimy algae curling around Piper's left foot as they pass. It's then that she realises she's lost one of her shoes to the depths.

"If you keep kicking, you'll lose more than just a shoe," Astrid warns.

Piper's heart slams open as if someone has punched right through it – not with desire, admiration, or awe, but with fear. She nods, incapable of forming words out of pure terror. Finally, the mermaid pushes her onto the nearest set of stone steps in an old wharf area.

Piper couldn't be more relieved.

Astrid remains in the water, rests her arms on the bottom step, and cocks her head. "That boy is very rough," she muses, casually turning her hand to the side to observe her sharp nails again, pointed and claw-like; stronger keratin than any human's, and an iridescent black-green colour that shines enchantingly in the light. "You could have been badly hurt, you know? You humans are so fragile. I'd stay away from him in the future if I were you."

Piper coughs violently, her chest burning. Her bleeding lower lip makes it difficult to speak, but she attempts a response anyway, a simple "Okay."

"Tell me your full name," the mermaid requests.

"Piper Tourneau."

"Hm. It's a pretty name, but does not suit you."

The girl looks surprised by this comment, but that is expected; she's not used to the bluntness and raw honesty of a mermaid. "Oh right…er…well…I didn't choose my name, so…is that a normal thing for mermaids or something? To choose your own name? What's yours? Your full name?"

"Yes. We choose our names. And I already told you mine. It is Astrid."

"Just Astrid? That's it? No last name, or anything?"

"No last name, although if I really wanted one, I would use…hmm…yours."

"What? Why?"

"I just would - it sounds good. Astrid Tourneau."

"Ah, yeah…I guess it does."

Piper smiles awkwardly, wondering whether it would be possible to befriend Astrid. She's never really had a friend before, at least not one she can rely upon. In the past, when she attended primary school, she often hung around with a small group of girls that tended to exclude her from out-of-school meet-ups. Still, she went out of her way to get them all birthday gifts or help them with their homework. It is only now, when she thinks back to it, that she realises she was wholly taken advantage of.

Who cares if her first *real* friend is a mermaid? Actually, stupid question - *everybody* cares. Not only could you be arrested for appearing too close to a mermaid, but there are some very questionable 'treatment' programs in Illyria for it. And for some unfathomable reason, the mayor supports it all completely. If he didn't, he would put a stop to it.

Wouldn't he?

Then again, her aunt works in close collaboration with the Ministry of Information as a therapist, specialising in said 'treatment' programs. If they were to be eradicated from society, she'd lose her job. And Piper knows her well enough to know that she'd take her anger out on her…

She clears her throat and in a sudden flurry of confidence, asks: "Do you … perhaps … want to be friends, Astrid?"

There's a moment's silence, in which Piper finds herself becoming increasingly anxious, before the mermaid responds. "Alright, Piper Tourneau," she answers coolly, "friends."

Suddenly, Astrid pulls herself onto the steps. Her tail splits behind her, a ripping that tears so strongly through her that even Piper, sitting before her, believes she can feel a body splitting in two, a flash of pain. And then like before on the pier, she no longer has a tail at all. Two smooth, glistening legs have replaced it, feet that push her upwards so quickly Piper scurries back and onto the step above to avoid a collision.

"Astrid!"

The mermaid presses a finger to Piper's full, blood-smeared lips and then brings it to her own. For a second or two she does nothing, merely studying the crimson stain on her skin. But then – her slick tongue slides against her finger, urging it into her mouth between those sharp, serrated teeth. The action is slow, needlessly provocative, and Piper swears she can feel her soul leave her body as she watches. Astrid notices, judging by the cat-that-got-the-cream look she's wearing.

"Mmmhh," she quavers, "your blood is good. Someday you're going to have to give me more of that, *friend.*"

Piper laughs nervously. "Er…erm…sure…haha…you can have my blood or whatever."

"I wasn't asking for your permission."

Piper falls silent, her cheeks - her entire *face* - burning so much that she feels it has been wrought from flames. "I ju – just you know, was just saying," she stammers eventually, "I wasn't erm…trying to control you, or anything…you know?"

"Oh, I know. But don't worry, I'm not going to take your blood from you, Piper. I enjoy your survival; otherwise I would not have rescued you from those other humans back there. And I admire your desire to befriend me, despite knowing that it is probably a dangerous thing to do. You live dangerously, don't you?" She leans forwards, causing their chests to press together. "I like that."

"Y-you do? I mean, I erm…I'm not a confident person really, I just…aha…I just thought you looked so nice and…different…to the other mermaids. Somehow?"

Astrid looks amused by this comment. "Different?"

"Yeah…I – I don't know why, but you're…different."

"I'm the same as every other mermaid."

"But you - er - you saved me. The newspaper always says mermaids…don't *save* people, they…you know…get rid of them."

"You believe the newspaper?"

The mermaid slides upwards further, her hands gripping hard at Piper's bony hips. She kneads into them for a moment enjoying the girl's dazed and stupefied expression, and then slips away and back into the water. She looks back. "Don't believe everything you read, Piper," she says smoothly, "writers will say all sorts of things to make their stories exciting, especially that Valentina Victory. Not everything in the newspaper is necessarily true, you know?"

"I – I just – wait, are you leaving?"

Astrid nods. "Mmhm. Even in an old unused wharf like this, anybody could see us playing. I wouldn't want to get your sweet little self in trouble."

Piper sits up, dishevelled. Every part of her body tingles like ice, an uncomfortable sensation but one she knows she wants to experience again. For a moment she is unsure of what to say. As Astrid stares forwards at her with those ebony black eyes she can think of nothing more than how much she longs for them. For Astrid as a whole. Just Astrid.

Finally, she gathers her senses. "Yeah…playing."

The mermaid laughs. "You'd better be getting home, *Piper Tourneau*," she bites teasingly, "or people are going to start wondering where you are."

"I'll see you again though, right?"

"Of course. We're friends now, are we not? You'll see me again soon. Very soon."

"Oh…well…okay. Goodbye then…Astrid."

"Goodbye, Piper."

And with that, the mermaid slips below the surface and vanishes. At first, her legs kick aimlessly and weakly with little power, but after they have once again melded together and her tail is reformed, she picks up impressive power and speed. It's not long before she finds Piper's boot; nestled between clumps of kelp. It already appears to have become a micro habitat. She bats the small creatures exploring it away and takes it in her hands before continuing onwards.

A few hundred metres from Illyria she slows and looks around at the oceanic scenery. Everything is wonderfully vibrant, as it always is on rainy days. Life blossoms in many colours. In the depths, blue octopuses spin like stars as they make their way across the sand and into small crevices between algae-covered rocks. Glistening stones and shells dance across the seabed with the flow of the water, skimming over slow-moving starfish.

The bones of numerous Illyrians clutter the seabed. It's hauntingly striking, though; seaweed and kelp grow around femurs in curls, fish dance in and around skulls in a ballet of colour, and barnacles decorate broken ribs. Death can be very pretty indeed.

Swooping down to the seabed, she runs her hands over some of the bones and notices a small crab making its way across the sand beside a human spine. She catches it by its left pincer, dangles it in her hand, and throws it casually between her cold lips. Normally, she would wait a little bit before biting down in order to feel the struggle of the creature behind her lips. Today she doesn't. She shatters its body quickly, savouring the satisfying crunch. Once it's entirely consumed, she spirals up towards the surface where the rain continues to fall upon the waves. Her lungs fill with the familiar scent of washed-up seaweed, salt crystals, and decay as she sniffs the briny air.

Illyria always smells the same.

Some things just never change.

CHAPTER FIVE

"Well, look what the tide dragged in," Elvira sneers as a soaking wet Piper stumbles through the front door, "you took *hours*. The dishes from breakfast are still not washed, there's no food in this damn house, and I've had three – yes, *three* – people come here, to my house, to tell me that you've been seen messing with a mermaid. Care to explain yourself, Bait?!"

Piper shuffles her feet awkwardly, closing the door behind her and walking into the hallway. She feels like the ghost of a drowned sailor; her clothes are wet and dishevelled, her hair is thick with salt. The floor creaks with each step as if she is haunting this miserable, anguished house. Her left foot is bare; the floor is cold underneath it.

"I'm...er...sorry."

"You're sorry."

"Yes...?"

"That's it. You're sorry."

"Am I supposed to say something else?"

Elvira narrows her eyes, and the girl silences herself. She lets the quiet sink into her with all the weight of an angry, disapproving guardian, and clasps her hands together behind her back to hide the fact that they are shaking.

At first, there is no response. Her aunt simply stares at her with her finger rubbing over her lower lip, and for a moment it looks like she is actually worried about her. The tense silence doesn't last. Elvira opens her eyes wide, throws her head back, and laughs. *"Am I supposed to say something else?"* she exclaims mockingly.

Piper's jaw stiffens as she takes half a step back in fear. "I didn't mean to mess up," she whispers, "I got distracted! The mermaid, she was -"

Elvira's lips clamp shut. "So there *was* a mermaid," she cuts in, her words far too pronounced to be anything but condescending. "And here I thought you knew how stupid it is – how utterly *brainless* it is – to get involved with those little vermin beasts. Did you learn nothing from your foolish father's death? Or, perhaps, your wonderful mother's? Nothing at all? Tell me about your mermaid, Bait. Tell me what exactly you were doing speaking to it."

Piper shrinks back even more, her voice softening in fear. "I…just…erm…it - it was charming me," she lies, "it was charming me and I was under its spell, I didn't want to go over to it and talk to it…but…it happened! And I barely escaped alive! You can see I'm wet – it dragged me into the water! And – and I lost a shoe! In the water!"

Thankfully, Elvira seems to believe this. She sighs, leaning her cheek upon her hand . "I am not surprised, my darling," she states, "it is so very difficult to keep a level head when in the presence of one of those disgusting creatures and their asinine songs. See, this is why we use earplugs - so we don't get caught up in listening to those dreadful mermaids. It's how they get you, you know. With the *singing*."

She leans forward slightly, as though she is divulging a secret. "They lure sensible, good people into making very insensible, bad choices. Do you want to make bad choices, Bait?"

The paradigm is something Piper has heard numerous times. Hearing it explained like this as if it *needs* explaining again is a rather chastening, shameful experience. Still, a wave of relief rushes into her chest as Elvira talks. The trouble she could have been in, if she had not thought so fast… "No, auntie, of course not."

"Am I to assume that this little…incident was only a momentary lapse in your judgement, Bait?"

"Yes, yes. Of course."

"Good girl. So," she dips her hand elegantly, "put the groceries away, and then go to the bathroom and wash yourself. You look a mess. Consider this a lesson learned, Bait."

Piper bows her head. Somehow, beneath all the discomfort of her aunt's disappointment in her, she is glad. She's not being severely punished and has earned herself nothing more than a light scolding. That in itself, is something to be happy about. She turns to pick up the bags of fish and such that she got from the market, and cringes.

Oh.

Oh no.

Instead of the shopping bags she expects to see at her feet, all that covers the floor is a small puddle of water formed from her dripping clothes. *She didn't buy anything.* Astrid grabbed her list when she dropped it, and she never went back to the market once she'd retrieved it.

Elvira prowls over to her, her gaze vivid and searing. "Let me guess," she starts, watching as Piper's heels shift against the floor as if she wants to back away but is too afraid, "you were too distracted by little miss mermaid to buy anything I asked you to? I suppose you didn't take the time out of your *busy schedule* to look for Falké, either?"

"I-I Just! I was going to but – but erm – no, I can go get it now and look for him on the way! I can go…er…run! And get it. I'll go run and get it now! And see if Falké is around!" Her voice is wavering. She knows she's in trouble. She knows she's going to get hurt. She's cowering against the inevitability of it all, waiting for her punishment. Any moment…any second…

"Aww," Elvira says, somehow finding humour in the situation, "it looks like you're scared of me, Bait. Are you scared of me?"

The girl swallows dryly as she tries to form a response. Her words come out in a jumble of mixed phrases. This is not going well. "N-no. Scared. Not. I'm er…scared. Not scared. Not scared of you."

"You know how I feel about liars, Bait. Tell me how I feel about liars."

"You…don't like them."

"Wrong. I *hate* them. Did you see a yacht then, or not?"

"What?"

"Did you see a yacht at the main pier or did the concept of looking for it similarly slip your mind?"

"I…no…no, I mean yes! Yes, there was a yacht there. It did look royal…it was really elegant."

"And did you see a prince?"

"I…er…I wasn't close enough…there were a lot of people bundling to see it so I stayed back. I'm sorry."

With a sigh, Elvira announces her next statement as if it is the biggest inconvenience in the world: "I'm just going to have to punish you for all of this stupidity, aren't I?"

Piper darts backwards frantically before her aunt grasps for her, dragging her back. She knows it is coming. She knows, she knows, and yet it doesn't make it any easier when Elvira is close to her, her hands clasping at mounds of brunette hair. A thin and wounded noise escapes Piper's throat.

"Pathetic, you are," Elvira states, kneeling down beside her. She runs her hands down Piper's back, rubbing it comfortingly, and the girl moans in pain. "Does your back hurt, dear?" she questions, "poor you. Why don't you cry for me? Show me how much it really hurts. You know I like it when you cry."

Piper shakes her head. Mistake.

Every inch of her feels stiff and frail as she is repeatedly hit until the tears come. Until Elvira is satisfied. "The things I have to do," she comments casually, "to keep you in line. If you weren't such a bad girl, this sort of thing wouldn't have to happen, would it?"

"I'm sorry," her niece repeats endlessly. "I'm sorry. I'm sorry. I'm sorry."

CHAPTER SIX

Midnight.

Piper stares out of her open bedroom window, her breath turning to vapour in the bitter air. Night in Illyria is always cold. The thin film of tears on her cheeks feels as if it will freeze any moment, so she rubs her face with the back of her hand to prevent herself from becoming a human ice sculpture. She already feels like one, honestly - every part of her wants to break off in shards and shatter.

She's never truly deserved the abuse she's been subjected to, and yet believes she has. Not only that, but she's now convinced of her apparent stupidity, her self-hatred growing with every passing minute. That's the problem with her aunt; she is a master manipulator. It's her *job* to change people's minds, to mess about with their heads and alter what they think. Nobody subjected to her cruelty stands a chance, really.

Suddenly, a sound. Her name.

"Piper."

Again.

"Piper."

Quickly, she inspects the surroundings. The dusty

lamplights illuminating the decking outside of her house cast shadows of their own, but the most prominent one is that of a person. It belongs to a tall, slender figure whom Piper recognises instantly.

"Astrid?" she calls softly, her voice breaking a little.

No reply.

She clears her throat, turns away, and heads to the door of her bedroom. *How did Astrid find me so fast? Did she follow me back home?*

The house is silent, unnervingly so. Piper's door creaks as it's opened, and she automatically winces and freezes on the spot. Luckily, the sound doesn't appear to have woken her aunt so she continues forwards and heads to the staircase.

Due to costly electricity bills, Elvira refuses to keep any lights on in the house at night. It's for this reason that the two desk lamps sitting on their small tables in the upstairs hallway are switched off, and Piper is left to navigate in the dark. All curtains have been drawn except for one, but the glass is so covered in grime that the gentle moonlight struggles to penetrate through. She makes a mental note to clean it tomorrow as she passes.

Upon tiptoeing down the hallway, rushing (as quietly as possible, of course) down the stairs, and opening the front door, she is greeted with nothing but the soft lull of waves.

"Astrid?"

"Yes?"

The mermaid steps out from the blackness, her head tilted and hair flowing in the cold wind. In her hand is the boot, laces undone and tangled. It looks so ugly compared to her; she is unmistakably the most beautiful thing Piper has ever seen. Every angle of her body – the slope of her cheeks, the jut of her hips, her slender legs – is shrouded by starlight, glistening like crushed diamonds. Piper's jaw stiffens. She shouldn't be looking at her like this, like she is an expensive piece of artwork. It's wrong. It's wrong.

It's…so right.

"Astrid," she begins, tugging at her own hands, "I'm r-really pleased to see you again. I – er, I missed you. Does that - does that sound weird? I hope it doesn't. I just – I haven't had a f-friend like you before. I haven't had a friend at all, really…but…you understand, right?"

Astrid holds her gaze as the girl trips and stumbles over her words. When Piper finally stops talking, she peers past her into the house and inquires, "Can I come in?"

Piper steps back to the side and nods rapidly. "Yeah, just…er…we have to be really quiet. My aunt gets mad if I'm too noisy at night."

Astrid nods. "Alright."

She steps inside, glances around, and closes the door quietly behind her as if she had lived in the Tourneau residence her entire life. Every step looks smooth and calculated, strangely precise, and as she heads down the corridor and towards the stairs Piper realises in shock that she seems to know exactly where she's going. Not only that, but she's moving confidently…*in the dark.*

"H-hey," Piper whispers, "you know where to go?"

The mermaid pauses, looking over her shoulder. "You were looking down at me from your bedroom window were you not?" she asks, "I'm heading in that direction."

Piper nods and follows after her, telling herself 'that makes sense.'

The moment the two enter the bedroom, Astrid's confident stride is abandoned and replaced by a slow, melancholic wander. Her eyes, now glassy as if peering into a memory, survey the surroundings. "You have a nice room," she states wistfully, brushing her fingers along the wallpaper. She places the boot down on the floor, takes a seat on the edge of the bed, and laces her fingers together at her thighs.

"It used to be my father's study. There's still quite a bit of stuff that belonged to him in here…like, his books and such. You know, this house belonged to my parents, not my aunt. She just moved in here after they…yeah. She just moved in here with my cousin and stuff."

"I see."

"How did you know where I live?"

The mermaid pauses for a moment before answering. "I followed you."

"Oh right."

Piper looks down at the floor as she hears the sound of Astrid's skin brushing against the bed. She's getting up; her light footsteps draw increasingly closer and suddenly slender fingers are dancing across her jaw, tilting her gaze upwards. The mermaid gazes upon her with a look that she very much feels is pity. Cold hands soothe the bruise along her jawline. "You've been hurt again," she muses. "Worse this time. Your aunt?"

The girl releases the breath she's been holding in a single, shuddering rush. "Yeah," she admits, "but it was my fault. I…didn't do everything she asked."

"No. It was not your fault."

"But -"

"It was not your fault."

"But I -"

Astrid cups her face with her hands, and then allows them to slowly retreat back to her sides. "Repeat after me: *It was not my fault.*"

"It…was not my fault…"

"Good. Next time she hurts you, think of me."

"Think of – think of you? W-why though? For comfort…?"

Piper stares into her new friend's eyes, their breaths mingling as cold onyx meets bewildered emerald. She gulps dryly. "Y-your eyes," she stutters.

"What about them?"

"They're beautiful."

"Complimenting a mermaid," Astrid observes. "What a dangerous thing to do. If your aunt were to find out…"

Piper gulps, shrinking in on herself. She shouldn't be doing this. She *knows* she shouldn't be doing this. Somewhere deep down there is a voice inside her, begging her to abandon this friendship. But it's already faint, and her desire for Astrid overrides it until it's nothing but a whisper she can ignore.

"I'd be in trouble if she found out," she murmurs, "so much trouble… I'm told – I'm told all the time that you mermaids…you're bad."

"Oh?"

"Y-yes…bad…very bad."

"Ahauh. Well, just being told something doesn't make it true. Why don't you find out for yourself whether I am bad or not? Seeing, or rather *experiencing* is believing, Piper."

The mermaid plucks at the little bow on Piper's nightdress collar and leans in shamelessly close to study the girl's every plane and angle. The inquisitiveness does not go unnoticed and Piper blushes a violent crimson before slipping sideways to escape the source of the newly formed frustration inside of her. "You er...like this nightdress?" she asks softly, "my aunt doesn't let me see other people while wearing this. It shows the bruises and things, that's why. She likes me to cover them up so people don't ask questions. Something like that."

"I like the nightdress," the mermaid confirms. She runs her hand down Piper's bare arms, feeling the goosebumps. "Are you not cold, wearing this? You have the window open."

Cold? Piper shakes her head. If anything, she's much too hot right now. She shouldn't be – she really shouldn't be – and she is well aware of that, but there is something about Astrid that she simply cannot overlook. Most importantly, there is something about Astrid that she *wants*. That she *needs*. She leans a little closer to her.

Astrid arches an eyebrow, noticing the subtle movement. She appears to consider a shunted impulse for a moment or so, but then relaxes and moves closer with a soft coo of: "Something you want?"

It doesn't work. Piper tenses up when she realises the quickly diminishing space between them, and the closing gap becomes stagnant. "I should..." she begins, her voice diffident, "I should go to sleep...soon..."

The mermaid moves away, seemingly unaffected by this decision. It's as if she knows that Piper will come to her in time, as every human she has ever desired has done. She moves towards the bed once more, pulls the covers back, and pats the mattress softly. "Get in, then."

Piper frowns, secretly disappointed in herself and regretful of her decision to retreat. She can almost hear her cousin calling her pathetic for rejecting whatever advances she was being offered. Whatever advances she *herself* was trying to offer, come to think of it. Still, she obeys the awaiting Astrid, climbing under the sheets with a quiet "I'm sorry. Goodnight…Astrid."

"Goodnight. Sleep well."

"Astrid?"

"Yes?"

"How old are you?"

The mermaid halts on her way out of the room, looking over her shoulder at the brunette. "I stopped counting after 570."

And with that, she leaves. Piper listens to the gentle rhythm of her footsteps as she moves downstairs, to the soft click as the front door is closed, and to the splash that follows this all from outside her still open window.

Sighing, she turns on her side and blows out the candle on her nightstand.

CHAPTER SEVEN

"Baiiit. Wake up, darlingggg. Baiiit. Bait. Wake the hell up. *Bait.*"

Piper stirs at the sound of Elvira's persistent words, groaning under sore muscles. She's reluctant to open her eyes initially, convinced for a moment that last night was all some kind of wonderful, frightening dream and doing so will make it vanish from her mind forever. A mermaid right in front of her. So close in fact, that she could feel her cool breath on her skin. Reach out and touch her.

"*Bait!*"

When she finally opens her eyes her vision swims before her. It fades in and out for a few moments, running like watercolours, and it's only after blinking a few times that things become clear. The room is dim, the curtains still closed. The candle on her nightstand has not been relit since she extinguished the flame last night, but still leaves a pleasant aroma of 'ocean breeze', a scent that is definitely not reminiscent of the *real* ocean breeze outside.

She notices her aunt and bolts upright.

Elvira scoffs, turning away from her and adjusting her gloves. As usual, she's clothed entirely in black; although her sister has been deceased for several years now, she remains in mourning. The outfit she wears today however is one that Piper recognises as the uniform for the Health Centre. The fitted twill blouse has a small cape attached, fastened in the front with double-breasted brass buttons. It matches the skirt perfectly in a set. She must be heading to work soon.

"Why is it so cold in here?" she sneers, directing her gaze to the window. "You left the damn window open, you bleedin' useless child! And get up, I'm starving. Is your alarm clock broken?! It's nine. *Nine*. I have been up since *eight-thirty* waiting for breakfast. I have to deal with a patient in just over an hour, you know! But of course you wouldn't care about that, would you? You only care about yourself."

"I'm sorry."

"Is that all you ever say, Bait? *I'm sorry, I'm sorry*. Pathetic."

Piper crumples like a wilting flower underneath her sheets. Her fear is obvious, yet she tries to disguise it as exhaustion and pulls the blankets up to her chin once more. "I'm just so tired," she lies. "I think – I think I might be getting sick…or something."

"You're not getting sick," comes the woman, rolling her eyes as she glances outside to watch a couple kissing behind the top window of the house parallel to hers. Jealous, she clears her throat and turns away. "You're *fine*. Get up. Wretched, you are."

A stern look is all it takes; the girl rises from the bed with a pitiful moan. "Get dressed and make breakfast. Maybe then I'll forgive you. I want you to wear that brown underbust pinafore dress. Actually no. The olive coloured one. The olive underbust pinafore dress, and the black collared blouse with the long sleeves."

"Okay," Piper agrees, "can I-"

"No."

"Okay."

"Oh, and some stockings. Black stockings. You need more black."

Piper sighs. When her mother and father were around, she wore whatever she wanted. Colourful dresses, skirts and short-sleeved blouses were all options, and not one aspect of her personal 'style' was dictated by Elvira. She misses those days. Days when everything was much less constricting, much more vibrant. Days when the harshest punishment she faced for what her parents classified as 'bad behaviour' was simply being told to go to her room and think about what she'd done.

Things are so different now.

Elvira squints suspiciously as she watches Piper sorting through her drawers, her mind obviously elsewhere. "You *are* going to wear what I told you to?" she queries, and the girl turns to her, holding up a pair of black stockings.

"Of course, auntie."

"Good. Hurry up. I'm starving."

She exits the room yet her harsh words and unspoken hatred linger in the air. Piper wishes she could ignore it, she really does, but it's overwhelming. Before she realises what's happening, a lump has formed in her throat and swallowing back the oncoming tears becomes painful. But suddenly:

Next time she hurts you, think of me.

The words burn through her, leaving hazy longing

in their wake. She can't explain why this memory of Astrid is affecting her so. Why her heart suddenly feels heavy and her face feels warm. It isn't a pleasant warmth either; a sickly, feverish heat crawls over her like she's been infected by a pathogen. Unexpectedly, all at once, she is too aware of herself. Her dry mouth. Her numb lips. The salty sting of tears in her eyes. Astrid's touch last night…

Astrid.

What is it about Astrid?

She shakes her head quickly, pulling on the clothes her aunt has approved for her to wear. She decides then and there that she cannot focus so much on the mermaid, for she has far more important things to worry about. Things like breakfast.

It's not too long before she's dressed and downstairs. Two quick bowls of porridge are made, topped with various nuts and a meagre spoonful of honey which had begun to crystallise. Elvira doesn't complain about the food, most likely out of hunger, and neither does she. At one point, the general creaking and settling of the house sounds like her cousin emerging from his room and heading downstairs, but luckily nothing comes of it.

Falké used to join the rest of the family for breakfast, but now tends to be extremely hungover most mornings. He doesn't bother getting out of bed early enough for such a meal, and sometimes doesn't bother coming home at all after a night out. Piper worries about him, honestly. Occasionally, when he's home and leaves his bedroom door open, she catches a glimpse of him sitting on the end of his bed, his head in his hands. His shoulders trembling. Muffled weeping, or quiet cursing.

She wonders what's wrong, but dares not ask. The last time she did it went badly – instead of being comforted by her he yelled at her to leave him alone. She hasn't attempted to talk to him about his feelings again since, out of fear that the same thing will happen.

"So, there probably *is* a prince in Illyria after all." Elvira's gaze on Piper is calm, implacable, and without an ounce of care. She places her spoon down in the now empty bowl before her, runs her tongue over her teeth, and leans forwards. "You are to stay away from that ship from now on. I'm not having you embarrass me in front of royalty."

"Yes, auntie."

"And you'll go get groceries – and bring them back this time – after you finish eating."

"Yes, auntie."

"And I need you to stop by the mayor's place at twelve and drop off some notes he requested. You'll do that for me, won't you?"

Piper looks up at her. "Yes, of course. But - erm - about the groceries?"

"What about them? You don't need me to write another list, do you? Or is the other one all soggy from when you got thrown in the sea by that mermaid or whatnot?"

"Er…well, yes…but…er…I don't have any money left…for the groceries."

Elvira simply stares at her for a few seconds, processing this information. The creases in her forehead seem deeper than they'd been when she was upstairs; it isn't hard to tell she's displeased. Unexpectedly, however, she smiles. It is a wicked smile, one that could put even the most confident of people on edge.

"Then, my dear little Bait…go make some," she croons, leaning back in her chair as Piper tries her very hardest to endow herself with vacancy. She doesn't want to look so terribly uncomfortable, but it's out of her control and her aunt is aware of that. The thing is, she could be face-to-face with a predatory, most likely *very* dangerous creature like an Illyrian mermaid, probably staring death straight in its cold black eyes…and feel nowhere near as fearful as she does when confronted with Elvira. The woman's warped sense of care, jeering looks, punishing hands, and looming stature terrify her without a doubt. She would rather be with Astrid. She would rather be under the sea.

"I could…fish. Sell some fish? That I catch?"

Elvira stands. The pats she places upon Piper's cheek are condescending at best, and Piper restrains a flinch as she receives them. "Good girl. Hmm…and let me think…I was going to give you something else."

She hums to herself, tapping a finger to the side of her forehead, and then reaches into the pocket of her skirt to retrieve some earplugs. "There. Don't want you getting into another 'mermaid problem' do we, Bait?"

"No…no we don't. Thank you, auntie."

"I hope you're good at fishing," she scoffs as she walks past Piper towards the kitchen doorway, "because you're going to have to catch a lot of fish very, very fast to make even *some* profit this morning…and you know how upset I'll be if you don't get me my groceries."

Piper gulps, pocketing the earplugs.

Elvira leaves.

CHAPTER EIGHT

There's going to be a storm tonight, Piper can tell.

The sun is a dull ache behind a miserable veil of grey, the sky shifting between gentle gleams and dismal darkness. It's drizzling with rain, as usual, but she's thankful for that. At least it's not a heavy downpour just yet – she'd rather be a little wet than absolutely soaking.

Under normal circumstances, she'd fish at the dock by the back entrance of her house. Today, however, she considers a new factor: Astrid. If *she's* around, it would be unwise of her to stay here and risk her aunt seeing them together. Ever since her sister's death, Elvira has despised the mermaids more than ever. She'd lose her mind.

"Not here," Piper mumbles aloud to herself. She stops for only a second, bucket and fishing rod in hand, and then continues walking.

The restless sea moves between foam and water, dark and light, twisting and swirling with white-crested waves. It would be easy to mistake them for the sharp fin of a mermaid or similarly great fish, but Piper knows better than to do that. She's been watching the water for her entire life, longing to be a part of it as the mermaids are – as Astrid is. The things her father told her about the depths have always enthralled her, from the spiny spider crabs among rocks and seaweed to the large, yet harmless rhizostoma jellyfish.

After a short walk around the back alleys of Dreracile Decks, she decides on a shadowed and secluded pier-like path in-between two rows of dilapidated houses. Although there are several mooring posts only two boats are docked, both of which look very much empty and/or abandoned. It's ideal – not only will nobody disturb her here but fish – especially mackerel and pouting – tend to go where the water is calm, where they're safe from predators. Well, where they *think* they're safe, at least.

Her father taught her that. It was rare, but when he wasn't busy studying the mermaids, he took her out with him on his little boat to fish. She never got bored waiting for a bite, and when it did come it was exciting. Every creature they caught was thrown back into the water to continue living its days. At the time, she thought that was merciful – now, she realises the blood of the animal most definitely attracted larger ones…possibly even mermaids. Hungry mermaids.

She places her fishing rod and bucket down. Still no sign of Astrid.

Mermaid song in the distance captures her attention, and she quickly dips her hands in her pockets to find the earplugs. Really, she doesn't want to have to use them but there is a general belief in Illyria that given the opportunity, the mermaids will attack and kill humans. The singing, as beautiful as it is, is thought to serve as a fair warning for danger to come. And not every mermaid is bound to be as friendly as Astrid…

Curling her fingers around the earplugs, she brings them into the light and stuffs them hastily into place. The gentle crashing of waves, seagull calls, and soft singing are abruptly subdued and replaced with an unsettling – yet necessary – quiet.

She baits the end of the fishing line with a lure from the bucket, casts it into the water, and waits. Her arms are aching and sore. With any luck, she won't be out here in the rain for too long and will catch a reasonable amount of fish to sell. That, or she's going to have to find a different form of money-making…fast. If her father's boat was still accessible, she could have sailed a little out to sea. The larger fish are there; they sell for higher prices at the market and are much more valued by fishmongers. Sadly, however, the vessel is no longer around. It lies on the seabed in splinters, jutting from the sand with its mast and sail tilted like misshapen limbs. It belongs to the ocean now and, unbeknownst to Piper, Astrid too. She can picture it laying there in the dark, cold water, black sea urchins and spiny starfish plastered onto the rotting wood on its prow. And somewhere in that boat, or near to it, fish fluttering around the bones of her lost parent.

A morbid thought. She regrets thinking it almost instantly.

She's being watched.

Astrid presses her palms into the cold, limpet-covered rock it sits on. It's her favourite rock out of the many protruding from the waters around Illyria, shielded from the wind by two others in front. Two brown-striped dog whelks begin to cross over her tail but she makes no effort to remove them. Instead, her attention is held firmly by Piper, who fishes in the distance.

Piper's skin is ridiculously pale, so much so that Astrid finds it comparable to cuttlefish bone. The bruises on it are more obvious because of this, but today she is wearing black tights to hide the worst of them. Her hair, like yesterday, is messy. It blows around her face like strands of seagrass, unkempt and wet in the rain. She is nothing like her father, and yet they are practically the same.

Astrid sinks beneath the waves, her eyes darting across each stretch of dull, grey-blue water around her. It takes her a moment to recognise the lure Piper is using as bait, but once her gaze is locked onto it, she can see nothing but its vivid green colour. Such a design would fool no mermaid, and not many fish either. Then again, a lot of Illyria's other fish are remarkably stupid. If Piper sticks it out on the deck for a couple of hours, perhaps she might catch one.

Perhaps.

She circles the lure for a minute or so before positioning herself vertically, and with casual grace raises her hand and presses down on it with an index finger. Sure enough, it moves away. She laughs; she likes this game. Curling her finger carefully around the lure and avoiding the hook, she applies a consistently light and steady pressure, then waits until it ascends to the surface.

One quick push and from her waist downwards a jagged line forms, renting her apart. Her beautiful, strong tail is replaced with feet, calves, thighs. Every movement is like glass for a second or two; sharp-edged, then the feeling is gone. All these years of switching forms and still the transformation is uncomfortable. Still, it's necessary.

Soon enough, she's reached the path. Piper notices her as soon as she starts climbing up onto it, and grabs her arms to assist her. The contact is broken once Astrid's knees are against solid ground. She stands up slowly, holding the lure, and runs the tip of an index finger across the hook. "I like these."

Piper removes her earplugs, and stuffs them into her overcoat pocket. "The hook?"

"Yes. I would like to pierce the tip of my tail fins with some. Would you like to help me do so? Would you gather me some hooks, so I may use them to decorate myself? I am rather bored of my earrings."

Tentatively, Piper moves her hand upwards with the intention of looking at the earrings. Astrid's hair is in the way, and will need to be moved. Then again, Piper is well aware that a mermaid's hair is not *hair* per se, but barbels like that found on certain types of fish. Whisker-like sensory organs often used to search for food in dark or murky conditions. Sometimes they even house taste buds... not in a mermaid's case though. At least, she hopes not. That would be weird, considering she is about to touch them if Astrid allows her -

"Can I?" she mutters, pausing.

The mermaid chuckles and urges her softly to continue with a smooth: "Mmhm. Go on."

The silvery wet strands (*surprisingly soft for hair that isn't proper hair,* Piper thinks) are pushed aside and then – as expected – Piper can see them; the skeletons of two very small fish – perhaps anchovies – garnish what seems to be Astrid's earlobes, dangling from fishing hooks and held together with fishing wire. Makeshift earrings, mermaid style.

Piper's eyes widen in fascination. Do all mermaids have such interesting methods of decorating themselves, or only Astrid? First the wrist barnacles, now this. And for what? To express creativity or individuality? To signify position amongst other mermaids? Do mermaids even *have* a hierarchy or class system as humans do? She has so many questions, and yet she asks none of them out of fear of looking stupid.

"Sure," she agrees finally, and is rewarded with yet another of Astrid's sharp grins. "I'll help you with that…but er…I gotta catch fish first. And stuff."

"You *want* to catch fish?" Astrid goads, "I thought you were just swinging that lure about for the fun of it. Why didn't you say you actually wanted to get something?"

Piper turns away, her back to Astrid. She places the fishing rod down and crosses her arms, pouting. "You're being mean to me," she mumbles childishly.

"Oh, please. Piper…"

Without warning, smooth, cold arms make their way around the girl's waist and hold her tightly. The embrace is comforting at first, and she doesn't object to it, but the minute Astrid's fingers wander down to the hem of her dress and begin tugging at her tights she pulls away. "Astrid!" she cries angrily.

The mermaid retreats, tilting her head. "Yes?"

"You can't just do that!"

"Nobody can see. This is a very…secluded place."

"That's not the point!"

"It's not?"

"No…"

"Oh, Okay. I apologise. I'll get you fish."

And with that, Astrid dives into the water and

disappears.

Minutes pass.

Guilt washes over Piper's frame like a tidal surge. She stares at the water expectantly for a minute or so, becoming increasingly stressed and then buries her face in her hands. What a headache it is to keep up a friendship with a mermaid...perhaps she's not cut out for it after all. The 'I'll get you fish' thing was clearly an excuse to leave...Astrid isn't coming back. She'll never come back.

"Here."

She came back.

The low timbre of her voice is an instant comfort. "Astrid," Piper breathes, frail-hearted. She steps forward as the mermaid climbs onto the deck to greet her once again, parting the wet strands of hair now clinging to her face. In her clawed hands are several large fish – mostly pollock, as far as Piper can tell – with distinct gnawing in their sides. Other than that, they are in perfect condition.

Something shifts in Piper's chest. She gasps quietly, suddenly realising just how powerful – and more importantly, how dangerous – Astrid is. "Woah..." she breathes, watching as each fish is dropped into the pail, scales stained crimson. "You're *really* good at fishing."

Astrid nods in agreement. "Oh, I know - all of us are. Mermaids, I mean. Anyway, now you have fish. You can eat well for a significant while an-"

"Eat?" Piper interrupts, "no, no. I gotta sell them. My aunt, she...er...yeah. She wants me to make some money. If I don't, she'll kill me."

"Seriously? I got you all these fish just so you could sell them?"

"Yeah, I guess."

The mermaid hisses, a sound that puts Piper instantly on edge. She jumps back violently in surprise, hands splayed out before her defensively. Astrid merely frowns, irritated, and picks at the barnacles on her wrists. "If you wanted money, I could have given you some had you bothered to ask. I have an abundance of it."

"Wha-how? You don't even use money, do you?! Do mermaids use our currency?"

Astrid studies her nails. "No," she answers plainly, "but humans do. And when humans die, they leave coins in their pockets and such. I have built up quite a collection over time. I have modern currency, and…ancient currency. From many years ago. You could probably sell it for a high price to a collector. Now here's a suggestion, Piper: keep the fish to eat and take some money from me. Elvira won't be mad – she won't even know. It can be *our little secret*."

Piper pauses.

Astrid knows her aunt's name? She can't remember ever telling her. In her head, soft alarm bells sound and hazy distrust nags. "How do you…?" she begins, caution creeping into her voice, "how do you know my aunt's name?"

"You told me," comes Astrid's immediate response.

For an instant, it's as if another mermaid stands before her; distant, calculating, and impossibly cold. Then, suddenly, Astrid's expression brightens again and the impression splinters and falls away. "You remember telling me," she adds.

The girl picks at her lower lip, thinking carefully. Yes – yes, she remembers. She's not sure when, or how, even - but she definitely remembers telling her.

"Ah, yes...I *do* remember that. Sorry. For a minute I – I don't know. I just forgot. Well, thank you Astrid, I really appreciate it. Maybe my aunt won't kill me after all."

"Well, I doubt she would have *literally* killed you anyway, even if she is rather psychotic," Astrid notes matter-of-factly, "perhaps just hurt you. Humans do not tend to kill each other...the mayor's police force is much too powerful. Crime rates are surprisingly low here actually, aren't they? Hm. One thing that man has done right. They used to be appalling back in the past. The crime rates, I mean."

Piper listens intently. "You know an awful lot about Illyria's history, Astrid."

"Of course I do. I have lived here for a long time. Anyway, stay here and I shall go get you some currency."

"Okay," Piper agrees. "Ah! But – er – I have to go to the mayor's at some point, I need to drop off something for my aunt. Notes or something."

The mermaid raises a brow. "Hm. Alright, well...you might as well go there now, since you're already out and such. I will return to you later with some money from your new underwater bank. It shan't be much at first, a few handfuls, but there is more."

Piper smiles. "Thank you, Astrid."

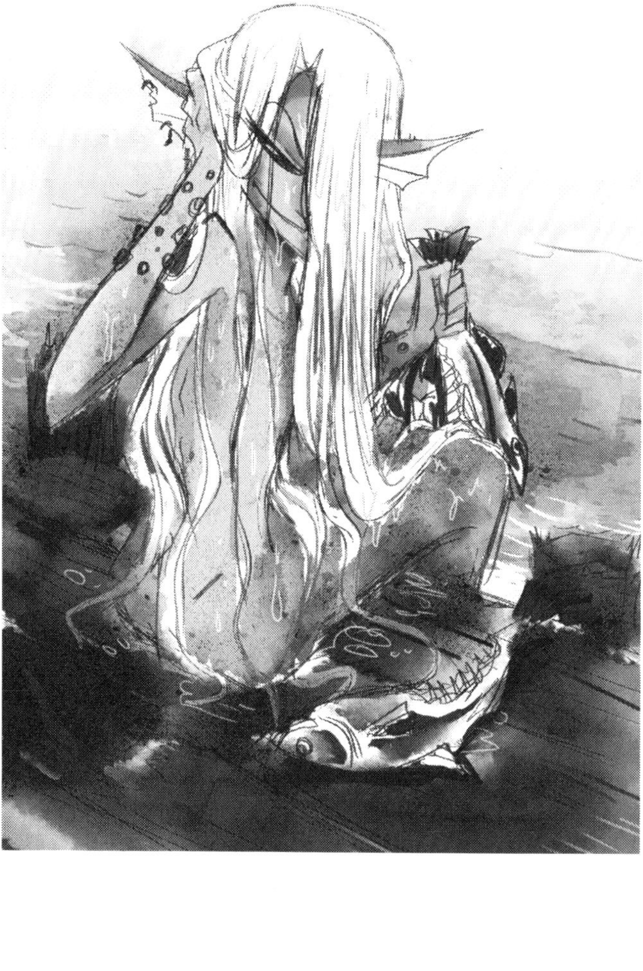

CHAPTER NINE

*F*alké stares out of his bedroom window in frustration, his lower lip swollen and bleeding. He left the nearest bar (and the secret fight club in its basement) only half an hour ago and was *so* ready to sleep through today. It was only when he passed that one block of run-down houses near Bysage Beach that he saw *them,* and hasn't stopped thinking about *them* since.

The harsh throbbing from the alcohol he consumed earlier hijacks his frontal lobe and adds to his aggravation. It's ridiculous. His cousin – his pathetic little cousin – out there in broad daylight speaking to a mermaid as if it's the most normal thing in the world. As if it's somehow natural. He ought to tell on her. He *will* tell on her as soon as he's had some sleep. She knows what she was doing is wrong; why else would she be in such an out-of-the-way location? She's not one to just loiter about in Illyria's back alleys.

Carmen's voice drags him back to the present. "What's with ya?" she asks casually, a cigarette between her ebony-painted lips. "This 'cus ya didn't win the fight a' the rin'?"

Falké shakes his head.

"This 'bout ya cousin 'gain then? I told ya, Falké…I got no idea what 'appened to 'er. Alrigh'?" Closing the jade curtains, bringing dimness to his bedroom, he turns to face her. Of all the Illyrians he is even slightly friends with, Carmen is the only one who never seems to get drunk; she can definitely hold her liqueur, that's for sure. She lays on his bed on her stomach now, propping herself up by her elbows, her chin resting in her hands. She doesn't look at all exhausted, and nowhere near as lethargic as him. How is she so physically stable right now?! He's almost jealous.

The girl turns over onto her back, exhaling a ribbon of blue-grey smoke and looking over to the side. There are several bottles collected on the bedside table to her left – empty of course. She grabs one, squinting her eyes as she attempts to read the label out of pure curiosity. It's difficult in the dark, so she gives up and brings it to her nose instead, sensing a yeasty aroma. Some sort of beer?

"This 'bout Kyran and me?"

He watches her and shakes his head slowly. Even doing *that* hurts. "Na. Aint 'bout Kyran an' you…just…feel like crap."

Two candles are lit on top of his dark-oak dresser. He walks over to them, observes the wax dripping down from the bright flames, and blows them out. This simple action is even more painful than shaking his head, and he clutches his throat for a minute as he makes his way towards his bed. Carmen moves to the side and he slumps down beside her, bringing a hand to his head and rubbing his temples in attempt to quell the pain lingering there. It doesn't work.

Carmen laughs, blowing more smoke from her plush lips.

"Wan' me to leave ya, Falké?"

"Nah…you stay…"

"Can't for long though, ya hear? Meetin' up with Kyran."

"Ah, 'course ya are."

He still doesn't understand what Carmen sees in the guy, and it's been a long time that the two have been…exclusive now. It's not that he likes her romantically and is jealous, it's that she's his best friend and he honestly wants what's best for her. Still, she seems to be happy hanging around Kyran and those other *delinquents* all day. She thinks it makes her look cool to be bad, and he has to admit that it sort of does. Whatever.

"My bleedin' cousin," he mumbles, and she raises her eyebrows and pulls the cigarette away from her face, holding it out to him. He gladly accepts the offer, taking a long drag and exhaling a thick cloud of smoke. Unlike Carmen, he isn't as…artful with his smoking. He doesn't have the patience for making pretty shapes like she does.

"What 'bout 'er? Sure she's fine."

"I know, just saw 'er and…euuugh."

"Wait, what?"

Carmen freezes, shocked into silence. How is that possible?! She literally *watched* one of those blue mermaids attack the kid. There's no way in hell that Piper survived such an ordeal – she would have been drowned and eaten the moment she was pulled underwater, surely?

"Just now?" she finally inquires.

He hums in affirmation, handing the cigarette back

to her and laying down. "Ya. Talkin' to a mermaid. Chattin' away…"

He stares at the ceiling. Mermaids are splendidly vicious beings with minds immeasurably more extraordinary than any human's could be. Why would one *willingly* talk to Piper? Out of all the Illyrians…why her? She's not special. She's not pretty. She's just…Piper.

"Ya too drunk right now, talkin' 'bout chattin' to mermaids and stuff," Carmen jests, smiling tightly and sliding off the bed. She puts her hands on her hips and purses her lips as she presses the cigarette back against them. "Get some rest. I'll see ya tomorrow?"

A hoarse sigh emanates from his sore throat. "'K. Seeya."

She ruffles his hair playfully. He bats her hand away weakly before forcing a tired smile. "Go 'way," he moans, "just get outta here already."

She winks. "Ya the boss, Falké."

Even after the sound of the front door closing no longer echoes around the house, and the quick beat of footsteps outside vanishes into nothing, Carmen's presence lingers in Falké's bedroom like the smoke from her cigarette. Usually, he likes this; it makes him feel much less alone and serves as a reminder that even somebody as remarkably stupid and deadbeat as him has a friend. He may hate himself, but Carmen doesn't. If she did she wouldn't hang around with him so much - that alone is a comforting thought.

Somehow, it doesn't seem so today.

He tries to relax in attempt to ignore the raging hangover but can't. Piper and that mermaid invade his thoughts to the point that it's impossible to even *try* to think of something else. Discomfort lodges itself inside him, pushing into his head, and finally he sits up in defeat, his hand fumbling over the night stand and finally finding a small handle. Pulling on it, he opens the drawer beneath and shuffles his fingers around the half-empty compartment until they close around his most prized possession.

Her pendant.

Now this never fails to relax him. He brushes it softly with his hands, running his fingers over the sharp shell edges and the smooth mint-coloured sea glass. The memories it holds alone are enough to help him find ease in his sluggish, pained state. He doesn't like keeping it away from view, hidden in that drawer, but it's what has to be done. If it were to be found by Elvira, he's not sure what would happen. It's so obviously mermaid made, he'd be questioned for sure. He's seen the patients of his mother, he's seen the vacant look in their eyes and the slow, pained gait of their walk. He can't become one of them.

Perhaps if it looked more like a silly little Illyrian souvenir trinket, he would wear it every day and keep it close to his heart. He likes jewellery – the stud in his ear, the piercings under his lower lip, the leather bracelet on his left wrist. If he were to wear a simple necklace, he doubts anybody would bat an eye. But this…this pendant is different. No matter how much he likes the mermaids – the mer*maid* that gave him this necklace – he can't let it show. Not now, and not ever.

He was eleven when he met her for the first time. She too was fairly young then, slender and perfect with sterling locks just past her shoulders, pale green from the mid-lengths onwards. Her hair hid her eyebrows from him initially, but with every gust of bitter wind the strands were thrown upwards and dark, expressive arches were revealed.

Her name was Esther.

Like now, thinking of mermaids as beautiful back then was…wrong. It was strange, it was stupid, and it made you look a bit peculiar. He couldn't help it though. He liked her the minute he saw her; her mint green, naked torso shifting to glistening wet emerald as waist flares to hip, the green fins on either side of her head sparkling. Her lips were turned down in pain. The hook caught in her left fin was disabling and bright crimson blood spread across the sand like a flower opening to the sun. "Help me," she had pleaded as he approached, the air humming with rain, and he did as she had asked. She was gone before he had the chance to do anything other than free her from the cruel torture of the steel, the necklace in his hand as a token of thanks.

It was the start of a beautiful friendship. And several years later, upon discovering that she had to leave Illyria, the end of one too. It's been two years now since he's seen her; two years of struggling terribly with his mental health - he's found himself quite suicidal on more than one occasion. He hadn't realised how much his life had become centred around her until she'd gone. Suddenly, he was lonely. Socially incapable. Lost…

Like Carmen, Esther had made her presence known, and it lingered long after she left. *She'll be back soon,* he used to tell himself, *every mermaid has to do it when they come of age. It needs to happen. She could get attacked if she stayed here. It won't be long until she's back.*

He stopped telling himself such things a while ago. He knows deep in his heart now that she will never return for if she wished to do so, she would have by now. Clearly, she's decided that she likes the warmer waters to the east, or the cooler ones to the south, better than Illyria. Better than him.

Who wouldn't?

He can still hear her voice. "Help me," over and over and over. Playing on repeat, an endless loop.

It's the drink, he thinks to himself, awkwardly moving under the sheets and closing his eyes. *I'm drunk and that's why I'm thinking 'bout her. I'm so goddamn pathetic, moping like this over a mermaid. I'm mentally sick, I know I am.*

It's moments before he finally falls into a sore, hungover sleep.

CHAPTER TEN

Despite her aunt's connection to him, Piper has never met the mayor in person. She has seen him at a distance, surrounded by guards and police, but never in close proximity. If not for the several pictures in school textbooks and the newspaper – Valentina Victory has written about him on more than one occasion – she wouldn't even know what his face looked like. As she walks towards his house, anxiety bubbles deep in her stomach as if it's a physical thing.

She's nervous.

A trio of friends wander past, and their enthusiastic chatter distracts her from such negative thoughts. Two girls and one boy, apparently so deep in conversation that they don't notice her; one of the girls bumps shoulders with her as they pass. Piper is instantly jealous of her mature-looking outfit; she studies the long, brown jacket hanging from the girl's shoulders, unbuttoned and almost touching the floor. The copper- coloured corset on her torso. The short, form-fitting skirt.

How wonderful it would be to buy and wear whatever she liked…

The girl catches her staring, and nudges the boy

beside her in the side with her elbow. He glares daggers at her for a moment, unaware of what's going on, and then follows her gaze to an embarrassed looking Piper. His eyes, she can see, are a very dark brown and for a moment she's reminded of Astrid and her jet-black irises. These are far duller. The pupils dilate before narrowing onto her, and then – he winks. His mouth curls into what she interprets as a mocking smile, yet is most likely just flirtatious.

Embarrassment overcomes her, prickling over her cheeks and down her neck. There's something about Illyrian boys that just makes her…uncomfortable. Perhaps it's because she associates them with Falké who, although nice in the past, is only full to the brim of alcoholic dependency and bad coping mechanisms now. She feels concern for him, as one would expect, but still doesn't trust him with anything.

She picks up pace in order to get away from the group, trying to ignore the very unpleasant feeling of being watched. "Loser," one of the girls calls after her, chuckling, and she visibly cringes at the insult before wrapping her arms around herself and breaking into a jog.

Loser.

By the time she's reached the gates before the mayor's house, her heart is thumping so rapidly against her chest that she feels it might hammer its way through. Cheeks flushed, she takes a moment to catch her breath both emotionally and physically. And then, after the word *loser* reduces to a whisper rather than a shout in her head, she approaches the nearest guard and drops into a polite curtsy. "I-I'm here to see the mayor," she says quietly, "d-deliver some papers. For-for my aunt, Elvira…"

The man stares down at her. "Speak up, girl."

"S-sorry. I'm here to deliver some papers for my aunt. Elvira. The mayor asked for them but she is busy so she sent me -"

Before she can finish explaining herself, the gate is opened and she is pulled through by the arm. Fingers splaying, she almost drops the compilation of Elvira's notes. Thankfully, she manages to grasp them again as she stumbles alongside the guard.

"He's been expecting these. Very important, these are. Very important. And none of us is to touch 'em – so you're going to have to hand them to him personally, you hear? Think you can do that, kid?"

"Y-yes. Yes. Of course."

Another group of guards approaches as she arrives at the door. They quickly assess her, check her clothing for weapons, and then move to the side.

"Do I just…?" she asks, gesturing to the door, and they nod.

She loops her fingers around the large brass knocker, raps it down three times, and waits. The door is opened surprisingly quickly, as if the mayor were simply standing behind it, waiting for her. "Can I help you, child?" he questions, and she finds herself straining to look up at him due to his height.

"I'm here to…give you some notes. From my aunt. Elvira?"

"Ah, you must be her niece, yes?"

"Yes."

"Piper Tourneau, am I correct?"

"Yes."

"How charming. Come in, Ms Tourneau."

He waves his hand, gesturing for her to move forwards, and she obliges. Seeing him up close feels almost unreal – just to think that this man governs her nation, controls everything around her…

His photographs don't capture him well enough. Despite being rather old, he looks far from it, and has sharp and angular features almost comparable to Astrid's. His grey eyes shine like twin moons under dark, arched brows, and his *hair*…it's practically white, short and tailored to the nape of his neck. Not grey, as she has always believed, nor salt-and-pepper. White. It's as if the man is imitating the mermaids.

Observant of her staring, he rests a pensive hand on his chin for a moment. "You look very deep in thought," he remarks, and then snaps his fingers together and gestures to his head. "It's my hair, isn't it? It's natural, you know. Extraordinary, I've always admired it. Almost … mermaid-like, don't you think?"

"Ah, yes," Piper agrees, "mermaid-like."

A saccharine sweet smile plays upon his face, one that she knows all too well from her aunt. It seems fake but that's expected from somebody so important; the mayor most certainly doesn't want bad publicity. Not more of it anyway. He already has enough issues as it is. "Do you like mermaids, Ms Tourneau?" he asks her unexpectedly.

"I mean…they're okay? I guess?"

"I see. I like mermaids, dear child."

"Oh?"

"So you can be honest with me. We'd be in the same boat."

"Well then…er…" she smiles bashfully, digging the ball of her left foot into the carpet, "…I guess I do."

He takes stock of this comment with idle

fascination. "Excellent. I feel like we could be friends. What do you think? Do you think we could be friends?"

Piper taps her index fingers together, impatience overcoming her so aggressively she cannot help but take action. She holds Elvira's notes up to the man and gestures to them with her free hand. "Sure. But – er – the notes? Just my aunt likes me to get things done quickly, an -"

A female voice, musical and breathy, interrupts her before she finishes her sentence. "Jasper!" it calls, "Breakfast is ready!"

She turns to look at the doorway, and her eyes rest upon a woman with hair as red as open wounds. The crimson curls foam luxuriously about her head, styled and glossy, and when she notices Piper staring, she raises a hand subconsciously to them and twirls a strand between her fingers. Her dark teal dress looks lavish to say the least; the taffeta skirt is long and bustled and the fitted bodice has small, golden buttons accenting it all the way up to the collar. She most definitely isn't a servant.

The mayor too directs his attention towards this new face. "Ah, Scarlett," he announces smoothly, "meet our guest. It's Elvira's niece, Piper Tourneau. Isn't she a sweet little thing?" He pauses for a moment, and Piper swears that his tone shifts to sinister when he continues. "She likes mermaids. Just like we do."

The woman looks around at her, clearly hesitating to comment. There is a longing in her eyes for a moment, a sombre melancholy which Piper recognises instantly as a look she herself wears often. It is a look that can only be described as *defeat*. As quickly as it appeared, however, it is gone and Scarlett has folded her hands together demurely with a soft, "Will she be staying for breakfast, then?"

He shakes his head. "I highly doubt it. She's just here to give me some notes. Aren't you, Ms Tourneau?"

Piper nods. "Y-yes. Yes."

"That's right. Thank you, my dear."

He takes a hold of them finally, removing them from her grasp so quickly that she's given a paper cut. She yelps at the sudden sting of pain emanating from her ring finger; the noise causes both the mayor and Scarlett to look down at her in concern.

"Oh dear," the man states. "I am *so* very sorry. Scarlett – go fetch a bandage for our guest here. She appears to have given herself a nasty little cut."

Piper shakes her head, finding an immediate need to decline any form of aid – "No, no. That won't – that won't be necessary. It's just – just – a *small* thing. I have had much worse before without treatment, it's fine, but thank you."

"I insist. Now, Scarlett -"

The woman falters for a moment. "Y-yes. Of course. And then are you going to come to the table? I have everything set out and rea-"

"Did you not hear me? I said go fetch a bandage."

Scarlett fidgets with the lace-trimmed bell sleeves of her dress, swallowing nervously. Her shoulders tremble with a fear Piper doesn't understand, but very much notices. She looks…shaken, all of a sudden, and the girl does not allow herself to think of what it might mean.

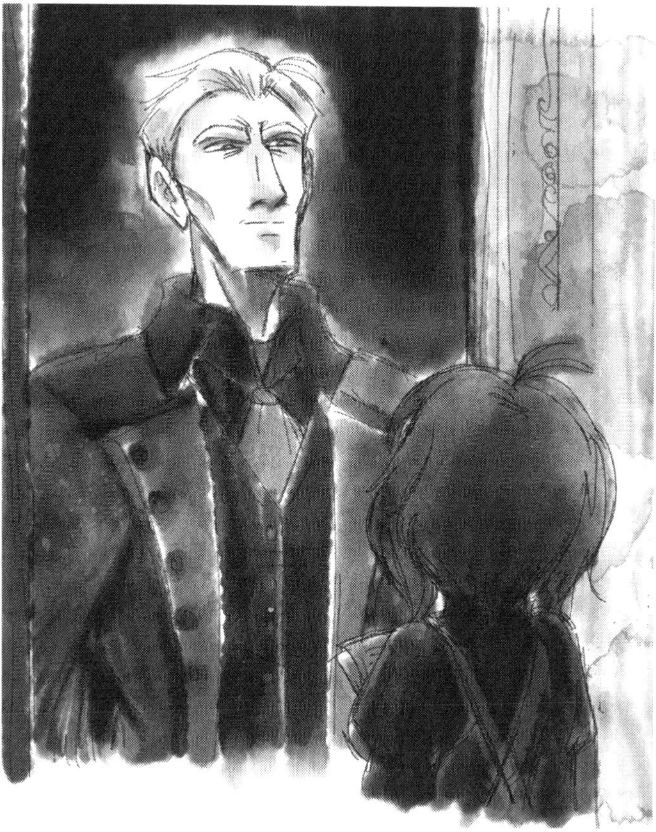

"Yes," she repeats quietly, "yes, I shall. One moment, please."

And with that, she leaves.

The mayor rubs at his brow. "I apologise on my partner's behalf," he comments. It makes Piper uncomfortable; she steps back, clutching her injured finger, and looks towards the door as if silently requesting permission to leave. No permission is given. Instead, he moves to the side, directing his attention towards a clock on the wall. It's five minutes slow – he taps it twice with his fingernail and hums in discontent. "We'll have to fix that," he mumbles, and then turns around quickly with a loud: "*Scarlett!* What is taking so long?!"

The woman appears in the doorway within seconds, carrying a small leather case. "I'm sorry!" she apologises, throwing it open and grasping a small bottle of what Piper assumes is a form of antiseptic. "It took me a while to find the medical kit – here, Piper, was it? Here you go, sweetheart. Hold out your hand, will you?"

Piper does as instructed, reluctant to go against the mayor's – or his partner's – wishes any further. As Scarlett drips the liquid onto her wound and begins to dress it with a small amount of bandage however, she feels something...warm inside. It's been so long since she's had a loving guardian who is willing to care for her like this and treat such minor injuries...it's...nice.

"Thank you," she whispers.

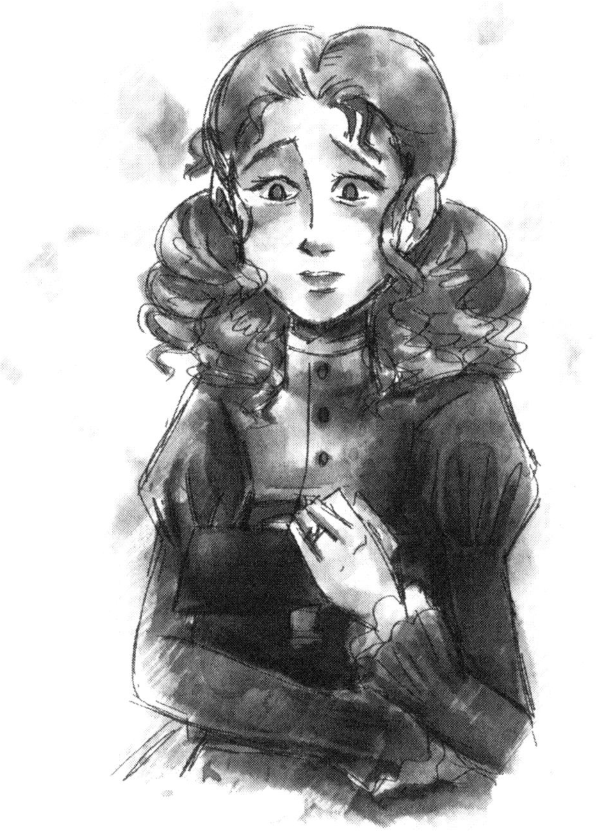

The moment is short-lived. As soon as the bandage has been secured, the mayor clasps his hands together and proceeds to escort a now weakly smiling Piper to the door. "It was a pleasure meeting you," he states, opening it, "and I do hope to see you again soon. I shall tell my guards of you so that, if you are to return with more notes or something of the sort, it shall be a little less of a trial to get to me."

"Oh…okay. Thank you very much. For everything."

"Goodbye," Scarlett interjects softly, earning a pointed look from the mayor. He moves forwards, waits patiently for Piper to leave the house, and then closes the door behind her. And that's that.

CHAPTER ELEVEN

Jasper Vanguard sieves through the sheets of paper Piper gave him with a small frown. Unfortunately, it seems nothing in Elvira's notes is of particular use today – there are various comments on mermaids and why patients find them attractive, which is interesting. Unhelpful, though. Same with the observations on mermaid/human interaction with romantic intent.

Bothered, he exhales slowly, and pauses on one of the sheets. "It is possible," Elvira has written, "that the mermaids are capable of controlling humans with their voice. Nine out of ten patients have commented that after hearing them sing or speak, they were willing to follow any instruction."

Hmm.

Well, she's not entirely off the mark, he thinks to himself, closing the notes and glancing out the window. Piper Tourneau is merely a figure in the distance at this point, unrecognisable. He wonders what exactly she knows of the mermaids, and whether she would be useful to him in the future. There's certainly a chance she will follow in her aunt's footsteps and become a therapist. That, or a researcher…something in the Ministry of

Information, at the very least. He has high hopes.

The delightful smell of breakfast begins to drift around the house then. He notices both the scent and his undeniable hunger at the same time, turning on the ball of his foot to make his way to the dining room. To have such indulgences – pork and eggs, that is – is rare in Illyria, for there are no farms. The vegetables and plants grown on the island are considered much too valuable to feed to animals. Fresh products such as meat and dairy must be imported into the nation, and unlike the grains Illyrians usually eat, they're definitely not low cost and are considered luxury items. But he is the mayor, and one of the lucky few who can afford such things.

Scarlett sits at the far end of the dining table, her hands folded modestly at her lap. She dares not glance up to meet his eyes as he walks in and takes a seat, but does say tenderly: "Ah, there you are."

"Eat," comes his simple command, and she does so.

The food is, as usual, exquisite. Today's breakfast consists of several things: A hearth-cooked omelette sprinkled with herbs, three rashers of bacon, two slices of fried bread, and a generous helping of cooked mushrooms. Scarlett has not always been such a good cook - when she first came to him, she practically burnt water. But the staff of the house assisted her in learning upon his request, and she's splendid now. He can't complain.

"What a dear little girl," he announces nonchalantly, studying the silver knife that now rests in his hand. It's sharp, as most cutlery in the manor house is, but not sharp enough to do precise damage. Scarlett nods in agreement, yet keeps her painted lips sealed as she slices through her omelette.

He stabs his fork into a rasher of bacon. "Do you ever think about having a child?"

Scarlett almost chokes on her food in surprise. Her face flushes a soft pink hue. "Y-yes," she admits quickly, a flash of hope crossing her expression, "why? Do you, Jasper?"

Normally, he would find this kind of response from her amusing. He's known very well since the moment they begun this 'relationship' that Scarlett has yearned for a child. That she's spent hours seated at the window upstairs wishing for a family. Sung lullabies to the air, read stories to the walls. Her enthusiasm is as tragic as it is entertaining.

But, today he is much too low-spirited to enjoy her behaviour; the yields from the mines, the *primary* export of Illyria (and the only source of foreign currency and economic stability), is declining. Not only that, but he's no closer to fixing the problem. The nation has no fossil fuels, and the limited supply of wood is used exclusively for construction…he must gain access to more resources, and it's not going to be easy –

"Jasper?" Scarlett repeats.

He blinks twice. Oh…the conversation about children is still happening. What did she ask again? If he wanted children? It was something along those lines. "Not particularly," he responds, "they would get in the way."

She looks down. "Ah…I see…I suppose you are too busy to look after them, aha…I would mostly have to raise them myself…"

"And you wouldn't be willing to do that in order to let me work, Scarlett?"

"Wh-what, no, I - I would, I would, just – just they would want to spend time with their father, surely? They would want both their parents -"

"Mmhm. I'm not interested in this conversation anymore, pet."

She chokes on her words, shuts her mouth so hard that her teeth click, and then continues eating in silence. It was a stupid idea to even think he was interested…

Stupid Scarlett.

CHAPTER TWELVE

The water's cold again.

Piper isn't surprised - regardless of the abundance of hot water (thanks to the island's numerous thermal vents), Illyria's plumbing system is in a constant state of disrepair. The pipes that access her house must be broken for the third time this month…she cringes at the thought of having to inform her aunt.

For now, she just deals with the cold. It's because of it that when she closes her eyes and thinks, *thinks hard*, she can imagine being in Illyria's sea instead of the grime-covered shower. The currents closing their maws around her, dragging her into the depths amongst shimmering fish and hungry mermaids. Being tossed and turned like a doll, thrown back and forth with no awareness of direction. And then, perhaps, the strong grip of a hand closing around her wrist, a fearsome angel dragging her to the light of the surface.

Astrid.

She awakens from the thought with freezing water cascading over her shivering form. Her lungs ache. She realises then that she's been holding her breath, and the imaginary abyss into which she willingly threw herself is gone. She's always had an over-active imagination. Her teachers used to tell her so in school – it's frowned upon in Illyria to be creative like that. It's not useful to anybody.

A small puddle of water collects at her feet, dancing over her toes with each splash from the showerhead. Looking down, she tells herself that unblocking the drain is a priority. But lots of things are a priority at the moment, like this shower in general. The house seems to be empty right now – she thinks Falké *may* be home, but is sleeping – and the one bathroom she shares with her family was not in use when she returned from the mayor's. Showering at this time is ideal, as she cannot be yelled at for taking too long.

Astrid.

She can't stop thinking about Astrid.

Reaching back, she turns off the shower and stands in silent thought for a few moments. Her skin craves heat. It's adorned with thousands of tiny goosebumps and stings with cold, but she ignores the sensation.

"Piper."

Astrid's voice breaks the peaceful quiet. Piper's reaction is instant – she jumps in surprise, grasps onto the side of the bath for support, and then reaches for her towel. Wrapping it around herself, she coughs awkwardly and screeches: "Astrid!"

The mermaid seems to have entered the bathroom a short while ago and is sitting comfortably on the edge of the toilet seat with her legs crossed. In her arms there's some sailcloth wrapped around a bundle. It's the same colour as her clothing; an off-white shirt that's clearly intended for a man at least five times her size hangs over her slender frame. It's much too big for her, and therefore acts as some sort of dress instead of a top.

She looks marvellous in it.

The notion of mermaids wearing clothes is not new to Piper. She's seen many doing so before, perhaps after stealing them from victims? It wouldn't surprise her – they display the material on their bodies like it's some sort of trophy. Illyrians tend to assume it's a warning. Of course, mermaids don't *have* to wear clothes. They care little about the human concept of modesty.

Piper shakes her head, adjusting the towel that's now around her body. "When did you get in here?!"

"Hmm…a few minutes ago," Astrid answers, "but you seemed to be in a daze, so I abstained from shocking you by speaking. Only now did I decide to get your attention -"

"D-did you see me?!"

"Obviously yes. I am seeing you right now."

"No, I mean like-like d-did you see me naked?!"

"Again, obviously yes. I just said I've been here for several minutes."

Piper flushes a deep and vicious crimson. "Urg man…okay, yeah…er…pretend you didn't see, okay?!"

"Why? I did."

"Because!"

"Because what?"

"Just because!" Piper responds with exasperation, climbing out of the shower. "And keep it down, Astrid! I think my cousin's sleeping in his room and hc's hungover…so…yeah…"

Astrid places the sail down and rises to her feet. "I *am* being quiet. You're the one that's speaking loudly."

"Oh…"

For a few seconds, the only sound is the soft drip-drip of the bathroom sink's leaky faucet. Piper leans her head against the mirror above it, a shadow passing over her face, and allows her eyes to slip closed. "Sorry," she mumbles, "I just - I didn't realise I was shouting. Just – urg – I'm tired. The mayor was sort of weird…and he treated his wife really bad. At least, I think she was his wife…maybe his girlfriend? I don't know. I don't remember. It was just…uncomfortable. Made me feel weird."

Astrid watches her, expressionless. From where she stands, she can see herself in the mirror; the bathroom window is closed, but the shutters are open, and light falls in over her. Her body shimmers underneath its dull glow. Piper's does not.

"What happened to your finger?"

The girl looks down at the small (and now wet) bandage around her finger. "Oh…I got a paper cut. It was just a small one, but the mayor overreacted and had the woman, his wife or girlfriend of whatever, clean the wound and treat it and everything. I'm fine."

"I see."

Piper turns to her slowly, shivering. The pair do not match heights since Astrid is exceptionally tall, as all mermaids are, and she is short. That doesn't bother her though, and she tentatively reaches forwards and presses her palm against Astrid's fingers. The action is reciprocated – the mermaid takes her hand and holds it.

"Astrid?"

"Yes?"

"Why did you save me?"

"Hm?"

"Back when Kyran and his friends were messing with me…why did you save me?"

Astrid lifts her shoulders, looking into her eyes. "We are friends, are we not? That's what friends do, they help each other. Besides…I liked you."

"Do you like me now?" Piper asks quietly, holding her breath out of pure nervousness.

Astrid lets go of her hand. Then, she leans close – so close that when she swallows, the girl can watch the way her throat ripples. Her fingers brush her cheek delicately, like water on silk, and when at last Piper exhales, shaking and wide-eyed, she sees her breath stir locks of moon hair. A strand falls forward from where it had been smoothed back.

She can only look at that lock of hair, only watch as it sways gently. It brushes softly against Astrid's glistening skin, tangles once in the lashes of her black eyes. Suddenly, her attention is taken away from it; Astrid leans forward and closes the gap between them with a kiss to her cheekbone. Her cold lips stain the girl's skin with a barely noticeable glitter, one that she doesn't notice until the light catches it. And then, after pulling away, she says: "Does that answer your question?"

Piper shrugs, her cheeks still flushed. "N-no…you're p-probably going to have to do it again…"

The afternoon passes quickly. Piper is kissed – not on the lips, but her cheeks – a total of thirteen times, and she is positively enamoured with the feeling by the time the sun begins to set. And when it does, sinking into the water on the horizon and throwing the surroundings into a combination of orange and pink, she decides she *definitely* has a crush.

Eventually, she becomes tired. She throws herself onto her bed, sighing blissfully, and Astrid joins her with a grin. "You want to go to sleep already?" she asks, amused, "It's only just sundown."

"I know, I know," Piper moans, a small giggle escaping her, "but no, I don't want to sleep yet. I'm just…resting."

"Resting."

"Yeah."

"Hah. Okay. Well…how do you usually 'rest', Piper Tourneau?"

"Er…I read books and stuff."

She reaches up to Astrid's face to poke her cheek, but the mermaid simply grasps her hand and kisses it. At first it goes unnoticed, but the array of colours from outside highlights it, and Piper gasps softly in shock –

"My hand is glittering," she states.

Astrid raises an eyebrow. "Oh, did you not know about that? I thought every Illyrian was taught this in school – perhaps they have stopped. Well, let me recite it: '*A mermaid's kiss is classified fatal. In the extremely rare case of survival, a dull shimmer and/or highlight will appear on the area of infliction.*' And that, Piper, is why your hand is glittering."

Piper presses her fingers to her cheek, almost on instinct. She imagines them to be Astrid's fingers, suddenly – smooth, cold fingers. And not just on her cheek, but on her arms, her stomach, her thighs. Gentle and relentless, touching her with focused earnestness. And she would allow them, of course, and watch as they press against her warm skin. And her breath would come calm and hot against Astrid's hair, her starlight hair…

"So, if you…kissed me…anywhere else…" she breathes, tracing invisible patterns on the leaflet with her index finger, "would I get the same shimmer ther-"

"Yes," the mermaid interrupts bluntly, "you would. I could leave your entire body shimmering if I wanted to. I could leave no patch of skin untouched. You would shine just like I do - like all mermaids do."

The girl lets her hands slide together. And…w-would y-you…?" she stammers, "do that, I mean? Would you do that?"

"Perhaps. If I wanted to."

"And do you…want to…?

"What do you think?"

"I…think y -"

Elvira's voice interrupts from the doorway, and Piper freezes mid-sentence. For a sickening moment, she feels as if she is barely existing, barely alive. It's as if somebody has stolen the breath from her lungs, and her head spins with fear as she slowly manages to turn her body to the source of the sound.

"Astrid," her aunt whispers, her voice shaking with horror but also deeply jaded. She takes a deep breath, steadies herself, and crosses her arms. "Get out of my house. You are not welcome here and you never were."

Piper moves away from the mermaid quickly and stands. "Auntie, I was just -"

"I don't care what you were doing," Elvira interrupts, her voice now nauseatingly calm.

"Because I don't think this is quite allowed, is it? Perhaps it would be a good idea to say goodbye to your mermaid friend now and have a little chat with me about this instead?"

She directs her attention to Astrid once again. "You just *love* breaking my family apart, don't you? I must say, though – I'm surprised. I assumed you would go for Falké, but that was silly of me, wasn't it? He doesn't have as many of Zachary's traits, does he?"

Astrid raises her eyebrows. "No. He doesn't. Now we've had this conversation, you are goi -"

"Shut up! Don't you dare open your filthy mouth and tell me what to do, you ocean vermin. You know she has nowhere else to go, and if you dare sing – or even *speak* to me – from this second onwards I will kick her out. She will be on the streets. How are you going to deal with that, Astrid? How are you going to look after her when you live underwater and she doesn't?"

The mermaid stares forwards at the woman in silence, straight-faced.

Elvira continues to speak, darkness stitched into every callous word. She points at Piper, seething. "I wonder how long you thought you could keep this up without me finding out, Bait. You lied to my face, didn't you? And I thought I could trust you for once. But no, of course not. You're just like your father. A liar. A cheat. A *mermaid lover*."

Elvira herself is amazed at how soft and yet pervasive her own voice is. It sounds like mockery; it is supposed to be mockery. It's a quiet lampoon of the intimacy she just watched her niece and this mermaid share. She sucks in her breath and narrows her eyes. "Get out of my house, Astrid," she orders, "or I'll get everything Zachary – and Piper – have ever owned and I will burn it all. You know I will."

Piper looks around at her friend, confused. This is the third time Elvira has said Astrid's name now. How does she know it?

"Go..." she whispers desperately, "please, Astrid...just go..."

CHAPTER THIRTEEN

When the vibrant hues of sunset threw themselves over Prince Holt Davori's family palace in Caldisa, he routinely sat on his balcony to admire the glow. Every evening, weather permitting, he would watch the vivacious sun disappear behind rolling mountains of lush green. The whole experience is beautiful in Illyria, in miserable little Illyria, just as it's beautiful in Caldisa. But as he stares out of the porthole window, watching the sunset, he feels tremendously homesick. There are no green mountains, nor are there little orange-roofed houses dotted about, the scent of cotton and flowers on the breeze…

He sighs softly.

If he had just accepted Izzy – oh, sorry – *Princess Isadora Petrova of Paliron* as his bride, he wouldn't be in this situation. It's what his parents wanted. In fact, it's what the entire kingdom wanted. If he had just proposed to her on that warm and sunny Tuesday afternoon like everybody so desperately desired him to, he wouldn't be alone now. He wouldn't be on his yacht in the middle of nowhere, surrounded by a merciless sea of mermaids that are undoubtedly unlike the ones he read about in storybooks when he was a child. And out of all things, he wouldn't be clinging to memories for some sort of solace, moping like a ghost.

He *would,* however, be tremendously unhappy.

Isadora is beautiful. Her smoky-topaz eyes, dark cinnamon skin, and glossy onyx curls are the envy of every noble in the land, of every peasant even. There is a kind of faultlessness in her that simply cannot be replicated, not even in the mermaids he's managed to catch glimpses of outside the boat. She is sweet, and kind, and very much enjoys royal things like elaborate tea parties and exquisite balls. She is of royal blood, and can dance, and play several instruments. She is the perfect match for him and marrying her would bring the two kingdoms of Caldisa and Paliron together in seamless harmony.

Then why is he here, in Illyria, and not back home with her?

The answer is simple, really: he doesn't love her. Isadora is a best friend at *most*. She has been so since they were children, a playmate that he affectionately nicknamed "Izzy". And that is all she is to him: Izzy. Not Isadora, not the Princess of Paliron, and definitely not his future *wife*.

She is perfect in many ways, yes, but that's what makes her so extremely…unsuitable. There's no fire in her, nothing unique or fun or wild. If he were to marry her, his entire life would be an endless drawl of boredom and having to be – how does his father put it? Ah yes - "seamlessly refined" every second of every day.

Her handsome, more audacious cousin Judas, however…

Unfortunately, he is engaged; a noblewoman from the north by the name of Adelaide holds his heart. Still it hasn't stopped Holt from thinking of him often. The rich, dark comfort of his warm vanilla skin, the wild – yet somehow tamed – coils of black upon his head. Unsavoury, nasty thoughts. Like his stifled gasps against his mouth or waking in his embrace while the sun is fresh and white with first exposure.

Terrible, terrible thoughts. Ghastly, he thinks to himself. *Still, Adelaide is lucky.*

Naturally, he loves being royalty. He loves being treated like the prince that he is, being waited on hand and foot, and enjoying the best quality products possible. But, forever with Isadora? Never leaving the palace, ruling a kingdom – wait no! *Two* kingdoms – with her, a girl he doesn't feel romantically attracted to whatsoever? Not appealing. His parents would never understand should he try to explain himself. They would be insulted at best, positively appalled and repulsed at worst. He *had* to run.

"Your Highness?"

He turns his head at the sound of his handmaiden, Lenka. Today she has opted for a frock of lavender to go beneath her apron; usually, she chooses a soft blue to match her eyes. Aside from this change of colour she looks the same as always. Her strawberry blonde hair is pulled tightly into a bun atop her head, its full bangs curled neatly inwards just above the eyebrows. "Would you like me to prepare your evening meal now?" she inquires politely.

He shakes his head and sighs.

"No…I am not hungry, Lenka. I may go for a

walk, actually."

The girl looks surprised. "In disguise again? I thought you said that the experience was most uncomfortable! But, if you are so keen on doing so, shall I prepare your clothing?"

Holt nods. He rises from his chair, straightens his shirt, and twists his lips into something he supposes might pass for a smile. "Thank you, Lenka. Yes. Oh, and it's getting a little darker now so I shall not sacrifice as much of my comfort in order to blend in. I would be extremely grateful if you could keep that in mind."

"Alright…I shall tell your guard…"

"No, no. I can handle this myself."

"Your Highness, please do not take this as an insult to your capability, but you really should have Cadmus with you.".

He sighs, throwing his head back, and gives in with a snappy: "Fine. Fine! But he must follow a few metres behind me at all times…not walk right beside me."

"Yes. Understood. And shall I fetch your rapier? I have read some most troublesome things in the nation's newspaper…things about *mermaids*…"

"It is nothing I cannot handle. But yes, please fetch my rapier."

Sunset is over, and the rich colours have been replaced by sheets of velvet black and indigo when Holt emerges from his yacht. Illyria is quiet in the evenings. There are no bustling crowds to bundle through, and no cameras being aggressively pointed at his boat after the slightest hint of movement. It's extremely satisfying for him to be able to wander the deck alone, in peace. At least…*almost* alone. His guard, Cadmus, walks behind him stiffly, looking from side to side constantly for any sign of threat. He sighs. Well, it's better to be safe than sorry.

He would have thought that such a place would be quieter in general. It surprises him that there's such an active population, considering the area is so dangerous. If the volcanic activity wasn't problem enough, there are mermaids swimming about, too. And from what he's heard about them, they don't exactly have a sterling reputation amongst the public. But Illyria's unattractiveness is a good thing for him, really – nobody would think to come look for him here.

He turns his head to observe the rolling water surrounding him. It's peaceful at the moment, moving like glass over an endless expanse of blue-black. The waves crawl up the sides of the pier beckoning, and he watches them gradually retreat as he slows to a halt. It's not until he hears the sudden splash of what he assumes is a large fish – perhaps a mermaid, in hindsight - that he starts moving again, his hand over the hilt of his rapier.

Remember your training, he thinks to himself. *Feet shoulder-width apart. Elbows bent, close to the body. Keep your balance.*

Honestly, he never particularly enjoyed fencing. It's a hobby – and technique – that was forced upon him from an early age, together with boxing, dressage, and croquet. Stereotypically 'rich people' hobbies and activities that, if he were not a prince, he would most certainly not be interested in. At least fencing has a use, though; he can defend himself in the case of an emergency even if he does have guards, too.

His stomach calls for food, churning

uncomfortably. Hunger is a nasty thing, something he'd rather not experience for long, so he turns and heads back to the yacht. Rejecting Lenka's proposal of dinner was a bad idea, he realises that now.

But suddenly, he hears *it*.

Crying.

And there is the source, in the distance; somebody crouched over, their body wracked with sobs. For a moment, he's worried that this may be some sort of trick. It seems out of place, somebody crying alone at night. But before he has the chance to decide whether or not to approach the figure, his footsteps cause the decking to creak. The person sits up straight like a shot, and he can feel his pulse in his throat as they turn their face to his.

Every beat of his heart echoes through him like a drum, a droplet of sweat runs down his neck. He places a hand on the hilt of his rapier as his bodyguards quicken their pace…

It's a girl. She's been hurt.

He takes a deep breath, relief showering his mind, and raises his hand. He can hear the man behind him slow down upon seeing this silent command, and then stop. He rushes to the girl's side.

"Miss?" he asks gently, "are you quite alright? May I assist you in any manner? Has somebody hurt you?"

"N-no…just…leave me alone!"

"What is your name?"

"Please just - just leave me alone…"

"I am H-henry. Henry. And you?"

"…Piper."

"A beautiful name."

His brown eyes soften as he kneels down before

Piper and tentatively holds out a hand for her to take. "Please, let me help you," he says, and she nods and rubs her eyes with the knuckles of her left hand, using the right to take his own. "What happened, Piper?"

Illuminated by the dim glow of Illyria's dusty lamplights, the girl forces a smile through her tears. "A mermaid happened."

Chapter Fourteen

"What am I looking at?"

Jasper's question seems much more like a statement. His head surgeon, Ms Margo Santi, stands at rigid attention. "W-well, it's a dead mermaid, sir," she begins, nearly frantic at whatever expression steals across the mayor's face. "And you wanted to hear about progress on the mermaid venom…so I called for you!"

For a few seconds, he says nothing. His eyes narrow as he stares down at the deceased creature. Its long, silvery hair, golden brown at the ends. Cold lips, slightly parted to reveal the sharp teeth behind. Smooth, yellow skin, shimmering in the light. Clearly, it perished in its human form, for it has legs rather than a tail.

"You insisted that I come down here and stop my research to look at a dead mermaid. As if I have never seen one before. This is progress how exactly, Santi?"

"Well…it's dead, sir."

"I can *see* that."

"Well yes, I know, but -"

"But *what?*"

"W-what I'm saying, sir, is that what you have asked me to do is impossible."

Jasper sucks on his teeth, dragging a finger along the side of his face. His voice is flat as he paces back and forth and asks, "And why exactly is it impossible? I asked you to do one thing - extract the venom out of the mermaid without causing immediate death. Is that really *so* difficult?"

"Well, I regret to inform you that it is. It truly is - you simply can't remove it without killing the creature instantly! I have tried with several mermaids now, and it's always the same result. It's not possible - it can't be done."

He groans quietly, coming to a standstill. "Right."

"Just…the organ that produces the venom is very deep within them, sir. At the end of a tube," – she raises her hand and runs it against the mermaid's body as if to demonstrate – "that runs alongside their equivalent of our oesophagus and trachea. Removal results in death every single time. It's a very complicated surgery."

There's a moment's silence while the man rubs his temples, visibly tense. And then, slowly, he turns away and waves his hand dismissively. "Sort it out, Santi," he commands plainly. "I don't care how many mermaids you have to kill. I don't care how many surgeries you have to perform. Sort. It. Out."

Margo watches him leave, lips pursed. "Yes, sir. Of course."

He throws open the doors and ascends the stairs, making a low sound of disapproval as he does so. Capturing mermaids regularly is problematic enough, but killing them for venom would be noticed for sure.

He'd be discovered, and they'd come after him…

By the time he's returned to the west drawing room (which is where he was before the surgeon *insisted* he come down to her surgical workplace) he's almost ready to gouge his eyes out in frustration. There has to be some way of getting that stuff out of their bodies without killing them. There *has* to be.

Scarlett, as usual, is feeding the fish. It's something she likes doing, and *has* liked doing since the moment she arrived at the house. And that was such a long time ago – he expects she can barely remember the touch of rags and cold now, the ache of hunger and the taste of cinders. She had blonde hair then – ash blonde hair – and now it is red, a blood coloured cascade of curls. Her previously shivering form covered with scraps of dirty material now is decorated in elegant taffeta. She's a different woman now, a better one. More attractive.

She turns her head to look at him as he enters with a gentle smile. "Oh, hello, Jasper," she says, diverting her attention back to the tank. And ever so quietly, adds, "you look stressed."

"I am stressed," he confirms. "I am stressed and I am tired and I am sick to death of this nation having *nothing* -" He knows that his voice is climbing. He makes no effort to stop it. "- Nothing but a mine that is running dry and a city decaying more every day. Why would I *not* be stressed, Scarlett? Answer me that. Why? Why would I not?"

The woman's brow creases as she slowly closes the lid of the large tank, almost the size of a small pool, watching him in the reflection of the glass. "I'm sorry, Jasper. Can I help?" Her voice is soft, soothing. "Why don't you watch the fish swim around for a little while…it's calming, I think."

"No. Come here." He sighs into his hand as it rests against his lips in thought. "You can help me by coming here."

She does so, carefully placing the fish food to the side and approaching. There, beneath the soft light of affection within her, he can see a certain sadness, a weariness that reminds him too much of his late mother. He hated that woman. Pathetic and weak, she was…no wonder she fell sick and passed when he was a child.

"Jasper -" Scarlett breathes, but he rises to his feet, presses a finger to her lips, and silences her. Wrapping an arm around her waist, he begins to slow-dance with her, eyebrows furrowed in concentration. "I am at an impasse, Scarlett," he comments, "it seems everything I want is constantly out of reach, no matter how hard I work for it."

"W-well…I am not. I'm not out of reach…and you want me."

He presses close then, almost over-eagerly, one hand snaking around her waist, the other grasping and possessing her flesh. She can feel the solidity of his chest against hers, as his mouth rests against her collarbone. The air he exhales is warm against her skin. A moment passes in which she can feel the thud of his heartbeat, a familiar and comforting rhythm, and nothing else seems to matter. But then…he clicks his tongue, running his hands up her hips, and sighs. "Scarlett, Scarlett, Scarlett," he croons somewhere behind her ear, his breath now against her neck, "if I wanted you right now, I would have taken you."

Silence.

"Ah...y-yes, yes I know," comes her meek response. "Just...I wanted you to know...that there is something you want that you *can* have...so you don't feel so...bad?"

Silence again, and suddenly...laughter.
She hardly has time to react before she is pushed violently away from him and into the side of the tank. The fish inside dart around in panic as her body hits the glass and slumps down into a sitting position. He advances towards her. "So I don't feel so bad?" he bristles, "you honestly think that telling me I can have you is going to make me feel better? I can have you whenever I goddamn want! What I *can't* have is a stable nation, Scarlett! And I think that is much more important, wouldn't you agree?!"

Her throat tight, she begins to stammer an apology as he kneels before her. A hand is pressed against her mouth and he says, angrily, "If you are going to be so unbelievably foolish, you can leave this place and go back to living off cupped coins! Why must you make such stupid comments?"

He removes his hand so she can speak, and she does.

"I just - I'm sorry, please forgive me, I'm - I'm so stupid sometimes."

"I know you are!"

She withers under the heat of his snarling gaze.

"You senseless woman! I am trying to fix Illyria and all you do is tell me I can 'have you' like that will make it all better!"

"I'm sorry! I'm sorry. Jasper, I..."

He steps back victoriously, glancing up at the fish tank. Watching the little creatures inside move around frantically, unaware of what's going on. And when he looks back down at Scarlett, poor shaking Scarlett, he takes satisfaction in the fact that she is not looking back at him anymore. Her eyes are averted to the floor instead. She is scared of him.

"You're a terrible mess, my love," he comments nonchalantly, beckoning. "Come to me."

She does. He takes her hand gently, pressing his lips against it like a true gentleman. "I apologise for frightening you. You know how passionate I get sometimes; you must forgive me."

"I forgive you, Jasper. I will always forgive you."

He presses his lips against hers. "Wonderful," he hums softly against her mouth, "I forgive you too."

CHAPTER FIFTEEN

Mermaids don't reproduce very often. After all, there isn't a particular reason to do so. They live for a very, *very* long time and would probably self-destruct if their population kept increasing dramatically. But three young mermaids pass Astrid's 'house' as she counts out a pile of coins for Piper. Two oranges, and one red. They'll make up part of a proper shiver one day, a fighting and attacking cluster. Strong, powerful, and ravenous. For now, they are carefree and laugh and chase each other playfully like the children that they are. Astrid lets a few small coins slip between her fingers, drifting down onto the table before her, and watches the group for a few moments.

Some forgotten human's skull embellishes the sand they move over, and the red mermaid pauses to take note of it. After a few interested comments to their friends they have it in their hands, pressing their palms against the cool bone. One of the orange mermaids quickly snatches it from them and within moments the item is no longer a lonely relic of the past but a plaything. The young mermaids take turns throwing it to each other in the water, forming a makeshift game out of the whole situation. Astrid's lips curve into a smile. She looks around at the skeleton beside her – belonging to this wreck's late owner – and taps her sharp nails against the tabletop in thought for a moment before sliding closer to the bones.

"You know," she says idly, "unlike you humans, we don't have a particular attachment to our young. There's no need *or* desire to coddle them until they are 'old enough' to go about the world themselves. They're born, given two or three meals, and that's the end of it. Isn't that interesting? Only a short while and they're leaving to pave their own future or form a shiver if they're a group-type mermaid. You know, like an orange or red. Ah, what am I saying? Of course you know. You're an *expert*."

Silence.

She continues.

"I remember my mother; her name was Diamorte. She was splendorous. A mermaid of several colours, the first of her kind. She…abandoned me after a week. It was hard, you know. There were no other mermaids around, nothing but open ocean as far as the eye could see and trenches of mysterious creatures unknown to both mer- and humankind. She left me in the darkness amongst ferocious megalodon sharks and expected nothing from me but survival. Isn't that miserable? Don't you feel so sorry for me after hearing that?"

She studies one of the coins in particular with intrigue. It has a unique design; she concludes it must be a collector's edition variation of the others.

"You know, I think it's because of that harsh abandonment that I spent longer than usual with my first offspring. I remained with them for almost three months before leaving them to their own devices, can you believe that? They were wonderful little beasts, though – none of them group attackers, but solos with shades of blue and violet. Pretty things. Their first kill was virtuous. They very nearly devoured the entirety of two large sharks with only the slightest amount of assistance from me. How those sharks thrashed and how merciless I and those perfect children were! It was a long time ago, though. A *very* long time ago."

She moves away from the desk piled high with shimmering currency and takes in the enormity of the cabin's contents. There are trunks brimming with everything from the mundane to the extremely valuable, broken and damaged shelves encumbered under the weight of the stock piled atop them, and masses of coins and coral and scales. She never realised how full the place was getting. Perhaps it is time to clear the ship out a little and dispose of the things she has no particular need of.

She picks up a pile of random items and pauses upon noticing one particular shell. It scatters underwater rainbows when she holds it up. They dance upon her face in a very alluring fashion, and the closer it comes to her cheeks, the more the light sways and twirls. It is a beautiful seashell, iridescent. When she holds it in her hands, her blue skin glows like a dying galaxy. Nova colours, solar flares…

It is a perfect specimen: unmarred, not a single scratch. She glides through the wreck carrying the shell with both hands. Its size justifies that, really. Zachary's skeleton remains sitting in his chair. He wasn't there when he died – he was floating in the water after a successful suicide – but she positioned him here shortly after eating the majority of his sweet flesh. The thing about human flesh is that it's such a delicacy, such a luxury…it's unlike anything else, an acquired taste for some but undoubtedly sought after. She finds it delicious. Better than fish, anyway…

She took scraps of him only now and again after his death in an attempt to preserve him for as long as possible. Eventually, all the meat was gone however, and she re-assembled his skeleton with wire in order to pay homage to him. All sorts of beautiful items adorn his bones now – sea flowers and brightly coloured shells, fishing nets woven through with grasses plucked from the sand. Gold, silver, bronze. Precious gems.

She poses and positions his skeleton, pushing the shell into his ribs, and then stares into the empty sockets where his striking green eyes used to be.

"A gift," she announces simply, running her fingers down his skull, "for you to keep with you here. Remind you of me while I'm away."

Quiet.

She lowers her gaze to the shell shimmering away in his remains. Her voice becomes soft.

"I've been thinking of you a lot recently," she begins, her hands wandering across his bones, "your daughter is wonderful and is so much like you. I am going to make her my next connector, and I am sure you will be pleased to know that I will be looking after her from now on. She will not meet the same fate as you, I can assure you of that."

Still quiet.

It's expected, of course. She furrows her brows together and moves away from him in the cool water.

Even if he were alive, Zachary would not be able to comprehend such ancient Mermish. It's a language that he never fully grasped despite hours of practising various phrases with her. At least he was capable of learning and understanding some basic, modern Mermish.

It's understandable - the human vocal cords are simply not designed for making such noises. To them, a mermaid's simple underwater communication sounds like a series of disturbing shrieks and squeals, with strange melodies and lullabies dotted throughout. Humans cannot harmonise with themselves like mermaids can either and need to sing in a group to achieve a similar sound.

Pathetic, really.

CHAPTER SIXTEEN

"The island nation of Calawi is approximately four hundred nautical miles away from Illyria, has over five times the landmass that we do and a significant amount of natural resources, especially wood." Jasper's primary political advisor, Tobias Wren, gestures to a map laid out on the table. "The northwest side is primarily agriculture while the east is where the city is -"

"I want it."

Jasper leans forwards in his chair, tapping his fingers against the wooden desk before him.

Tobias clears his throat dryly. "Although it would be the perfect nation for us to conquer, sir, there is one major problem – overcoming it in battle would be, ahem, challenging. Both its navy and army are huge and powerful. They have significantly more ships and more fighting men than us. In short, we would be wiped out in an instant."

"Mermaid venom."

"E-excuse me?"

"Mermaid venom, Wren. Delivered in very large quantities, it will render a human permanently brain damaged…or even kill them. Take it out of the mermaid, put it in a weapon. *That* is how we take over Calawi."

The room floods with conversation suddenly, advisors and military leaders talking over one another in order to voice an opinion on the matter. This isn't the first time the mayor has mentioned 'mermaid venom'…he's been interested in it for a long time, just as he's been interested in the mermaids themselves for a long time. But, unlike him, none of them knows enough about it; he's been extremely secretive regarding his discoveries while experimenting on the creatures and has informed nobody of his findings.

"Quiet! All of you! This is not up for discussion. I know what you're all thinking – what's mermaid venom anyway and just how effective is it? Well let me tell you this, my fellow Illyrians: have you ever wondered how mermaids lure you in? Every report from those obsessed with them states that they felt inclined to do whatever that mermaid said? For crying out loud, just read the notes from the Illyrian Health Centre nurses – it's all the same. Well, it's the venom."

Tobias is quick to interject. "But sir," he begins, "is it not the singing that allows the mermaids to control people?"

"That *is* the common assumption, yes. But it's incorrect, Wren. An old wives tale, Wren. Something to amuse children with, or frighten them perhaps. But most definitely fiction."

A beat passes while everybody exchanges glances with each other. Honestly, no one believed Jasper's hobby of studying the mermaids would be fruitful in any way. It was always just that – a hobby. Not something serious enough to attack another nation with…

Jasper continues.

"They expel it through their mouths," he states, starting to pace the room, moving his hands in grandiose gestures as he speaks. "In the water, it's released to partially disable marine life and make it easier to catch. On land, it can either be spat out…which is lethal…or released in gaseous form through mermaid breath which intoxicates animals – including us humans. And once intoxicated we *will* respond to auto-suggestion. Why not make this useful to us, I say? Why not make this a weapon?"

Tobias wrings his hands. "With all due respect, sir, we can't just…capture mermaids and have them swim into Calawi. How are we supposed to know they're trustworthy enough to fight for us?"

"We're not. And that's the problem. We need to remove it from the mermaids and then put it into some kind of delivery mechanism. A weapon. Are you paying no attention to me whatsoever?"

"I – I am, just…I'm unsure of how we could possibly disperse such a thing…how much we would need…how many people it would affect, and *how* it would affect them -"

"Then find out."

"We would need to test the venom, sir."

"Then do it."

The room falls silent again. So silent, in fact, that it's uncomfortable. Eventually, somebody speaks up, and that somebody is one of the military leaders. "Sir," he begins cautiously, "people would have to die. We would need to find out exactly how much of this venom is enough to disable a human. To disable a group of humans. There would have to be several experiments, numerous tests..."

"Fine. Make the weapons, get test subjects, and test. The place is a hazard anyway, nobody will notice if a few people go missing. Especially people in prison, or in the asylum, or those dying already...and we *will* have this figured out by the end of the month. That will be all."

By the end of the month.

Jasper groans, rubbing his temples in agitation as he sits at his favourite desk. What vivid memories he has of that meeting....and yet it's been an entire year since it occurred. Illyria's extremely limited resources are deteriorating at a speed he simply can't keep up with and still Calawi is nowhere near being his. The sheer number of problems he and his team have run into has annoyingly put the mission concerning its seizure at a standstill.

The most prominent issue is the degradation. It's been a problem from the beginning of the tests and continues to be. The moment the venom leaves its host's body, it's only viable for a few hours. This is particularly challenging to deal with, as the journey to Calawi is far longer than the viability of the venom and it would be useless by the time his ships arrived anywhere near the island. No matter what he tries – all sorts of combinations of chemicals – nothing seems to make it last longer. Acids, Alkalis, alcohols...all ineffective at prolonging the viability. It's only a matter of time before his nation falls apart entirely, both economically and physically, and just the thought of it sickens him.

He believed for a while that bringing the mermaids

along with his army and extracting the venom on site might be an option – but now Santi has informed him that it simply can't be done without killing the mermaid.

He buries his head in his hands, mentally exhausted. At least the capturing of test subjects has been successful – no Illyrian seems to have even noticed, even if the list of names in the newspaper's obituary section has been steadily increasing over the past few weeks in particular. He thanks the stars for that.

Chapter Seventeen

Mount Saphielle is more difficult to climb than Piper remembers. She hasn't ventured up its side for what seems like forever though; the last time was with her father. It was a weekend and the sun was shining brightly on the roaring waters of Illyria below. She can remember the white-crested waves gleaming, crashing against each other. It's a similar scene now, but everything seems…darker. Colder.

"Are we stopping here, or are you just taking in the scenery for a moment?"

Heat rushes to her face, and she nearly stumbles. She almost forgot Astrid was walking behind her – she's so quiet. "N-no, not stopping," she responds, shaking her head, "I was just…remembering something. The last time I was up here…it feels so long ago. I was just a kid. What about you?"

The mermaid shrugs. "I don't think I ever climbed this high," she admits, pushing some hair out of her face, "I never had much reason to. Mermaids usually just stay in the water. I am far more familiar with the underwater caves and sunken boats in the waters around Illyria rather than the land. Exploring on foot was never very appealing to me."

Piper nods in understanding. She assumes the only reason Astrid is even present *now* is to spend time with her. At least, that's what she hopes. Maybe she just got bored of swimming around.

The wind is strong so high up, carrying the scent of the sea. Irrationally, Piper thinks how cold the mermaid must be, standing there unclothed with it dancing through her silvery hair. She slips an arm out of her jacket almost taking it off and asks, "Do you want this? To keep you warm?"

Astrid shakes her head. "It's not cold for me."

Of course it's not, Piper thinks, feeling like a fool. Mermaids have a layer of blubber beneath their tough skin and it clearly does a fantastic job of keeping them warm considering they live in such frigid waters. There's no reason Astrid would be cold because of a little breeze. She shrugs the jacket back on, adjusting it, and continues forwards. That was embarrassing.

Suddenly, another thought comes to her mind. It's hugely unwelcome and causes her to blush severely -

Is this a date?

For a moment, she finds herself wondering what it would be like to press her lips to Astrid's mouth. She doesn't doubt her soul would take flight at such an occurrence – to be able to kiss a mermaid whenever she feels the desire to! But no...no. She shakes her head and presses her fingers into her palm as she walks. That's wrong. She shouldn't desire things like that...not from Astrid. Not from a mermaid.

But then – her hand is cupped and her fingers moved outwards as Astrid weaves her own through the gaps between them. She looks around at her quickly, surprised. At that moment, a cloud moves past the sun, and the warm light shines upon them and illuminates Astrid in all her glory. Piper can't imagine a sweeter sight and stares in rapture. "Y-you want to hold hands with me?"

"If I didn't, I wouldn't be doing so right now. Why? Do you have a problem with it?"

A few seconds of silence pass. Piper gazes up at the mermaid in nervous joy. It washes over her face, taking over her expression entirely, and for a moment she forgets her problems at home. Her alcoholic cousin, aggressive and resentful. Her abusive, patronising aunt. Neither of them matters right now – what matters is Astrid.

"Astrid," she says. She loves the way her name feels in her mouth.

"Yes?"

They continue onwards, scaling the mountain, hand in hand. "Is this a date?"

"If you want it to be."

"I want it to be."

"Then yes."

Piper can't help the smile that spreads across her face at the confirmation. She squeezes Astrid's hand, moving slightly ahead and looks up at the sky. Two seagulls scale the breeze above, flying inverted arcs around each other. "Hey, look," she gestures up at them, "they're lovers, too."

"Are they now?" Astrid replies, following her gaze to watch the birds wheeling overhead. She watches briefly before seemingly getting bored, and shifts her gaze back to Piper. "They'll come to us as soon as we start eating," she notes, listening to their brazen cries. "They'll want the fish."

"You know I brought fish with me?!" Piper meets

her gaze, astonished. "That was supposed to be a surprise! I was going to set up a little picnic at some point – I wrapped some fillets up for you and made myself a sandwich."

The mermaid laughs quietly. "What, you really thought I wouldn't smell fish?"

"Ah…yeah, that's a good point. Haha…well, do you wanna eat now? This is a good place to stop, actually."

"Alright."

"Should we sit down here then?"

"Alright."

They do so. As Astrid proceeds to unpack Piper's backpack for her, the girl looks out into the distance again, at the decaying city stretching into the blue water. It isn't very beautiful, but it's all she's ever known. She doesn't doubt that past the horizon, there are far more beautiful places. Places like Caldisa, where that Prince Holt Davori is from. She tries to picture what it's like there. The waters aren't as dangerous looking, she decides. They sparkle cerulean blue instead, and you can see everything underneath them they're so clear. But even though her image of Caldisa is stunning, it doesn't have any memories attached to it like Illyria does. Illyria may be run-down and plain at best, but every part of it tells a story. It's still her home, after all.

"It's cool up here, isn't it?" she asks softly, taking her sandwich from Astrid's hands.

"Yes."

When she looks back around at Astrid, she's greeted by the sight of her eating. Her sharp teeth bite the edge of the fillet that's currently impaled on her equally sharp nails. She rips at it, closes her full lips around it, and chews firmly. Piper can't take her eyes off of her – her powerful jaw, those shark-like teeth, her throat as she swallows…

"D-do you like it?"

"Mmm, yes," Astrid growls, her tongue running along the top row of her teeth. She looks directly into Piper's face as she eats, her gaze so intense it's as if she's devouring her with the same intensity as the fish. "What else is on the menu?" she asks, grabbing a second fillet.

Piper swallows hard. "Well," she starts, looking down at her sandwich to avoid Astrid's piercing gaze, "I didn't bring anything else, but we can always go pick something up at the store once we get back down."

Astrid raises her eyebrows. She gulps down the second fillet, and then grasps Piper's chin with her slender fingers. She lifts her face, forcing their eyes to meet. "What's for dessert?"

"I…well…what do you want?"

"I think," – the mermaid leans in close, her breath cool against Piper's ear, "I'll have you."

"What?! Astrid-!"

"What?"

"You can't be serious?!"

"But I am."

Piper shuffles back slightly, shaking her head. "But I- I'm your friend now! You said so!" she cries, noticeably upset. All admiration for Astrid all but evaporates in an instant, replaced by fear -

"Hmm…I don't think you understood. I was toying with you, not saying I wanted to kill you and consume your flesh. It was supposed to be suggestive. Never mind. Should we head back soon?"

Oh. Embarrassed, Piper brings her knees up to her chest and nods. "Y-yeah," she stutters, "jeez…I thought you wanted to actually kill me for a second there."

"No. I like you."

Astrid moves close to her again, her lips brushing Piper's left collarbone, frozen silk against warm velvet. She sucks gently on the skin. Her hands sweep up Piper's arms.

"Astrid?"

"Mmm?"

Piper clears her throat softly, wondering how to approach the question she so desperately wants to ask. No words come out when she opens her mouth, though, so she takes a deep breath and tries again: "Can mermaids fall in love?"

Astrid blinks twice, but otherwise seems unfazed by the prompt. She crawls on her hands and knees around Piper in order to get behind her, and then kneels down and proceeds to rub soothing circles over her shoulder blades. "Some of us," comes her response.

"Some of us?"

A bouquet of silvery-blue locks falls across Piper's back as Astrid leans forwards. "Surely you know this already?" she asks, "green mermaids partner up, and stay with their chosen ones for life, and -"

"Blue mermaids. What about blue mermaids?"

A beat passes. Piper turns slowly to face Astrid again who lowers her hands and lets out a particularly withering sigh. She knows where this is going.

"No."

Although she tries desperately to hide it, the

disappointment that overcomes Piper is painfully clear. Groaning softly, she turns her face away from Astrid, her brows buckling inwards. It's too late to retract the question now, but she wishes she never asked in the first place. It was foolish. It fact, it's foolish to be *so* obsessed with Astrid in the first place; she hasn't even known her for that long.

"Oh right, of course," she whispers, chiding herself, "I should have known that."

"Did your father ever tell you about 'connections,' Piper?" Astrid presses her hand against the brunette's cheek with insistent gentleness, her eyes full of desire. "I think you might be fond of the idea."

Piper falls silent, abashed. Suddenly, she's ashamed by her lack of knowledge. "N-no? What are they?"

"Well, we may not experience what you humans call 'love', but we have our own version of it in which you become emotionally connected and linked to another person – or persons – of interest."

"Kind of like marriage?"

"Hmm…similar. This emotional link is called a 'connection' and is powerful. Once it has been formed, one should seriously avoid breaking it because to do so is physically painful and can cause emotional damage."

Piper laughs nervously, weakly. "It sounds like love, alright…"

"If you say so. So, do you want to form a connection with me, Piper Tourneau?"

"For one single heartbeat, it seems to Piper that her soul hangs transfixed, balanced as though a weight of feathers has fallen onto one side of a scale and lifted the other out of a dark abyss. And now, in perfect equilibrium, it stands. A connection with Astrid. No matter how the mermaid phrases it, to her it's a relationship. Astrid will be her *girlfriend*.

"Yes," she breathes.

I don't even know you that well, but yes.

Chapter Eighteen

Unlike having to deal with the usual bustling afternoon crowd, Falké has no need to jostle his way through the Gilded Gull bar on this Tuesday night. Usually, he sits at the bar itself, slumped forwards and clutching a glass of something he often can't even pronounce. He doesn't really feel like doing so today. Instead, he locates a solitary booth near the window after ordering a couple of drinks, slackens into the leather seat, and sighs deeply.

This bar might as well be his second home now, considering how often he finds himself here. He knows every inch of the place. Every glass. Every scratch on the wooden tables. Every tear in the leather-padded stools. His depression is buried in the onslaught of knowledge he has about this building and its components, and it's a welcome distraction to say the least.

If there were more people here then maybe the little fight ring they have below this place would be in operation. If it was, he'd probably find some solace in throwing a few punches at a random opponent. It's not though, and he's too emotionally weak at the moment for fighting anyway.

He sits alone for a long time, drinking in the quiet and staring at the table in attempt to disguise his wretchedness. The people that occasionally look over at him still seem to notice, and that does nothing but make him feel worse about everything.

Crystal and blue number three. He brings the glass to his lips, knowing deep down that he should really slow down with the drinking today; it's barely past midday. Then again, if he were to slow down…he wouldn't be able to mask any of this ridiculous sorrow he feels. Who cares if he's hungover tomorrow? At least he'll be more distracted with the physical pain, so much so that he might, just *might*, forget the mental stuff for a while.

All of his problems flood his consciousness in one big tsunami. Piper and her mermaid friend, Carmen and her boyfriend. His mentally and physically abusive mother. This stupid drinking problem he *knows* he has. Oh…and of course, Esther. How could he possibly forget about Esther? She's the reason he's really here, he knows that for sure. He clutches at the necklace hidden under his shirt, almost pulling it from his neck thanks to his slow and thoughtless movements.

"Falké, my guy."

Eugh, no - he'd recognise that voice anywhere. Carmen's squeeze, Kyran. What is he doing here? He doesn't normally frequent the bars around here…he's typically getting into trouble somewhere else. The boy grumbles under his alcoholic breath, nursing the drink in his hands. "Yo, Ky," he greets lazily, "what ya doing here? Ya ain't hanging with Carmen and the others?"

Kyran moves forwards and sits beside him, grasping at his unfinished drink. He invites himself to a sip of it, and Falké creases his lips in disdain. He's never been a fan of Carmen's boyfriend, mostly because he's such a bad influence on her. "Do ya mind?" he asks in a less than hospitable tone, and Kyran shrugs. "Nah."

For God's sake.

"I ain't hangin' with nobody today," the dark-haired boy says, and Falké genuinely contemplates correcting his grammar. He doesn't. Instead, he snatches his drink back and takes a ridiculously large gulp in some attempt to make the conversation more interesting. When he's drunk enough, even the most stupid chats seem at least *slightly* tolerable.

"A'right. Whatever," he scoffs, trying to stay focused on his surroundings despite the now very off-putting blur on everything. Kyran gives him a slow once-over, portraying what Falké instantly perceives as a very patronising smile on his face. "Ya don't look so good, Falké," the guy notes, "ya drinkin' cusa ya cousin?"

Falké narrows his eyes. He is about to say something, comment on Piper and her obvious interest in the mermaids, but he gets sick without warning. He loses what must be at least two of his crystal and blues on the floor with a miserable, throaty moan.

"Look at ya, upchuckin' everywhere in a winda' booth of the Gilded Gull. Ya mama must be so proud," Kyran cackles, "dunno what Carmen sees in ya."

Falké glances at him with boiling hostility. He's never liked the guy but has been dealing with the prospect of him for Carmen's sake. But now, now he hates him. Despises him. *Loathes* him. He tenses his fists in preparation for throwing a punch but the only action his body undertakes is throwing itself forwards as he heaves and throws up again. Kyran laughs scrappily, and that is the last sound Falké has the great displeasure of hearing before he blacks out.

Darkness.
Dull grey light.
Darkness again.
Slightly brighter light.

Falké opens his groggy eyes slowly, a few violent coughs escaping his lungs. His fragile, weak body still lies on the ripped-up leather seat of the booth, yet the bar is empty. It's not too hard to decipher what happened – clearly, Kyran didn't think of supporting him in such a time of need and just left him to his own devices. But that doesn't explain why the place is empty apart from him. There's no way the bartender would have allowed him to just crash here all night. And thinking of night, what time is it? How long has he been here?

"Your friend abandoned you."

That voice.

He adjusts his positioning with a low whine of pain, sitting up and staring forwards at the girl sitting opposite him. "Wassgoin' on? Waappened?" he slurs, and she twirls a strand of silvery green hair around her finger in silence for a while before responding.

"You were sick. You passed out, and your friend just left you, laughing to himself. If I were you, I would refrain from hanging around such stupid humans who clearly do not care for your health and well-being."

"Not my friend," Falké says abashedly, feeling like an absolute fool for getting so damn drunk in the first place. He raises a hand to his forehead and rubs at it in a desperate attempt to quell the awful pain persisting there.

The mermaid sighs. "Anyway," she starts, "the bartender kicked you out before closing. Once he left, I broke in via the back door and took you back to this booth. I would take you home, but it would be too risky. I couldn't leave you lying on the decking, though."

"…Esther…?"

She leans forward and places her elbow on the table, propping her head against her hand.

"Yes?"

CHAPTER NINETEEN

Jasper Vanguard loves mermaids. He loves the carnal fire in their eyes, the sharp, shark-like teeth hidden behind their plush lips. He loves their smooth, glistening skin and powerful, beautiful tails. But there is nothing – *nothing* – that he loves more than their venom.

"You'll let us out now, you'll let us out."

"You won't keep us trapped here anymore."

"You want to let us out *so badly*."

The newest captives, three red mermaids, cling to the bars above their tank with ardent desperation. Lips pressed against them, breathing their sweet words into the air as their tails move from side to side in the water. They all react in the same fashion upon being captured, he's noticed over time. They all try the same method, they're not used to not getting their way.

"You want to let us out."

"You'll put us back in the ocean now."

"You don't want to keep us here anymore."

"It won't work, my dears," he states wistfully as he taps his finger against a vial, glancing back at the creatures in the tank behind him. "You can attempt to persuade me or command me all you like. But I have this," – he places the vial down and gestures to the mask he's wearing – "and your intoxication won't work. You see, there are filters in this mask I wear – filters that block your venom gases."

In spite of the explanation, the mermaids clearly don't understand. They continue with their smooth, musical encouragements and he hums to himself as he turns back to his work. He doesn't expect them to understand, really – they've never seen a gas mask before, after all. How are they supposed to know how it works?

He's been down here for a while now. Seven hours, ten minutes, and… fifteen seconds to be exact. Timing is so very important when dealing with mermaid venom. Out of all the chemicals and substances he's tried mixing it with, nothing has been as promising as this recent attempt: sulphur extracted from an area around the thermal vents in Illyria.

The idea came to him last night, as he lay in bed thinking about the recent upsurge in 'deaths related to volcanic activity'. Some of them faked (for in reality they were people taken as test subject for his weapons), but some of them very real…

Pressing a spray nozzle into the vial he clears his throat and smiles. There is excitement within him, growing with every minute. Where before a cold stone sat, now a wonderful ball of heat is lodged in his chest, burning, and he can't wait another moment before he stands and rushes to the door.

"Let us see if this works, my loves," he tells his captives, who begin thrashing violently in the water as he approaches the exit, "and if it does, you are going to unlock a whole new world of possibilities for

Illyria. Think of it as serving your nation. Heh."

Scarlett awakens from her afternoon rest tangled in an excessive pile of silk blankets. The last vestiges of her dreams cling to her – married to Jasper, a child they both love running around at their feet. Happiness.

An ache gnaws at her cheek from where she was hit earlier, but she doesn't audibly complain; such a thing serves as a reminder that she ought to stop questioning Jasper. She has told herself more than once that aches like this are useful because she's so utterly *brainless* she's bound to forget her place without them. They make her remember.

She reaches for the cream she keeps on her night stand and rubs it onto her face. The soothing sensation that follows provides a strange mixture of relief and numbness. Sometimes, she wonders if she truly loves Jasper.

"Scarlett, you fool," she whispers to herself, frowning at the way her tongue is strangely heavy in her mouth and lips annoyingly dry. She's thirsty, she realises after a moment of deliberation and, blinking sleepily, finds that there's glass beside her lamp. She hadn't noticed it before when reaching for the cream, but is relieved to see it now.

I love him, she reminds herself as she sips the water, *of course I do. I deserve to be punished for thinking otherwise. He helped me become who I am today.*

When she first came to this place, to Jasper, she knew nothing of comfort and riches. She lived alone in a crumbling house on the south-west side of the city and was sick. Had an infection or something of the sort; antibiotics, although available in Illyria, were too expensive for her to afford thanks to the nation's enormous taxes.

Everything is so different now.

She finishes the glass, and heads towards her vanity chest. The golden comb that sits there was a gift to her from Jasper on her last birthday. She puts down the glass, picks up the comb, and runs it through her crimson hair slowly as she stares in the mirror. She didn't like red before, when she was new to this place. Blue was her favourite colour by far, baby blue. But Jasper liked red, and he named her Scarlett, and she didn't want to upset him. She still doesn't want to upset him.

"Scarlett, my pet,"

Jasper.

She turns quickly on the stool to face him, smiling. "Hello, Jasper. I hope you are having a nice day. I just woke up from a lovely dream."

"That's nice," he cuts in, stepping into the room with a smile. "But I'm not interested in listening to you talk about your dreams. I *am* interested in having you," he points to the bed from which she just moved. "On the bed."

A light, anxious chuckle escapes her. "Right now...? I just woke up, Jasper! Perhaps we should later? I don't think I'm particularly ready for it this instant. Oh, but I will make it worth the wait tonight, I promise."

"Right now."

He moves over to her, brushing his thumb over her lip. She shivers under his touch, and rises from the stool with a sudden, "I will pleasure you in another way if you like."

Disregarding her cacophony of muttering he presses his fingers against the atomiser and tilts his head to the side. "But you don't *want* to pleasure me in 'another way,' Scarlett. You want to in the way I want. Don't you? You really do."

For a moment, nothing happens. And then, ever so slowly, she clutches at the sides of her nightdress with a low sigh of need. "You're right," she whispers, "I do. I do really want to."

Jasper laughs in delight. It's the longest he's ever managed to prolong the efficiency of the venom — and it's all thanks to that *beautiful* sulphur! Seven hours, fifteen minutes, and forty-five seconds and so far, it works. He can only hope that further experimentation will mean minutes and hours will turn into days.

"Yes. That's right. That's right, my pet. Just climb on up there, like you want to, and everything is going to be wonderful."

He revels in his discovery, joins Scarlett on the bed, and celebrates. What an excellent day.

CHAPTER TWENTY

A very small part of Prince Holt feels silly for turning up at the house of a girl he has only spoken to once. A much larger part, however, is brimming with excitement at the prospect of seeing her again. He has never had a peasant friend before – although he feels this terminology doesn't suit Piper in the slightest – and especially not one that likes him for *him*, and not his status. Thrilling.

It wasn't too difficult to find this place. Out of the several nearby Illyrians his guard questioned, pretty much all of them knew the girl's name and location. Piper Tourneau, niece of therapist Elvira Tourneau, and cousin of Falké Tourneau. All live at Dreracile Decks, Mahina house, Number 130. He didn't get much information on the girl's parents, but assumes they're deceased or otherwise absent from her life.

Straightening his posture, he clears his throat and adjusts the brown wig upon his head. Prior to this trip he had very limited experience in wearing wigs – so limited, in fact, that he had never worn one *at all*. He decides at this very moment that he hates them and the itchiness and general discomfort they cause.

He clutches the small bouquet in his hands with a series of deep breaths. It had been a tremendous challenge for Lenka to get these flowers. She had wandered Illyria's shops yesterday for what seemed like hours but discovered that flowers simply weren't sold anywhere. In the end, she had resorted to cutting a few buds from some of the potted plants on the yacht. It was very difficult as Holt adores his flowers, but it was a sacrifice worth making for the sake of impressing a lady like Piper. After all, if bouquets are *so* rare here, she'll be even *more* impressed to receive one.

She will adore them, he thinks, *all ladies love flowers; it will be worth the trouble. Definitely.*

It's not very polite to turn up at somebody's residence uninvited. He knows that. After all, he is a prince and has spent numerous years training in etiquette. But there is a desire within him that overrides mere etiquette. Piper looked in such pain the first – and last – time they spoke, and he can't help but want to help her. Fix things. Stop the pain, at least a little. Befriend her.

What was it she said when they met? Something about mermaids. He can only assume one of the creatures did something to her. He knows very little about them; the national newspaper isn't very informative in regards to them. Mermaids are clearly a dark subject, portrayed as sinister and dangerous but never really confirmed to be. There's clearly not enough fact, only speculation. Still, he's willing to protect her from them as best he can. He raises his hand nervously to the door, feeling his heart beating in his ears.

"Who are you looking for?"

The voice is smooth and dark, and comes from behind him; he pivots quickly on the ball of his foot, and is faced with one of *them*.

She stares at him almost threateningly, standing perfectly still as if she is but a statue carved from blue alabaster. Cold and hard, with eyes made of polished obsidian. Even the way her lips purse gives the impression somebody has captured a fleeting, delicate expression in stone…but then there are the fins on the side of her head; like wet leather in the light, shimmering and strong. Shining like diamonds. They're too glistening, too *real,* to be part of a sculpture.

She smiles at him wryly. He licks his lips nervously and then, as confidently as he can, says, "It is none of your business, mermaid."

"It is. Tell me."

Before he knows it, the words are slipping out of his mouth. "Piper Tourneau."

The mermaid raises her eyebrows. "Prince…Holt Davori, isn't it?" she asks, watching his eye twitch slightly as he realises his secret is not so secret after all, "I don't know what you want with Piper, but she is my connector. You have no chance with her."

What on Earth is a connector? he thinks. *Well, it is of no matter – I can deal with this. I will protect Piper Tourneau.*

Curling his lip, he grasps for the rapier hidden under his jacket and holds it out towards the creature. Still holding the flowers in one hand, he takes a deep breath and cries, "Begone, mermaid!"

She doesn't recoil, staying perfectly placid. This only heightens his nerves – "I said begone! You shall do no more damage…and my name is Henry!"

"Oh yeah? Henry what?"

He swallows dryly. "Henry…Brown! Henry Brown. Yes. Why, it is a very plain and ordinary name. Not special or regal-sounding whatsoever. Henry Brown, not Prince Holt Davori or whatever you just said! If that even *was* it! I can barely remember because that is not my name and I just happen to be bad at names, so there!"

"Mmhm. Alright, Henry Brown. I am Astrid."

"Fine. Astrid - I am Henry Brown and I am telling you to stay away from my Piper!"

Astrid laughs sourly, seemingly provoked by the boy's attitude. "Your Piper," she repeats.

"Yes! My Piper."

"I think you will find…" she starts, "that she is *my* Piper, not yours. I have a history with her family, and I am not having some random royal from a far-off kingdom come here to *my* Illyria and try to steal the affections of *my* Piper. I would eat you, you know. But one, I am not hungry, I just ate, and two, it wouldn't be a very smart idea of me to do so at the moment."

Holt scoffs. "This place doesn't belong to you. *My Illyria*, ha! You do not own it. There is a mayor, you *do* know that, correct? And you can stop trying to frighten me – mermaids do not eat people."

She says nothing for a few seconds, then smiles. "You know nothing of us, do you? All you know is what you have read from newspapers or heard in fairy tales. The rumours, the speculations, the wild guesses that we mermaids are drowning Illyrians. Not eating them, *of course*. If the stories don't mention it then it isn't happening. Right? Drop the flowers, Prince Holt. You won't be needing them."

She tilts her head to the side and draws so close to the prince that the point of his weapon very nearly pierces her stomach. He clutches the bouquet tighter for just a few seconds, and then stares down at it as his hand loosens and it falls to the ground.

Astrid steps on the blossoms. They crumple under her feet.

"You honestly believe that I'm unaware of the fact that Illyria has a mayor?" she jabs, "how stupid do you think I am, little human? Anyway, it is of no matter to me whether there is a mayor or not. Illyria is still mine, and so is Piper. Now… kindly lower your sword."

Slowly, ever so slowly, she presses her hand against the foible of the rapier and pushes it downwards. Holt allows his arm to fall to his side and lowers the weapon as instructed. Astrid breathes deeply, and then begins to laugh. "Pathetic. Perhaps I will attack you after all." She reaches out and forces up Holt's chin, baring her fangs.

"Astrid! Stop!"

Both the mermaid and her victim glance up at open window. Piper sticks her head out, imploring: "Stop! Don't hurt him, Astrid!"

Astrid raises her eyebrows, lips curling in frustration. "Why? Do you like this boy, *Piper*?" She emphasis her name angrily as she calls up to her, "Is that why?"

The girl pauses, shaking her head. "Not like that, Astrid," she calls back, "but he's nice…he helped me a while back…"

"And?
"Please don't."
"You like him."

"Astrid…"

"Fine."

Piper's face disappears from the window.

"Do not try my patience," the mermaid warns, raising her hand. She tightens it around the prince's neck until he gasps for breath, her sharp nails digging into his skin. That is not the most startling thing however; she lifts him off of the ground with only one arm, displaying an almost impossible strength. His eyes widen in shock. *How can a creature be this strong, yet look so like a human?*

"I'm leaving now," she says. "Tell your girlfriend she ought to think carefully about who she spends her time with. Who is more important."

"I – will do so – my lady," he chokes out in response, his voice full of terrible surrender. Then, suddenly, Astrid's hand releases him and he steps back, wheezing for air. A long moment is lost to the relief of filling his lungs once more, and when he manages to raise his reeling head again, he realises the creature has gone.

Suddenly, the front door opens and Piper rushes out. She's wearing a brown, pinafore-style dress today over a white shirt. Long white stockings. No shoes.

"Astrid, wait!" she shouts. Realising her words are useless she directs her attention to Holt instead. "I am *so* sorry, Henry! She doesn't usually behave like that, please forgive her!"

He rubs his neck, a confused look on his face. "No, no. It is my fault. I apologise profusely, my lady."

He doesn't recall doing anything wrong, only being near-strangled to death by a beautiful creature he couldn't help but follow the directives of. Nothing was particularly *his fault*. But he doesn't want Piper to feel bad, and if that means defending her mermaid friend's actions, so be it. He clears his throat, glances down at the crumpled bouquet on the ground, and bends down to retrieve it.

"You must forgive me for being so rude to it, I mean *her*, and riling her. I just couldn't bear the thought of you being hurt and I was under the impression that she was the cause of your suffering the other night. Do you understand?"

She sighs, watching as he rises back to his feet and holds out the flowers. "Yes, yes, of course. Sorry. I was so vague that night, I…I didn't mean to worry you. Please be careful around Astrid, she's very strong."

"I know for future reference. Anyway, I brought you these. It would make me happy if you were to accept them -"

"Oh…wow, yes…thank you," comes her surprised response. She takes the bouquet, looking down at it, and lightly dances her fingertips against the petals of one of the flowers. They're beautiful. Flowers are so rare in Illyria. "Where did you get them?" she asks softly.

"Ah, well, I was not able to find any bouquets in your…lovely…city. So, I cut these blossoms from my own potted plants. May I come in?"

Her gaze snaps upwards to his face. "My aunt will be home any minute now…I'm not allowed guests."

"I will speak to her."

"No! No. Don't do that. She's not very nice."

"I am sure I can handle it. I am very good with people."

"She's one of the therapists at the Health Centre. You know, the ones that work for the mayor and stuff."

"Oh! I have such respect for people who spend their days healing others. It is a wonderful thing to help other people."

Piper grimaces slightly, interrupting. "You're not from around here, are you?"

Not from around here. He dabs at his brow instinctively, nervous. Is it really that obvious? After a long, tense moment during which he can practically *feel* his heartbeat in his throat, he speaks again. "Ah. Yes. I am a visitor. My family docked in Illyria only a few weeks ago in order to sell fish we caught on the open seas. We are sailors."

This earns a small laugh from Piper, which pleases him. She shakes her head and shrugs. "Aha. Good luck selling fish here. We have so much of it already. But seriously, my aunt is gonna be home soon. So, if you don't mind, I should get back inside."

His brow creases, but he relents and stands back. "Alright, if you insist. I shall return another time if you do not mind. I have been thinking about you a lot since we met - I am worried about you, you know?"

Before she can respond, he turns and leaves.

CHAPTER TWENTY-ONE

The remainder of 'Henry' and Piper's conversation does not last long. Astrid observes the end of it from the shadowy underneath of a nearby jetty, running her nails up and down the wood to her left so hard that it leaves marks. And then, once she notices Elvira coming home out of the corner of her eye, she shifts her attention away from it entirely. The woman is carrying her 'medical' bag as usual, stuffed to the brim with notes upon notes of her patients' thoughts, feelings, and concerns in relation to the mermaids. Notes that Astrid is well aware will go straight to the mayor. Not that he does anything with them – nothing ever changes around here.

She doesn't stay any longer. Curving her body downwards, she dives underwater and towards the seabed through the cobalt deep. Thrusting her hands in her pale hair, she pulls until the physical sensation distracts her from such a frustrating event.

Schools of glowing silver fish pour past her. She grabs one of the smallest by its tail, stuffs it into her mouth, and chews on its sweet flesh. Crunching the small bones gives her momentary satisfaction, as does the feeling of it sliding down her throat. It's nowhere near as tasty as human flesh – but then again, very little can compare with human flesh. There is something so delightful about its soft, rippable texture, the fat and blood...

She squints slightly, looking around. There's a human body somewhere in the water nearby; she can smell it and the blood seeping from it. The suspicions are confirmed when a small shiver of red mermaids darts past her, swirling around each other in a quick display of adrenaline-fuelled excitement. In the centre of this group is a middle-aged looking man, clearly already deceased and bleeding crimson clouds into the water. He's missing an arm and a leg.

She purses her lips as she swims to Zachary's boat and darts through the gaps between rotting planks of wood to reach him. He too coloured the sea red with blood. Of course, he's not bleeding now. That was in the past.

"I saw a dead body just now," she says calmly, lowering herself onto the skeleton's lap. "It made me think of you. But then again, I didn't dare let another mermaid have you when you became a dead body. *Especially* not an entire shiver. They didn't have the right to you like I did, like I still do, and it's for that reason that I took you for myself. But you always belonged to me really, though, even if you *were* married. Marriage is merely child's play in comparison to a mermaid's connection, inconsequential and silly."

She sighs.

"Besides, Elisa Tourneau was nowhere near as beautiful as I was – as I still *am*. She was plain and ordinary at best, and her only redeeming quality was her gentle, weak soul. Definitely not something I would be proud of, but a feature that humans seem to like very much…you were a fool for choosing such a woman over me. You should have known that I would claim you no matter what, even if you ended your life. And even now, as you sit here at the bottom of the sea, you belong to me. Not Elisa. *Me.* I won, and I will always win. I will win your daughter as I won you."

Slowly she leans back, lounging, and allows her eyes to slip closed.

"It's pathetic, really – this boy thinks that he can impress *my* connector with some plants and a few sweet words? Piper's not that easily led. On second thought, she probably is. But still – can you believe the nerve he has? He may be beautiful, but he's nowhere near as gorgeous as I am. He may be smart, but he's nowhere near as wise and ancient as I am. Everything he can do, I can do a thousand times better. He isn't a threat, no matter how bothersome and persistent he appears to be."

She stretches out. Several glittering fish scurry past but she cannot see them; her eyes remain closed as she shifts on top of the bones, her powerful tail curling from side to side. She pushes her palms against her waist. Feels at her cold skin, runs her hands down over the curve of her belly, across her tail, and then exhales slowly. Here in this body, she is practically permanent.

"When I was young, around seventy perhaps, I thought maybe it would be a relief to feel things like love and jealousy: to be more human, cut myself open and let other humans sift through the offal. But I have matured since then, and wretched human-style emotions are in no way a relief. If anything, the burden of them grows heavier and constricts in my chest until I am crushed by the weight of pure *feeling*. I'd much rather be wholly ethereal, separate from that type of living. Do you understand what I mean? Of course you don't. You always liked *feeling*. Well, feelings die as the years pass just as the creatures in the water and the humans on land do. Just as you did. Unlike me, you all wither and age quickly. You don't look youthful and perfect for centuries, like a mermaid does. It's both disappointing and wonderful, really."

She opens her eyes.

"There's nothing wrong with connecting with humans when you take it all into consideration. They live such short lives anyway, growing old and dying within, what, eighty years on average? It's barely any time at all, really. Your daughter is mine. And so are you."

CHAPTER TWENTY-TWO

"It's strange, isn't it?"

Esther adjusts her positioning on the armrest of the worn couch in Falké's bedroom. She sits side-saddle, perfectly idle, and combs her fingers through the boy's hair. It's a pleasant feeling, for she only lightly grazes his scalp with her sharp nails, and he smiles in contentment with a "hm?"

"Well, we green mermaids gravitate towards bonds with others, yet the other colours tend to reject love and romance. But what we just witnessed highly suggests *Astrid* and your cousin have formed a connection now. Did you see the way she nearly killed that boy for just talking to Piper?"

"Wasn't lookin' at 'em," he responds. Esther may have been watching the events outside unfold from the window, but he certainly wasn't. Why look at anything aside from Esther? Nothing else matters.

The mermaid purses her lips. "Well, the whole concept of it is…practically impossible. Blue mermaids cannot feel love…like I can." She leans forwards holding his head back, and finds his forehead with her lips. She kisses there just once, above his eyebrows. The action catches Falké off guard and he looks up at her, his cheeks hot with mortification. After a moment, he drags his head away from her hands. "Don't wanna talk 'bout my cousin," he grumbles indolently, his own hands clenching into his thighs until they are sure to leave bruises.

Esther nods in understanding, her fingers creeping across his shoulders, dancing over them. And soothingly, empathetically, she whispers, "Alright then."

He breathes in deeply. "Sorry."

"It's alright. You look awful, by the way - you really shouldn't have drunk so much. I would have thought you learned your lesson after that 'friend' of yours left you. You could have choked to death on your own vomit. What a wonderfully stupid way to die."

He moans in indignance, the unwanted memory of Kyran's nastiness pushed forwards in his head. Why would she bring him up? She knows the mere thought of that guy has him seething. Does she *want* to get a negative reaction out of him or something? Also, why must she, and everybody else, criticize him for drinking so much? It's not his fault. It's an addiction. It's not exactly easy to just *stop*.

If he wasn't feeling so exceptionally awful today he probably would've shouted at Esther by now. He tends to have difficulty managing his anger. When he was back in school, he was encouraged to seek help concerning his emotions on more than one occasion. The school nurse was entirely useless when it came to mental health issues, as he assumes all Illyrian nurses are, and only gave him leaflets to read as support. He threw them in the bin on the way home and never spoke of it to his parents. After all, seeking any form of 'therapy' is nothing but bad in Illyria, and that's the way it always will be.

"Geddoff my back," he bites. It's not as effective as shouting of course, but a lot less painful. Even so, a slightly wounded look falls upon Esther's face, and his forehead crumples with guilt. He's waited for years to speak to this mermaid again, let alone be this close to her. He doesn't want to mess it up this early on. Besides, she's right – he did drink too much, as usual.

He groans softly, avoiding her gaze. "Eugh, I'm sorry. Just…it ain't that easy, Esther. I can't just quit. I need it, I need it so badly and -"

Esther interrupts, her finger pressing against his lips in an effort to silence him. She drags it down his chin to his collarbone and allows it to rest there for a few seconds. "I can help you stop drinking," she hums, "all I need to do is tell you to stop, and you will. But…that is an easy way out, isn't it? It would be much better for you to go through the process of quitting yourself. In the end, you'll come out of it much stronger. Once you admit to yourself that it's in your control, it'll be much easier."

"I'll try."

"Good."

"Will ya 'elp me?"

"Yes. But Falké?"

"Yeah?"

"Do you want to touch me?"

She knows the answer already - if she didn't, she wouldn't have asked. Still, hearing the words from him gives them more power, more meaning. It makes her feel in control, and for the past few years she has felt nothing but out of it. A green mermaid without a connector is barely a mermaid at all, all things considered. They *need* a partner.

There is a moment of silence. Then Falké shifts, the couch creaking in protest. His breathing changes, becoming quicker and shallower, and he swallows dryly before responding: "Y-yeah. Yeah. I wanna touch ya. I wanna touch ya, Esther."

"Then touch me. Go on, touch me."

This incentive is all he needs to grasp for her and with a sharp inhalation, skim his fingers across her smooth, mint-coloured skin. He moves her closer to him with a tug, and she lands with her knees planted on either side of his hips. "Very forward," she observes, laughing.

He feels the sudden need to apologise. He does so regretfully, the words tumbling from his mouth and falling upon her slender, perfect frame. She collects them in her hands and dips them right back between his lips with one simple phrase: "No need to say sorry."

He nods in understanding.

"Kiss me," she commands, "please? Kiss me here?" She bares her neck to him, and he embraces her. His mouth finds its way to her skin, pressing against it, and he sighs happily as he kisses his way across her throat and down her chest, huffing hot puffs of air. She breathes his name, and he scorches a mask of desire into her throat, a splotchy ring of red. Finally, *finally* Esther is here with him, her voice like a song, her entire existence so very like a dream. He looks up at her from the jut of her sternum and feels entirely enamoured.

"Ya so beautiful," he whispers tiredly, picking her up and scooping her into his arms. Damn, he feels dreadful. His head is pounding, his muscles are exhausted, and bile seems to rise in his throat every few minutes. Despite this, he sure as hell isn't going to stop making love to the mermaid he's been fantasising about for the past few years. Who cares if he's outrageously hungover? What matters is that Esther is here, and not only that, Esther is here and *she wants him to touch her.*

"You are beautiful too," comes the mermaid, and Falké can't help but smile. Not once in his entire life has he been called such a thing, and a strange tremor shakes through him for a moment before he realises he is laughing. A lot. She laughs too, and he holds her close, burying his face into her perfectly straight locks of starlight and emerald.

"I wanna be with ya," he says suddenly, "I wanna date ya. Can I? Esther."

She chuckles, wrapping her arms around him as she is held. "Yes. Let us be connectors, Falké. Let us be together."

"Yeah…"

"Oh, and Falké?"

"Yeah?"

"I'm going to love you."

He places her down on his bed gently, flinging himself beside her, and rests his hand against her cheek in a moment of weakness. "Imma love ya too," he murmurs, "think I already do."

Esther perches herself atop him, straddling the thinnest part of his waist, and plants both hands upon his chest. "No, you don't," she supplies, shamelessly running her fingers under his shirt and across his skin, "it's been a while since you last saw me. I've changed a little, as have you. When you get to know this new me, then, and only then, can you love me. Okay?"

He nods after a second's consideration. It doesn't matter to him if he has to wait to love Esther properly. He's happy enough knowing she wants to be with him and the time they are spending together isn't just some fantasy he's forging for himself late at night in a drunken haze. This is real. "I missed ya," he whispers. "Why'did ya have to leave?"

"Coming of age."

"I know…why though? What dya do? Why'd ya have to leave Illyria?"

"We change."

He looks up at her, basking in the warmth of her company, and a certain contentment settles on him as she stares back with a smile. "Ya look the same."

"Our bodies change. Mature. Remember when I was younger, and I had to stay in the water all the time? I was unable to change my physical form to walk upon land. I couldn't have legs, like you."

A small grunt leaves him. "And ya 'ave to leave for that long just to get legs? Stay in Illyria."

"No. We need to go to a secluded – and safe - cove that is partly in water and partly out of it. The process renders us practically immobile – it's dangerous to go through it here. Besides, it's also tradition, I guess. They say the first Illyrian mermaid went through their coming of age change there, and now we all do."

His eyes holding hers, he sighs softly and nods in understanding. "Did it hurt ya?"

"Sorry?"

"Changin' and stuff…did it hurt ya?"

"Yes."

"What was it like?"

Esther pauses for a moment, leaning back slightly as she recalls the events of her coming of age. It's not something she particularly *wants* to remember, but it happened, and she should be glad of it, really. There's no use pretending things didn't happen when they did. How are you supposed to learn and grow from things you've experienced, otherwise? She traces little patterns on his chest with her fingertips and sighs softly.

"It started a few days after I reached the cove. When it began, I thought I might die. And some of us do you know. Some of us don't survive the change, it hurts so badly our bodies shut down. I remember clutching at my tail and screeching to the sky, lying just beyond the shoreline with the warm water washing over me. It reminded me of you. I thought of you a lot for comfort's sake actually. Especially when I had to watch this jagged, vivacious line rent me apart down the middle. I couldn't stop it. It wasn't fast-moving. It was slow and painful. And I felt like a mussel without its shell. Weak and unprotected. And then I was creating *bones*. I could feel them piecing together slowly, rearranging. And it made me feel sick. Eventually, I could form legs. Legs with bones, and muscle, and everything else they need to work. I practiced walking on them for a while. I was so bad at it."

She laughs weakly. "...*So* bad. But anyway, as soon as I felt comfortable moving between forms, I headed back home. Back home to you."

Falké frowns. Every mermaid has to go through this? It sounds horrific. "Wish I was there to help ya through it."

"You were in my heart. Besides, it doesn't matter now – I'm home. We're home. Both of us."

He nods, closing his eyes. "Yeah. Home."

CHAPTER TWENTY-THREE

For three days, Scarlett drifts in and out of quiescence. Time seems to pass in a strange, fragmented fashion, which is stressful to say the least. She has always liked being organised; creating calendars and to-do lists is one of the few things in life that makes her feel... accomplished.

She has no idea what the date is now.

Her head aches, as if it's held at the mercy of a crackling storm struggling to settle within her skull. It has for a while now. Despite this, Jasper refused to take her to the Illyrian Health Centre. He brought in a doctor yesterday to look at her instead, one that she remembers was named Doctor Margo Santi. A very smart-looking woman, with a very smart-sounding name and an assured manner.

Strangely enough, the doctor didn't speak to her about the 'illness' – instead, Jasper handled the situation himself having an extremely intense conversation with her next door that Scarlett could only vaguely overhear. Something about being exposed to far too much of something in a short amount of time.

Scarlett doesn't recall coming into contact with anything dangerous over the past few weeks, but who knows? Illyria is full of all sorts of hazards, hazards that she sometimes forgets exist at all. It's so safe and cosy in the mayor's house and she only rarely leaves. Still, she chides herself for being so foolish, she should be really be more aware of her surroundings. Getting sick like this is only wasting Jasper's time. He has more important things to do than speak with doctors and check up on her every few minutes.

She can't help but feel she's disappointed him.

Again.

Sometimes she opens her eyes and he is facing her, watching. Sometimes he is turned away, asleep. Sometimes he is absent from the room and his side of the bed is cold. Every once in a while she can feel his warm body arched over hers, his legs straddled on either side of her hips, his hands caressing her skin. She opens her eyelids and meets his gaze, when this happens he averts his stare and observes the whole length of her body, snagging his lower lip between his teeth. "Back to sleep," he says to her simply, and she obeys as best she can.

It's a grim and rainy Wednesday afternoon when she finally feels well enough to rise from the bed. The headache she had previously suffered is finally gone, and she makes a mental note to be more vigilant next time she ventures outside to avoid anything that might cause her to get sick again. Whatever it might be.

She glances in the mirror and groans softly at the state of her hair. It streams from her scalp in thick curls like strands of DNA, twirling around itself and over her face. It's uncombed and knotted. She reaches for the comb, but the door opens suddenly and she turns her attention towards it instead.

Jasper carries a tray in his hands. What looks like sushi has been placed upon it, alongside a small glass of cloudy-looking water. Probably containing dissolved medication, she decides. He looks surprised to see her moving around, and then nods his head in the direction of the bed. "Go sit down. Don't strain yourself…how are you feeling?"

"I'm feeling a lot better," comes her response. "I don't have a headache any more. I'm sorry for worrying you."

"I see." He watches her take a seat, places the tray down, and presses his fingers against her brow with eyes full of intrigue. The woman falls silent, abashed. As he draws his hand away, she licks her lips and reaches for the glass of water, realising that her throat is very much dry.

She sips it, and then gestures towards the sushi. "Can I-?"

"Yes."

It's delicious. It contains what she assumes is crab meat alongside white, medium-grain rice and soy sauce. The entire thing is salty, extremely so, but she likes it. It's not long at all until the entire tray is empty, and she almost finds herself begging for more. Needless to say, she decides against doing so. It would only make her sound even *more* pathetic.

Once again, he asks how she is feeling. This time, she responds with "much better," which seems to please him immensely. He stands, preparing to leave but she quickly reaches for his sleeve and tugs on it. The action causes him to stop in his tracks and look down at her questioningly. "What?"

"Don't go yet, Jasper."

He takes stock of her with idle fascination. "Mmmh," he drawls, "why not? I have a lot of work to catch up on you know. I've been putting it aside to look after you."

She smiles. "Do you love me?"

He crouches down a little, holding her by the chin, and returns the smile. He runs his hands over the cusp of her breasts, down her chest, towards her thighs.

"Do you love me?" Jasper asks in response.

Scarlett's eyes follow every movement that his hands make across her frame. Something inside of her runs in excited circles at the thought of him touching her like this, and it causes her to blush profusely. "Of course I do."

"Well there you have it then."

Chapter Twenty-Four

"Do you like the mermaids now?"
"No!"
"Now?"
"*No!* Stop, please!"
"Say they're vermin. Say it with me: *The mermaids of Illyria are all vermin, and I hate them.*"
"Please, please…"
"Piper!"
"The mermaids of Illyria…are all vermin…and I hate them…"

Piper's eyes shoot open as she rouses from the memory. It's unsettling to replay the events of last night in her mind, but every time she finds herself pausing to think they return to her, unwelcome. Despite the clothes she is wearing, and the fact she is not actually cold today, she shivers as she imagines herself at Elvira's mercy.

Before her, a bowl of porridge bubbles on the stove. She locks her gaze onto it, her breath laboured by pain, and sighs quietly. Everything hurts, physically and emotionally – but what feels the worst, what *really* digs at her, is the fact that she's said such terrible things about Astrid during her aunt's 'therapy'. Even if the mermaid never hears those words, it makes her uncomfortable to know they have been spoken.

She shouldn't really be making food now. Elvira is giving her very small rations during the day, with the intention of starving her into submission, and is bound to notice if she eats. Not only that, but the house's porridge oats supply is noticeably decreasing.

Astrid hasn't made an appearance since Henry turned up at the house. He, however, has visited several times. His offers to buy meals or purchase gifts have gone unclaimed as she doesn't want to seem so pathetic in front of him.

He tries his best.

She stirs the porridge slowly before hearing the sound of footsteps, and the kitchen door opens to admit somebody who approaches her from behind. She inhales sharply through her nose, her eyes wide, and dares not turn around. Her body burns in feverish panic. Blood scalds her veins from the inside. Her heart beats in a quivering rhythm. Her aunt shouldn't be home yet; she just left to give the mayor more notes. It's impossible. And Falké is upstairs, passed out drunk. Again.

"Piper," Astrid greets. She sighs in relief, the hot fear dissipating as she feels hands on her body, cool and firm as they slide over her skin, taking possession of her with unavoidable tenderness. Astrid breathes softly against her neck, kissing her, and she trembles as those hands smooth down her chest and come to rest on her hips.

She wants to beg for more. She *will* beg for more, she decides, as Astrid's touch is intoxicating in every way. The light grazing of her nails on bare skin makes her shiver uncontrollably. It's an unrivalled sensation and due to Astrid's absence for the past few days she has been painfully devoid of it. But, before she manages to speak, the mermaid continues, "I heard you screaming last night. I didn't like it."

"I'm sorry," she murmurs, trying to appear unfazed by the closeness of Astrid's body to her own. Her breathing is traitorously heavy, though, and she's almost positive Astrid notices.

"Don't apologise."

"Okay. I haven't seen you…in a while."

"I know. I was *thinking*."

"Thinking? About what?"

"Well," Astrid starts, "thinking about many things. But what matters is that I have come up with a solution to your issues. As much as I like this house, and the history it holds, it is time we both move away from it. You can just leave. Leave Elvira. Together, we can pack your things."

Piper whirls around in surprise, brushing Astrid's hands away. "Are you joking?" she snaps, "I can't just leave, Astrid…that's ridiculous! And what do you mean the 'history' this house holds?! You don't even live here. I live here, and where am I supposed to go if I stop doing that? Are you expecting me to just come underwater with you or something? Because, news flash Astrid, I am *not* one of you…vermin!"

For a moment, everything is painfully still. Astrid, stunned into silence, raises her brows and takes a graceful step backwards.

Piper coughs awkwardly. "I…" she starts, quiet, "I just…sorry, I just…"

The apology goes unfinished. Astrid crosses her

arms over her chest and interrupts with a low chuckle. The chuckle becomes a laugh, condescending and hostile, and once she has finished, she clears her throat and shakes her head. "Excuse me?" she questions, bitter amusement thrown into her tone, "Did you just call me *vermin?*"

Piper's breath hitches, and she struggles to respond to the question. Instead, a series of stammered, jumbled words escape her: "I-I didn't...I j-just...call you...I-I'm sorry..."

"Is this because of Henry Brown?" the mermaid raises, leaning against the counter and crossing her ankles casually, "has he been convincing you that I'm a problem? Has he?"

"N-no! Not at all! Henry has nothing to do with this, it's the stupid therapy I have to go through! It's messing with my head, Astrid!"

"I can tell," Astrid bristles, gesturing to the girl's bruised collarbone and arms. "This is getting ridiculous - I cannot believe you stand for such treatment. I have had enough of this, anyway. As soon as I leave, you'll want to pack your things."

Piper interjects, fuming with pent-up emotions, "Stop telling me what I want to do! Why do you always do that?! And if you haven't realised by now, the entire reason I'm in this mess is because of *you,* Astrid. Because of you and your ridiculous connection business."

This seems to strike a nerve with Astrid. She looks genuinely offended for a moment, a shady, sullen look darkening her expression. "So, you don't want to be connectors anymore?" she asks, her voice rumbling low like thunder. "This is because of that boy, isn't it? You like him better. He has nothing that I don't."

"Astrid, I don't like him! Oh my God! I like you, I do! I'm sorry, just ignore all of this stuff I'm saying okay?! I need to get back to cooking this stupid porridge."

The mermaid presses her lips together and frowns in scorn. Scepticism burns cold in her eyes. "If you don't like him," she begins, watching Piper suck on the insides of her cheeks, "then why did y-"

Piper cannot truly explain what happens next. All she knows is that suddenly, Astrid's mouth is soft and hot as it opens to her own. She grasps her shoulders, pulls her forwards, smashes their lips together, and Astrid reciprocates. The sensation of Astrid's tongue slick and smooth against her own makes her heart beat painfully fast, half-swallowing a gasp. It's dreamlike, just how she imagines being drunk to feel; Astrid's breath filling her throat, Astrid's taste filling her senses to the point that she feels she could die should their lips part.

When they do, she's relieved to find herself still alive. Astrid's grip on her tightens when she attempts to pull away, her glistening nails pressing into her skin and reminding her just how fragile she is. She looks at her questioningly, innocently, and Astrid flashes her a smile as if she has won some sort of game. In a way, she has. She brings both her hands up to Piper's face, sliding them over her cheeks and down her neck. They settle there for a moment like shackles, her thumbs stroking over the column of the girl's throat. Unexpectedly, Piper bats them away and inquires: "Do you still think I like him more?!"

"I suppose not."

Piper's heart lurches, pauses, and then starts again.

She lowers her hands slowly from Astrid's shoulders, her fingertips trembling with both embarrassment and awe.

"Well then." The words are cautious, but her eyes are warm and cheeks flushed, head spinning with adrenalin. She turns back to her porridge, grasping the stirring spoon, and watches Astrid stare at her in her peripheral vision. It was a dangerous move, kissing her like that, without any warning. And now her lips shimmer like diamonds – her aunt is bound to notice.

Astrid's hands settle on Piper's hips and begin to slowly and sensually knead. "I should go," she whispers in her ear, "leave you to your…porridge. Tell me goodbye."

She drags a palm upwards along the contour of Piper's bruised ribs through her clothing, just barely brushing her chest. The girl persists with stirring her food, willing herself to refrain from making an obvious reaction to this behaviour. *Astrid can't always get what she wants,* she thinks. *She's had a kiss from me, that's more than enough.* "Goodbye, Astrid," she mutters, and yet the words sound stale and wrong as if they shouldn't have been spoken.

"I'm going to leave now then."

"Good. My cousin will probably turn up soon and I don't want him to catch us down here."

"Alright. Bye-bye for now, *beautiful.*"

Astrid spins on the ball of her left foot gracefully, turning away from Piper. She blows a kiss over her shoulder when she notices the girl is watching, and then proceeds to run her hands down her own body alluringly.

Piper swallows dryly. She turns off the stove, puts

the spoon down, and makes a helpless gesture with her hand. She's not even certain herself what it's supposed to mean. Astrid's absence is an ache, and she yearns again to kiss her, to draw her close enough that she can feel her heartbeat against her skin. If she leaves, it's impossible. And who knows how long she will be gone for this time?

"Wait, Astrid!"

Astrid grins. She turns around again, hand resting thoughtfully at her chin. "Mmhm?"

"Could you stay...for a while? I'm sorry about snapping at you."

The request is established. Within seconds Astrid has swung herself up onto the kitchen counter beside Piper, one leg crossed over the other. She pushes some papers that were in her way to the side and they float gracefully to the floor in a quick tumbling dance.

Piper doesn't notice anything but Astrid's grin. It's unnaturally wide, so much so that she finds it necessary to reach forward and push at her cheeks in attempt to make it stop.

The mermaid laughs loudly. Playfully, she sticks out her tongue and licks the hand in front of her face, which the girl pulls away quickly with an annoyed: "Astrid!"

"Ha. Do you find my smile frightening?"

"Sorta."

"Adorable."

"Your teeth are just...so sharp."

"I take pride in that. Thank you."

Piper looks away, pouring the porridge into a bowl. Despite her great hunger, it doesn't look particularly appetising. She's afraid to use any honey - or even simple sugar for that matter - to sweeten it in fear of her aunt noticing. She moves to the side in order to fetch a spoon from the right, but her foot slips on one of the papers and she tumbles forwards.

Astrid jumps gracefully down from the side, catching her before any further damage to her body can be done. "Be careful," she warns, slowly letting go as the girl kneels down to pick up the sheets and gasps.

"What is it?" she queries, cocking an eyebrow.

"My aunt's notes, Astrid! I hadn't even noticed – Astrid, she's going to make a fool of herself if she turns up with no notes! She'll take it out on me- Astrid- Astrid what do I do?!"

The mermaid pauses. "Well, she hasn't been gone long. I'm sure you can catch up to her if you run. You know where she's going and the direction she will be heading in, so -"

Before Astrid has finished her sentence, Piper is at the door. "Look after my porridge for me!" she shouts, "I'll be right back!"

CHAPTER TWENTY-FIVE

"Esther?"

The whisper earns the faintest of answers. A little groan, almost, comes from behind Falké, and the fingers at his right hip stretch to life, pulling him closer. Esther is cold, but her body is smooth and perfect; he can feel it against his bare back as she snuggles up to him under the covers.

Everything is good. Everything is *great*.

She won't be here for very long. It's morning already and sunlight has been forcing its way through a small gap in the curtains for a while now. She never stays too long into the morning – sleeping on land dehydrates her.

For now, she is here, and that's all he cares about.

Closing his eyes again, a small, sleepy smile plays upon his lips. For once, his head is not throbbing from an excess of alcohol. His stomach is not heaving with the desire to throw its contents out of his mouth. Even better, Esther is with him and he is with her. He shuffles snugly against her; she makes another sound that he interprets as his name in response.

"Sorry," he mumbles sleepily, his eyes still closed, "wanted to see if ya was awake."

"You were…"

"Eh?"

"…If *you were* awake…"

He chuckles lightly. "Sorry."

A comfortable silence falls upon the pair again. Actually, Falké can't remember the last time he felt so content beside somebody. He's seen several girls in the past, and even had the occasional one-night-stand, but they haven't been particularly memorable. None of them made him *happy,* not like Esther.

Carmen used to sleep over, and despite being his best friend (and nothing more) she's the closest thing to a romance he's ever had. She rarely stays any more though; she's always at Kyran's place in the evenings. Falké can't really complain about that; the pair are in a relationship, after all.

Esther snuggles her face into the nape of his neck, planting a gentle kiss on his warm skin. He sighs blissfully. This is all he has ever wanted: the sound of her breathing. The softness of her long hair against his skin. The knowledge that she belongs to him, and he belongs to her.

Elvira – and Piper, for that matter - think he is still drinking, that he is here in his room suffering from a hangover like always. But, that cannot be further from the truth, because he hasn't had even a drop of alcohol for several days now.

His long trips to the bar? Esther.

His hungover days in bed? Esther.

Everything Esther.

Within moments, he finds himself falling into a contented and peaceful quiescence once again.

When he awakens a few hours later, she's gone.

It takes him a while to fully adjust to the morning and he simply stares at the ceiling for several minutes. His first action is to bring the sheets to his face and take a long inhale. It smells like Esther, like brine and sea flowers; it somehow makes him feel...at peace.

It's laundry day - Piper will be fetching his bedsheets sometime this afternoon. Esther's scent will be gone, but that's all right; she'll return again tonight, and everything will smell like her again soon enough.

Scrambling into a sitting position, he runs a hand through his messy hair, and finds himself wondering what his cousin is doing now. It's no secret that she's in some sort of a mermaid-human relationship, too. He's seen 'Astrid' hanging around the house on more than one occasion. Not only that, but despite Piper going through therapy at the moment, *the meetings between them have gone undeterred.* They must be very close.

A dark feeling passes through him, guilt curling in his stomach. It's hard to admit, but Piper is tough. Tougher than he is, for sure. Tougher than he will ever be. His mother isn't exactly the nicest person and he's often used Piper as a scapegoat to avoid being on the receiving end of her emotional, and now often physical, abuse. Piper's dealt with it for years in silence, all by herself, and he never really considered how hard that must be for her. Even now she's undergoing treatment for her interest in the mermaids, something that he himself would have to endure if anybody (especially Elvira!) were to find out about his connection to Esther. Really, he should be kinder to his cousin since she's not as unlike him as he used to think.

Perhaps it's time to be a better cousin.

He blinks twice, rubs the sleep from his eyes, and rises from the bed with a low and satisfying yawn. When he leaves his room and traverses the hallway, he notices that Piper's door is closed, as usual. It never used to be when they were children - she kept it open at all times, even during the night because it made her feel safer. She was afraid of the 'monsters' in her closet and under her bed, and they were less likely to come out if she wasn't enclosed in such a small space.

He can understand why things changed, why she keeps the door closed now. The monsters are no longer in her room, and never really were – they were wandering the house in the forms of him and his mother. He didn't *mean* to become one of them, it just…happened.

He inhales sharply and knocks twice on her door, swallowing his discomfort as best he can. It's always been hard for him to own up to his mistakes and apologise, but if Esther has taught him anything over the past few weeks it's that he has the potential for goodness inside him. A fresh start, built upon a sincere apology, is necessary.

Bai-Piper?" he asks in a falsely confident voice, "y'alright in there?"

No reply.

Strange.

If he remembers correctly, his mother told her last night to stay in the house today. More importantly, she told *him* to make sure she did. Piper knows better than to disobey Elvira like that, surely?

He waits for a short while, tapping his fingers

against his thighs restlessly. Soon, he loses patience and flings the door open wide. His fears are confirmed – his cousin isn't inside. A groan winds its way up from his throat as he turns and hurries down the stairs. Perhaps she's in the living room or the kitchen?

"This can't be happening," he mumbles aloud, taking his head in his hands. Dragging his palms down his face, he can't help but whine pathetically. The living room is empty. The kitchen, however, is not. Instead of finding Piper though, he's greeted with the sight of a blue mermaid. Astrid. She's absent-mindedly stirring a bowl of porridge on the side, looking bored. "Oh. I thought you were out," she states when she notices him, annoyingly calm.

"Where is Piper?"

Astrid waves her hand dismissively. "Out. She'll be back soon."

The words hit him like a ton of bricks. Piper is gone. He let her leave, just exactly as his mother told him *not* to. "Get out of our house," he orders, "get out! Who do you think you are?"

"I think I am Astrid. And I'm not going anywhere. I'm waiting for Piper to get back. *Then* I'll go."

CHAPTER TWENTY-SIX

*T*he latest research report from Dr Margo Santi displeases Jasper.

The moment he opens it up and smooths it out before him on the coffee table for review, his brows draw together in frustration. The summary page alone is disheartening to say the least – the most recent experiments regarding toxicity level are good, and appear to be honing in on what quality of venom is needed to create different reactions. Yes, there have been many losses of life and several cases of moderate or severe brain damage, but the high numbers of successful intoxication are promising. But, the *venom harvesting*…the venom harvesting experiments continue to disappoint. As it stands, the survival rate of subjects contributing to the tests remains at 0%. *All* donor subjects die the moment the venom is removed from their bodies. Every single one.

"Jasper? I brought your coffee."

The concern in Scarlett's voice makes him focus on the paper rather than the words on it. He'd crumpled it in a sudden fit, and his cheeks flush with annoyance as he smooths it out again. "Good. Put it down there. That's right," he says stiffly.

"Can I help with anything?"

"No. Go."

"Are you sure?"

She slowly raises her hands to his shoulders with the intention of massaging them, but he merely bats them away. "I said go."

"Okay."

She does.

He peruses the content of the report once more. Stares at the data within the tables. Terrible. Awful. Discouraging. What a waste of time and effort.

"Somebody get me Santi!" he shouts, and upon receiving no response, storms out of the drawing room to find her himself.

CHAPTER TWENTY-SEVEN

Elvira is nowhere to be seen. Piper bites her lip hard as she jogs down yet another jetty, her hands clutching at the set of papers her aunt left behind. It hasn't been long since she left. She should be just reaching the mayor's house now if she walked at a leisurely pace. Yet when the girl arrives at the gates and asks the security guard if there have been any recent visitors, he shakes his head.

"Ah – you again. Not yet, girl. Nobody today."

She groans softly. Perhaps it would be wise to go inside and drop off the papers beforehand, explain to the mayor what happened and that Elvira will be arriving shortly. It will save everybody a lot of stress that way, and she did bother coming all the way here. There's no point just going home with the notes.

"Can I come inside, then? I have more notes."

"Alright."

She probably stopped at the store on the way or something, she tells herself as the gates are opened and once again, she's given a quick pocket-check. *That's why I didn't see her on the way here.*

The door is opened by Scarlett this time. "Oh,

hello," she remarks softly, "welcome back. It's Piper, right? I'm sorry if that's not right. Do you have something for Jasper? I mean – the mayor?"

Piper nods.

"Okay. He's a little busy right now, around here *somewhere*, but I'll go look for him. You can just wait in the drawing room, if you like. I'll have one of the staff make you some tea."

"Oh, I'm not – I'm not planning on staying that long, just here to drop off some papers."

"I insist. It's very good tea. It's from Araslan!"

"Araslan?"

She turns the name over in her head as Scarlett leaves the room. She's never been particularly good at geography (she very nearly failed the subject in school) but is almost certain that Araslan is a warm nation somewhere in the south. Or was it west? A mountainous region. Probably.

"Here you go, my dear. Lift your cup, would you?"

Snapping quickly out of her thoughts, she studies the teapot that's now being held towards her by a lady wearing an apron. It's the colour of bleached bone, hand-painted, and adorned with royal blue swirls that remind her of ribbon seaweed. "O-oh. That was so fast," she remarks, surprised.

The woman raises the teapot somewhat, clears her throat, and smiles as she repeats: "Lift your cup, would you?"

The smile suggests that it's not irksome to repeat herself. Piper is well aware that it is, though, as she has become rather good at reading negative body language over the years thanks to her aunt.

"Y-yes. Yes, sorry."

She glances at the small coffee table in front of her, on which a trio of small cups have been placed. Choosing one with a pretty, navy coloured pattern, she does as requested and watches the woman pour in some steaming tea. And then, without another word, the woman leaves and Piper is alone once again.

Minutes pass.

Piper's eyes wander slowly to some clocks on the wall to her right. There are three of them, just as there are three teacups, each showing a different time. She assumes that they are for different continents yet doesn't know which ones. She watches the steady movement of the hands on the central clock for a few minutes and then directs her attention to the door.

Her aunt still hasn't arrived and Scarlett hasn't returned from looking for the mayor. What's worse, she's making Astrid wait far longer than intended. Just the thought of the mermaid standing there patiently in her kitchen for what feels like *hours* is stressful. What if she gets angry? What if she breaks up with her for making her wait so long? Is it even possible to just break up with a mermaid or do you have to somehow revoke the connection? She nurses her teacup, pressing her fingers against its thin porcelain walls with a nervous little whine. The heat soaks into her hands. When she brings it to her lips and tries to drink, she recoils suddenly from shock and almost spills it on herself. It's still much too hot.

Her brows buckle, and eventually she stands, placing the cup down with a resounding clink. She told Astrid she would be right back…this is going on forever. Clasping the papers once again, she walks to the doorway and peeks her head out of it with a frown.

"Excuse me? Scarlett?" she calls, "Is it alright if I just leave the notes here? I told my friend I would be back soon."

Nothing.

"Scarlett?"

Nothing.

Eventually, and with a loud sigh, she walks back into the room. Thankfully, it isn't plain whatsoever – there are numerous things to look at to distract her from her growing impatience. The vast, glazed wooden cabinet filling the wall behind her is the most interesting by far. Its lower shelves are given over to a whole manner of books dedicated to science, mathematics, and languages. The upper ones are filled with a manner of pottery and small bronze figures. On the very top shelf behind a thin sheet of glass there are two skulls, their deep, hollow eyes darker than shadow.

Piper's eyes widen with a mixture of surprise and curiosity.

There is a ladder beside the cabinet – with its aid, she finds herself face to face with this macabre display and upon closer inspection sees that they aren't human skulls. Although very similar, they are far more angular and contain extremely sharp teeth and jutting cheekbones.

Mermaids.

The sound of a door closing – not in the room she's in, but one that's clearly close by – causes her to step down quickly in fear of being caught. In her attempt to rush back to her previous position, she almost trips over her own feet and practically dives onto the sofa. Once she's adjusted herself she notices that it's actually rather uncomfortable; it's clearly intended for decorative purposes rather than to be actually sat on. That, or whoever happens to sit here is not supposed to stay for long. It would make sense. The mayor probably doesn't have the time to host people for hours on end.

The tea has cooled down significantly when she picks it up and tentatively takes a sip. She finishes it, tapping her fingers gently on either side of the cup, and stares at the door. Nothing.

How long is this going to take?! I said I'd be right back.

The inactivity within the household leads her quickly to boredom. Reluctant to snoop around and explore the drawing room further on her feet, she resorts to reading a small stack of papers that have been left on the table. They all look very professional as she leafs through - a compilation of graphs and notes. Some sort of scientific report, perhaps. Data. Numbers. Tables. All in all not something she would normally read, but there's nothing else to do.

As expected, she's rather confused at first. It's only when she looks more closely at the information in front of her that a small knot of dread lodges deep within her stomach. And slowly, ever so slowly, it dawns on her: this isn't just a random scientific report – it involves Illyrians. People. Some of whom, a *lot* of whom are being killed in the process of some disturbing sounding experiments. Death. Brain damage. Heart failure. Insanity. Intoxication.

Her heart beats a harsh rhythm in her chest as her body freezes in shock. None of these deaths has been accounted for in the Weekly Illyrian; there's never been any speak of experiments or tests as a reason for death. Just speculation of mermaid attacks or volcanic activity. Drowning. Drunken fights.

She gulps dryly, trying to steady her breathing.

Or maybe the increase of deaths in the obituary her aunt spoke of have not been due to any of those things. Maybe, just maybe, they were because of something far more sinister that the mayor is involved with. Something that he – and the newspaper – are covering up.

CHAPTER TWENTY-EIGHT

"Not one, Santi? Not one?!"

Margo frowns. "I'm afraid not, sir. They die instantly. As I explained before, there is simply no way to extract the venom without killing the merm-"

"There has to be an alternative method."

"I have tried."

"Jasper?"

Jasper and Margo turn their heads quickly to the doorway where Scarlett now stands. She wrings her hands nervously, and then forces a smile. "Er...Jasper. I'm so sorry to disturb you, but Piper Tourneau is here? She brought you some papers."

Jasper exhales deeply, pressing a thumb and forefinger to his brow. "Just tell her to put them down and I'll come get them later."

And with a sudden strike of panic, adds, "Where did you leave her?"

"Ah...the drawing room? I figured it was the most appropriate place for a guest to wait-"

He rushes out of the room before she can finish her sentence, leaving a rather stunned and confused looking Margo and Scarlett.

He enters the drawing room and Piper stares up at him like a frightened, trapped animal. Her eyes are wide. Her hands are shaking. She places the research report quickly back on the table where she found it and rises to her feet. Her mouth opens and closes as if she's trying to say something but cannot quite find the words, and eventually she just mutters a meek, "I- I have some p-papers for you."

He looks down at Margo's papers and then back up at Piper. She follows his gaze in horrified silence.

"N-not those. T-these ones, these ones."

She presents a collection of notes from beside her on the sofa. He ignores them.

"How long have you been down here, child?"

"Only a few – only a few seconds I just – I -"----

The man moistens his lips and sucks at his teeth, his back arching from the way his muscles now tense.

She saw it. She saw it all. She knows too much.

He takes one step forward, alarming Piper further. She hops in place for a moment as if trying to figure out what to do, and then turns on the ball of her foot and runs for the door. Jasper's face loses colour and twists into something similarly as panicked. "Wait!" he shouts, his heart pounding in his chest, "Wait, Ms Tourneau! I just want to talk, my child. I just want to talk."

And then, in a lower tone, directed towards Scarlett: "Don't let her get away. Tell the guards to stop her. *Stop her.*"

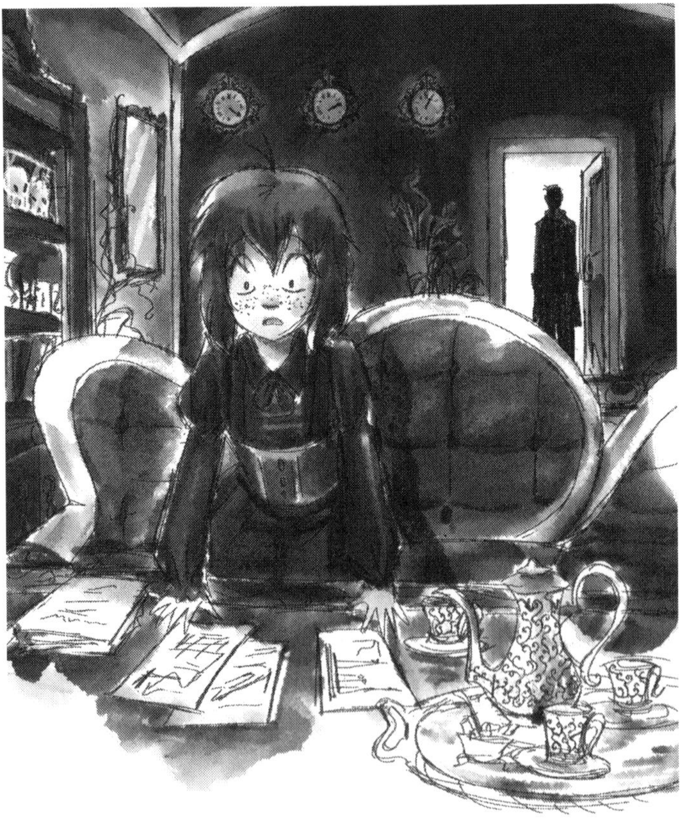

Piper sprints past him and doesn't look back. Not when the outside guards open the gates for her, clearly still unaware of Jasper's new order. Not when she hears shouting behind her. Not when she passes a confused, and then furious-looking Elvira on her way to the manor house after some quick grocery shopping. Not when she almost slips on some stray seaweed that has somehow found its way onto the path.

The moment she arrives home, sobbing and frightened, Astrid emerges from the kitchen with a frustrated-looking Falké behind her. "Ah, there you are," she remarks calmly, and then pauses when she notices her partner's horrified expression. In unison with Falké she adds, "What's wrong?"

With a panicked lump in her throat, Piper flings herself onto the mermaid, out of breath, and cries a quick and terrified explanation of her extended absence into her chest. "I read something bad, Astrid!" she begins, her voice shaking, "I read – I read something really bad. A report. He's experimenting on people, Illyrians. Testing on them with some kind of venom taken from some animal or something. Astrid, he's *killing them*."

Astrid stares. "The mayor?"

"Yes!" she sobs, her breathing erratic, "yes. Yes! He's doing something in that manor house, Astrid, and it's not good. People are dying, people are getting hurt. There was something about intoxication? Brain damage. Something. I'm scared. Astrid, I'm scared."

"Shh." Astrid wraps her arms around Piper tightly. "Listen to me and answer everything you can. Did he see you reading this information?"

She nods. "Yes…yes. He saw. He knows. He knows I read it. Please don't let him take me away! Please! Please protect me. You'll protect me, won't you?! Please!"

"What did he say?"

"He – he asked how long I'd been there and then – and then – said he just wanted to talk when I started running, but I know he didn't. I know he didn't just want to talk! I know. I know…"

"Shh. It's okay. It's alright. Is he coming? This is important. You need to tell me if he's coming after you."

"Yes. Yes, I think so. Yes. Yes."

Astrid wastes no time in picking the girl up. "Right, okay. We have to go. We have to go right now."

"W-wait! Ya can't just – what?! What's goin' on?! Ya can't just *leave*!" Falké cries, looking around desperately, "Ya didn't do nothin' wrong though, right? Ya just read some stuff, it ain't a big deal, Bai-Piper! Ya fine, alrigh'?"

"No," Astrid responds, running to the door with Piper in her arms. "No, she's in grave danger and you know she is. Say goodbye to your cousin, Piper. We need to get out of Illyria. And fast."

Piper nods, crying in panic. "Goodbye Falké!"

"Hold on! Hold on! Where are you going?! What ya doin' Piper?! Don't run! Piper!"

Before he can say anything else, they are gone. Blinking twice, Falké attempts to register what just happened in a brief bout of dread. The dread lasts mere seconds before being replaced quickly by terror when a group of men dressed in Illyrian military and authority uniforms crashes through the door. He barely has time to react; three hold him back while others search the house.

Discovering nothing, the leader of the group shouts in Falké's face. "Where is she?"

Falké shakes his head, struggling against the men holding him. "Wh-who?"

"You know who. Where's the girl?"

Falké falters. His initial thought is to just tell them that Piper's just left. Get them out of the house. But a small voice in the back of his head rejects this idea, and replaces it with something else: loyalty. Love. The knowledge that Piper has suffered her entire life, and deserves something better. Something good for once. And with that realisation, he swallows thickly and exclaims, "I – I dunno. I dunno who ya mean, I just got 'ere from the bar."

"Liar! I'm not asking again, kid. Where is she?!"

"I dunno!"

The man now standing before him narrows his eyes. "Listen, kid, you're gonna tell where the girl went or we're gonna break every bone in your goddamn body. Your choice. What'll it be?"

"I can't tell ya 'cus I dunno!"

Another man pipes up. "Hit 'im, Treston," he says coldly, "We ain't got all day."

Treston is more than happy to oblige; he punches Falké brutally before repeating, "Where is she?"

"I dunno – I dunno."

Falké barely acknowledges the second hit, a punch to his stomach, as he's still reeling from the first. When a fistful of his hair is grabbed, and he's forced to look up, he splutters another, "Dunno."

The man scowls. A third hit. A fourth. A fifth. And with that fifth, Falké finally relents. He takes a deep, shuddering breath, and with a voice rough with pain, exclaims, "Okay! Stop! She said something about going to Saphielle". Honestly, he has no idea where Piper's going. What he does know, however, is that Mt. Saphielle is in the complete opposite direction from where they ran.

At last, the men release him and he falls to his knees, coughing. Treston orders the group to go to Mt. Saphielle immediately and get Piper. And with that they leave, but not before kicking Falké a few times for good measure. "You're lucky today," Treston whispers darkly, "you got to keep your pathetic life. But just know if you're lying, I'll be back. And next time, I won't be so…gentle."

Falké doesn't look up when Treston leaves. He just listens to his footsteps get quieter, then forces himself to his feet and closes the front door.

I'll be back.

He shudders.

Chapter Twenty-Nine

*D*aily bubble baths, drawn by his maids and lavish with perfume and salts, was something Prince Holt grew rather accustomed to in Caldisa. Out at sea, things are different - such constant luxury is rare, and fresh water is much less readily available. Still, every now and again he gives in to temptation and has his handmaiden Lenka draw him a tub of steaming, fragrant water.

This particular bath, the one he relaxes in now, is suspended slightly from the ceiling with strong wires. That's expected on a boat like his, for if it were to be mounted on the ground the perfumed water would slosh about everywhere as the vessel sails over the waves. He's not *adverse* to his bathroom smelling of geranium and rose (that's what today's bath is scented with) but it *would* be an awful mess.

Rose has always been his favourite aroma; it brings fond memories of his childhood, his warm and gentle grandmother in particular. She very much surrounded herself with rose in all its forms. Rose flowers and water in her hair, rose perfume on her inner wrists, rose quartz crystals around her neck and on her fingers. Her favourite colour was rose. Her *name* was Rose.

She was there for him when King Nicolai and Queen Delilah were not; they were far too busy with their responsibilities, and neglectful in comparison. Unlike her, they didn't spend much time with him and hardly – if ever, in fact – had in-depth conversations with him. If it weren't for Rose, he would have been dreadfully lonely and starved of real, proper affection.

Allowing his eyes to fall closed, he visualises her in his mind. Soft, white candy floss hair, shoulder-length and pouffy like dandelion fuzz. Friendly blue eyes like blueberry cordial. A laugh comparable to wind chimes. She's probably holding a tray, or a mixing bowl, for she loved baking, as did he. Sunday mornings were normally spent creating things such as red velvet cupcakes and decorating them with pastel pink icing and tiny roses made of sugar. It was something they enjoyed doing together despite the fact that baking was – and still is - supposed to be done by the kitchen staff.

She died when he was ten years old.

Although her passing still upsets him, recalling such lovely memories brings him a sweet, near perfect, calm. It's for this reason that he's almost, *almost* asleep in the hot water when a frantic distant knocking drags him from his peaceful state. His eyes shoot open and gaze towards the bathroom door, and a soft, exhausted groan leaves him.

Do these bothersome Illyrians have nothing better to do than disturb him? He's been docked at this place for a while now, surely the public are bored of waiting for him to make an appearance?

"Lenka?" he calls, "could you *please* send those

Illyrian commoners away? I am trying to have a bath! I simply cannot relax with this incessant knocking!"

No reply.

He exhales slowly and tries again, raising his voice a little further: "Lenka?! Could you send them away please?"

"Ah, yes! Of course, your highness!"

He sighs in relief at the sound of her muffled voice behind the bathroom door. Sinking under the warm, scented water again, he allows his eyes to slip closed and his head to sink back. Lenka has always been good at politely declining people's requests to see him. He has complete faith in her to get rid of these people.

"Your highness, I've let them in. They need your assistance."

What?!

He sits upright, rubbing his face stressfully. Is this supposed to be a joke? She just let random Illyrians onto his boat, despite telling her to tell *them* to go away? What sort of servant goes against a prince's orders like that?

"For goodness sake, tell them to leave, Lenka! Is there a problem here? And could you please go gather up some groceries? There have to be some stores here *somewhere* and some fresh oysters would be just lovely for dinner today."

"Of course, your highness!" comes the woman's response after another long pause, "I will tell them to leave, your highness - and get that shopping right away!"

For a few seconds, everything is quiet and still once more. In spite of this, he can't get comfortable again, opting to stay seated upright in the tub. At the moment he's unsure if Lenka will carry out her duties. And he *has* been in here for a while now, anyway. Perhaps getting out soon would be a wise decision. Oh – and he can make a quick visit to Piper in a little while, and perhaps bring her another small gift. Then again, doing so would most likely mean having to speak to her dangerous-looking mermaid friend as well. Decisions, decisions.

"Your highness?!"

He throws his head back in aggravation. Suddenly, however, he hears another girl's voice. It snaps him into an instant state of concern.

"I'm really sorry for intruding on your ship, prince, but we really need your help! Could you please just hear us out?"

Piper. That voice. That voice is *Piper*. Not only is she here, on this yacht, but she *needs* him. Something's wrong. He can tell by the tearful, despairing tone with which she speaks. Perhaps she has been beaten again as part of that 'therapy' she talked of. Perhaps that mermaid – Astrid – attacked her. Perhaps both. His nostrils flare in anger and he flings himself upwards, grasping for the soft white towel on the handrail to his left.

Whatever the problem is, he's concerned.

Wrapping the towel around himself and drying as quickly as possible he throws his bathroom door open and with still wet feet, enters his dressing room before shouting a response: "Yes yes, that is perfectly fine, and I will be just a moment. Please await my arrival in the main cabin!"

A 'moment' in Prince Holt's time ends up being around fifteen minutes. Honestly, even that is a record for him when it comes to getting ready; his hair alone normally takes half an hour to style since there is a particular way he likes his crown to sit upon it. When he finally enters the main cabin he's not even completely dressed. As beautiful as the garments of gold, pale yellow, and white that Lenka had laid out for him are, they don't look especially striking when put on so hurriedly. Still, Piper appears to be impressed with the outfit; her glimmering, emerald eyes are wide with shock as he approaches, popping the shining line of brass buttons down the front of his jacket.

It's not until he notices her lips curl with a mixture of discontent and irritation that he realises his outfit is totally wrong for the situation. Before her stands a boy she has come to know as Henry, just another commoner living on the outskirts of Illyria. A commoner wearing what he can easily assume are the most luxurious clothes she has seen in her entire life. A commoner with a crown upon his head. A commoner being referred to as 'your highness' by a handmaiden.

Silence.

Astrid stares at Piper. Lenka stares at Astrid. Piper stares at Holt.

"Henry?" she murmurs, "you're…the prince?"

CHAPTER THIRTY

"It's an outrage.

Her niece, her own *family*, on the run from the mayor for – what was it again – ah yes, thievery?! What will the neighbours say? What will her *clients* say? If she cannot keep tabs on a child that is supposed to be her responsibility, how is she supposed to keep her position at the Health Centre? She could be fired for something like this!

Elvira groans. Can this day get any worse? The pure embarrassment of it all. As if her niece's wayward behaviour wasn't bad enough, Falké *lied* to the men that came looking for her! They had to punch the words out of him! It's times like these when her head practically begs her for a drink to drown the shame. Then again, she doesn't doubt that a few people are going to be turning up at her door today, and it's probably not a good idea to answer it in a drunken state. That would only ruin any shred of good reputation that she has left.

"After everything I have done for you two," she starts, anger colouring her voice, "you are a worthless alcoholic *liar*, and she is a mermaid-obsessed fool that you just let run away? I told you to keep an eye on her, didn't I?! *Didn't I* Falké? And you seriously couldn't just tell them the truth straight away?!"

Falké takes a deep breath, fearful sweat beading against his sweeping dark brown hair. "Didn't even know she left," he mumbles, turning his head away to avoid eye contact, "I just looked in 'er room and she wasn't the-"

Elvira interrupts him with a sharp, piercing tone. It cuts like blades. "Don't lie to me, too! You had one job!" she screeches, "one job! Can you not follow orders?! Are you brain-dead, Falké? Are you?!"

"I didn't mean to, it all happened so fast -"

"You're just like your damn father! Both of you are idiots! Absolute idiots!"

Falké blinks twice. He hardly remembers his father; he and Elvira had an extremely toxic relationship and the man left when Falké was just a young child. He can remember them arguing a lot, especially concerning his uncle Zachary's job working with the mermaids and the effect it was having on his aunt, Elisa. It was never physically violent, he knows that, but verbally abusive. But, to be compared to a man that abandoned his wife and left her as a single parent is extremely offensive –

"I ain't like dad!"

"You are! An absolute idiot, just like him!"

"I'm sorry, for God's sake!"

"You *better* be! I bet she's gone off with that mermaid now, bothering random Illyrians for somewhere to hide – Illyrians that are going to come right here and humiliate me!"

"Piper'll come back, ya know she will! She always

does, every time she runs off. This time is gon' be no differen -"

The open palm against his cheek shuts him up before he finishes his sentence. It's not a hard slap, but his face is bruised and sore from the previous beating he suffered and the impact sends a shock wave through his body. "This time she has a bleedin' price on her head, Falké! Get outside, you *imbecile*, and look for her! I don't want to see your stupid face in here a minute longer! Get out!"

"I didn't mean to, I jus -"

"I said get out!"

He wastes no time in leaving and she wastes no time in heading to Piper's bedroom. She doesn't realise it at first, but once she catches a glimpse of herself in the small mirror on her niece's closet door, she sees she has tears in her eyes.

This child is ruining my life, she thinks, staring at the wet, black tracks forming on her face. It's going to be a pain to rub off. Illyrian makeup is pretty much always made using ocean products and isn't as easily removed as brands seen in more landlocked areas. The particular eyeliner she is wearing now is predominantly squid ink, and the stuff *stains*.

As she looks at herself, and at the fat droplets of ebony-black on her cheeks, she wonders if she'll throw up because of how furious she is. The internalised anger is making her feel *sick*, and something inside her trembles with white-hot heat as she grits her teeth and throws a punch at the mirror. It cracks, and shards of silver fall from their place like splinters of melted pearl. She looks down at them on the floor, at her now disjointed reflection, and screams with years' worth of rage. She screams so hard that her ribs jut from her chest like vaulted, stark columns and her voice cracks and splinters into a thousand shards.

Like the mirror.

How happy she could have been if her husband was kinder and had stayed by her side. If she wasn't forced into the role of a single mother, barely coping with an entirely out-of-kilter work-to-home ratio. If her beautiful, unfortunate sister hadn't married a fool. She warned Elisa of Zachary the moment she met him, but Elisa didn't listen. He strayed from her, had an affair with that disgusting, vile creature from the sea. And she warned her – she warned her *countless* times that playing with such vermin would be the death of him.

And she was right, as she always is. It was only a matter of time before he was torn apart by that ravenous beast he thought so beautiful. Did he ever even call her sister, his own wife, beautiful? She can't remember.

Poor, poor Elisa. She should have done something. She should have been there for her, stayed by her side every moment so she couldn't leave this godforsaken world. But she focused too heavily on work, on looking after Falké, and before she had time to do anything it was too late and her sister was gone.

Days and days of grief and furious wrath have struck her so suddenly it hurts. Kneeling down on the floor, surrounded by shimmering debris, she takes a sharp breath and throws her head back. The small shards of glass cut her hands as she shifts them on the floor, and she looks down at the wine-red blood emerging from her pale skin as if it is personally offending her.

I hate Astrid.

In a way, the pain feels good. It makes everything physical, so physical. It brings the emotional pain out into the open, into a place where she can grasp it by the throat and choke it until it begs for forgiveness.

I hate Zachary.

With trembling hands, she grasps her hair and drags it roughly out of its bun. She discards the sticks once protruding from it onto the floor where they join Piper's broken mirror.

I hate Piper.

The chestnut locks tumble down in strings and then clumps, falling just past her shoulders, and she tugs at them with a miserable, exasperated moan.

I hate this place.

She just can't stay here all day, in her niece's room. She can't stay kneeling on the floor, her hands bleeding and cheeks black with ink. She has to go to work. Redeem herself. Get a drink or some tablets or *something* that will distract her from Astrid. From Zachary. From Piper. From everybody and everything.

She knew that girl was trouble the moment she took her in.

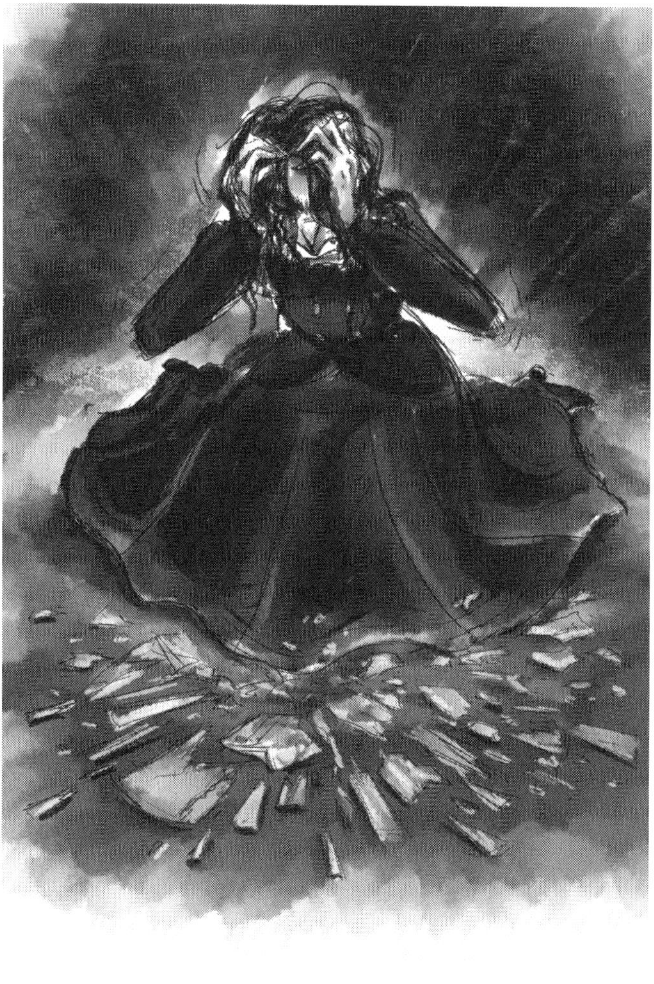

Chapter Thirty-One

"Mayor Vanguard, we went to her house, as you requested."

Jasper pinches the bridge of his nose. Why is this man even talking to him right now?! He didn't ask for a report. He asked for Piper to be seized and brought to him. Are his staff really so horrendously incompetent at following simple orders?

"And you found her, I assume?" he asks impatiently, "bring her to me. I told you to bring her to me! Why are we even having this conversation!?"

The man shakes his head. "Well, no, we haven't found her yet. But there's been some significant progress – we got the location she's heading outta her cousin. He was at the house, but she wasn't. Don't worry though, the team is heading after her now as we speak."

"And where exactly *is* she heading, Treston?"

"The mountain, sir."

"Saphielle? Mt. Saphielle?"

"Yes, sir."

"And you got that information from her cousin?"

"Yes, sir."

Grinding his teeth, Jasper turns away and crosses his arms, tapping his fingers against his wrist before turning back. "Check the harbour."

"But the boy said the mountain-"

"I'm well aware what the boy said, Treston. I just heard your report. Now, check the harbour."

"But sir, that would surely be a waste of men."

"This is not a debate. Check. The. Harbour. And do it *now*!"

There's clear reluctance in the man's body language as he steps away from Jasper and towards the door. "Of course, sir," he states, bowing, "we'll send some men to the harbour right away."

And with that, he leaves.

Jasper sighs loudly, rubbing his temples. How on Earth did that little girl manage to escape the manor so quick?! She's like a slippery little *rat*. Still, even rats get caught eventually. They may be quick, but they're small and weak; it's only a matter of time before they run into a trap. But, even with the knowledge that his army – that his entire authority force, even – are after Piper, a small seed of doubt lingers in his chest. It's beginning to grow with every second that passes, tearing a small hole as if someone has stuck a knife into him. If word gets out about his plans he's all but finished.

He slips his eyes shut and practices his breathing, remembering something Scarlett told him about meditation. In and out. In and out. In and out. The stress lessens, and he finds himself more relaxed as the seconds pass and turn into minutes. He sits, and the minutes pass, too. Eventually, the door once again opens.

It's not Piper.

Treston has returned.

"An update, sir," he says, clearing his throat. "We checked the harbour. She's definitely not there. And…there's no sign of her on the mountain paths either, but we're still looking."

Jasper groans softly, closing his eyes once again. This is pointless. "Has anything changed at least?"

"What do you mean, sir?"

"Are there any signs of her changing direction. Footprints, clothing, personal items she's dropped. Anything?"

The man sucks in his cheeks. "Ah, well…no, not yet. Oh, but Prince Holt Davori's yacht has left the docks, we noticed that. I wonder when he departed? He didn't even inform us."

For a moment, Jasper feels as if he's been punched in the chest, or the breath in his lungs has been somehow stolen from him. His eyes snap open, fury churning in his mind.

"You bloody idiot," he whispers, his voice rising in intensity until it's nothing less than a yell, "she's on the yacht! Get everybody on the water *right now* and *get her back*!"

It doesn't take long for his navy to get involved in the situation. As Holt's yacht, grand and striking, slices through the sea like a beacon of light upon the darkness of roaring water beneath, the navy gives chase. They are larger, more powerful, and prepared for a fight – but Holt is faster and already heading towards the horizon.

"I'm impressed," Astrid states, watching Illyria become little more than dusky, dim hues in the distance as the yacht speeds ever further from her home. The colour of soot and decay, misery and grief…replaced by an almost endless expanse of blue water. Picturesque. "I haven't seen somebody so good at sailing for a long time. You have a natural affinity for the water."

She leans back, hands resting on the starboard side of the yacht. "You seem to like this," she adds, directing her attention towards Holt. "The chase, I mean. Do you find it exciting?"

He doesn't respond to her, nor does he look in her direction, but appears to be concentrating much more now. That's fine. She watches him for a while and the boats behind them, and once she's confident that he knows what he's doing (which is around twenty-five minutes into the chase) she turns and tromps over to the main door of the yacht, and peers inside. Sure enough, Piper is wedged in the back of the central cabin between a luxurious looking white sofa and a very polished cabinet. Her arms are wrapped around herself, and when she hears the door open, she lets out a strange little whine.

"It's just me," Astrid insists, walking over and reaching out. "I think your prince friend has this pretty under control. He looks like he knows what he's doing…I doubt they'll catch up. They're going to give up at *some* point."

"He told me he was called Henry, Astrid. I actually liked him, I thought I had a made a friend…for once I didn't find an Illyrian boy insufferable…no wonder. He *wasn't* an Illyrian boy at all."

The mermaid raises her eyebrows. She rests a hand on the girl's shoulder, being careful to not scratch her. Her nails *are* very sharp, after all.

"As much as I don't like Prince Holt, I see why he

played this silly charade," she states simply, "he is a prince. To reveal himself to somebody so quickly would be dangerous – you could have attacked him or something. Demanded ransom. Perhaps he wanted to ensure his 'friendship' with you was real, and not because you wanted status or money. I don't know. He probably had to lie."

"Lie!" Piper cannot help but echo, feeling a short burst of indignation that's soon drowned in a sorrow so profound that for a moment she thinks she'll further increase her humiliation and break into tears in front of Astrid. "I can't believe I didn't realise, though! He speaks like…like he's the noblest person in the world, Astrid! It was so obvious!"

She raises a hand, pressing it hard against her eyes, and then lowers it again. "It's embarrassing that I fell for it…"

Astrid shrugs. "You couldn't tell he was a prince, so what? He has revealed himself to us now. And as we speak, he's rescuing you from a very dangerous situation. He is really putting out for us. He didn't have to help us but he did. He still is now."

"Yeah, but about that *dangerous situation* – I don't even know why they want me, Astrid. All I saw was some graphs and some data, I told you that! And suddenly they're chasing me? Why? What's going on in that house?!"

Astrid blinks twice. She leans back a little and breathes deeply before responding: "I don't know. I genuinely don't. I never even considered the mayor as a potential threat in the past. I don't know what he's doing, Piper, but you clearly were in the wrong place at the wrong time. He thinks you read something you shouldn't have. That's all we can deduce."

"I'm scared," the girl confesses. Her voice is soft and shaking with the hint of tears she has been so desperately trying to suppress. "I'm scared of the mayor, and the people working for him, and his ships. There's something going on in that house, Astrid. Something bad."

"I know," Astrid supplies.

"I see why that woman acted so nervous around him. Scarlett. I see why. She knows he's doing something bad, I'm sure of it."

Astrid cups Piper's face and looks at her with half-lidded eyes. "Don't panic. It's going to be alright, Piper. We're going to escape the mayor. Do you want to kiss me? It might make you feel better. You want to kiss me, don't you? You do."

Her voice is low and beautiful. It has a playful resonance to it, like thunder in the distance during a rainstorm. Compelling. It's the finest symphony to Piper's ears and is so alluring, so promising and perfect, that she obeys without a second thought. She presses her lips against Astrid's, her head swimming and vision blurring with need. The rising flood of desire within her is all-consuming, all-powerful, and before she realises it her hands are on the mermaid's chest, pushing, shoving, heaving her away.

Astrid simply clicks her tongue. Slowly, she rests her hand gently upon the girl's head, the light brown hair soft against her palm. "Holt is a very good sailor. I have faith in him to get us out of this mess."

A little kernel of doubt forms in Piper's mind as Astrid's fingers slide through her hair. She fears that it will sprout any moment and prays inwardly that it stays small. If it doesn't, Astrid will weed it out, and –

"Astrid, can mermaids…influence people to do things?"

Astrid looks surprised for a moment, and then her lips curl into a grin. "I think you know the answer to that already."

Piper glances down at the deck, disorientated. Did she really want to kiss Astrid just then, or was she *made* to want to? She loves Astrid. She loves her from the very depths of her heart, and yet…

"You made me do that…didn't you? I didn't want to, and suddenly – suddenly I did. How many – how many times, Astrid? How many times have you done this to me? Is our whole relationship… fake?"

Her voice is soft and helpless.

Astrid shakes her head, looking concerned. "No. Not fake. You chose this. I'll…explain in greater detail. Alright?"

"Astrid…"

"Let me explain."

"Alright."

The mermaid drags her thumbnail over Piper's lips, savouring the hot breath that brushes her palm as she does so. "We can intoxicate animals – humans included – with our breath, Piper. We can breathe out a little mist. It's barely noticeable, but works very well; it makes them so easily influenced. It's how we get food. How we make creatures bigger or stronger than us put down their defences. And how we get humans to do what we like. It's not the singing, Piper. It's the breath. But," she moves her finger in a spiralling circle, fixated – "you've chosen to stay with me, to love me, even when I am not in direct contact with you. Even when you are not in contact with this mist. You like me because you want to, not because I want you to. Yes, I can ask you to do things, and you will do them. I would be lying if I said I haven't controlled you at all, because I have."

A small, innocent noise escapes Piper. She closes her eyes, serenely passive in receiving this attention. It doesn't matter if she's doing Astrid's bidding. It doesn't matter if she just *thinks* Astrid is perfect. What matters is that she is in love and even though blue mermaids can't experience such an emotion in great depth, Astrid feels whatever is the next best thing towards her.

"But we make a perfect pair, don't we? Of all the connectors I've had, you are my very favourite. And if you want, I will try to stop using this intoxication. It's just natural, though…it's *instinct*. But I will try, for you."

When Astrid pulls away and stands up, the girl frowns in disappointment. She was happy here with Astrid, blocking out the rest of the world. "Oh, Astrid," she whispers, "you can't help it if it's instinct…but I appreciate you offering to try." She extends her hand, and Astrid takes it, helping her up.

"You know, once upon a time I lived here in the open ocean," the mermaid comments, shifting the topic of conversation. "Human and mermaid civilisation was sparse at best and deep, sapphire water stretched all around me so far that I was unable to distinguish between sea and sky."

Piper forces a smile. "Did you prefer it?"

"No. I decided a long time ago that Illyria is far better. There is an abundance of sea life due to the presence of undersea volcanic vents, which makes food plentiful. There are humans which are entertaining, and, well, you're there. At least, you *were* there. Now you aren't."

"Yeah," the girl mumbles, "I guess I'm not."

Chapter Thirty-Two

"I've received several concerned comments from your co-workers. With this in mind, I think you should go home, Ms Tourneau."

Elvira stares at the CEO of the Illyrian Health Centre, shuddering with manic intensity as a string of stuttered laughs drop from her lips. Go home. Is he insane? She just got here. She has work to do. She has patients to fix. She can't go home – not now, at least. She places her extremely overpriced bag on her desk, picks it up again, turns it over, and pours the entire contents down on the table.

Concerned comments?! Which idiots in this place spoke ill of me?!

The man looks at her disapprovingly, but there is slight worry evident in his eyes. It's not unusual to see depressed-looking Illyrians, but Elvira is taking the term 'depressed' to a whole new level here. She looks as if she's on the verge of a complete mental breakdown; her hair *alone* is an absolute mess.

It's a shame, really – Elvira Tourneau has always been one of the most professional and hard-working therapists in the centre. It's why she's a favourite of the mayor and why he always requests to see her notes in particular. At the moment, however, it seems as if she has lost herself entirely.

He sighs, rubbing his temples. "Ms Tourneau…this is not just a personal opinion of mine, nor is it a mere suggestion. I am politely asking you to leave - do not make me take disciplinary measures. Your patients will be seen by another doctor for the time being."

Elvira staggers back, clasping the sides of her head with shaking hands. A disturbed smile splits her face, black tears spilling down her cheeks and between her quivering lips, staining her white teeth grey. "It's not my fault that little brat ran!" she starts, but her words are rendered into little more than a helpless gurgle as she begins to weep openly.

"You know where the door is, Ms Tourneau. If necessary, I can have somebody accompany you to your house."

Elvira screeches, sounding like some sort of wild animal caught in a trap. She looks around the room – the cold, clinical room – and then back at him. Her office is as devoid of beauty as she is of sanity. "What if I told you, *Frank*, that this IS my house!" she cries deliriously, waving her hands in large, exaggerated gestures as she speaks.

The CEO raises his eyebrows, the sympathetic gleam in his eyes turning dull with agitation. "Dr Cuthbert," he corrects, "we do not use forenames in this building, as you know. You look unstable. Please do not take offence when I say that you are not…rational…enough to be here at the moment, especially considering your position here includes working with sick and mentally damaged patients."

She gasps dramatically, spinning around and shovelling through the belongings dumped from her bag. Finally, she finds what she is looking for; her fingers clasp around a small lipstick tube and flick the top off, revealing the dark plum shade beneath. "I'm perfectly fine," she assures him, turning the bottom of the tube and bringing the makeup to her face, "See?! I'm rational! I'm happy and smiling! That cheating husband of Elisa hasn't ruined me! Her idiot child hasn't ruined me! No, no, no. Not at all. Of course not. Of *course* not."

In one staggered action, she brings the lipstick across her cheek and over her mouth, a messy and desperate display. The colour – highly pigmented, raw and deep – stains her lower face in a jagged line giving the impression that she is grinning ear to ear. It's a disturbing sight, so much so that the man before her feels the need to look away for a moment.

"Can't you see how fine I am right now?!"

The man shuffles, uncomfortable and rather troubled. He looks at the cream walls and the three paintings on them – one of a little green boat, one of a seagull, and one of a pebbly beach – on them, and then back at her. He walks over to the window, moving the simple blue curtains that are drawn over them, and takes a deep breath. "Elvira. If you are unwilling to take orders, and leave the premises, I will have to have you escorted out."

Escorted out, she repeats in her mind. *Who the hell does this guy think I am? I'm not a patient, I'm a doctor. I'm the best doctor in this damn building.*

It's only when security appear in the doorway that Elvira grasps the full extent of what is going to happen to her. Her disturbed, malicious tone grows discordant and desperate as she reels back. "No, no, no, no, no!" She yells, her fingers jerking in sporadic terror as she struggles to gain enough cognitive control to coordinate them. "It's her fault! Piper! She's the problem - not me! Not *me*! Why can't you see that?! She's the one that's *broken*!"

The grip of the men holding her is impossibly tight. As she is dragged through the doorway, and down the hall of the Health Centre, she instantly regrets any vitriol she's ever emitted.

CHAPTER THIRTY-THREE

*D*eracile Decks, Mahina House, Number 130. It is a desolate place; Elisa's passing made it so. And yet never before has it felt quite so desolate as at this moment - when Elvira shouts within the thin walls and no one answers. She doesn't like being alone. She'd rather have her son upstairs, hungover and half-asleep in bed, than be alone. She'd rather have her niece downstairs, sweeping the kitchen floor or making food, than be alone. But Falké is no doubt at the bar drinking, and Piper is God knows where with that *vermin*.

The tick-tock, tick-tock of the grandfather clock in the downstairs hallway is usually comforting for her to listen to. But, at the moment it serves only as a reminder that time is passing by a little too quickly. She sits in her – no, in Elisa's, for this house belonged to her before she passed – living room, staring at the wide picture frame on the coffee table. It shows the whole family: herself, with Falké as a young child on her lap. Falkés father behind her, hand on her shoulder. Elisa and Zachary to the right, baby Piper in Elisa's arms.

Somebody – or a few somebodies, probably – knock on the front door sporadically throughout the rest of the day. She doesn't answer though, nor does she take her eyes off the glossy photograph.

What went wrong? What happened to ruin it all?

Astrid, she decides. *Astrid happened.*

CHAPTER THIRTY-FOUR

Creating a distance between Jasper's navy ships and Holt's yacht doesn't feel like Piper thought it would. She thought that she'd feel safer suddenly, like everything around her would snap into place like the final completion of an unfinished jigsaw puzzle. She thought that she and Astrid would stand on the deck with their heads held high, in each other's arms, laughing to declarations of victory. She thought that she would forgive Holt for lying to her, instead becoming filled with great admiration and pride for his noble service to her.

Instead, the moment the storm hits and the ships separate further in the rain, she only feels more lost. Illyria is gone now, far behind her, as is her home and her family. Her possessions, her entire life…it's all been left behind. All she has now is Astrid, some people she doesn't know, and a boy who isn't who she thought he was. It's a mess.

Astrid is out on the deck at the moment, assisting a man that Piper doesn't recognise with the sails or something along those lines. When she explained that she was going out to help, due to the windy conditions and large waves, she used technical terminology that Piper didn't really understand. But the word 'sails' was included somewhere in it, so she has a *little* information at least.

She'd been on her father's boat many times of course, but never paid much attention to how it all worked. She was always much too focused on the fish, or the sea birds, or whatever her father was saying at the time. She doesn't know much about sailing really, at least not enough to be useful to the yacht's small crew. It's sort of embarrassing, actually; she can't help but feel a little bit useless, pacing back and forth in one of the cabins while the sound of rain batters the porthole window. It's her fault they're even having to sail like crazy in the first place, and here she is all warm and cosy inside the boat.

"Prince Holt has it under control," she murmurs to herself, "and Astrid is helping. I'd just get in the way. It's better if I'm down here."

Speaking the words aloud is helpful. She closes her eyes tightly for a moment and takes a deep breath, clenching and unclenching her fists. When she opens them again, she sees Astrid walking past the porthole. She's holding a lot of rope for some reason, and her long hair is being whipped around her face due to the storm. She doesn't notice Piper, but Piper certainly notices her.

She's beautiful, she thinks. *So beautiful, so focused, so powerful. Astrid can do anything.*

In the isolation of the cabin, she presses a hand between her legs, bites down on her lower lip, and orders herself to stop being so ridiculous. Astrid could pick her up and press her against the wall. Astrid could kiss her everywhere, leaving a trail of diamond dust on her skin. Astrid's breath is cold like frost. And most importantly, Astrid is hers, and she is Astrid's.

She shakes her head quickly, dragging her gaze away to focus on something more mundane, something that doesn't have to do with Astrid.

There's an elaborate-looking light fixture – golden and polished, like most things on this yacht – to her right, next to a painting of a yellow and blue coloured flower that she's never seen before. The light is turned off at the moment. She approaches it with the intention of turning it on, but can't locate a switch.

His palace must be gorgeous, she thinks to herself, *if his yacht alone is so wonderful.*

The large, gilt-framed mirror behind her makes the cabin appear deceptively big. When she turns around to stare into it, she's momentarily tricked into believing there is far more room than there actually is. Her reflection puts things into a better perspective when she comes closer.

For what seems like the first time in her life, she's transfixed by the way she looks in the mirror. Shimmering silver encompassing her, framed by gold and blue-coloured precious gemstones. She can name them all – blue topaz, sapphire, tanzanite. Her eyes are like emeralds, complimenting them. But then there are the marks on her skin, and they aren't like gemstones at all; the bruises that had first spread dark and purple are healing, sickly yellow patches that fade slowly into pale cream. The scratches and cuts she wears are becoming raised, less pink. Whiter.

She wonders what Astrid sees in this weak little body, healing from all of these wounds. She's not a shimmering creature like her, tall and willowy with smooth skin and onyx eyes. She's frail and short, freckled and imperfect.

Perhaps that's why, though. Perhaps it's that fragility that makes her special to Astrid; perhaps her imperfections are what make her 'perfect'. After all, mermaids are faultless, and perhaps that can become boring after a while. Astrid probably got tired of all her potential partners looking the same, but in different colours. No wonder she's interested in something...different.

Without conscious thought, Piper moves away from the mirror and finds herself touching the curtains on either side of the porthole. They're silky between her fingers, smooth and cold like Astrid's skin. The elaborate golden lamps dotted about the room, however, are warm when she puts her hands close to them. They aren't like Astrid at all.

Stop thinking about Astrid, she tells herself. *For five minutes. It's a challenge. Starting...now.*

There's a tremendously fluffy throw blanket draped over a chair in the corner. After discovering how luxurious it feels to the touch, she can hardly resist; she picks it up, wraps herself in it, and settles down on the chair with a contented sigh. It reminds her of her duvet at home, but more decadent.

Her breath hitches.

Home.

Is home even home anymore? And if it is, will she ever be returning home? Will she ever see her aunt again? What about Falké? Will she ever see *him* again?

She curls up tightly, snug in the blanket. None of this was supposed to happen. She was never supposed to fall for a mermaid, to leave everything and everybody behind. To end up on some prince's ship in the middle of a storm. Then again, it was probably worth it to be with Astrid. Nobody can hurt her for loving Astrid out here on the open ocean. And Astrid is perfect.

I failed the challenge.

She sighs quietly and closes her eyes, listening to the sound of the waves and rain.

CHAPTER THIRTY-FIVE

"I'm sorry, you *what?!*"

Jasper narrows his eyes, utter indignation plastered on his face. Almost all of Illyria's funding has gone into the police force, military, and navy ships, and *still* they are so incompetent that they can't chase, catch and seize a slightly-larger-than-average yacht?! It feels as if his chest is going to burst. If this girl tells anybody, *anybody* about his plans, not only will his entire life go up in flames but the ashes left behind will be scattered around everywhere. No Calawi. No Illyria. No *anything*. Just fragmented hopes and dreams, forever lost…it's a mess, an absolute mess. She can't have escaped, it will ruin him.

Claud Treston lowers his head ever so slightly and clears his throat. "Well, we tried as hard as physically possible to bring the girl back, but a great storm hit. We have ships out looking, still, but the ocean is vast, sir."

Jasper has heard enough. His nose wrinkles with displeasure at the mere prospect of losing Piper and the precious information she most definitely holds. "Shut up!" he barks, his lips tightening into a gritted snarl. "Do you know how dangerous this is? For this girl to have this information on our plan – on *my* plan – and be let loose?! She has the prince of Caldisa with her, may I remind you! If he tells his parents, his kingdom, we are done for, all of us."

A wrathful fist slams down upon the table. Everybody in the room tenses up. The advisors shrink back slightly and turn their heads away. The military and police leaders shift, clearing their throats awkwardly. Tobias Wren is the only one to speak up, and does so with an air of nervousness as he steps closer to Jasper: "With all due respect, sir, they couldn't have possibly caught up to them in the storm – the rain was heavy, the waves high."

Jasper raises his arm. He pulls it back, palm open, and brandishes the man. "Figure this out!" he shouts, "you're my primary advisor Wren, give me *advice*! And for the love of God, don't defend them!"

Tobias draws back attempting to keep a calm demeanour. "I apologise, I just…well, I – I don't know. And as for advice…I…will have to think about this, sir. All of us," – he gestures to the other advisors in the room with a frown – "will have to think about this. Discuss it in detail."

"Fine! Go discuss it amongst yourselves and leave me alone. All of you! All of you leave me alone. And somebody fetch Scarlett. Bring her here this instant. This instant!"

Moving quickly in small groups, the people in the room dissipate like prey upon noticing a ravenous predator nearby. Jasper watches them, running his tongue over his teeth. How is he supposed to overthrow Calawi if his employees are so extremely appalling at their jobs? So appalling in fact, that the fighting men lose sight of a ship *right in front of their eyes* because of a few waves and some rain. And the advisors have no advice? It's disgraceful. He almost wants to subject them to the venom experiments as a means of punishment for their disservice to him, but that would be foolish. Despite their poor *at best* work, he needs them.

Once the room is empty and he's alone, he throws himself down onto his chair with a grunt of dissatisfaction. The only possible way that he can think of to work around this problem is to attack Calawi now, before word gets out. But as yet the projectiles are not entirely completed, and despite making good progress with the use of sulphur, the mermaid venom still hasn't maintained efficacy for longer than a few hours. There's no way this plan would be successful now. He needs more time, much more time. Time to experiment, to plan.

The door opens. Scarlett walks in slowly, her hands folded in front of her, eyes down. She knows Jasper's upset, and she knows that he's not going to be kind in this type of mood. Ever since Piper left Illyria, this has been coming. She's had time to prepare emotionally for it yet no amount of preparation is useful when it comes to being faced with Jasper's anger. She'd honestly rather it be a shock, for the waiting has torn her apart.

"Jasper," she says, "they told me you wanted me. I was just going through your mail for you…"

"Leave that job to the servants."

"But you said – you said you only trusted me with organising your mail."

"Well I changed my mind."

She clears her throat dryly. "Okay. I'm sorry.

What's wrong? Do you need…comforting?"

For a short while, he doesn't speak. But then, after Scarlett asks once again what's wrong, he stands and orders ever so quietly: "Come here."

She does.

It only takes a second. He grasps her by the wrist roughly, digging his nails into her skin. "You left her unattended," he bristles through gritted teeth, "you left her unattended and she got curious in your absence. What were you thinking, leaving that child unattended in my house?!"

"I'm sorry -!"

He grabs her face, and jerks it towards him as she whimpers in the back of her throat. Her soft, sad eyes stare back at him, searching desperately for some form of kindness that she can latch onto. He groans in frustration, and then releases her. "Well it's happened now. There's nothing you – or I – can do about it. You asked if I want comforting. I do."

She instantly falls to her knees before him, and a small grin tugs at his lips as he realises that this required no venom whatsoever. She's choosing to do this out of her own will, something he didn't even specifically request.

A pulse of heat runs up his spine in excitement and then turns to ice when she reaches for him. He pauses. No. He doesn't want this from her. He doesn't feel like this now. He smacks her hands away. "No, get up. Get up, you idiot."

"What?"

"Get up! Do I have to ask again?!"

"N-no. No."

When she does rise to her feet again, part of him considers laying her down on the tabletop and crawling over her. Taking her roughly and with reckless abandon. He enjoys the validation her cries grant him. Her body is responsive and oh so easy to pull close to his own and use. But no, not now. Not like that. Instead, he takes her hand in his and presses a kiss against her knuckles. A vibrant flush spreads across her cheeks.

"Wh-what? Jasper…?"

"Soothe me, my pet."

"Soothe you? I – I don't know how, I – you need to tell me what to do."

"Do whatever you want."

She freezes in shock. "Whatever I want? Jasper…"

"Whatever you want," he repeats, and with that, she lightly pushes him back into his chair and climbs upon his lap, straddling him. She buries her face in his neck, kissing him. It's loving. It's passionate. And what's more, it's a welcome distraction.

CHAPTER THIRTY-SIX

*T*he storm continues deep into the night.

Piper is awoken time and time again because of its impact on the yacht – sometimes, the boat rocks violently from side to side, causing everything inside to tilt. Sometimes a wave crashes over the porthole window so hard that she worries it might break the glass and seawater will flood the cabin. Sometimes the rumbling thunder, louder than anything she's ever heard, echoes through the air and lightning splits the sky, throwing her surroundings into bright white for a few seconds. There is almost constant shouting from the deck, too; she can hear it from inside the cabin, even when she curls into herself tighter, pressing her hands against her ears within the security of the warm blanket. Sometimes the shouting is Holt's. Sometimes it's from a man she doesn't recognise. It never belongs to Astrid.

Of all these things, however, none is as loud and jarring as the boat's violent jolt at quarter past three in the morning. It frightens her the most; eyes wide, she stares forwards into the dimness and clutches the blanket closer for half an hour until she feels secure enough to sleep again.

At five in the morning, with the rain still beating relentlessly, she wakes again with eyes heavy-lidded to the sight of Astrid standing in front of her. The oversized shirt she's been wearing for the past few days is gone now, apparently discarded in the storm, and her nude frame glistens like stars. There are three lights on in the cabin that illuminate her, the others are off. She's dripping with water, and as Piper looks behind her, she notices a trail of wet footprints across the floorboards. "Astrid…" she mumbles sleepily, "you're so pretty."

The mermaid moves closer to her. Suddenly, Piper feels so much safer, so much more comfortable. Like everything is going to be okay, and she can rest securely under the watchful eye of her 'connector'.

"You are too," Astrid responds.

"The storm's still going on…"

Astrid nods. "Yes, it's still going on. But, there's not much else we can do right now. We've got the ship trimmed tightly and we're running ahead of the wind with a sea-anchor. That's about all we can do…"

"Is it scary out there?"

"Not for me. I am used to ocean storms. But anyway, why are you on this chair? Is the bed not comfortable?"

Piper shuffles on the chair, hugging the soft material to her body. "Well…I dunno," she says softly, "I got comfortable here in this blanket, and it would be weird to be in somebody else's bed, I guess."

"So you slept on a chair?"

"Yeah, I guess. I just…I dunno, I'm so tired."

"Probably because you slept in a chair. Get in the bed, and sleep properly."

Reluctantly, Piper rises to her feet. She shuffles towards the bed sleepily with the blanket still wrapped around herself, and then falls onto it with a small sigh. "Can you lie beside me?" she requests, shuffling to the side to create room for the mermaid.

Astrid nods but doesn't move. Instead, she stays standing, staring at the girl in silence, observing her. The curve of her nose, where a sliver of light from the porthole spills across its bridge and onto her right cheek. Her plush, plump lips. Her soft, messy hair. Her clothes, mostly hidden by the blanket. As far as she can tell, she's taken off most of her layers, leaving only her undergarments, a thin white camisole and matching slip-like underskirt.

"You don't have any more clothes," she comments in realisation.

Piper nods, reaching out to Astrid, beckoning her to come over. "I usually wear my dad's shirt to bed," she notes, yawning, "but, we sorta rushed from Illyria so fast I didn't get to bring any clothes with me, so…yeah. Astrid, can you come here?"

"Yes. I'm coming. And we will get you more clothes soon. But they won't hold sentimental value like I'm sure your father's shirt does." She climbs onto the bed beside Piper, turning on her side. The girl closes her eyes, as does Astrid, and for a short while they lie together in silence.

"Are you close with your parents, Astrid?"

Astrid's eyes snap open.

"Of all the things I thought I might possibly discuss with you, Piper, my parents – and family, by extension – were definitely not one of them," she confesses, raising her eyebrows. "But to answer your question, not particularly. Why?"

"Just...I was thinking about my dad's shirt. Then I thought about how you must have parents too, but have never mentioned them. Ever. And I don't know anything about your family, or if you even have any."

The mermaid hums thoughtfully to herself. "Well if you must know," she begins, watching as Piper too opens her eyes again, "I only had one parent when I was younger, my mother. Her name was Diamorte. I always believed she was one of the first mermaids to exist. She was," she raises her hands, spreading her fingers as she speaks – "almost holographic, in colour. Had extraordinarily long hair, with a life of its own, almost, pulsating and moving up and down like a jellyfish's bell. It shone with all colours of the rainbow, at the ends, almost blinding when it caught the light from the surface. And she was huge – definitely over ten times my height."

Piper gasps softly as she pictures such a creature in her mind. "So tall!" she breathes, "you're already so tall. I can't even imagine a mermaid taller. She sounds wonderful, Astrid, and so beautiful! A rainbow mermaid, I've never even heard of such a thing."

"Well you have now. I have no idea if she is even still alive – but we are in the open ocean now. Who knows? Perhaps she will sense I am here and come to me if she is still living. Perhaps not. I don't think she cares very much about me. She abandoned me very quickly after I was born. She abandoned all five of my siblings in the same way."

Piper purses her lips. "At least you had each

other."

"No. We didn't. Not for ages; Diamorte dropped each of us off in separate seas over an extended period of time rather than have us all together. She was too perfect, too flawless to be weighed down by silly things like offspring, I think. To my knowledge, there are six of us. I have three sisters, Nysa, Alula, and Calliso. I also have two brothers, Perseid and Altair. I found them and mated eventually, so I wasn't lonely for *that* long - only ten years or so. Still, I never saw my mother again. It's strange to think she may still be out there, shimmering in all her splendour."

"Oh…that's sad. That's really sad, Astrid."

"It is?"

"Yeah. It is. Are you not sad about it?"

"A little, maybe."

Instinct makes Piper reach for the mermaid's hand. When it makes contact, she realises just how longingly her heart beats from nothing but Astrid's closeness and the coolness of her skin. "I'm sorry you don't get along with her," she sympathises gently, "I know how hard it is being distant with your family. I mean, both my parents died when I was quite young, and my aunt despises me… I understand better than anybody."

She swallows, and for a moment, fears that Astrid will pull her hand away and rebuke her efforts to show compassion. But instead, the mermaid reaches out with her other hand, and her fingers come to rest on her cheek. Piper smiles weakly at the action, but her brows furrow after a moment.

"I think the prince has a crush on me," she confesses quietly.

Astrid shrugs, her fingers still resting against the girl's cheek. She draws her thumb down Piper's jaw, a gentle caress, and at last withdraws to focus her attention on her hands instead. Slowly, very slowly, she leans forwards and brushes her cold lips against Piper's knuckles. "And what do you want me to do about that?" she asks, kissing each finger. "Kill the boy and eat him? Proceed to steal this yacht afterwards, and take control of it?"

"No, no! No…"

"I thought not. So, what is the point of telling me this information?"

"I just want you to know that I don't have a crush on him too, Astrid. You seemed jealous before, so I'm just making sure you know that I don't lik -"

"I know you don't."

"You do?"

"Mmhm. I am a mermaid, he is a human. I am objectively better. You *have* to like me more."

Piper sighs in relief, but guilt gnaws deep in her core. She doesn't have a crush on Holt, that's true, but she doesn't *dislike* him. In fact, she would go as far as to say she's enjoyed the limited time they've spent together. Not in a romantic way, but still.

"Just so you know, Astrid," she utters, "I like you for more reasons than the fact you're a mermaid."

Astrid sits up, looking amused. "Oh? How so? Pray tell, Piper."

"Well, you're err, you're beautiful."

"Oh, I know - but that is because I am a mermaid. Give me reasons that aren't because I am a mermaid."

"Er…you're…smart. Really smart?"

"Mermaid."

"You're strong…?"

"Mermaid."

Piper yawns again, clearly too tired for such thinking. "You're...passionate."

Astrid licks her lips and nods, turning the word over on her tongue. *Passionate*. "Yes. That is a good reason to like me," she muses, looking down at her. "You should try and sleep now, Piper."

The girl nods. Comfortable and warm beside Astrid, she closes her eyes and allows sleep to overcome her once again.

Darkness.

Silence.

Peace.

Nightmare.

"Come back, darling."

Astrid's singsong voice twists through the air like a smooth blade. Its tip grazes Piper's back as she runs down the crumbling jetty nearest to her house, the wooden planks splitting and cracking below her feet. *Leave me alone,* she internally begs, fear seeping through her limbs. *Please Astrid. Please.*

A choked cry for help forces its way up through her as she turns the corner, knowing very well that the mermaid isn't far behind.

Snap. Snap. *Snap.*

The planks directly beneath her split in half before she can react. Freezing seawater tumbles over her thrashing, flailing body like sheets of glass, and shredded silver waves crash over her head before throwing her downwards into the mermaid's domain. Astrid's domain.

She screams as loud as her hoarse, painful throat will allow. Soon enough, however, the screams are nothing but muffled vibrations in the water, blending in with the shrieks and calls of Illyria's mermaids. And then – cold hands plant themselves firmly on her waist, pressing against the delicate bumps of her hipbones. The muscles in her stomach shift as she struggles for air.

"I knew you'd fall in."

The grip around her tightens. Cold, wet fins brush against her feet, and then, in a smooth and smoky voice: "I can't wait to taste you."

No. No please no. God no. I love you. I love you. I love yo-

Sitting up quickly from the bed, Piper is met with no dark water or hungry mermaid but the gentle rhythm of waves pushing against Holt's yacht. Other than that, and some distant seagull squawking nearby, the only sound seems to be her own pulse throbbing in her ears. The serenity of quiet surrenders to the sound of shuffling as she adjusts herself and the blanket falls off her shoulders and down by her sides.

Astrid lies beside her still, the silver and blue streams of her hair spread around her face like a cobweb. She looks…peaceful.

The girl sighs softly, and suddenly that peace is broken. Astrid's eyes open faster than an anchovy caught in a riptide, staring up at her, and Piper draws back in fright. She grasps the pillow behind her on the bed, and holds it out before her like a shield.

Astrid laughs musically in response to this action. She draws her lips up from her sharp teeth and shakes her head, rising to a sitting position as well. "Did I frighten you?" she asks, amused, "put the pillow down, Piper."

The command is followed. Piper looks to the side. "I had a nightmare, and -"

"Nightmares are not real."

"Yes but…it freaked me out. Can you…?"

"Can I what?"

"Hold me?"

Astrid doesn't need to be asked twice. She draws closer, wrapping her arms around Piper and kissing her neck softly. "Do not be afraid," she says calmly, staring up at the ceiling. "There are much more terrifying things in this world than nightmares…"

Piper's breathing gradually steadies and slows as she calms down.

"…Like, for example, sleeping beside a mermaid."

CHAPTER THIRTY-SEVEN

*M*oney.

Falké meticulously counts his notes and coins for the thirteenth time. One hundred rials in notes, sixteen in coins. It's barely enough to survive on; he's going to have to take drastic measures soon to get more money, or he and his mother are going to lose their house and starve to death all in the same month.

Every time his fingers card through this cash the amount seems to be less. *So why do I keep counting?* he thinks, suddenly recoiling his fingers with a small shriek of pain. He's cut himself on one of the notes and a small bead of blood has emerged from his index finger. "Bloody 'ell…" he complains quietly, clasping his hand around the wound and throwing his head back in pain.

Can this day get any worse? He wouldn't doubt it, honestly.

Elvira is crying again. Her loud, tearful screeches are so incredibly powerful, hard and obtrusive, he can barely focus on counting anymore. Rising from his bed, he grumbles softly to himself and goes to her.

Ever since she lost her position at the Health

Centre, her sanity has slipped dangerously. It's got to the point where he can no longer spend time with Carmen or even Esther for that matter - the last time he tried to, he returned home to find Elvira bleeding from self-inflicted injuries and laughing hysterically through black, inky tears.

He moves downstairs to find her kneeling between the meagre rays of morning light spilling from the sitting room window. He scoffs as he crouches beside her, but the bite in his voice is soft as he says: "Mother. You don't have to cry. I'm here, you're not alone."

It isn't fair. All the anger and rage he's felt towards her over the past few years, since his father's death, has been replaced by pity. And he doesn't *want* to feel sorry for her - she deserves to suffer after all the suffering she's put him and Piper through. But she's his mother, his guardian, and to see her in such a state is…disturbing, to say the least.

"We have no money. I'm *hungry*," she whines.

"I know. I – er - imma get you some food later. And some money now, alright?"

"Don't leave me!"

"I have to or we'll be starving in no time. I'll be back soon, kay?"

Elvira sniffles. "Alright."

And with that, Falké strikes out on his own, leaving the woman kneeling there on the floor of the living room.

CHAPTER THIRTY-EIGHT

Piper has been gone for a while now. She left Illyria with her mermaid friend– *connector*, most definitely, come to think of it – on the yacht of that supposed prince and has yet to return. Honestly, he doubts she ever will. If she really *is* sailing with royalty, *and* her partner, there would be no reason to come back to such a miserable place. She's happy now, probably.

Hopefully.

The worst thing about it all though, aside from the fact that he'll never see her again and apologise for his past wrongdoing, is the fact that everybody in Illyria seems to know what's happened. Every passer-by glances at him with a look that screams a mixture of antipathy and morbid curiosity. As if, for some bizarre reason, this is all his fault.

News certainly does travel fast in the area. He doesn't doubt the neighbours, Roberta and Hetty, are behind at least some of it – they're renowned as the local gossipers and they live close enough to find out such things before spreading them like wildfire. Once upon a time, he actually rather liked Hetty. She made some very good fish pies and seafood coleslaw when he was a child, and often brought them over for supper…but that's beside the point.

The Gilded Gull is busy this morning. People have crowded outside to smoke and drink together, and drunken laughter mingles with the screeches of seagulls overhead. Falké blinks, bewildered by the sheer *happiness* of the people now surrounding him. It's almost unprecedented to see such joy in Illyria, even on national holidays and events. Still, the location's popularity is a good thing.

He shoves the door open with a grunt, steps inside, and halts in his tracks. There, at the bar, sits Kyran and his friends, beer bottles in their hands and smiles on their faces as they talk. As expected, Carmen is with them, perched on a barstool holding out her pocket mirror and touching up her makeup. As usual, she's wearing lipstick – this time a deep maroon colour – and thick winged liner.

Falké sucks his teeth.

She never used to be so vain, not before Kyran came along and started imposing standards on her. In fact, she never really cared about beauty before becoming one of the Illyrian delinquents. It's sort of sad how much she's changed, but at least she's happy, right? That's all that matters to him really.

For a second or two, she pauses as if she's seen his reflection in the glass. He hesitates for a long moment, sudden anxiety bubbling urgent and hotly beneath his skin as his nerves tense like bowstrings. With bated breath, he waits for her to turn to him, to approach perhaps –

She shuts the mirror with one hand, grins at her boyfriend, and joins in the conversation.

Falké sighs, unsure of whether he is feeling relief

or disappointment. Perhaps it's a mixture of both. If she were to come talk to him, he thinks, Kyran would too, and he's definitely not in the mood for that sort of confrontation right now.

He tears his attention away from the group and proceeds to weave his way through clusters of joking, tipsy Illyrians. There's no point in just standing around and watching Carmen's 'friends' like some sad little geek in school wishing he was a popular kid. It's not going to help him feel any better.

Two very large men, looking stereotypically suspicious, stand on either side of a closed, heavy-looking door at the back of the room. Unlike the majority of people in the bar, they are well-coloured, dark-haired, and sport a certain degree of five o'clock shadow. Both stick out like a sore thumb, but in a way that makes them seem a lot more powerful than everybody else. They regard him with a slight smirk as he approaches, crossing their arms. "Well if it ain't Falké Tourneau," the one on the right muses, "what yer doin' 'ere so early in the mornin'?"

The boy responds flatly: "Lemme in."

They comply, and he heads through the door without a second glance at Carmen, her boyfriend, or the rest of their troublesome little squad.

The bar's underground fight room is a cesspool of aesthetic displeasure - grungy, dark, and messy. There are only four lights in the whole area, and one of them is flickering desperately, barely holding onto life. Several chairs are scattered haphazardly around, some taken, some empty. They are all aimed towards the arena in the centre, though, which also looks shoddy. It's basically a stage enclosed in rope and fencing.

At the moment, two men are fighting. They're

using mixed martial arts and constantly shout at each other over the uncomfortably loud, heavy music. Falké recognises them as regulars but as he approaches the announcer to get his name down for the next tournament, he can't remember either of their names.

Of course, he's well aware that he shouldn't be anywhere near a fighting ring like this. But the winners are rewarded generously, and there's no waiting around to get paid. If he succeeds in any match, he walks out of here with plenty of cash in no time flat.

It's not too long until his name is called and he eagerly climbs into the cage, a few audience members cheering in support, a few yelling vulgarities. He's entirely unfazed by this though, and takes a seat in the corner of the arena with a confident grin on his face. If he wins this, he and his mother won't be struggling with their funds for at least a couple of weeks. He might even be able to get something nice for Esther.

Esther.

His smile falters. What would she think if she knew he was here, sitting in the very centre of this adrenalin-filled circus of violence? She'd be angry. She'd be upset. She'd be…disappointed.

He takes a deep breath, tightens his fingers, and looks up as his opponent enters the cage. A grimace of distaste crosses his face when he realises who it is: Kyran, his eyes filled with a gleam of petty satisfaction and lips curled into a sneer.

"Kyran…" Falké grinds his teeth, his heart aching in his chest as though the boy has forcefully reached into him and squeezed it with a powerful cruelty. "Since when did you fight?"

"I 'ave been fer a while, Falké," comes the boy's response. "Carmen told me ya come down 'ere sometimes. Thought I'd 'ave a looksie. See if ya were down 'ere."

The bell is rung to signal the beginning of a new match, and Falké rises to his feet. His mouth opens and he tries to speak. Tries to shout even, but finds he can't. Instead, he gapes, his head shaking, and runs towards Kyran. He fists a hand into his shirt, rage flaring in his chest, and throws a punch, which his challenger dodges easily.

Kyran laughs. "Ya ain't very good at this, are ya, kid?"

Falké ducks to the side and travels around him. Deep down, he knows that Kyran is right, though. He's never been a good fighter despite years of practice. He almost always loses, and it was a stupid idea to think he had a chance.

No.

He clenches his fists, snarling. He can't let Kyran win. Not again. Quickly he gets behind the boy and grabs one of his calves, squeezing it with all the strength he can muster.

Surprisingly, he is able to yank Kyran hard enough to throw him off balance, and the audience gasp in shock as he falls onto his back.

Falké crawls atop him, spurred on by adrenaline. He lands the first blow to Kyran's face hard; a drop of blood runs down his chin and with a wild look of hatred, Kyran throws Falké off after five or six blows.

Panting, Falké watches as his tongue touches the small wound on his lower lip. "Stop callin' me kid," he snarls, and is about to attack again when he notices a familiar face in the crowd – Carmen. She notices him staring and in helpless fury cries out: "Stop it! Stop fightin' like this, both of ya!"

For a moment, he sees Esther there instead of Carmen. Esther, who cares about him more than anybody in the world. Esther, who he saved the life of and who has saved his life by coming back into it.

The adrenalin inside him evaporates faster than he ever thought possible and suddenly, he's hit square in the stomach. The very strength of the blow forces him to retch, pain blooming hot across his body. He blinks dazedly, the taste of bile in his mouth, and staggers back with visions of Esther swimming before his eyes.

Another hit comes. And another. Sweat gleams on his brow, strands of hair stick to his skin and he desperately swallows against the shriek that wants to break free from his throat. He doesn't want to look weak here. Not around Carmen and especially not around her jerk of a boyfriend.

He raises his hands to fight back, but before he can get in a jab, he's grabbed by the wrist and another punch is thrown right into his mouth.

"Falké!" He can hear Carmen screech from somewhere to his left, "Kyran, quit it! Ya won, quit it now!"

He collapses on all fours, out of fight and breath while the crowd cheer for a smug-looking Kyran. It's embarrassing, kneeling on the floor like an idiot, chest heaving as he struggles to breathe. A sound of pure anguish escapes him, and it reverberates through the room like the howl of a dog.

I lost, he thinks, brushing Carmen away as she practically materialises at his side, *I always lose.*

After he leaves the bar, it takes Esther less than

ten minutes to find him. The sea breeze dusts her with tiny, glistening sprinkles of salt as she approaches. The normally hidden sun peeks from the clouds and scatters golden light all around her, silhouetting her in a soft glow. *An angel,* he thinks when he sees her. *A sea angel.*

He falls forwards into her arms. She is strong and capable; without any sign of effort, she carries him to the back-alleys and places him carefully down on the decking. Here, they are sheltered by the shadows of the waterfront properties running adjacent to them, and are less likely to be seen by passers-by. Still, they cannot be out in the open for long. Just in case.

"I'm fine," he says. The words come out as little more than a groan, and Esther's eyelashes flutter and lift as she looks at him with a combination of sympathy and anger.

He's willingly hurt himself, and for what? Money? Thrills? Idiot.

Her gaze moves down to the crumpled-up paper bag he's holding. She's almost positive that it contains a pathetically small amount of money for participation. A consolation prize. It's ridiculous. Falké refuses to make his love for a mermaid public out of fear, yet seeks pain and violence though fighting.

"Why are you doing this to yourself, Falké?" she asks simply, "I don't understand. You humans are so fragile as it is. Why are you putting yourself in harm's way for such a small amount of currency? It's so stupid. Why?"

He facepalms and drags his hand down his cheek in attempt to strangle the tears surging behind his eyes. Everything aches, and his body sits tense and trembling beside her, slick with sweat. He knows she's right.

"Falké, talk to me. Why?"

"Had to."

"You *had* to?"

"Yeah."

"I don't believe that for a second," she counters, sighing deeply. "You're bleeding. You're bruised. Does this feel good to you, Falké?"

"I need the money. And sorta…it - it helps to distract me."

"It looks to me like you're *not* making money from it! Is there no other way? And if you want to be hurt," she mutters, "then you might as well just confess to being with a mermaid. Can't you see just how stupid this is? Just how idiotic you are being by participating in these human fights? Can't you see that?"

He swallows hard. "Sorry."

"No…I'm sorry. For letting you get caught up in such things. Listen…I know where Astrid's little boat is underwater, and I know she keeps precious things in there, including money. If she's really gone, like everybody thinks, I can try and take some things from her. I'll be discreet…she won't even notice when, or if, she returns to Illyria. Hopefully."

Tears begin seeping from beneath Falké's now closed eyelids; Esther can see the flutter of his pulse at his throat, and the heaving of his chest as he sobs. "You'd do that?" he asks, his voice weary and gentle, "steal? For me? But you…you're so good. Don't do bad things for me"

"Falké…" Esther hesitates for a moment. "…I would do anything for you.

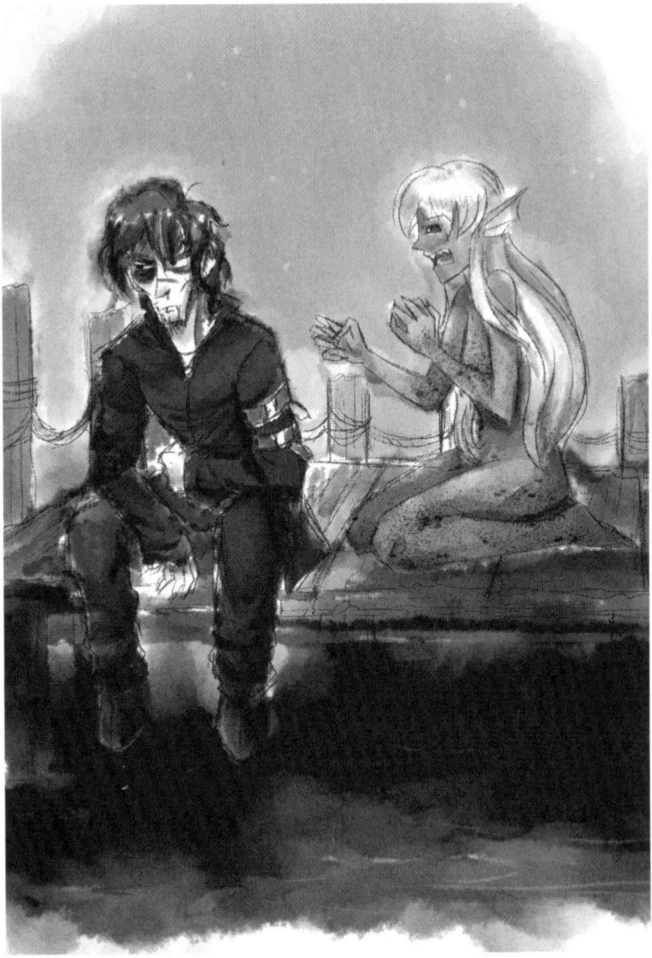

CHAPTER THIRTY-NINE

The moment Astrid wakes from her rest beside Piper, she groans in discomfort. The cabin is a far warmer temperature than she's used to, the heat practically pounding through her. A deep, low throbbing reverberating and rushing up her spine. When she shifts on the sheets, moving her aching legs, she realises that the heat is from her own body, originating from somewhere below her stomach. It sizzles up the inside of her soft thighs and stays concentrated between her legs.

Lust.

"Hm."

Her eyebrows raise causing a surprised – yet impressed – look to steal over her elegant, angular features. Sliding her tongue over her teeth she runs her hands down her body for a moment, the tips of her sharp nails only lightly scratching the skin. The suggestive, licentious cast of her eye towards Piper goes unnoticed; she's still asleep, comfortable and content with half of that fluffy blanket on her body. The other half of her is exposed. With a long, slow exhale, Astrid moves herself so that she's nestled more perfectly against it.

"Wake up," she commands Piper huskily, "can you hear me? Wake up." And after a moment: "Please wake up. For me."

Piper yawns softly, signalling her awakening. She mumbles something along the lines of "Mmmh…hello Astrid," as she stretches her limbs out. Almost a quarter of her freckled, pale face is obscured by the blanket but it's easy to see her eyes are closed still. Her light brown hair is rumpled and messy, streams of it ribboning her brow.

Astrid smiles.

She rests her hands on the crook of Piper's waist, skimming over her hips and the dip at the small of her back to cup her closer. Emerald eyes open half-lidded and stare forwards at her, every blink slow and sleepy. "I'm up," the girl mumbles tiredly, "sorry…what do you need? Astrid?"

"You."

"Me?"

"Yes. Do you need me too?"

"Dunno, I'm sleepy…"

Astrid groans low in her throat and kisses the girl firmly without another word, chasing the flavour upon her tongue. It becomes passionate very quickly, and turns into something much more carnal, much more possessive. Devouring, perhaps, but not kissing. It doesn't last long. Piper pulls away, laughs weakly, and wipes her lips with the back of her hand. "Wait – Astrid. I just woke up! Hold on…"

"And?"

The mermaid leans in for another kiss, but Piper presses her palm against her lips and shakes her head. "No, Astrid. You gotta, you gotta learn no means no.

Okay? Boundaries…consent."

Astrid frowns. 'Boundaries and consent' aren't exactly important to mermaids. But still…

"Boundaries…consent," she repeats, nodding. "Alright."

Relief floods Piper's expression, and she rubs the sleep from her eyes before speaking again. "I'm sorry to stop your fun," she sighs, "perhaps later. I do want to, just not now. And I…was thinking about something yesterday during the storm. I forgot to mention it."

"Oh?"

"Yeah. So, can I ask you about it?"

"Well I don't know what it is – but okay. Go ahead."

The girl takes a deep breath, unsure of how she should approach such a subject. "Did you…" she starts, looking away from Astrid for a moment, "did you know my parents at all?"

Astrid looks surprised by this question at first. Her black eyes widen, her lips part. It isn't long before this expression falls into a more knowing, calm one. "Yes, yes I did. Zachary and Elisa Tourneau, correct?"

"Yeah, that's them…do you know what *really* happened to my father?"

"Excuse me?"

"The death certificates say my father was killed by mermaids, and my mother committed suicide. I know what my mother did was true, but I don't believe my father's cause of death whatsoever. I think there was more involved. The mermaids wouldn't just attack him for no reason, would they? He was close with them. He studied them. He was even friends with one. He told me about them."

A moment of silence passes.

"He killed himself, just as Elisa did. Took his boat out to sea and did it there, I saw him jump into the water with blood on his wrists."

"Why?" An almost imperceptible sob escapes Piper's lips, and she makes an effort to swallow it back. She can't start crying now – she needs to know what happened. Now is the time for learning, not crying. Now is the time to be mature about this.

"I suppose that mermaid he was 'friends' with was part of the reason…I assume he fell in love with them and the guilt within him that stemmed from the relationship was the final straw. So, we, the mermaids, didn't kill him per se. Although I think that it would be fair to say that we *contributed* to his death."

Piper stiffens. A deep inhale rushes into her chest all at once. She stares around at her connector, her hands clasped tightly together and her breath shudders out again. She taps on the duvet for a few seconds in silence, processing this information. Before she manages to speak again, Astrid rises from the bed.

"Wh-where are you going?" Piper asks, a crease forming in her brow. Her eyes flicker back and forth across the room. "I didn't upset you, did I? I wasn't accusing you of anything, I hope you realise that!"

The mermaid shakes her head. "No. You didn't upset me," she confirms, "I am *tremendously* dehydrated, so we will have to move this conversation to the head. I simply can't stand another minute out of water; I've been in this form for much longer than I can usually tolerate and it's starting to take its toll."

"Oh. Oh good. I thought – never mind. What's the head? The front of the boat? So you're just going to jump off the boat and swim around for a bit, right?" Piper stands too, trying to push all thoughts of her father to the back of her mind. She glances out the porthole – the sky seems to be clearing up a little, but the sea remains rather turbulent as its waves peak and arch towards the sky. Astrid follows her gaze and then says, "No. It's too much effort climbing on and off a boat in these conditions, especially considering I need to switch forms. Also, the 'head' is what you call a bathroom on a ship. Our 'handsome prince' has a bath in there so I might as well use it."

"Ah…okay. So you're just going to have a bath? In freshwater?"

"Precisely."

"Huh. Okay."

Despite Astrid referring to it as the 'head', the plaque on the door states 'bathroom'. She is going to make a comment on this but decides against it, instead becoming rather flustered when Astrid looks over her shoulder at her and suggests they bathe together.

Piper waves her hands frantically as a tense energy overcomes her. Of course, part of her wants to agree to this proposal. She can easily recall her behaviour last night in this very cabin, practically lusting after Astrid and her strong, perfect frame. Wanting her, *needing* her even. But now the opportunity to be so intimate with Astrid has arrived, she's scared. She's not entirely sure she's prepared. "N-no thank you," she declines, flushed. "That's okay, Astrid. I don't need one – besides, your mermaid form is longer, right? Taller, I mean. It's taller. Your tail is longer than your legs. There won't be a lot of room, surely."

"Your choice," Astrid responds, shrugging her thin shoulders. She moves through the door and towards the ridiculously luxurious looking bath, and then proceeds to turn on the taps (cold water only) and watch the water cascade down. The 'bathroom' itself smells strongly of rose, and upon close inspection both girls notice almost every product – soaps, shampoo, conditioner... – are rose-scented.

"He must be a fan of rose, huh?" Piper comments as she watches the mermaid slink into the now filling tub, the cool water encasing her stiff legs.

"Yes. He must be." Drawing a hand across her eyes, Astrid shifts into her regular form, tail curling to the left and fins brushing the side of the white bath. Thankfully, the tub is large and accommodates her reasonably well, despite her tail's length. It's not too hard for her to get comfortable. Sinking under the ever-rising water, she stares up at the now blurry ceiling and blows bubbles before surfacing again and asking, "So, shall we continue our conversation about your parents?"

Piper doesn't manage to answer. The moment she opens her mouth the boat lurches violently, causing her to lose her footing and fall

forwards onto her hands and knees.

Astrid sits up straight. "What was that? Are you alright? You fell."

"I – I don't know," Piper admits, carefully getting up again and rubbing at her knees, "but I think we just hit something. I don't know. I'm gonna go check, Astrid. Hold on – you stay here."

"No, I'm definitely coming. I'll meet you on the deck in a minute – you go ahead."

Chapter Forty

The first person that Piper runs into is not Prince Holt Davori. Rather, it's the member of Holt's crew that she doesn't know. A broad-shouldered, light-haired man who looks as if he could battle a mermaid underwater...and win. The floor is damp as she gets closer to the steps up to the deck and as he passes holding a thick bundle of rope and a life jacket, she stops him to ask what's happening and where Holt is.

She learns his name is Cadmus, and he informs her briefly that 'his highness' is on deck trying to free the yacht. Before she can question this, he's already headed up the steps. A skittish and restless looking Lenka emerges from one of the cabins and quickly follows.

Free the yacht? From what?

Once she gets outside, the wind whipping her hair across her face, she learns exactly what. The yacht is not moving whatsoever and Holt, with his hands in the air, is complaining loudly about how the "weight is simply not shifting!" and they're "going to be stuck here forever on this godforsaken reef."

She moves over to him hurriedly and clears her

throat to get his attention, placing a hand on his shoulder. "Excuse me? Prince Hol- Eek!"

She jumps back in surprise when his warm hand grasps her own, soft lips pressing against her knuckles as he turns to face her. They linger for an instant before she reels back in shock and looks down at Holt, who is down on one knee. "What on Earth?!" she cries, before realising Astrid might have heard from below deck and lowers her voice as she continues: "what are you doing?!"

He raises an eyebrow. "Why, I was kissing your hand," he responds, confused, "like any true gentleman. I'm terribly sorry if that offended you?"

She groans softly, the panicked beating of her heart resounding through her body. Every thud is like the tolling of a great bell, or something similar. "You frightened me," she finally states, trying to regain the breath stolen from her lungs. "You can't just grab my hand like that and kiss it with no warning! I almost fainted. I just wanted to ask you what's going on!"

"I apologise profusely. Startling you was never my intention… please forgive me. And I must say, I find your choice in pyjamas very charming."

Piper reddens, subconsciously moving her hands to tug at the underclothes she's wearing. In her hurry, she hadn't dressed before coming out onto the deck. It was fine being around Astrid wearing such little clothing, but she has seen her in every state possible at this point. This is different. Suddenly, with *him* staring at her, she feels uncovered. Exposed.

"Ah. Yes. Well. I didn't bring my actual pyjamas with me," she points out quietly, a clear vulnerability in her expression, "these are just my underclothes.

We didn't have time to get anything from my house before we left."

She knows he's noticed the scars, the bruises, the cuts. She knows he's decided not to mention them, and for that she is grateful. She glances over his shoulder as he stands, looking at the sparkling water. Lenka, hitching up her skirt, has waded onto the rocks where Cadmus is currently positioned. The man instructs her to get back on the boat. She declines.

"Have we...crashed?"

"Hmm. Well, the proper term is 'run aground' actually! But do not panic, I am working on fixing it -"

"Wait, is the boat going to sink?!"

The boy's elegant hand brushes the question away with an expansive gesture. "No, no," he replies, shaking his head, "*my* boats never sink."

Piper makes a concerned noise at the back of her throat. She looks over at Cadmus attempting to dislodge the vessel from its reef prison to no avail. He stops after a minute or so, standing with arms crossed, further assessing the problem at hand. "Are you sure?"

"Absolutely positive."

"Just, the ship seems to be leaning to the left a little."

The prince directs his attention to the horizon. She isn't wrong; the boat is listing to port and it seems to be getting worse. "Well," he starts with mock confidence, "that is simply because of the storm. There was a lot of wind, and a lot of...wave. We are definitely not sinking, not at all. Everything is *fine*."

Cadmus finally speaks up. "We need to shift the weight your highness! Everybody should move to the area farthest away from the point of impact – so – starboard. To be honest though, I'm not sure this is repairable outside of a boatyard. The hull is badly damaged and when the tide comes up, we will be taking on water."

"Wha-?! Taking on water?! We *are* sinking!" Piper cries, putting her hands on either side of her head. "I'm gonna go get Astrid. Maybe she can do something."

"No need. I have arrived."

The pair turn around quickly, greeted by a rather reproachful looking Astrid. Some wet strands of hair have plastered themselves to her face; her eyes are somewhat hidden. She raises a hand and plucks each one away individually and then says, "Am I right in assuming that this vessel has run aground?"

Holt nods in confirmation, his eyes flicking to the side.

The mermaid looks over the side of the boat, her brow pinching for a moment before smoothing again like ripples on the surface of water after throwing a pebble in. "Well that is a problem. A serious problem." Her voice is flat, unimpressed with the entire situation.

Holt moans in displeasure, pacing in a circle as he grumbles to himself. "What a nightmare," he comments with a surly mutter, "we must have been blown a long way off course and have no way to take a proper reading."

"So what are we going to *do* about it?" Astrid taps her nails against her hips as she watches Cadmus' useless attempts to free the yacht. The sun shines from behind departing slabs of cloud, hitting against the wet rocks he and Lenka stand on, causing them to glisten.

Chapter Forty-One

It's an hour later when the ship is spotted; as if by divine intervention – a distant angel, a saviour.

Piper is the first to see it. Restless, she grasps onto Astrid's arm and shakes it ever so slightly. "Will it see us?" she queries, her lips widening into a smile of relief.

For a minute or so the mermaid is silent. Her eyes, fixated on the horizon where the vessel pushes forward, don't even seem to blink. Finally, she diverts her attention to the girl and dips her head downwards with a simple, "Yes."

For a while, the calmness of Astrid's words soothes the crew. When the oncoming vessel grows closer however, torrents of doubt rush through every one of them. It's in no way small; the masts climb to the heavens with an air of grandeur, and the ship itself is large and powerful as it carries out its steady approach. The water at its prow parts like a curtain. Hollow-fronted, rolling waves snarl around its sides like the hungry jaws of a great sea creature, and are only pushed back by its greatness.

It seems…imposing.

"It's so big. We should be cautious," comes Lenka's immediate, concerned observation. She stares at the advancing ship with great trepidation, her eyes wide and nervous. "What if this boat is dangerous? What if it belongs to pirates?"

Cadmus raises a hand to his face, palm flat to shield his eyes. "We can only hope that it doesn't."

Relief returns once the ship has drawn closer. It looks very clean and well cared for, signifying a well-tuned and considerate crew. There is no jolly-roger flag indicating piracy, either. Only gigantic masts and slightly off-white sails that bulge with wind like the great wings of an angel. Like Holt's yacht, it is grandly carved with a proudly bowed hull. On its bow is a figurehead – a mermaid with sharp features like Astrid and extremely long hair, surpassing her waist with ease.

Once it's about a quarter of a mile away, Holt flashes signals with a small, hand-held mirror and is greeted with a quick response: small explosions of light, a return signal. He sucks in air, holds it, and then lets it all out through his nose as he lowers the mirror. "They are coming," he states, the relief in his voice clear as day. Mixed with it is something despairing, which seems very much like defeat.

To his left, Piper remains clutching onto Astrid like an anchor. Honestly, it baffles him that she and that creature are a couple in the first place. Well, that's what they seem to be, at least; he's not entirely sure he understands the term 'connector' that's been thrown around, but it's probably Illyrian slang for *girlfriend*. Part of him wants to ask what exactly it means and part of him doesn't really want to know.

He swallows convulsively. "Well, this is certainly

not how I intended your rescue to pan out, Piper." As much as he attempts to add a light-hearted, jovial tone to his words they end up rather stale. "Of course, it is not *my fault* though. Not in the slightest. I refuse to apologise for that reason."

"You were the one sailing, though," Astrid points out shamelessly. "So, it is your fault in a way."

"Astrid!" Piper hisses softly, squeezing her arm. "I'm so sorry, Holt. We know it's not your fault, you didn't know the reef was here or whatever."

Holt crosses his arms. "No, no, Piper. Do not apologise for the mermaid," he trifles, "you have a very disagreeable temperament, Astrid. Besides, the ship has very nearly reached us. We ought to make a good impression upon our rescuers. So…do behave yourself please. No more snide comments."

"It was hardly snide. Just fact."

The vessel, in all its grandness, stops eventually to avoid the reef. The reef that Holt unfortunately did *not* avoid. With slumped shoulders, he watches a small rowboat depart from it and begin a short journey towards his damaged yacht. The two burly looking men on it fill him with sudden, intense unease. Although the ship looks far from slovenly, the crewmates don't exactly seem…*un*pirate-like.

Glancing over at Cadmus, he feels somewhat reassured to see that the man clearly feels the same way. He most definitely looks on guard, his fists clenched at his sides. Lenka stands behind him with a nervous, stressed stance, peering out at the approaching boat. "Stay behind me for now," he warns her. She nods.

"Yer seem to be in a bit of trouble there, mateys!" one of the men calls. "Our cap'n be mighty gen'rous though – saw yers in the distance and sailed all the way o'er here to help! An' what a mighty fine piece o' work this boat be! Shame 'bout the damage. But…yer win some, yer lose some. That's what me cap'n says."

"Is tha' a siren?" the other adds, "I ain't sure we should be bringin' one of them on board."

"I am coming on board" Astrid calls.

"Okay." The men chorus. They don't seem to want to argue with her, which is encouraging. At least they don't seem to be set on starting a fight or anything of the sort. Once they get close enough to the rocks, one of them climbs onto the reef and makes his way over.

Cadmus is quick to step in. "Thank you for your rescue," he states simply, nodding in the direction of the great ship. "Your captain truly is kind."

"That he is, meartie. That he is. Now yer and yer crew can get offa this wreck and onto there." He gestures to the rowboat his crew mate sits on. "An' well, yer don't 'ave to worry about yer things…we're gonna handle that. Get it all offa there. No worries, not at all."

There is a somewhat malicious glint in his eye then, which causes Holt to shudder involuntarily. Despite the fact that not only are he and his crew being saved, but so are his extremely valuable possessions, he can't help but be wary. What the men are going to do with them – and his things – he has no idea.

"Alright," he relents with a soft sigh, "let us go."

The stranger grins like a Cheshire cat.

Aside from Astrid and Cadmus, there's a noticeable twinge of anxiety in everyone's steps as they make their way off of the yacht and across numerous limpet-covered rocks to the rowboat. Each of them carries a bag of items such as clothes and shoes, but are reassured that they have no need to. Their new captain's crew will empty the yacht soon enough.

"How do we know that they are…safe?" Holt whispers to Astrid, "that they will not…murder us perhaps…or harvest our organs? *How do we know*, I say?!"

"They won't," she responds. "Calm down. And walk slower. Some of these rocks are slippery – lots of algae and seaweed. You too, Piper."

Holt huffs. Crossing the rocks does prove to be very challenging, though; he realises soon enough that the mermaid was right. He almost falls twice, and notices that up ahead Piper does actually slip. With all the desperation of somebody drowning, she hooks her hands around Astrid's arms and scrambles upwards, complaining about scraping her knee. He can't properly hear her, for he has fallen significantly behind –

"Piper?!" he cries, "Are you quite alright?"

"I'm okay!" comes her response, and within a couple of minutes they are all on the rowboat. Astrid needn't travel on it with them, but does so anyway, humming to herself.

The humming, Holt decides, is actually very soothing. He's almost disappointed when they arrive and she stops.

CHAPTER FORTY-TWO

Seven hours, five minutes, and seventeen…eighteen…nineteen seconds.

Jasper scribbles the time in his notebook, his hands shaking with adrenaline and excitement. It's the longest he's ever managed to keep mermaid venom viable by far – he almost wants to cry with joy in light of this accomplishment. But still…even now…even with the sulphur, the *miracle* component, it's not perfect yet. It has potential to be, of course, and it's the best he's ever done, but it's not ready. Not quite ready. He can make it last longer, he knows he can.

With eyes bright and full of determination, he closes his hardback journal with a resounding thud and looks around at the group of people before him. They stand rigid to attention, hands planted firmly at their sides. Some look proud and confident. Most, however, seem worried, for Jasper's true moods are notoriously difficult to determine; there have been countless instances where he's appeared perfectly content but is actually seething with rage. This may easily be one of those situations…

He nods at them all, tapping his fingers against the

cover of his notes. "Perfect! Absolutely perfect. Well done, team. Seven hours prior to use, a fairly small amount, and still the venom has completely disabled a human!"

There's a quiet, yet collective sigh of relief from each team member.

Jasper doesn't seem to notice this. But, his smile does fade as he looks down at the deceased man on the floor. He grimaces when he taps the body with the tip of his shoe. "Dispose of him," he instructs, moving back towards the door, "and tell our lovely newspaper – Miss Valentina Victory, in particular - that the death was due to drowning. He was a terrible drunk. He had one too many, and fell in the water. Unfortunate, so unfortunate. But sometimes these things happen."

The people nod and chorus: "Yes, sir." It's all too normal by now.

Jasper heads back to his study and throws himself into his chair, eager to start work on another batch of venom. The red mermaids in the tank behind him are gone. They died quite a while ago, actually – Margot's surgical experimentation was more successful with the second one, but the first perished instantly. Venom was extracted from both of them, though, and that's what's important for the time being.

In their place is a violet mermaid with long, moon hair ending in a soft lavender. She was caught two days ago by his 'apprehension crew,' a small team of workers dedicated to capturing mermaids for research and experimentation purposes. In an ideal world, the crew would be much larger. After all, more men means more mermaids caught. But no – if the team were to grow any more, there's a much higher chance of word getting out that mermaids are getting…taken. That would be nothing but problematic. But despite the diminutive size of the group, they have managed to pluck several mermaids from the sea. This one was an unexpected – but in no way unwanted – capture. She got extremely trapped in fishing net, so much so that even her sharp teeth and nails did little to help her. Her venom and voice served no purpose either, for his team are masked and prepared for such things. It was a very pleasant surprise to get her. He's always been fond of the violet mermaids, for they are the most beautiful in his opinion -

And she certainly is, without a doubt, extremely beautiful. When he looks over at her, she blinks and mewls, a look of contemptuous indignation on her face. Her hands are folded into her chest, she clutches at something partly hidden by her floating hair, and unquestionably moving. Jasper doesn't notice them at first, for he is far too busy with the venom – she hides them, shies to the back of the tank. Of course, he sees them eventually.

Two baby mermaids. They're newborn, from what he can tell. Small. Tiny, yet moving their little tails side to side quite powerfully. They're clinging to their mother's torso and most likely nursing from the two inverted nipples that sit within her mammary slits.

"Oh, I didn't even notice you had these little things," he confesses, moving over to the tank and tapping against the glass, "aren't they cute?" "Do mermaid babies produce venom, or does that develop a little later? We may just have to find out, hmm? I thank you for your contribution to my scientific discoveries, mermaid."

The creature doesn't seem to understand him, yet a look of horror tugs at her features anyway. She makes a loud whine-type noise upon realising he's staring at her young, and then turns her back to him in the water.

"Aha. You can hide, but you can't run. There's nowhere to go. You and your babies are trapped here, my dear. But think of it as supporting Illyria and its community, hmm? No hard feelings. I understand you mermaids don't stay very attached to your young, anyway."

A grin dimples his cheeks. The feral coil in his silvery eyes burns with curiosity. What an amazing, wonderful coincidence, to have a mermaid captured that happened to be pregnant? He's never experimented on the babies before, for they are terribly hard to get a hold of…it's a sign. A sign that everything will be okay. That Illyria will be reborn soon enough, and Piper Tourneau will be a problem of the past.

He turns, heads towards the door, and makes his way into the main hall of the manor house. Scarlett is upstairs – he knows she is, for she has nothing else to do today. She'll be staring out of the window as usual. When he walks into her bedroom after ascending the stairs, she turns to him with a look that makes his grin widen even further. Melting, devoted eyes and a soft smile. Her hair is done up in a low bun at the nape of her neck, a few curly tendrils loose and framing her face. She's wearing a green, short silk robe, is barefoot, and looks at him as if he is her whole world. Then again, he sort of is.

"Well, look at you," he comments as he strides over to her, "sitting there looking gorgeous. What are you looking at, my pet? Is there anything interesting going on outside?"

"I'm looking for mermaids."

He pauses, a look of confusion chasing the shock that sparks in his expression. "For mermaids, eh?" He entitles himself to touch soon enough, playing with the loose red curls on either side of her cheeks. "And why is that, my dear?"

"I hear you talking about them a lot...and I know you like them. How is work going?"

He doesn't bother questioning her sudden interest in the mermaids any further. It's something to occupy her, and whatever occupies her is fine as long as it doesn't hinder his work. In fact, having her look out for mermaids might be beneficial in the long run – there's always a chance she'll spot one that's injured or vulnerable, and inform him of it.

"Good. Very good," he responds, cupping her cheek. "I believe I'm getting somewhere now. And it's all a good distraction from thinking about that foolish child – I think she'll come back, I truly do. We just have to be patient. Her family is here, in Illyria, and she seems too...weak to go without them. She already lost her mother and father. She won't want to lose her aunt and cousin, too."

"That makes sense."

He moves over to the mirror on the wall, shimmering glass encased in an intricately carved frame. He examines himself and then looks at her in the reflection with a smile. "How are you feeling today?"

Her clear hesitation in answering causes him to raise his eyebrows. "Well?"

"Unwell."

"Unwell? Unwell how?"

"My head hurts. I'm nauseated."

"Is this a *womanly* matter?"

Thankfully, there's no hostility in his voice. Scarlett can see the hard edge to his gaze in the mirror though, and it unsettles her. "No," she responds. "No, it's not that. I thought at first it might be, for I had a little blood but…"

"But what?"

"But it was only a little."

He turns back to her. "This is bound to be a womanly matter; the blood will come properly soon. Be patient. If it gets worse, tell me. Is that it? Just the headache and nausea?"

"But it has never been this bad before, Jasper! And I'm tired. And…I'm sad. I feel as if I am going to burst into tears at any moment."

His eyes, fastened on her still, soften as he chuckles. "Everyone is sad in this city, my pet," he remarks, "this place is a disaster. Go make yourself a dessert, something sweet. That'll cheer you up, give you something to do as well. Maybe you're just hungry."

"Maybe," she parrots. Her gaze is downcast.

The moment he leaves the room she dashes to the bathroom and vomits into the toilet bowl. Convinced she has somehow made herself ill *again* she leans back on her knees and cries in shame. Since her last bout of sickness, she's taken it upon herself to avoid anything potentially harmful at all costs – and yet here she is, vomiting. Dizzy.

She forces herself back onto her feet and wipes the sweat from her brow with trembling fingers. If this sickness continues, she must hide it. Be discreet at the very least, so Jasper doesn't find out. He's bound to get upset with her if it lasts longer than a few hours…

CHAPTER FORTY-THREE

"My yacht," Holt chokes out, his words ragged and despairing, "my beautiful, splendid, gorgeous yacht. I *loved* that yacht, do you hear me? My mother – that is Queen Delilah Davori of Caldisa to you all – presented it to me for my fifteenth birthday. How will I *ever* live now, knowing it is at the bottom of the ocean, laying on the sand in *pieces*. We should have done more to fix it!"

Cadmus clicks his tongue, smacking his large hands together. It makes Holt jump in surprise. "With all due respect, your highness," he announces, "the hull was quite irreparable...we *had* to abandon it. There was no chance it would be able to be fixed fast enough; the tide would have risen and overtaken the vessel before we managed to do anything even remotely helpful."

The prince's lower lip starts trembling. He lets out a shuddering sigh, looking as if he's about to burst into tears. "And now look where we are," he whines, gesturing around to the dimly lit storage cabin the group currently sit in. "This is far from luxury! I am sitting on a barrel, Cadmus! A barrel! Have these people never heard of a chair?!"

Piper takes initiative; she places a comforting hand on his shoulder and offers a small, weak smile. "Sorry, Holt. It's just, well, you told me to attract the attention of any ships passing and so...I did. A-and all of your possessions have been taken off the yacht, so you're only really losing the vessel. Think of it as a good thing! We could have...well, we could have all been trapped on a boat with a broken...er...hull, was it? Yeah, hull, 'run aground' or whatever. But no! We're all safe and comfortable on this ship instead."

"Well I wouldn't quite call this comfortable," he grunts, "and my yacht was worth more than a hundred – no – a thousand musgravites! What a waste."

Piper wrings her hands. "That's er – that's very expensive," she murmurs in attempt to console the boy, "one of the most expensive in the world...and I assume a firm favourite of yours. You have musgravites embedded into your royal crown -"

"And where *is* my crown, speaking of such matters?!" Holt interrupts, slamming a fist against the bulkhead in frustration. "Those devious, disgusting sea peasants stole it from me! Do you know how utterly important that crown is to me? Do *any* of you know? This is what happens when you get involved with pirates!"

"They're smugglers, Holt," Astrid corrects. "Not pirates. I don't doubt that pirates would have killed us all instantly. Well, killed you all at least. I would have been able to escape such a fate..."

The sound of footsteps descending a stairway attract the group's attention. They echo with a maddening staccato for a short while, and then stop abruptly. Holt squawks out a rather undignified noise of terror; his gaze darts from a stack of wooden crates to a pile of scrap and finally to the doorway. Darkness lies beyond the threshold, but it's not too difficult to make out the shape of a person approaching. Before he can react in a way he sees fit in this situation (hide behind Cadmus, probably), Astrid speaks.

"Captain Tyrian," she says, rising to her feet and extending a hand in greeting. "It's been a long time. A pleasure to see you again – and thank you for the rescue."

Piper looks quickly from the deeply tanned man to Astrid. She guesses he's in his mid-thirties. He easily matches Astrid's height, is grinning from ear-to-ear, and stands with an air of confidence that she can only dream of possessing. He removes his tricorn hat for a moment, bowing courteously, and his raven hair is revealed to be wild and spiked from the salty air. It sweeps to the side in such a manner that it covers his left eye.

"Wh-wait what? Astrid, you know this guy?" she asks.

The Captain answers for the mermaid, placing the hat back upon his head and adjusting it. "Aye, medear. Known Astrid fer a long, long time. Many a year, sailin' the seas. An' yer can call me Cass, Astrid. No need fer the fancy long version, usin' me last name an' such."

"Perhaps a middle ground," Astrid supplies. "Captain Caspian, rather than Tyrian *or* 'Cass' as you suggest."

"Aye. If that's what yer want."

As he talks, Piper notices there is a little calico cat at

his feet. It's trilling, wanting affection, and eventually he picks it up and places it on his shoulder. It purrs loudly when he pets it, craning its neck at the attention. Despite her confusion at the situation, she can't help but smile a little - she's always wanted a pet, but her mother was allergic to fur and Elvira hates animals. "I-I see…okay…"

"That's right. Cap'n Cass, and ye be?"

Piper blanks for a moment. "Eh…Oh! Oh, sorry. Er…yeah. This is Prince Holt Davori, his handmaiden Lenka, and his guard Cadmus…they're all from Caldisa. You know Astrid, obviously…er…I'm Piper. Piper Tourneau. From Illyria."

"Illyria, yer say?" Caspian raises his hands, moving them apart in a downwards arc. "The nation of jewels, eh? And I can tell ye be one of them, Piper Tourneau from Illyria." He winks.

Holt narrows his eyes, uncomfortable with this man's behaviour. "She is far from interested, *smuggler*. And I am requesting the things taken from my ship to be given back to me this instant, please."

An intrigued expression flashes across Caspian's face. A smuggler like him – a captain, nonetheless – expected to return stolen things? What an amusing thought. Stupid, but amusing. "Well, me'artie, we *smugglers*…we don't like givin' back. And yer owe us fer rescuin' yers."

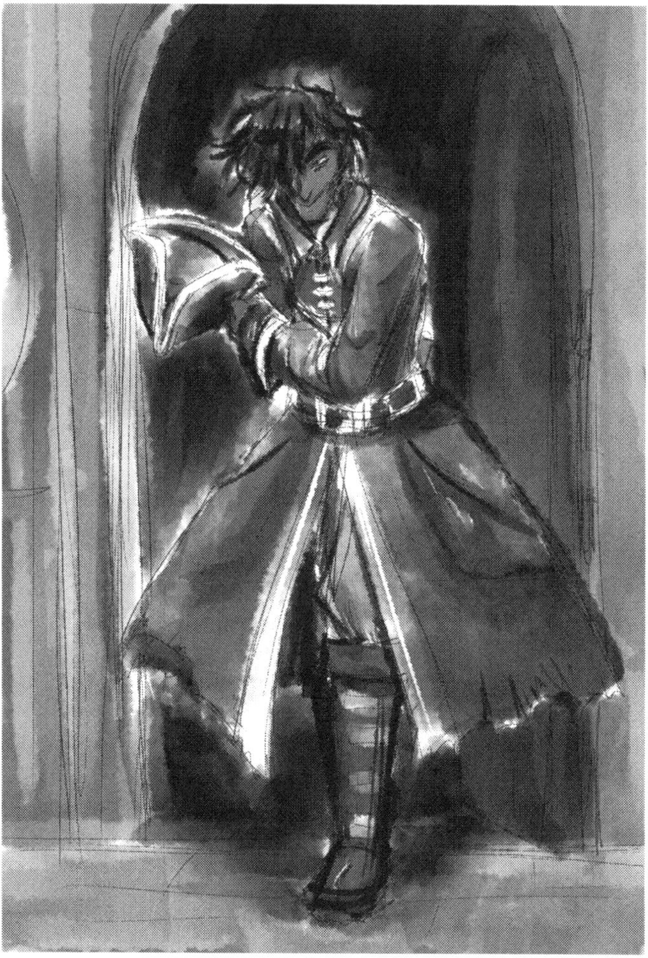

Holt gasps dramatically. "Excuse me?!" he cries, "how dare you! And you are not to address me as 'me – heart – lee' or whatever peculiar made-up word you just attempted to use. You should refer to me as 'your highness' like everybody else. Also, Astrid is right. 'Cass' is far too informal so I shall not be calling you that - we are *not* friends, simply acquaintances, so formality is key. And may I add that Cass is far too…feminine for a man such as yourself"

"Them friends of yers may call yer that, but I certainly ain't gonna," Caspian responds, chuckling to himself, "And what's it to yer if I got a 'feminine name,' matey? If I didn't like it, I'd get meself a new name. Yer can call me Cap'n Tyrian if yer want to so badly, like the rest of me crew when they use me name. And yer better start actin' a bit more grateful! I be yer hero, yer know?"

Holt turns his head to the side, pressing his lips firmly together and avoiding eye contact. "Whatever. Thank you for helping us, truly, but I simply cannot socialise with rude little thieves. Cadmus, back me up."

Cadmus rubs his temples and says nothing, much to the prince's frustration.

Caspian laughs. "I be the rude one?" The cat on his shoulder climbs down his arm and jumps to the deck, proceeding to rub against his ankles. He motions towards them. "This be Vivo, me little lassie. That be a masculine word, yer know. Vivo. I hope that's alright with yer, princey."

"Vivo? What a ridiculous name for a cat." Holt raises an eyebrow, directing his attention towards the feline, and the smuggler glares daggers at him in response. He reaches for what seems to be a cutlass at his side and says, oh so furiously: "Me' mother named that cat! Ye'll meet the rope's end for that, yer scurvy infested, yellow-bellied, rotten cored -"

"He's sorry!"

Caspian glances around at Piper quickly, his hands falling to his sides. He sighs softly, takes a deep breath, and regains his composure. "Ay, lassie. Just…I love me cat, yer hear?"

"I'm sure you do."

For a moment or so, Piper considers mentioning the scratch on her knee. But she's had so many wounds before, and it's so minor she fears she'd be laughed at for making such a fuss over something so small. Still, it stings; she discreetly reaches down and presses her fingers against it, flinching ever so slightly. Predictably, Astrid notices her discomfort. She moves closer to her, grasping her wrist. "What are you doing?"

"Nothing. I just – I got a scratch when I fell over."

"Alright. That's all?"

"That's all…it's fine. It just stings a bit."

"Fine. Don't keep touching it."

Suddenly, Caspian speaks again. "An' ye be heading where?" he asks, directing the question towards Piper. At first, she doesn't seem to notice that he's speaking to her, and doesn't look up. But, after he repeats the sentence, she directs her attention towards him with a soft: "Pardon?"

"Where were yer goin' lass? Before yer ship struck the reef?"

She pauses. "Oh…honestly, I don't really know…not Caldisa, and not Illyria."

"Definitely not Caldisa!" Holt agrees, "and to answer the question, *Captain Tyrian*, we were just sailing, going nowhere in particular…why must you know, anyway? Such things are none of your business whatsoever. That is private and confidential information shared only between myself and my crew."

"I wanted to know if ye be wantin' to get anywhere. But if not, ye be welcome to stay 'ere on me ship, become part of *me* crew…you and yer friends 'ere. The lasses, the lad, and…"

He stares intently at Astrid.

"I am female as well," she confirms for him. "And yes – we shall all stay on this vessel for the time being Caspian. After all, Piper and I are in need of the protection, and you, Holt, are in hiding, are you not? Nobody from your kingdom is going to think you're on some random ship, are they?"

"I – I suppose not. They will expect me to be on my yacht."

She hums thoughtfully. "Then there you have it. Cadmus, Lenka, are you in agreement that this would be the best solution to our current predicament?"

While Cadmus makes some sort of affirmative grunt, Lenka speaks. "Seems fine to me," she agrees, "I am more than happy to stay on this ship for the time being. If it helps, Captain…Caspian? Cass, I am quite good at cooking! Perhaps I could help in the galley to repay you for your kind rescue?"

Caspian taps his chin thoughtfully, and then snaps his fingers. "Yar, me head chef be mighty talented – he'd be happy to 'ave someone to teach his ways to. Ye be interested in bein' a porter or commis chef at first? Then if yer like workin' with everyone and all, yer can be more. Go up in rankin' an' all! An' speakin' of food…we– me an' me crew, that is - be all 'aving lunch soon, ye be welcome to join us, all of yers."

"I'd really like that," Piper confesses, "we didn't get to eat breakfast before this whole 'run aground' situation…Astrid? Thoughts?"

"Yes, we shall join the crew for lunch."

CHAPTER FORTY-FOUR

The overwhelmingly salty tang of brine. Tobacco. Whitewood.

Holt crinkles his nose at the smells drifting around this new vessel. They are most unpleasant, he decides, and as he follows Caspian, Piper, and Astrid up the narrow and almost vertical ladder he can't help but cover his lower face with his hand. He much prefers the scents he had on his yacht...predominantly vanilla, rose, and raspberry. And none of them were so disgustingly *potent*. A groan breaks free from him. "Has anybody on this vessel heard of air freshener before?!"

Lenka and Cadmus make no comment from behind him. He assumes that they're on their best behaviour in order to avoid any possible conflict with Caspian or his fellow smugglers. It makes sense, of course, but doesn't make him any less annoyed at them for neglecting to stand behind his every word. "Absolutely preposterous," he adds casually, "can barely breathe."

Astrid turns her head, looking over her shoulder at him as he ascends. "Hm...I find the scent rather appealing, actually. But then again, I have become accustomed to such things. I assume you find that Illyria is not the most wonderful smelling location on this planet?"

"Pft. You assumed correctly." Holt moves upwards with confidence, but a sudden loud mew at his feet shatters his poise – caught off guard, he lets out an ungodly screech and almost jumps out of his skin. A chuckle comes from behind him, of which he definitely knows belongs to Cadmus, and then Lenka scolds in a voice barely higher than a whisper: "Don't laugh at him!"

Yes, don't you dare laugh at me! I am your prince, for goodness sake, he thinks, pursing his lips together. *How rude. Does this boat have magical properties that cause everybody to lose their manners or something?*

Upon hearing his cry, everybody in front pauses and looks around at him in concern. He clears his throat, turns his head to the side, and mumbles something about 'being spooked' before urging them to continue on. How embarrassing. He tilts his head downwards to look at Caspian's cat and sighs in irritation, gently nudging her to the side with his ankle. This doesn't discourage her in the slightest; she starts weaving between his legs, causing him to stumble forwards. "Shoo, feline," he hisses, trying to be quiet, "Vivi? Or Via. Vivo. Vivo, yes. That's your name, is it not? Shoo, Vivo."

No change. The calico continues matching pace with him. He makes a conscious effort to bend down and push her gently away with his hands but this only worsens the situation - she rubs her body against his palms, longing for affection, and he sighs quietly and gives in. Crouching, he strokes her and attempts to continue upwards as he does so. Her fur is much thinner than he expected.

"Ahem. Smuggler -"

"Cap'n," Caspian corrects.

"Fine. Captain *Tyrian*. Your cat looks too thin, you ought to take better care of it, you know."

"Do yer 'ave a cat, matey?"

"No, I do not."

"An' 'ave yer ever 'ad a cat?"

"Well not really, no."

"Is me cat yer cat too?"

"Why would I have even slight ownership of *your* cat? What a ridiculous question, of course not."

"Then yer don't know nothin' and ye be in no place to tell me how to take care of it. Me lass be fine, yer hear? She be very 'appy an' 'ealthy."

Holt scoffs, crossing his arms.

Humiliated, he stands up straight and continues walking, heat having rushed to his face. "Why, I was only trying to help. And voicing my opinion on things."

Honestly, he's never looked after a pet before. Any animals in – or around – his family's home in Caldisa were taken care of by servants. The horses in their stables, the koi in their ponds, the fancy birds of different colours in the gardens…he never paid any of them much attention. He was never given such responsibility.

Caspian stops suddenly, as do Piper and Astrid. Holt almost walks into them upon reaching the top of the ladder; he wasn't paying attention and was more focused on Vivo.

"Right then. 'ere we arrr."

"The dining room?" Piper questions, and she is answered as a large door is opened and the smell of heavily spiced food floods the air. Holt welcomes it, as it disguises the earlier scents, and waltzes past the group into the room without a second thought. But, the moment he does, he is greeted by numerous faces staring around at him, judging him. He coughs awkwardly and steps back.

"The newcomers be joinin' us!" thunders a voice.

"Mighty *pretty* newcomers," another exclaims.

Caspian jumps onto the nearest barrel, waving his hands. "Avest ye, all of yers. These be our new shipmates – Piper, Cadmus, Lenka, and Princey 'ere. They be part of our fam'ly now, yer hear? And yer to treat 'em accordingly. Oh…and yer know Astrid. If yer don't, and yer new, then she be me lifelong friend."

Holt bites back the urge to correct Caspian, to announce that his name is not 'Princey' but Prince Holt Davori of Caldisa. He's not sure that doing so would be wise, however, for there are an awful lot of people in this room, and none of them look at all weak. Provoking any of them would be…problematic.

"Cap'n be lettin' Astrid *in* the ship? Not just on the deck? What a turn'o events!" announces one of the smugglers rather indistinguishably, as he has a particularly full mouth, "haven't seen 'er in a long time! Ye be the most beautiful lass on the planet still, Astrid!"

"Thank you," Astrid replies calmly.

"Ain't aged a day, have yer?"

"Barely."

"Hahah! Funny as ever!"

Most of the crew explode into salty, energized expressions of amusement as if Astrid has just told the funniest joke in the world. A small number of them, however, do not seem so eager to see her below deck. One in particular, a broad-shouldered man with sharp, blue-grey eyes and short, coarse hair, shakes his head and lets out an irritated laugh. He stabs his fork into a hearty chunk of salt beef, and with it, gestures towards the mermaid. "Ye be lettin' our deaths in by bringin' that siren on board, lettin' 'er stalk aroun' the lower decks."

"Oh, she – she's not stalking, I promise, she's wonderful!" Piper assures him, curling her arm around Astrid's.

He raises his eyebrows, observing. "Ye be a fool, lass."

Caspian shoots the man a warning look, and there's no further talk on the matter. At least, not to his knowledge. He jumps off the barrel, sits down on it cross-legged, and slaps his thighs as he turns to face his new shipmates. "Now yers just take a seat anywhere and eat whatevers yers want. An' I hope yer enjoy the food."

Holt opts for the empty chair at the very end of the table. It clearly belongs to the captain, but at the moment he seems more than happy to sit on that barrel. *Well, I am the most important person here anyway*, he thinks, *it only makes sense that I would have the best seat.*

Astrid watches him ever-so-gracefully slip into the chair, and elects to merely observe the humans eating rather than actually join them. None of the food looks particularly appealing to her – cooked meat is strange at best, and heavily spiced food seems ludicrous. Why not just eat the food raw? Pressing her tongue between her teeth, she sits down on one of the large dining benches and says, ever so confidently, "Excuse me. There is very little room."

The entire line of smugglers on it shuffle up as far as they can so she has more space. Piper follows suit, sitting too, and Astrid places a hand on her thigh under the table.

"Astrid!" she witters bashfully, "your – your hands are cold!"

"I know. Mermaids are always cold. And you are warm. Is there a reason for you making that statement? Would you like me to remove my hand from your thig -"

"No! no, it's fine. I – I don't mind."

"Alright."

As they speak, a man donning a white chef's hat – perfectly complimenting his heart-shaped face, Piper thinks - begins to pile aromatic parcels of food onto plates before them. "Errr…" she drawls, "what's this, sorry? And this?" She gestures to the meal, and taking a fork in her hand, impales a mound of fragrant, brown rice.

The man clears his throat. "It be spiced rice, lass. With thyme, turmeric, an' a hot pepper sauce. And tha'…tha' be spring onion an' coconut soup with scotch bonnet chilli."

"I…er…I see. Thank you."

Tentatively, for she fears the food might be too spicy for her, she takes a small amount of rice into her mouth. Sure enough, it is very hot – but thankfully, not unpleasantly so. The chef watches her, and once she makes an affirmative "mmm!" sound, steps away and continues serving the crew. At one point, he drops into a crouching position and places a full dish - meat, rice, and all – onto the ground for Caspian's cat. The small creature lets out a small, raspy meow before accepting the meal.

"How cute is Caspian's cat?" Piper asks Astrid, eating another forkful of rice, this time more enthusiastically. "Look at her go, eating away! She really likes this food, huh? Well, I can relate. You gotta try this - it's so good!"

The mermaid shrugs. "I shall take your word for it."

"Are you not hungry?"

"Hm...a little hungry, perhaps."

"Okay...?"

Dipping a spoon into her soup, Piper makes a conscious effort to collect several slivers of onion and pick them up. Once she has done so successfully, she holds the cutlery up to Astrid's face and nods encouragingly as if to say: 'try it.'

Astrid does. She opens her mouth, displaying her teeth, and takes the spoon between her lips. The warm, pungent liquid causes her to grimace instantly in revulsion. "Disgusting," she confesses, grasping for the closest pitcher of water. She pours the entirety of it down her throat, much to Piper's amusement, and shakes her head. "Blegh."

"Don't you like it?" Piper giggles, wiping some soup from the corner of her connector's mouth. "I guess you're just used to cold food, huh? Like raw fish and stuff. That's probably too rich and hot for your tastes."

"Mmhm. That's right."

The hour that follows is full of enthusiastic chatter and stories – the majority of which come from Caspian. They are silly, yet entertaining somewhat, and the new crew members listen for a while. Eventually, it becomes boring to Astrid in particular.

It's about the fifth variation of 'how my crew and I survived a megalodon shark attack' when she decides to speak up, rising to her feet and clearing her throat to attract everybody's attention.

"I am tired. Captain, I would be thankful if you could show my friends and I to our sleeping quarters."

Caspian pauses, nodding. "Aye, lass," he responds pleasantly, rising to his feet and heading for the door. "I hope yer don't mind sleepin' in the storage cabins. There be two available with enough room fer sleepin'…yer can sort yerselves out and organise sleepin' arrangements, I hope. Harhar!"

"I'll go with Cadmus!" Lenka exclaims, perhaps a little too enthusiastically. Cadmus doesn't object, though, much to her relief. "And His Royal Highness," he adds calmly, "I am his guard, after all -"

Holt sighs dramatically. He would have much preferred his own private quarters. This boat is huge, surely there's enough room! *Well, it's not forever,* he reminds himself. *As soon as we make port somewhere, I am getting off of this dreadful ship and starting a new life in some bizarre foreign destination.* He stands up and brushes down his jacket. "Fine…If I *must*."

"This way, then," Caspian calls, leaving his crew to their meal. Vivo rushes after him, padding along the floor with her tail high in the air. "An' I'll get yer some hammocks. Oh, an' ye be right on time to join me crew, yer know – we 'ave a special 'oliday comin' up.

The crew cheer from behind him at these words; such enthusiastic exclamations become muffled when the door is closed. Caspian chuckles. "They love it, we all do. An' yers will too! It be mighty fun. Yer know what? Come an' see me tomorrow when yers wake up, lasses. I'll get yer prepared for such an event."

"Just the 'lasses'? What about me?!" Holt cries.

The smuggler smirks. "What *about* yer, matey?"

CHAPTER FORTY-FIVE

*I*t's midnight.

Holt stands on the deck of Caspian's ship, blinking sluggishly as he watches the dark waves turn and fold over one another. Wreaths of grey, gloomy mist dance over them like spirits of the drowned, and an eerie loneliness has come upon the prince as he gazes out at the water.

His head aches with exhaustion and stress. It feels as though hot bands of iron are tightening themselves around it, and when he at last manages to open his eyes, they burn with a desire to rest. He did try to sleep – he tried *very* hard, in fact – but he tossed and turned in his hammock, and sleep would not come.

Maybe it's because his yacht is gone. Maybe it's because he has no idea where he is right now. Maybe it's because he secretly misses his family a lot more than he thought he would. Maybe it's because he knows he has to return home *eventually* and can't delay his marriage to Isadora forever. Maybe it's because he is on a *smuggler ship*. No matter what the reason, he can't seem to relax at all. "Oh lord," he says out loud, overcome by tiredness and anguish.

Nobody hears.

There are a few members of the crew nearby, but they are clustered in broken groups, and are brawling and laughing from alcoholic influence. They're throwing various profanities around and the boy wrinkles his nose in disfavour as he overhears a small snippet of the current conversation: "Blimey, an' what a beauty the lass was. Would 'ave taken 'er there an' then, if yer know what I mean."

Disgusting, he thinks, rubbing his temples. In a way, he's jealous of them, though; they're out here carousing on the deck because they want to be. They're not like him, struggling to sleep with a throbbing headache. Even so, he hopes they're quiet soon, since the noise they're making is terribly annoying and only contributes to his pain.

He plucks at a loose string on the sleeve of his silk shirt and frowns. At least he has his pyjamas - earlier in the evening, after much complaining, Caspian relented and gave him back most of his things taken from the yacht. These pyjamas were one of those things, and he was extremely thankful to retrieve them. He still is. But, even with his items returned to him, it doesn't feel like home in his new 'bedroom'. Then again, the royal yacht never really felt like home either. Home is Caldisa, in the palace, with his mother and father. Home is *not* bobbing about on the ocean with a group of sea robbers, that's for sure.

"I thought you would be asleep by now."

At the sound of Astrid's voice, Holt swallows against the discomfort rising within him. He turns quickly to face her, his eyes wide with surprise. She's sitting on the edge of the ship, her legs crossed. She's holding his rapier in its sheath, something Caspian had yet to return to him…

"I thought I would be too, but I was finding it much too hard to slip into a peaceful slumber. Not on a smuggler ship. At least you can just swim off whenever you want! And is that my rapier?! Apologise and give it back this instant."

The mermaid shrugs. "Sorry. And…fine. You can have it back."

Her tone is somewhat dismissive, but it's still an apology and Holt is far too tired to ask for anything more from a *mermaid*. "It is quite alright," he announces curtly, "I forgive you. And alright, I'm waiting." He holds out his hands expectantly, impatiently tapping his foot.

"Good."

Astrid slips from her perch. She starts moving towards him with graceful, long strides, a certain hunger flashing in her expression. Holt represses a shiver and curls his lip in disdain. He's familiar with this look – it's the same look she gave him when they met for the first time in front of Piper's house. The same look she gave him when she was almost definitely going to *kill* him. He shies back with a nervous: "Is something the matter?"

"Not at all, Prince Holt. Not at all. I want something from you, though…are you listening?"

A knot of suspicious doubt clenches deep in his stomach. "No, no I most certainly am not," he responds, putting his hands on either side of his head to cover his ears, "I know what this is, Astrid. I read about the Illyrian mermaids' siren songs and tempting words in the newspaper. That smart Valentina Victory made a big deal about it! And I am *not* falling for it. If you want something, you shall go get it yourself and refrain from tempting me."

A gentle hand on his cheek guides his gaze back to her stunning, shimmering face. Slowly, he lowers his hands back to his sides.

"Valentina Victory knows very little about us, you know. I wouldn't trust her 'knowledge' if my life depended on it. Neither should you...now, will you give me what I want?"

"Okay..." he mumbles dazedly, "...what do you want?"

"I want some fresh blood. It would be very kind of you to donate some to me, so I don't starve out here on the open ocean. You want to help me, don't you? Let me have some of your blood."

A strange throb of desire racks his entire body, colour dusting his cheeks. He can feel her dark, shadowed eyes boring into his very soul, searching for something, *anything*, to latch onto. Something vulnerable. And as she stares at him, waiting, watching, he believes she may have actually found it. Before he has time to think about what it may be, he's already speaking. Unplanned and unrehearsed words tumble from him like water - "Well, I don't see why that would be a problem...anything to help you. Of course. I am more than happy."

"Alright then," Astrid drawls, her tone low and soothing as she hands his rapier back to him. "Go on, just a small cut, just a small amount of blood for dear, dear Astrid -"

Those predatory eyes trail towards his fingers as they come to rest of the hilt of the weapon. Gradually, ever so gradually, he pulls it from its sheath and holds the blade to his arm. He is about to make the cut when Astrid whispers, "Wait."

She looks away from him and towards one of the

groups of crew on the upper deck. There are three men in it, one being the grouchy man from earlier in the dining area. The other two seem to be new crew members; she's never seen them before on this ship. They've gone from laughing drunkenly together to speaking in hushed tones. Tones that her highly trained ears pick up as particularly...*suspicious*. And then – even more shadily – they look around, gesture to a doorway, and head in its direction with the clear intention of having a more private conversation. A conversation that they clearly don't want to be overheard. A conversation that Astrid decides she will definitely overhear them having.

The prince stares forwards at her, frozen in place. "What? What is it?"

"Hmm...move aside," she bristles in response, brushing past the now confused looking young man and moving away from him. The suspicious trio have already passed through the door – she has to hurry to catch up with them. "Have a good evening, Prince Holt. I now have better and more important things to be doing than talking to you here."

Pressing his lips into a thin line, Holt shakes his head and follows. "Wha- what is going on? Astrid? Why, it is terribly rude to just leave a conversation like that. At least, I believe we were in the middle of a conversation. My mind is rather hazy, but I am very tired, so that makes perfect sense. Astrid. Astrid. Astrid?"

"Be quiet."

Together, they move towards the upper decks in silence, kneeling beside two crates before hurrying up a ladder and standing behind the door. Astrid presses the side of her head against it.

"An' don't yers agree our lurverly cap'n be puttin' us all in danger, lettin' such characters onboard? Eh? A siren, fer starters?! Wantin' us all in Davy Jones' locker, yer hear me! An' this ain't the first time he be puttin' us in 'arms way. He ain't fit to be a cap'n and yers know it."

A mumbled chorusing of "aye" from the two men.

"Yers know if I be cap'n it'd be much better. Fer all of us. An' no more sharin' sleepin' area with all the others – no, no. Yer, yer, and me, we'll be livin' it fine. I be havin' cap'n's cabin. An' yers can have storerooms, like our esteemed 'guests' all of yer own. Make it up all fancy an' nice fer yers."

More mumbled chorusing of "aye," but then: "I dun wan' a storeroom! I wan' cap'n's cabin too!"

"Fine. We'll sort somethin' out. So are yers in? Mutiny! An' first step, takin' them newcomers fer ourselves. I wan' the brunette. I love me them brunettes. Yer can have the sorta-ginger. Yer can have -"

One of the men interrupts, although Astrid doesn't know who they are. "The blond!" they exclaim.

"There ain't no blond! And the ginger lass you ain't 'avin' cus she's mine!"

"No, the boy. The blond boy!"

"…Oh. Alrigh' fine. I 'ave the ginger, though."

"Yar."

"Yar."

There's a moment's silence. "Now the two problems are the siren an' the big guy protectin' the royal boy. How we gon' get 'em out of the picture?"

"Kill em. We all got cutlasses, eh? An' sirens ain't strong outta water. She be goin' down fast if we all gang up on 'er an' she ain't seen it comin', yer hear.

Yers in, then?"

One final chorus of "yar," and that's that.

The sound of movement causes Astrid and Holt to stand rigid and rush to the side, hiding. The men emerge from the doorway, led by their self-proclaimed captain-to-be, and head towards the lower decks. This would be fine under normal circumstances, but the general crew's sleeping quarters are not located in that direction. The storerooms, on the other hand, are.

Astrid scowls. Before Holt can make a comment on the situation (which he does *want* to do, but instead finds himself speechless with shock), she's gone, bounding silently after the group. She moves with an elegant, smooth and rapid speed. He doubts it's anywhere near the swiftness she can achieve in water.

"Come on," she calls back to him, breaking him out of his stunned, somewhat disturbed reverie, "get your rapier ready – we need to end this mutiny plan. And fast."

Their pace is cautious, yet hasty. The caution is abandoned entirely, however, when a shrill little cry - undoubtedly from Piper – fills the air. The door to the storeroom cabin she shares with Astrid *has* been opened, but the trio of smugglers have barely made their way inside. The leader, of course, is it front. Cadmus has just emerged from his own sleeping quarters, dressed in his nightclothes, and is clearly about to start a physical fight -

Viewing this scene is all it takes.

Something inside Astrid snaps so quickly, nobody has time to react. She rushes forwards, stabbing her long, sharp nails into each man's neck in quick succession. While the two accomplices fall to their knees, gurgling screams, the leader gets more personal attention – one moment she is simply grasping onto him, her teeth grazing his neck, and the next his skin is ashen, his eyes are blood-shot, and his skin is being shredded like thin strips of tissue paper.

With hands raised, palms outwards, Cadmus curses and shakes his head. Off all the things he's been trained to deal with, this is definitely not one of them. He shoots Holt a look, one that practically screams 'what the hell do I do?' and Holt mumbles something about fetching the captain. He doesn't even hear his own voice. All he can hear is *death*.

Horrified, Piper tumbles out of her hammock and hits the ground, shuffling quickly backwards into the corner. There's blood. More than a little blood. Her breathing quickens with every pitiful wail emitted from the men. And there, in her corner, she looks like a little trapped animal, her eyes darting back and forth and lips quivering.

Holt notices.

Almost every part of him wants to run, jump off this cursed ship, and swim away from this creature, this *monster* from the very depths of the sea. But - he can't leave Piper like this. Terrified. Vulnerable. Panicked. He forces himself to move past Astrid and her victims, kneel beside Piper, and pull her close. She latches onto his sleeve and pulls urgently, a small squeak forming from the back of her throat.

"It's alright," he whispers shakily, "I have you. It will be over soon. You're safe."

Of course, he doesn't really know whether these murders – for they are most definitely murders – will be over soon or not. He doesn't dare linger to find out, and instead leads Piper out of the room and away from the harrowing sight.

By now, the noise has attracted a significant amount of attention from the crew. Several groups of men have made their way over to the scene, and upon Holt's request to Cadmus, the captain has too. After a quick explanation, including what was overheard of the mutiny plan, he enters the blood-soaked storeroom and proceeds to talk to a ravenous Astrid.

He's thanking her.

Holt doesn't stay to hear the conversation. He leads Piper, shaking like a leaf, to the other storeroom to bunk with him, Lenka, and Cadmus. Luckily, there's just about enough room for one more hammock.

"I – I n-never," she stammers, trembling as he assists her in laying down, "never t-thought this…would happen I-I almost for-forgot she can do this sort of thing."

"Try and get some sleep." Holt's voice is very quiet. He leans forward, touching her cheek softly, and his fingertips tremble against her skin. He too is afraid of what he's seen, fear throbbing through him with the relentless beating of a drum. "And from now on, remember to lock your door at night."

"I just – Astrid was out – I thought she'd be coming back soon s-so I left it open for her -"

He sighs. "Okay. But in the future…if we must stay on this Godforsaken ship for much longer, please be more careful. And be wary of the other crew members…and…be wary of Astrid."

She turns on her side and brings her knees up to her stomach in the foetal position. "She would never - no, no – she would never hurt me…never."

CHAPTER FORTY-SIX

*E*lvira looks down at her cup of coffee. It's the third one she's had this morning, and somehow, of all of them, it's the most bitter. It's strange but she doesn't mind that reduction of quality, really. Blaming Falké for his poor coffee-making skills would be pointless, as he's never had to create such a brew before. It was always Piper's job…

She doesn't rebuke him for the 'cardboard' toast either, or the plain cornflakes. At least he's making an effort to provide her with breakfast. He could be out with that friend of his – Carmen Chavez, was it? – or at the bar drinking, but no. He's here with her, keeping her company.

"Okay?" he asks from the opposite end of the table, and she glances up and nods in confirmation. Disgruntled and depressed, she mumbles some haphazard comment about the meal she has been given. "Thanks. Lovely. You're a good boy. Thank you."

"Welcome."

This is how it's been for the past few days. A certain awkwardness between them, an emotional wall keeping them separated. Of course, it's nothing new, just worse than before; whatever closeness there was between them in the past no longer blossoms.

For a long time, they remain almost motionless, staring blankly forwards at each other. There are no attempts made at conversation, and under normal circumstances both would find this extremely uncomfortable. But, now they seem to enjoy the peace and quiet. At least, until Elvira mutters, bitterly: "We're running out of money. I need my job back. I'm fine. I'm *more* than fine. It's not my fault she left me – left us – here to rot awa -"

Falké sighs, interrupting. "Mother."

He breathes in deeply, his voice sad and weary. She stops speaking and gulps down some coffee with a grunt, prodding at a stain on the table with her fingers as if it's only just appeared; it's been there for years.

Elisa and Zachary used to invite her over for coffee on Saturday mornings. Elisa was very good at making it – she worked as a server at one of Illyria's diner-style restaurants, and was well versed in all things 'breakfast'. At one point, there was an abundance of potatoes imported into Illyria, and the price was low enough for citizens to buy them in bulk. Elisa was very fond of making things with them at work, hash browns being her favourite. She was so terribly sad when the price was increased and supplies ran short…

Elvira spent lots of money on potatoes after that.

If she concentrates hard enough, she can almost perfectly visualise one those mornings spent with her dear sister. A generous spattering of raindrops against the kitchen window. The smell of coffee and hash browns. Elisa, her wispy, light hair sprinkling her arms, laughing at something her husband said. Something that's not funny, but she's laughing anyway. And as they all sit down at the table, Zachary says he's going to "Find something amazing today."

Ha. Find what, she thinks. *Another woman to spend your time with?*

Why Elisa let this man into her life she cannot fathom. Not only that, but they had a *child* together, a product of their 'love', somebody that should have never existed. Perhaps if Elisa didn't have Piper to look after, she wouldn't have felt the need to stay with her selfish partner. Perhaps she wouldn't have died. Perhaps Elvira wouldn't have inherited this miserable little house and moved in only to mourn for the rest of her life.

"Y'alright?" Falké asks. Concern twitches at the corners of his eyes, and quickly settles into his entire expression. When she doesn't respond instantly, he repeats himself, a little louder: "Y'alright?"

Suddenly, she sees Piper sitting there instead of him. And it returns – the pulsing urge to inflict pain. To exert revenge. To allow the fire of frustration to take over her. She snarls and throws her fists down onto the table, causing everything on it to shake. There is little coffee left in her mug but the small amount inside spills at the action.

"Awh man…" Falké mumbles, assuming this bout of rage will pass quickly, as it usually does. Elvira often has several such episodes most days, typically triggered by various memories or actions. But however short the episodes are, things always seem to get broken or damaged; he isn't looking forward to having to clean everything up this time around. He reaches for the paper towels with the intention of soaking up the spilled coffee.

Elvira watches, and doesn't think, only acts. Panting as anger floods her veins, she stands and approaches him with a loud and resentful: "You selfish, selfish, *selfish* little fool!"

Falké tenses. "What?!"

She grabs his wrist roughly, sneering, and his hand splays in surprise. "What'd I do?!" he shouts, attempting to pull away unsuccessfully, "mothe-"

She interrupts him before he can continue. Visceral disgust rises in her chest as she tightens her grip - "You think I don't know you are still hanging 'round that bleedin' vermin?! That slutty little beast that tears families apart!"

"Astrid? Piper's mermaid?"

"Do you know what I had to go through after you left on that fancy boat? Do you?!"

"What, I – I'm not Piper! I -"

"I was humiliated! Mocked! By everybody!"

And then, without warning, she hits him on the side of the head with the now-empty mug. He slumps forwards, stunned, and she grabs his head and slams it down on the kitchen table with every ounce of force she can summon. Once. Twice. Shouting. Three times. Light-headed mumbling. Four, and her eyes widen in realisation.

"N-not Piper," she stammers quickly, staggering back, and the tips of her fingers go cold as Falké slumps to the ground. She tucks her nails inwards, digging them into her palms, and wails a hopeless, stunned apology.

Everything is still, Falké included. He lies on the floor in a tangled heap, unmoving and frail there on the tiles. She can't see his face because of the position he's fallen into, yet knows that his head is bleeding profusely. Sticky redness garnishes the edge of the table, staining the wood like red ink.

A panicked lump forms in her throat. He should be moving again by now, a little hurt of course, but not…not like this. Not…gone. She wills him to move, to speak. "Nah ma," he would say and stand back up rubbing his head with a grimace, "not Piper. Just me."

It doesn't happen. Nothing happens.

"C'mon…c'mere," she whispers, falling to her knees beside him. The words come out garbled, chopped up between shaky, trembling breaths. Finally, she manages more: "Falké. Falké. My beautiful…my gorgeous baby boy. Such a good boy. Falké."

Her entire body quivers with an awful combination of horror and adrenaline as she reaches for him and pulls him close. After a moment's hesitation – out of fear for what she may see, really – she turns him over and chokes out a sob. Tear tracks carve thin rivers through blood on his cheeks. His nose is broken. Are his eye sockets fractured? She doesn't doubt it. She didn't mean to hurt him. Of course she didn't. She didn't mean for this to happen; why would she want this? She saw Piper, she didn't even mean to hurt *her*. She just lost control. Just for a second.

"He can't be dead. Can't be dead. Can't be dead." Her head is flooded with the same phrase over and over. No matter how many times it's repeated though, the situation stays the same. And in the dimly lit kitchen of Dreracile Decks, Mahina house,

Number 130, howls of misery echo and resonate.

CHAPTER FORTY-SEVEN

*E*arly in the morning, Piper is woken by the sound of shouting coming from above her. It hails from the upper deck, and it most definitely belongs to Caspian. She can't make out every word, but catches the occasional sentence: "All hands hoay...I be willin' to blow a man down meself if it 'appens 'gain!...if yer see yer fellow crewmates actin' strange, yer tell me!..."

She hasn't opened her eyes yet. Part of her doesn't want to at all, for she's not sure what she'll be faced with when she does. Will there be dead men around her still? Will there be Astrid, soaked in blood? What if there's nothing at all? Nothing but darkness and uncertainty? That's even worse. After a few minutes' hesitation, she forces herself to open them out of anxiety alone.

Ah.

She's in the *other* storeroom, the one belonging to Holt and his staff. There's a small lamp in the corner giving off a dull, yet warm, glow. She remembers now - being taken in here by Holt, lifted into her hammock; spoken to with soft words of comfort. When she turns her head, she sees him lying in the hammock closest to hers. His blond hair has fallen floppily over his face, and his lips are pursed. He sleeps with both hands cupped over his heart as if he's protecting it from harm.

She moves her gaze away from him. Cadmus and Lenka are in here too, but instead of resting separately, they're nestled together in one hammock. It looks rather silly, actually; Cadmus, burly and broad-shouldered, practically underneath thin and small Lenka. Her hair is out of its bun, tickling his face, and yet he doesn't stir. Somehow, they seem comfortable in such a position. She doesn't question it, for it's something she can see herself doing with Astrid. There would be more space with Astrid, though - she isn't a husky, muscular man.

Where *is* Astrid?

A certain...fear begins to bloom in her mind like a disease. Only when it overtakes her entirely does she realise it's not simply fear but memories - memories of last night. Last night she was looking into the eyes of a killer, not her lover. She was looking at black, soulless eyes. Lips dripping with sticky crimson; lips that she herself has kissed several times now. She lifts her fingers to her *own* lips and wipes them vigorously in disgust.

"Astrid," she murmurs aloud and feels unsettled by the sound of her own voice: a weak little croak, desperate and sorrowful as though she is little more than a spirit. She coughs once to clear her throat and sits up carefully. *She did it for me,* she tells herself, *she was protecting me and she was hungry. It was a no-brainer for her to kill them all.*

The whole situation is a bitter mouthful to swallow, but she forces herself to gulp it right down.

Honestly, she knows that she deserves to taste every last bit because she *chose* this. She chose Astrid, and she was more than aware from the beginning that that meant choosing a killer. Besides, it was defence...it was called for.

"Are you quite alright?"

She jumps at the sound of Holt's voice. It's sleepy and soft, for he has just awoken. When she looks back at him in his hammock she forces a smile and he returns it with soft, molten honey and cocoa eyes. A truly beautiful person, she decides, like a prince from a storybook. Not that Holt is part of a story, but he is most definitely a prince. A *handsome* prince. Still, no prince (and no handsome prince, for that matter) matches Astrid's strange, otherworldly beauty.

"Yeah. I'm just...I'm just thinking about last night and stuff," she whispers, trying to avoid waking Cadmus and Lenka, "thanks. For letting me sleep in here, I mean...well, and comforting me. You're a really nice person, Holt."

He props himself up with an elbow and laughs tiredly. "Why thank you. I try to be."

What time is it?" she asks, realising that the shouting from above has stopped, "Do you know?"

"I am afraid I do not."

"Right...yeah, it's fine."

A long period of silence ensues before Piper climbs down from her hammock. Doing so is troublesome; her left leg feels quite stiff and a little painful, and when she presses her hand against her knee where the primary source of discomfort is, she realises it's where she scraped it against the coral reef. It doesn't *look* bad, though - at least, no worse than any other wound she's gotten before. It's not worth complaining about.

I've had worse, she thinks.

She moves over to the door, and after a moment of attempting to open it, and failing, notices it's locked from the inside. The key is hanging on a small hook to the left. She takes it, opens the door, and squints as light floods the cabin.

Cadmus and Lenka shift in their hammock, clearly woken by this event. It makes Piper cringe. "Sorry, sorry…didn't mean to wake you guys," she mutters, edging out into the light and putting the key back onto its hook, "sorry."

Once she's left the warm safety of the storeroom, Piper stands in silence for a while, processing. She barely hears when Holt emerges from it too, walking up behind her. It's only when he clears his throat softly to get her attention that she snaps back to reality and says quite plainly, "Last night Astrid killed those guys."

The bluntness of this statement surprises him. He buckles his brows and sighs quietly, glancing to the side. "I am…afraid she did. Are you holding up alright? I was worried about you…you looked so afraid."

"It just…took me by surprise, that's all…I'm okay now. I guess."

"Pardon?"

"I said I'm okay now. Those guys…they were up to no good, right? Astrid saved me. So…I'm okay. I just wish she didn't save me so *violently*."

He grinds his teeth against the helpless ire building within him. How can she be so blasé now? Just yesterday evening she was shaking in his arms, tears in her eyes.

"Why, she murdered three men before our eyes! Are you not...disturbed by that?!"

Piper opens her mouth to speak. But nothing comes out, and before she manages to form a sentence there are footsteps coming down the ladder. And there, approaching them, is Astrid. Her heart clenches at the sight; how can one being drive blood through her body until her face flushes with heat, and her lungs ache with fear? How is it possible that she feels so many emotions just by catching Astrid's piercing gaze?

Holt speaks up. "A-Astrid! You practically *traumatised* Piper last night, you know? I strongly advise spending some time apart to let her...process things."

Astrid's eyebrows climb up somewhere beneath the volume of moon hair that frames her sharp-featured face. "Good morning to you too."

"You were much too beastly with those attacks." Holt's attempt at a scolding is pathetic, really – his voice is wavering and Astrid looks far from regretful. If anything, she seems amused now, which was definitely not his intention. As much as he doesn't want to admit it, she scares him. It makes no sense that Piper – or anybody else on this ship, for that matter – feels safe with her around. She's an animal, plain and simple.

Astrid notices how frightened he looks. She is going to tease him for it, embarrass him, but then, after a moment's contemplation, decides against it. Instead, she focuses on Piper, putting a hand on her shoulder and smiling slightly. "Caspian spoke to his crew this morning," she begins, "you can rest assured that nobody on this ship will dare attempt such a feat as mutiny again. And there is no way they will lay a hand on you, whether it's part of one or not – he's threatened to make them walk the plank. Although it's not *that* punishment they fear. It's that I will be waiting for them in the water."

Piper takes a deep breath and forces a smile. "Good, I'm relieved."

"I'm glad to hear so. Also, I apologise for scaring you last night…and you, Holt." She looks over at the prince and tilts her head to the side. "But everything's okay now."

"That makes me feel no better." There is hesitation in Holt's voice and regret on his face as he speaks. Still, he shakes his head, trying to keep his voice firm - "You murdered a trio of people right in front of my eyes. Everything is *not* okay."

"A trio of people that were going to assault your friend, your handmaiden, and you."

Holt grunts quietly. He knows she's right.

"Exactly. So again, everything's okay now." She shrugs and takes Piper's hand, circling the palm with her thumb. "Where are Lenka and Cadmus? Still sleeping? They should get up now – it's the 'Day of Sullivan's Serpent' and we're invited to the crew's celebrations on deck. Caspian wants to lend you and me dresses…and Lenka is wanted in the galley to help prepare the great feast."

"The day of *what*, exactly?" Holt asks, raising his eyebrows. "I've never heard of such an event. Suliman's Serpent?"

"Sullivan," Astrid corrects. "Caspian will explain it to us all, I assume. But for now, let's just assume it's a special day on the smugglers' calendar, hm?"

The pair nod. As Astrid and Piper head up the

ladder, Holt once again opens the storeroom door and apologetically informs Lenka and Cadmus that they ought to wake up now and join everybody on deck for some kind of a celebration. This instruction is met with soft, tired groans of dissatisfaction.

 He can relate.

CHAPTER FORTY-EIGHT

The Day of Sullivan's Serpent is already in full swing when Astrid, Piper, and Lenka finish ascending the ladder to the upper deck. The music and smells that quickly surround them serve as confirmation; the sound of accordions and flutes fills the air and the tantalizing promise of food, a rich and tempting array of scents, drifts from the galley. There's clearly going to be a great feast. Piper in particular is excited for such a meal, since she thoroughly enjoyed her last one and can't wait to try even more interesting dishes. That, and it's a welcome distraction from last night's terrifying series of events. There is, however, one other thing plaguing her mind that has nothing to do with Astrid's murders *or* the celebration today.

"Astrid?"

"Yes?"

"Do you think my family miss me?"

"Hm?"

"Do you think they miss me, or just…don't really care that I'm gone?"

Astrid stops for a moment. "Well," she muses, "I suppose they do. After all, you were the one doing everything for them. The cooking, cleaning, and shopping. What did Falké ever do for the household? Elvira has her career but she never actually *does* anything. Therefore, it's somewhat logical to assume that they'll miss you simply because your absence means they have to do things for themselves. Why do you ask, anyway? Do you, perhaps, miss *them*?"

Piper frowns. She pauses on the ladder, shifting her weight onto the balls of her feet and then back again to her heels a few times. "Not entirely - I'm just sort of worried about my cousin. Just...y'know, one of these days he's gonna find himself really drunk and stumble into the water or something. Nobody will even notice he's gone. His friends don't seem like they're really his friends. Do you know what I mean?"

"Yes. I know what you mean. But he chose that path himself, by becoming obsessed with alcohol."

Piper wrings her hands and starts walking again with Astrid behind. "I hope he's alright alone with my aunt," she mumbles nervously. "She can be so violent...Ah! Sorry, Lenka. I just realised we weren't including you in the conversation. Er...do you have family that you miss? Back in Caldisa?"

The girl waves her hand dismissively. "Oh, it's quite alright, I was much too tired to focus on the conversation anyway! To answer your question though, I have my parents back in Caldisa, and my older brother. I think about them sometimes, but not too much. We aren't really close. After all, I've always worked in the palace for the Davoris, and my family work in the city as bakers. They like it that way."

"Ah...that sounds nice. Bakers! Is that why you

like cooking so much?"

"Well, yes, I suppose. I grew up with baking and cooking. It's in my blood"

"What's your favourite thing to cook?"

"Oh…what a difficult question! Hmm, maybe, fresh pasta with basil pesto?"

The group all stop before the galley door. It wasn't too difficult to find, they simply followed the delicious aromas. Astrid gestures to it, nodding, and Lenka smiles before entering.

"Should we go in there too, just to make sure she's okay?" Piper asks.

"No. Again, the crew wouldn't dare try anything now. Not after last night. Let's get to Captain Caspian and see what he has in store for us."

On the main deck, the crew are spread out, bottles in their hands and smiles on their faces while they drunkenly sing of the great Sullivan and his daring adventures. Piper doesn't really understand much of it, and their dialect is quite hard to grasp in song form, but she giggles at the sights and sounds anyway. Unfortunately, a certain *ache*, slowly building in strength, has begun to throb in her head. It's only intensified by the noise; she finds herself covering her ears soon enough in attempt to quell the pain.

"What's wrong?" Astrid questions without directly looking at her partner, opting instead to stare ahead as she walks.

"I have a headache. I guess I slept sort of badly."

"Hm. Drink water."

"I will."

"Piper, Astrid! Mornin' lassies!"

When the two look up to follow Caspian's voice, they see that his cabin door is swung wide open. He stands leaning forwards with his hands resting on the upper door frame, donning a larger-than-average grin. "Come 'ere!" he calls to them, "I be ready to give yers some mighty fine things!"

Stepping into Caspian's cabin, Piper decides, can only be compared to stepping into some sort of fantasy world. It smells strongly of unfamiliar, exciting scents, there are all sorts of trinkets and other interesting items about, and beautiful, expensive-looking fabrics and clothes are strewn everywhere. But, they themselves seem to be the main focus; Caspian hums to himself as he selects two dresses from the mass of clothing closest to him, one gold and one silver. He holds them out and exclaims, "Try 'em on! Yers will look mighty fine, I be sure of that! An' there be petticoats on the bed fer yers, too. Actually, I think this one be a weddin' dress…forget that one. Yers can choose another -"

Astrid stares. "No. The wedding dress is fine, I shan't ignore it."

Attempting to ignore her headache, Piper takes one after little more than a moment's hesitation. She holds the dress to her body with a small "ooooh!" of approval, and then spins around slowly to admire the way it sways. Astrid, on the other hand, doesn't seem so impressed. She grasps the remaining outfit from Caspian's hands and stares down at it, scrutinizing it with a calm "Thank you. If I must, I will put this on my body for as long as I can tolerate its annoyance."

Caspian doesn't seem put out by this less-than-enthusiastic reaction. He didn't really expect a mermaid to like – or even appreciate – elaborate human clothing. It's not necessary for her kind. "Good enough fer me, lassie," he chuckles, "will yer need 'elp puttin' it on?"

"Yes, but I am sure Piper can assist me. You can go back to your crew. We will see you on deck once we have put these items of clothing on ourselves."

He nods and heads for the door. "Alright lass."

Once he's left, she studies her dress in more detail. The whiteish silver hue, the jewelled accents, the lacy white spirals overlaying the satin skirt. She can understand why a human would want to own such a thing – it's a lovely piece of work, after all - but why they would want to *wear* it? Incomprehensible.

She chooses the simplest looking petticoat from the downy collection on Caspian's bed and, after pulling it up to her waist, proceeds to slip into the dress. She fumbles with it for a moment before Piper steps in and helps her. "Yeah, these things are sorta tricky," she comments light-heartedly, lacing the garment up at the back. "I have a book on fashion that I got from the Illyrian library before it burnt down. It has stuff on dresses like this. The tops are basically a type of corset."

"Hm. I have never worn such a thing before. It's particularly constricting."

"Yeah, that's the point. It makes you really skinny and stuff."

"Bizarre concept."

Piper ties the white lace in a bow and steps back to admire her handiwork. "I think that's good! Turn around, I wanna see!"

The mermaid does so. Surprisingly, the outfit fits her beautifully. Despite the fact that she is much taller than the average human the hem is still low and a quantity of the material sweeps the floor as intended.

"You look like a princess," Piper whispers, picturing a tiara atop Astrid's starlight hair, shimmering with a hundred perfect diamonds. No – diamonds and pearls. Blue. Soft blue pearls.

Astrid raises her eyebrows. "I am not, though. I am a mermaid."

"Do the two have to be mutually exclusive?" Laughing, Piper pulls on her own petticoat and dress. It truly is a work of art; golden as wheat in the height of summer and adorned with frilled black lace. It's cinched and bustled in several places along the multi-layer skirt, and embellished with black ruffled tulle and organza roses at the top of the cinches.

She's never worn anything so beautiful in her entire life.

"You too look like a princess," Astrid remarks, and the girl smiles warmly, taking her hands. "I'm not though," she replies. "I'm just a normal girl. And they *are* mutually exclusive."

CHAPTER FORTY-NINE

'*olice have confirmed the murder of Falké Torneau was committed by his mother, esteemed Illyrian Health Centre therapist Elvira Tourneau. There were no murder weapons left at the scene of the crime, the kitchen of their house, but it has been established that -*'

Jasper folds the newspaper, uninterested in reading the rest of Valentina Victory's report. It's well written, as her stories always are, and he can see why it's on the front-page...but he's read enough. A mother murdering her own son in a fit of psychotic, anger-fuelled intensity. Nothing that interesting has happened in Illyria for a long time. At least, not to the public's knowledge. No wonder the entire city is buzzing. But it's just an irritation to Jasper. An unwelcome distraction.

What's especially frustrating is that there will be a lot of attention on the sanatorium where Elvira is now being held. Taking patients away to experiment on will be challenging. He's going to have to resort to reducing the jail's population instead.

"It's a shame, really," he notes, passing the newspaper to Scarlett, "Elvira was one of the Health

Centre's best doctors. I suppose this terrible little nation drives everybody to insanity eventually though, doesn't it? It's a miracle you and I haven't lost our minds entirely."

"Jasper…" Scarlett feels her heart struggle against the confines of her chest. She puts the paper down and rests her hand on his upper arm, her fingers tightening slightly. "I fear you might be! The shadows beneath your eyes deepen and darken every day. Have you been sleeping at all? I'm concerned."

The man snarls. "I'm busy with work. I don't need you to tell me I look tired, Scarlett, I know that already. How would you like it if I said you looked tired?"

"I-I was just worried about you -"

"Well stop it then," he cuts in with all the sublime calmness of an uncaring God, causing Scarlett's insides to clench with cold fear. He walks past her and towards the window, staring out at the ocean. The waves toss over each other in a swift, salt-laden waltz.

"But I -"

"Why must you argue with me?! Just behave for once! If I tell you to do something, you do it. Have I not made this clear enough in the past?"

"Jasper -"

He turns around then, facing her, and backhands her hard enough to snap her head around. Pain blooms hot across her face. Blinking dazedly and tasting blood in her mouth, she stumbles backwards and presses her fingers against her cheek. Still, she refuses to back down –

"No," she states, plain and simple.

"Excuse me?"

She looks up at him from beneath gently lifted eyebrows, and he can see that there is something either sorrowful or yearning in her dull, tired eyes. "No, Jasper."

"No," he repeats, blinking in shock. He breathes deeply, rage flaring up in his chest again as her eyes meet his. "No. You say…no."

His hand hovers over his pocket. Inside is an atomiser filled with venom - he's made it a habit to carry some with him at all times now, but the liquid may very well be expired and useless. It's been in there for almost twenty-four hours. Still, a *tiny* spritz isn't going to hurt. He learnt his lesson last time, and has dramatically reduced the dosage for Scarlett; he doesn't want his little pet getting sick again.

As she paws at her face to push away the tears, he makes one little spritz. It won't hurt to have one…and besides, it may not even work. Worth a try though, and he could do with some *loving* right now. "Care to explain your defiance?" he asks.

"I – I want to stay worrying about you, Jasper…because I love you."

He brings a finger to his chin in a good parody of deep thought. "I see, I see. Then…that's alright, isn't it? Oh, you know what we should do?" he asks, as if it's some amazing revelation, "we should go to the bedroom and you should show me how much you love me."

"Ah…" Scarlett swears she can feel a knot of heat clench deep within her belly. At first, she thinks it may be her sickness. What Jasper passed off as "womanly matters" – and yet the blood has still not come. After a moment she realises it is far from this, and instead she is filled to the very brim with deep lust and longing. Jasper's mood shifts are dramatic and cause her much emotional pain, but it's worth it for this sort of thing. For his attention and desire. "Of course," she whispers. "of course I'll show you. Just...let me get ready and then I'll call for you...okay?"

Jasper nods in response, but then, without warning, she's pushed against the wall. The impact is so hard that she sees stars and very nearly heaves on him, but she doesn't complain. He starts kissing her, and for a moment she believes that he'll take her right there and then -

Somebody clears their throat from the doorway. Jasper doesn't pull away, but does turn his head in their direction and sneers a, "What the hell do you want? Get out of here."

It's Tobias Wren.

"Two things to say, sir," he begins, "firstly, we've had a message from the kingdom of Caldisa – a letter asking us to inform Prince Holt Davori that they are most unhappy with his decision to leave and he ought to come home immediately. How should we respond? The boy is no longer here. Secondly, Dr Santi wants to speak with you again in regards to her latest operations."

Scarlett pauses turning the name Santi over in her head. She recognises it, but can't quite put a finger on who it belongs to. Santi. Santi. Santi. Eventually, it clicks – Margo Santi! that's the name of the doctor that helped her when she was sick a while ago. She hopes this news about her 'latest operations' is good.

Jasper pulls away, brushing down his waistcoat, and heads towards Tobias.

"I'll be back later," he informs her.

She's not entirely sure he will, but nods anyway as the burning fire inside her quells to nothing but barely smoking coals. When the inevitable tears come, she curses herself over how terribly overemotional she has become of late.

CHAPTER FIFTY

"Where in Heaven's name are my white trousers with the golden line down the side?!" Holt gripes, going through his pile of clothes for the umpteenth time. The trousers are not there, nor is the matching waistcoat, and after a moment's realisation he seethes, "Of course…Caspian" through gritted teeth and rises to his feet. "I cannot *believe* this. Did he not say we should be treated like family now? Do family steal each other's clothes, Cadmus? Of course not!"

Cadmus grunts, pulling on his own clothes by the light of the small lamp. Unlike Holt's, they're arranged neatly in the bag he brought on the ship with him and nothing is missing. Probably because the smugglers weren't as interested in his (humbler) outfits.

"I ought to go demand them back!"

Another grunt.

"You know what? I *shall* go demand them back *this instant*. Who cares if it's some fancy celebration day? I refuse to partake until I have all of my clothes."

Cadmus shrugs, lacing his boots. "I can do that

for you, if you so desire," he offers. After all, he *is* the prince's guard. It's his job to carry out confrontations on Holt's behalf. But Holt shakes his head in response to this, huffing, and puts his hands on his hips.

"No, no. You go - I don't know - have fun. Enjoy the 'Day of Sullivan's Serpent' or whatnot. Take it as…a vacation, of sorts. A small holiday. To serve as a distraction from that…mess last night. Because you know what Cadmus, I simply cannot let this rotten thief walk all over me! Captain or not, he is no better than me and ought to know his place, subordinate to a royal!"

Before Cadmus can make a comment, Holt leaves the storeroom in a strange mix of his pyjamas and a long blue jacket.

"I have to speak with that no-good smuggler!" he cries when he arrives on the upper deck, hands on hips. The music, laughter, and chatting of the crew on-board is extremely loud and animated so nobody takes any notice at all. It takes five obnoxiously loud *ahems* to get some attention, and even then he finds he must raise his voice considerably to be heard.

"Not all of my possessions have been returned to me! I was just sorting through my things, and – and I must speak with him this instant," he announces to nobody in particular.

"Harhar! Yer gonna 'ave to be a smidgen more specific, meartie! Which one of us are yer looking fer? There be an awful lotta us."

One of the smugglers has approached him, his wild russet hair sticking in all directions, stiff with salt. The stench of aged rum emanates from him so strongly that Holt finds the need to plug the bridge of his nose with his fingers for a moment. "I'm *looking* for your captain," he clarifies, grimacing, "where is he?"

"He be in 'is cabin fer now. But he be comin' out real soon if yer can wait fer a little while, 'yer 'ighness' aharhar."

"I most certainly cannot."

"Arrh. Well, the cap'n's cabin is that wayyyyy," drawls another smuggler who is sprawled on the deck and slurring his words as if they're liquid pouring from his mouth. There are two other men beside him, crouching and laughing over a joke that Holt didn't hear and wouldn't have understood even if he had. Something about a whale and a seagull. The man gestures to the side, pointing drunkenly at Caspian's cabin. "There ye goooo."

Holt looks down at this man with unveiled repugnance, taking note of the half-empty bottle in his hand. Disgusting, how much these smugglers drink. He clears his throat and nods, turning his head to look at the study in question with a curt, "Thank you for your assistance."

It takes five loud knocks at Caspian's study door to relieve the smuggler of his one-track-minded focus of annotating a large map. He opens the door, chewing on the end of his fountain pen, and the ridiculously strong odour of pine and smoke floods Holt's nostrils. "My goodness!" he exclaims, waving his arms around as he coughs uncontrollably, "are you people incapable of understanding pleasant scents?!"

Caspian shrugs, moving back towards his desk. "Do come in…yer highness"

He slacks into his chair with a sigh and picks up the cigar he's been smoking for the past few minutes.

Holt notes just how comfortable he looks – he's not wearing his overcoat or captain's hat at present, which is surprising, and he seems to be…drawing? No, writing notes. He looks quite handsome actually, in this lighting…

It is definitely just the lighting, he tells himself.

"Could ya've knocked any louda' by the way?" Caspian piques once he notices him staring. "Almost sent me to Davy Jones' locker, yer did."

"Oh, please," Holt says flatly, "I had to knock five times. *Five.* My cousin thrice-removed, Theodore, would have heard the first time – and he is deaf! I had to knock loudly because one, your crew are making an absolute racket 'celebrating' outside, and two, you seemingly didn't notice the first four times! Anyway, I want my clothes back. *All of them*, Caspian."

Caspian carefully places his cigar in an ashtray before throwing his head back in laughter and running a hand through his wild, raven-feather hair. "Oh, yer using me first name now? An' here I was thinkin' yer would use 'Cap'n Tyrian' yer entire life. But don't yer 'ave enough clothes already?" he asks, standing. "Ye be overreactin' I think, matey. Maybe yer should consider it as…payment. Fer rescuin' yer, and lettin' yer stay on me ship as part of me crew."

Holt throws his head back, letting out a high, thin whine. "But I *love* those clothes! That outfit set is my very *favourite*!"

"Ye be the most dramatic person on this planet. Fine, yer can 'ave yer clothes back." He gestures vaguely to a closet in the corner of the cabin. "But I be expectin' some others in exchange, yer hear?"

"Are you serious?! You already have so many!"

"But I want *yers*."

"Fine," Holt relents, splaying his arms in a grandiose manner before storming over to the closet and flinging it open. Sure enough, the white and gold clothes are in there, alongside an array of other clearly stolen outfits. He grabs them, folding them neatly in his hands, and then proceeds to walk back to the door. When he swings it open, he's met with even more rowdiness.

"What is going *on* out there?" Holt moans, "I swear, your crew are absolutely insane. You do know that half of them are drunk, correct?! How are you supposed to celebrate this 'special event' if everybody's bloodstream is ninety per cent alcohol and they barely understand an iota of what is going on around them?"

The smuggler moves past him, out onto the deck. He tosses a smirk over his shoulder. "Speakin' of the event, princey, why don't yer join me in tellin' the story of our brave and courageous serpent slayer, Sullivan Sands."

"A ridiculous name. Sullivan Sands…honestly! I think you all just wanted to use an alliteration…serpent, Sullivan, Sands…you cannot tell me for one moment that it's a coincidence."

Caspian shrugs. "Maybe, maybe naht. But yer see, it be fun tellin' the story, matey. An' sometimes that be better than cold, 'ard truths. Eh? Yer agree, don't yer? Now ye be plannin' to carry those clothes around all day wearin' this…interestin' look, or go sort out yer outfit in yer sleepin' quarters?"

"The latter."

"Well then…" He makes his way to the storeroom with Holt in tow, humming an unrecognisable tune that the prince finds increasingly annoying because of its repetitiveness. Still, he avoids calling attention to it, and instead clamps his lips shut and rolls his eyes. The deck is a little emptier now – *thank goodness* - for the crew have started filing towards the dining area en masse for the giant feast. But, the entire prospect of having such a feast at breakfast seems ridiculous to him. Honestly - who has the stomach for such a thing?

After a quick stop at the storeroom, where Holt carefully organises his clothes and changes into the gold and white trousers and waistcoat, they move to the dining area. Upon arrival, he's aware of several things: the beginnings of the great feast inside, Piper and Astrid – in beautiful dresses, no less – already eating, and a *lot* of men all in one place, just as last time. The crew have descended upon the feast as if they haven't had a bite of food in a millennium. They're loud and drunk, but clearly having a good time.

Holt pauses, his tongue darting out just enough to moisten his dry lips. He cares little for the meal (despite the fact he finds himself quite hungry upon smelling it) and focuses solely on Piper. He likes the oddity of her hairstyle, the freckles on her face, her bright emerald eyes. He likes her smile and her laugh. He likes the fact that they are friends most of all. He doesn't like Astrid.

Astrid.

His lip curls. *Astrid may be powerful,* he thinks, *but she isn't even human. What does she know of a proper romance? Not only that, but she is little more than a ruthless killer. What if she hurts Piper one day?*

It's actually surprising how easily last night has

been forgotten. Nobody seems to mourn the three crewmates Astrid murdered, instead seemingly celebrating their absence. He would have thought that the bonds between the men on this ship were stronger than that…surely, they had friends? Companions? Well, it is of no matter anymore – they're dead. And it's a good thing, really; if Astrid didn't stop them, it would have been a disaster. He shudders just thinking about it.

"So, what do yer think, matey? Yer like the gowns, eh?"

Caspian's question knocks him out of his thoughts quickly. He blinks twice, directing his attention to the gowns in question. Piper's dress is golden, like the sun. Astrid's is silver and is most definitely a *wedding dress*. But, neither belonged to the girls before coming on this vessel - he turns his head to Caspian and asks a question he most definitely already knows the answer to: "Did *you* give them those?"

"Aye."

"Do those dresses even belong to you?!"

"They belong to the lasses now."

"No! I mean – I mean you stole them, didn't you? Just like you tried to steal my clothes!"

The smuggler only grins. Holt scoffs, shaking his head in disappointment. "You are absolutely terrible." He moves towards Astrid and Piper, being careful to avoid several groups of rowdy sailors who have yet to sit down, and Caspian follows. "A very good morning to you, Piper," he says, and then clears his throat and adds, "Astrid."

Astrid doesn't seem to care about this curt greeting. "Good morning, Holt," she responds. She glances to the side at Piper, expecting her to reply, but instead sees she has changed her position on the bench to curl over her knees, pressing her fists against her stomach. Pushing on it hard. As if she can reach in there and grab whatever hurts, and then give it to Astrid to destroy. "Are you sick?" she states, but it sounds more like a statement than a question.

"No" Piper instantly denies.

"Tell me the truth."

"A little. But it's nothing terrible. I think I just didn't get enough sleep, so I have a headache and a bit of a stomach ache now but it's not a big deal Astrid, I promise– oh, and sorry, sorry! Hello Holt, Caspian. I didn't mean to ignore you. Isn't this feast wonderful?" she pauses for a moment. "Oh, and the dresses! Look at the dresses! Aren't they wonderful too?"

Despite his concern for Piper's wellbeing, there is a wide smile upon Holt's lips. "They very much are," he replies, nudging the girl playfully. "I assume you like them then, Piper?"

She concurs with a hum.

"Well then," Caspian cuts in, "may I 'ave this dance, m'lady?"

Holt shoots him a look. "Oh please. You cannot speak like a royal to save your life. And can you not see she's eating right now? I highly, highly doubt she wants to start dancing midmeal with the likes of y -"

Piper takes Caspian's hand, and Holt's voice falters. He watches her stand and whirl into an inelegant (yet very fun-looking) waltz with him with a small, pitiful groan. "You have to be joking," he mumbles to himself, looking around at a particularly expressionless Astrid. "Ahem. Astrid? Are you annoyed by this? Your girlfriend is d-"

"Connector," Astrid corrects, following Piper and Caspian with her eyes. There is something calculating and cold within her gaze, and Holt (wrongly) interprets it as jealously. "Connector then, whatever! Your connector is dancing with a smuggler?!"

"That is *hardly* the problem. She shouldn't be dancing – she feels ill."

"Well – well yes, sure! That too?!"

"No matter. If she wants to dance, she can dance."

"With him?!"

"Yes."

Loud music quickly fills the air, replacing the sound of chatter and drunken laughter. Other smugglers stand and join in this sudden dancing, linking arms merrily. Some of them continue to eat while spinning around, which makes Holt grimace at the mess of it all. "Can you believe them?" he asks Astrid over the noise. "At least you and I have enough self-respect to refrain from such unstructured dancing, Astrid. I must give you credit for that."

Astrid tilts her head to the side with an uninterested sounding "Mmhm," as they both observe Piper being swung from Caspian's arms and into another sailor's, and another, and another. "If you will excuse me, Holt," she says eventually, noticing Caspian is beckoning her over, "I believe 'Captain Cass' wants my attention."

"Wha-hold on! You cannot just leave me standing here!"

She does. Once she reaches Caspian's side, he places his hands on her shoulders and whisks her into the festivities with a grin and an eager, "Just wanted to 'ave yer in on the fun!"

"I haven't danced in many years," she claims in a monotone as they begin to spin around the deck. This makes Caspian laugh. "Well, lassie," he responds, "ye be mighty fine fer somebody who 'asn't! And yer know…me motha' used to tell me mermaids be the best singers and dancers in the world. An' she was always right, yer know?"

Astrid chuckles. "Oh she was, was she?"

"Yar. Now listen, lass, listen. To the story of Sullivan and 'is serpent!"

"Alright, captain. I'm listening."

And with that, Caspian lets go of her and jumps onto a barrel, waving his hands. At first, nobody notices him, much too caught up in their dancing, but then he starts practically shouting over the music - "Alrigh', Alrigh' mearties! Take yer seats, there be more time fer dancin' after yer food…an' after the *story*."

At the mention of the story, enthusiastic cheering ensues. Holt covers his ears, as do Piper and Lenka (who has just emerged from the galley with yet another plate of food). Cadmus however, doesn't seem to care and happily joins in with the raucous cheering.

"Avest ye! Now," Caspian starts, grinning, "'twas a long, long time ago…an' the seas were a dang'rous place fer everyone - smugglers, pirates, merchants, the lot. They be feedin' the fish a lot after travellin' 'cross the waters…and there were only rumours of why 'cus dead men tell no tales, mateys."

Silence. Everybody seems absorbed in the story.

"So…a smuggler, a cap'n like yers truly, thought to put an' end to such problems. An' 'is name was Sullivan Sands. He 'eard the rumours, he did. 'Eard there be a sea serpent in the depths, devourin' entire vessels that dare cross its stretch o' the water. And after a while of learnin' 'bout the beast, he figured somethin' out. It only attacked ships carryin' precious jewels - diamonds, in particular. Us smugglers, we carry such precious booty! It be importan' we continue to do so…so he thought he'd go slay the beast. An' so he took all sorts of things – jewels, mirrors, all that fancy cargo – an' travelled day an' night to fin' the serpent."

"I can barely understand him through all this…smuggler lingo," Holt whispers to Cadmus, who is now standing beside him, "can you?"

Cadmus merely grunts as usual, but it's an affirmative grunt. Holt groans softly to himself. He could have at least pretended not to in order to show some comradery.

"An' then, one day, it showed up – the serpent! 'Shiver me timbers!' the crew cried, but Sullivan, he wasn't scared. He tol' 'is crew to batten down the 'atches an' bring a spring upon 'er. An' they did, they turned that ship aroun' an' the serpent followed…but Sullivan, he was grinnin', he was. An' yer know why? 'Cus he knew 'is way aroun' the seas, he did…knew everythin' about currents, an' reefs, an' rocks – an' that foolish serpent was too focused on 'im and 'is crew that it paid no attention, mateys. Sullivan led 'em to a reef, a mighty perilous area, in the bright sun, almost blindin', it was."

Caspian pauses for a moment to take a larger-than-average swig of rum, and the crew urges him to continue.

"An' Sullivan took the largest mirror he brought with 'im, he did, and held it up to the sunligh'…it reflected onto the reef, yer see. Made it sparkle like any jewel would. An' that serpent, it be run a rig. Fooled. Swam right into the reef, thinkin' it be precious gems, glitterin' in the light. An' then, while it be surprised, 'is crew all launched spears at the beast… killing it where it writhed in confusion! Victory fer Sullivan, an' smugglers everywhere!"

Everybody erupts into cheering once again, clapping and stamping their feet. Caspian bows, enjoying the attention. "Glad the beast be gone now, princey?" he asks Holt, chuckling, "it'd be attracted to yer with yer fine, jewelled clothes."

Holt rolls his eyes, but can't help but smile and chuckle a little. It *was* an entertaining little tale.

Chapter Fifty-One

"He's gone alrigh', solid gone."

Frank Miligan – at least, that's the name written on his Illyrian authority badge – begins without preamble. He takes one look at Falké, nudging his side lightly with the end of his black, glossy boots and turns away. "Ya would'a thought the kid would'a been offed sooner, honestly. Always hangin' with them delinquents. Kyran an' that."

His colleague, a man by the name of Evan, kneels beside the dead body. He presses his fingers against the boy's neck and clicks his tongue with a barely noticeable shake of the head. "Sure is. Been gone for a while. He's cold as ice."

"Then let's beat it. No reason to be here anyway, really. Shoulda' had Claud on this case, ain't he the one that beat up the kid when 'is cousin ran off or whatever? Should be 'is responsibility, don't ya think?"

"Perhaps. But he's working on the Piper Tourneau case instead."

"Ah, 'course he is. He gets *all* the interestin' stuff, doesn't he? Doesn't 'ave to come stare at dead bodies all day."

Taking a seat, Frank kicks up his feet and rests them on the blood-splattered table. When he was a new officer, young and desperate to keep the position, he'd feel sorry for the victims of the often heinous crimes he was called to. In fact, he can distinctly remember quietly weeping to himself like an infant in the bathroom of some rundown little house on Sarvar Avenue; an alcoholic boyfriend had murdered his partner with a kitchen knife and oh, how deeply depressing it was to step inside that dark residency.

He frowns at the memory.

The past doesn't matter any more. He's tougher now and cares very little about the dead people he's sent to investigate. Because that's all they are – dead people, people that meant nothing to him when they were alive and mean nothing to him once they're dead. This boy is just one of those people; there's no reason to get upset about it.

"Get ya feet off the dang table!" Evan snaps unexpectedly, now looking at him, "It's a bleedin' crime scene 'ere, ya know."

Frank withdraws his limbs and scoffs, ignorant disdain crossing his face. It makes sense that Evan takes his position more seriously – after all, he's newer to the job and has only actively been on the force for around a year now. His heart is still in it unlike the others on the force, and Frank gets the impression he genuinely cares about the Illyrian citizens. Usually, officers are in it for the power. Still, he doesn't doubt that such passion will ebb away before long.

From the inner pocket of his coat he retrieves a

cigarette, lights it accordingly, and slips it between his lips. The smell permeates within mere seconds, and his associate looks over with an infuriated glare. "Do you 'ave to smoke right now?!"

"Yeah, actually. Come on, let's get outta 'ere. Obvious what 'appened. His mama went bleedin' mental an' hit his 'ead against the table. Nobody else involved. The newspaper'll write about it, them journalists will come flockin' 'ere soon enough. Surprised they ain't done so already. Why are we still 'ere, Eves?!"

"Evan," the kneeling man corrects in a sigh. Under normal circumstances, he'd get angrier about Frank's nickname use as he finds it extremely annoying and childish. But today he finds there is something intimidating beneath Frank's cocky attitude - enough to prevent him from challenging it so dramatically. Honestly, in general the guy is good at his job (when he wants to be, at least) - excellent at intimidating wrongdoers, shows little fear of the mermaids, and is not to mention very strong - but his attitude is something Evan can't quite get over. They can hardly claim 'friendship' status because of this, and he assumes they'll remain work associates for the rest of their lives. Nothing more, nothing less. He's fine with that.

"Right then," he says, rising to his feet and gesturing to Falké's body slumped in a sitting position against the wall. "Should we get rid of 'im, or…?"

"Yeah. Take 'im to the crematorium. His mama's still alive, so we can't just throw 'im to the mermaids."

"Got it."

Frank nods and exhales a thick cloud of smoke from his nostrils. He looks around for an ashtray and upon seeing none, simply throws the cigarette onto the floor and extinguishes it with the ball of his foot. He moves over to the corpse rather pensively, his head bowed, and helps Evan to pick it up. Together the two men lug Falké to the door of the dining room, down the hall, and towards the front entrance of the house.

Evan halts in his tracks, dropping Falké's legs. He is the first to see the figure; Frank has his back to them and lets out an immediate, "What ya doin'?!" the moment the boy's entire body weight is passed over to him.

"It's - it's one of 'em, Frank," his co-worker raises nervously in response, gesturing forwards with a shaking hand. He hunches in on himself and takes a step back, his shoulders round so that they nearly swallow up his neck. Of all the crime scenes they have witnessed, Frank has never seen him so disturbed, or afraid – he looks over his shoulder and is greeted with the sight of a green-skinned mermaid coming towards them.

"Indeed, it is," the creature says, a snarl simmering on its lips. "Drop him, and leave, or die. Your choice."

Of course, neither man really has a choice. After all, according to Esther, they touched her connector – her lover – without his permission. Nobody should be let off the hook for something like that. She bares her fangs fully, raising her claws in a threatening display, and Falké is dropped to the floor with a resounding thump as both men pull out knives.

Luckily, they are not too difficult to take down. The younger, weaker man is killed instantly, posing very little challenge to her. The other takes more time and is more experienced at fighting; his knife manages to cut a glancing blow across her chest as she twists out of his grasp with the agility of a threatened cat. Luckily, she disarms him quickly and snaps his neck. He slumps to the ground beside what's left of his partner.

The room smells of blood, sweat, and death.

Most of the time, it's easier to balk and deny the truth than it is to accept reality. It's for this reason that once she's shoved Frank and Evan aside, finally focusing on a similarly lifeless Falké, she finds herself imagining that this is all some cleverly executed joke. *What an awfully realistic tragedy*, she thinks, moving so that she is kneeling beside him on the floor, *he even smells dead.*

The front door is wide open. Outside, the air crackles with rain, fat droplets spinning through the sky and splattering onto the decks. Lightning splits the heavens and as it punctures the sky and forks down to the sea, realism strikes her straight in the heart.

It's not a joke. It's real.

A blend of dread and horror instantly takes root in her stomach, germinating with a disturbing urgency. She raises her hand to his face and when her trembling fingers come to rest on his bruised and bloody cheek, they are greeted with a certain coldness.

"Falké," comes a moan that most definitely belongs to her but feels rather detached. "No, no, no, no." Her bloodstained lips move with the words until it is undeniable they are her own. "No, please no!" The cries pitch in intensity, spark high and shake, and she grabs for his body and wraps her arms around it, clutching at the frame in desperation.

He's gone.
He's gone.
He's gone.
Who did this?

She spots the police report scribbled onto a stained piece of paper on a clipboard. It must have fallen when the man holding it had, and lies on the floor in a puddle of blood. Still, the words on it are clear in black ink – murdered by his mother. Head bashed against the table. Sign of little struggle so must have been struck beforehand. Mother has been put into isolation in Illyria's sanatorium.

Esther is repulsed by the mere thought of that human woman killing him. Slowly, she draws a ragged breath - it rattles uncomfortably in her chest – and lets out a desperate scream of pent-up frustration and despair. She takes another look at his body, at his dead body, and the hope is stolen right out of her chest.

Chapter Fifty-Two

The Illyrian Health Centre's sanatorium is unusually quiet this afternoon. Normally, the cold, clinical halls echo with desperate wailing or soft sobbing throughout the day. The noise, constant and overbearing, increases and decreases in volume sporadically and Elvira despises it. She appreciates the quiet.

She's glad today is different.

She'd long ago grown accustomed to the silence of her own house, when Falké was either at the bar drinking or upstairs hungover, and Piper was busying herself cleaning. Now the lack of noise is a welcome, soothing attribute of her world. Quiet is good. Darkness, too, is good.

But it doesn't last.

A pair of voices break the peace, trailing closer and closer to her room's door. They settle in front of it and she feels like screaming in frustration at the mere thought of her calmness being interrupted. There is a fumbling, clinking noise – she can only assume they're looking for the keys – and then more quiet mumbling.

She hopes they've lost the keys. These four walls

signify security to her now and she doesn't feel like leaving them any time soon. *Especially* if that would mean returning to Dreracile Decks alone. She's decided over the past few hours that the place is most definitely cursed.

Her shoulders shudder as she curls up tight, tucking herself into the corner furthest from the voices. She clenches her eyes shut, presses her hands against her ears, and nearly crushes her head between them. For a short time, this works – everything is darker and quieter, and she feels *better*.

It's not long before the door opens though, and her stillness and tranquillity is demolished. She opens her eyes and sees two figures framed in the light from the hallway. They both wear lab coats, as all doctors in the building do, and are holding various medical devices that do little to ease her stress. The look on their faces is uncaring, to say the least – devoid of sympathy or compassion, harsh and hard-hearted.

"Strange to think that she's now a patient here," one of them muses, approaching her. "Now, Elvira, don't hide from us. We need to test your blood pressure and such."

She squirms in her corner.

"Killed her own son," the other states sharply, his voice like knives in Elvira's stomach.

It was an accident, she thinks to herself, *I thought it was her. I didn't mean to kill him. I didn't even mean to kill her.*

"Oh, I heard about that. Bashed his head against the kitchen table, or something like that?"

"Yeah. Just kept at it 'til he died."

"Do you think it was because her niece ran off or whatever?"

"She did?"

"Yeah – Piper Tourneau. The mermaid lover."

"*That's* her niece?!"

Elvira hisses in anger. "Stop gossiping about me like that!" she snaps. "I can hear you both, you know!"

The two doctors look at her in surprise, and the woman dares to raise her voice louder, throat cracking and stinging from going so long without use. "Leave me alone!"

When it becomes apparent that neither of the two are going to do as she asks, she grabs for the closest and begins to rattle him violently. Voice hoarse with strain as she shakes him, she yells, "Leave me alone! Leave me alone! Leave me alone!"

Hands pull her away and shove her backwards. She gasps desperately for air, hyperventilating and crying, and for a short time nothing further happens. Once she has calmed slightly, her breathing less ragged and quick, the doctors go about their business taking measurements from her.

"Good girl," one says condescendingly, patting her head, and then they both leave.

The door closes, the voices become more distant, and silence wraps around her once again like a dense, heavy smog. It lingers comfortably, and then -

"Help! Security! *Security!* One of them! It's one of them!"

This desperate exclamation, followed by a series of disturbingly loud screams and gurgled pleas, causes her to sit bolt upright. The entire sanatorium is filled with sound now; fearful crying, angered yelling, and frantic praying emanates from every single room. Every patient afraid, without a doubt, including her.

She looks away from the door, her nails scraping against the floor in stress.

One of them. What's that supposed to mean? An escaped, psychopathic patient? A thug, or delinquent like the ones Falké used to hang around with?

That now-all-too-familiar sound of keys again. The lock to her door is tried once, twice, three times. Four. Five. Six. And then – it clicks open. Elvira stares, eyes widening and her gaze settles on the unmistakable silhouette of a mermaid. So tall. So frightening.

"He didn't deserve it," the creature says coldly as it steps into the room, its sterling and emerald hair glittering in the dim glow of the sanatorium lights. "You humans call *us* the monsters – but you ought to look in the mirror, you pathetic waste of space."

Elvira's breath hitches in her throat. "Didn't – didn't mean to," she responds, her heart beating violently in fear against her ribs. "Thought it was her. Didn't mean to."

Her fingers tremble as she buries her face in her hands, allowing herself a moment of weakness. It's all going to end soon so why bother fighting, anyway? The mermaid is right – she *is* a waste of space, useless like an old working animal that can no longer perform its tasks. She deserves the sharp hatred, the tormenting visions of Falké's kind hands and soft voice.

"You aren't even sorry, are you?"

As Elvira looks back up, she is greeted with the horrifying sight of the mermaid running towards her. She jerks back in reflex, clutching her hair in both hands and screams in shock and fear. Within microseconds, she is being attacked; the long, drawn-out wailing from her lips punctuates every time she feels nails scrape at her skin and teeth rip at her. She takes a great gasp, running out of breath, and screams desperately for help. Warm blood spills down her body like a shower. It's a strange and unwelcome feeling, being coated in its crimson thickness, but there's nothing she can do to stop it. As security rush in, she decides that this is undoubtedly the worst thing that has ever happened to her.

"Elisa…" she gurgles, her eyes filled with anguish. "Falké – Piper - my family…my family…"

The words come out as helpless warbles. As her surroundings fade to black, and a ringing begins in her ears, she remembers a lot of things. Zachary's 'other woman', her sister's suicide, Piper leaving with the very mermaid that destroyed her life. The death of her son that she herself caused.

And then, as she dies, she realises that this isn't the worst thing that's ever happened to her at all. In fact, it's probably the best.

Chapter Fifty-Three

The remnants of celebration cling to Caspian's ship far into the week following the Day of Sullivan's Serpent. The crew, as lively as ever, continue to drink and prattle on about their – and their wonderful captain's – personal achievements every chance they get. It's nice, really, and everybody truly feels like a family. There are no more incidents involving mutiny. In fact, there are no more incidents in general. Not that Piper is aware of, anyway.

She doesn't feel well again today. It might be because, although she is miles away from Illyria, she's worried about her cousin. It might be because Holt seems like he is still infatuated with her. It might be because she's in yet another dress Caspian so kindly gifted to her, and it's quite tight; she fumbles with the lace at the back of it while standing beside her hammock, ready to fling herself down onto it.

When Astrid enters the room, Piper barely notices. It's only when she speaks, a smooth and lovely sound, that she turns her head towards her.

"What are you thinking about?"

She doesn't know what an acceptable answer to

this would be, honestly. She doesn't want to admit what she's thinking about. It shouldn't even matter now. Falké shouldn't matter – he's not here. He's in Illyria. Prince Holt's apparent infatuation with her shouldn't matter. It isn't reciprocated. So naturally, she spews out whatever generic answer she can think of: "Just…Sullivan's Serpent. It was a good story, wasn't it? Caspian's good at storytelling. He had everybody hooked, and I bet they've heard it a million times before. I liked it. Did you?"

With luck, Astrid will believe this pathetic excuse of a lie. And believe that she does, for the mermaid nods and taps a slender finger against her chin, a sharp nail barely grazing her lips. "Yes, I liked it. It was a very nice little tale. And you're quite right – he truly is a master storyteller. You know, I am quite good at telling stories too. I have collected many over the years. Perhaps I can tell some to you."

"Sure," Piper says, somehow making herself sound even more tired and sickly than she genuinely feels. She lets out a low moan of discomfort. "Listen, I feel really sick right now, Astrid. I think I gotta lie down. Or take this dress off. Or both."

Astrid's interest is piqued. She leans towards Piper, shamelessly so, and laughs quietly. "Well, I can help with both of those things if you like. We can start by taking off the dress. Do you want me to get it off you?"

"What no! I mean, what? No, but…sure…okay…do you want to?" Piper's heart gives a flutter. Her cheeks are flushed and burning with heat, but she's unsure whether that's because of Astrid or her feeling of sickness. It doesn't matter. She's suddenly nervous, anyway – it makes no sense though, for it's not like Astrid hasn't made advances on her before, *welcomed* advances…

Astrid presses her fingers against Piper's mouth before she can speak any further. "I need you to make this decision. I am learning consent, remember? So…do you want me to, or not?"

Her fingers are cool against Piper's lips. The girl trembles, adrift in the storm of longing building inside her. Tentatively, she presses a kiss against one of Astrid's fingertips and smiles shyly. "Mmhm."

"Ha. You are cute. I need more than just a 'mmhm'…will you vocalise it?"

Caught up in the fact that she's just been called 'cute', it takes some time for Piper to realise she's being asked a question. It's because of this that her response is less than composed – "Y-yes. Yes, undress me. I mean, take it off…er…me, I mean. T-take the dress off of me. You know what I mean."

"I know what you mean."

Astrid reaches for the sash around Piper's waist, intending to pull it off, but is stopped. "W-wait. I want you to feel this…" Piper mumbles, grasping her hand and bringing it upwards, reverently pressing it to where her heart is racing in her chest.

"Your heart?"

"Yeah…"

She's so vulnerable. Only a thin layer of material, skin, and bone parts Astrid's hand from her most vital muscle. Hot and alive, pumping red blood that she knows by now that this mermaid would drink, drink and *enjoy* until there's nothing left. How intimate the thought is. How frightening, too. "You did this," she whispers as Astrid's fingers glide over the material, flattening and spreading. "You made it beat so fast."

Astrid grins almost maliciously and presses her hand, cool and firm, against Piper's chest.

"Your heart beats so differently to that of a mermaid."

Piper can imagine Astrid's heart beating. Thumping hungrily. The heart of a starved creature who has hunted her prey for far too long.

Astrid moves her hand from Piper's chest, ghosts a soft kiss on her shoulder, and with agonisingly smooth, slow movements unties the sash around her and throws it to the side. She grasps the hem of the dress, inching it up little by little, and a small, frustrated sigh comes from Piper.

"Astrid…"

Her breath is heavy. She wonders what Astrid thinks of her right now, in this state. Is it possible that she feels what she feels: a terrible mix of nervousness, desire and upheaval? That's what her world has consisted of since the moment they spoke to each other. Can she perhaps feel the aching expansion of new-grown muscle in her chest too, pulled beyond capacity so that it may have a chance of containing such love?

Hands pry at the gown, teasing with gentle tugs and careless brushing against her skin. "Someone looks nervous," comes the mermaid, drawing the girl further into her own anxiety. "Am I making you nervous, Piper?"

"N-no, Astrid, I'm fine."

"Really?"

"Yes…yes."

"If you say so."

With little effort, Astrid's fingers yank the clothing upwards to Piper's shoulders. She pulls it over her head, relieving her of the pressure it was causing, and tosses it, too, to the side. Piper can't withhold her gasp. *This is crazy*, she thinks, *how much more exciting it is to have somebody else undress you.*

No sooner has the dress been removed from her thin body, that a soft kiss finds its way to her lips, defusing any nervousness or biting tension instantly. "I feel sick," she mumbles against Astrid's mouth, "I don't wanna vomit on you."

Astrid shrugs, looking amused. "I'll take my chances."

It's seconds before the two are laced together in Piper's hammock, their bodies intertwined, Astrid's tongue trailing carefully across her connector's neck. This sensation is definitely strange to Piper – a warm, wet presence moving across her skin – but it is certainly not unwelcome. She shuts her eyes tightly, focusing on this feeling, the lips now treating her neck to some rather heated oral gestures. Hands trail down to her thighs, gripping, reaching, grasping. Sharp nails scraping her skin.

"Mmmh, you can't. Not there…" she breathes, shuddering with yet another gasp, droning in bliss, when suddenly, Astrid stops.

"Astrid…!" she whines, breathing a sigh of disappointment and frustration. She wiggles her hips expectantly but nothing happens. Honestly, she has in mind to just clutch the mermaid's hands and push them back onto her skin. But, before she gets the chance, an acute thrash of pain vents from her knee and clouds her mind in a throbbing haze. It snakes its way down through her leg to her foot and toes…she realises Astrid has poked at her wound suddenly, and lets out a little groan of despair.

"What is this," Astrid says, almost angrily. It's a question, but said as if it's a statement. "You told me this was alright. This is *not* alright – it's infected. No wonder you feel sick, you have an infection, you have a fever coming on. Why didn't you say it was hurting?"

"I – I just -"

Astrid groans loudly. "Piper, do you realise how serious this is?!" she asks, grasping her upper arms, "this could be fatal. Unless Caspian has antibiotics on this ship, we are going to have to get some elsewhere. And fast. I'm not sure where we are, but we'll need to make a beeline for inhabited land. Land that has medical facilities.

"S-sorry," she stammers, noticeably alarmed by Astrid's tone. "Will we - will we have to go back to Illyria?"

The mermaid rubs her forehead, and then climbs out of the hammock. "Well, unless Caspian has antibiotics on board, which I highly doubt, then we may, yes. Stay here. Don't move."

She leaves the storeroom without another word. Piper watches her go in silence, and then curls up, embarrassed and ashamed. How can she be so stupid? She didn't realise it would become so bad. It's a *scratch*. She's had scratches before and never had a problem. But then again, Elvira always had access to antibiotics at the Illyrian Health Centre and she remembers taking them from time to time.

Whatever lust had been born from this encounter with Astrid is now gone, leaving a hollow blackness in its wake.

CHAPTER FIFTY-FOUR

"Oh please. That is not how you do it. *This* is how you do it."

Holt leans forward gracefully and drops into a bow, an impish smile playing upon his lips. He keeps his eyes on Caspian the entire time, much to the smuggler's annoyance, and then straightens up again with a small chuckle. "You smugglers know absolutely nothing about such things, do you? Cannot even bow…ridiculous."

Caspian's face grows red. He crosses his arms, frustrated, and sighs heavily. How much more infuriating can this boy get? He wouldn't be averse to throwing him in the ship's prison hold. At least if he was in there, he wouldn't have to worry about him running about and fiddling with things on his ship. And that's why they're both in this room together now; Holt was positively obstinate and insisted on going inside Caspian's cabin to avoid the rain that's just started and, of course, the smuggler was obliged to follow. He doesn't trust anybody in such a place alone, not even a posh little prince who probably doesn't have the mental capacity necessary for thieving.

"Yer think I be needin' to know how to bow on me own ship, lad?!" he scoffs, regretting ever questioning the blond on royal etiquette in the first place. It was interesting initially, learning such things, but now it's just become a competition on who's better than who. He shouldn't have expected anything less, really.

Before either of them can say anything else, the door flings open to reveal Astrid, her silvery-white hair whirling about her face in the wind, wet with rain. Her eyes are wide, and her smooth blue cheeks have darkened with a certain flush. She seems...dishevelled.

The pair stare at her in shock. Caspian is the first to speak. "Yer alrigh' lassie?"

She shakes her head in response, a pinched expression crossing her face. "Not particularly. Do you have antibiotics on this vessel?"

"Hm...no, lass."

"Fine."

"Why? Ye be hurt? Do mermaids need antibiotics?"

"No. They're not for me. Alright then - we are going to have to take some steps. Set a course for the nearest land with medical facilities."

"We be a long way from anywhere right now. The nearest place with medicine would be back where yer came from. Illyria."

A small moan of indignation escapes Astrid's throat. "Fine," she repeats. "Mark the course with your navigator, and then put the course into motion as soon as you can."

Holt blinks twice. His heart is – and has been since the moment Astrid entered – pounding in his chest, fear and curiosity at war within him. The sound of his own heartbeat grows steadily in his ears until he can stand it no more and cries, if not to cover the sound with something else, "Illyria?! You must be mad if you think we should all waltz into Illyria! May I remind you, Astrid, that I risked my *life* sailing you and Piper out of that place because you were in danger there!"

Astrid ignores him and starts pacing back and forth in the cabin. "This boat must arrive in Illyria within the week, sooner if at all possible. You must command your crew to have all hands on deck, Captain Cass. I'm serious. Deadly serious."

"Aye," Caspian responds, nodding. He heads out on deck with her and Holt, calling for his navigator to aid him in a new course. Upon scrambling over to the group, and listening to Astrid's appeal with serious consideration, they highlight a particular obstacle, however: "Alrigh', lassie, but how do yer think we can enter the harbour?"

"I hadn't thought about it," Astrid admits, tapping her nails against her cheek. "We will probably need a nautical disguise."

"Merchant ship?" Caspian suggests. "Nobody e'er questions a merchant ship."

"Good. Yes. Fine."

"Some repaintin' will be necessary, cap'n," Caspian's navigator informs him, and Caspian nods in understanding. "That be fine, Williams. That be just fine."

Holt finally speaks up once again, something terrible and tender unfurling within his chest. "Why do we need antibiotics, Astrid?" he asks, fearing he already knows the answer. Fearing he already knows who is hurt.

"She has an infection."

"Who?"

"Piper."

"Shiver me timbers, lass!" Caspian cuts in. "She be that hurt? How did that 'appen?"

"She fell while crossing the reef to your ship and scratched her knee. I thought it was a minor wound and when I asked about it later, she assured me it was fine. She hasn't brought it up since, but it's become worse. The headache she had during the celebrations earlier in the week was clearly because of this, as were the stomach pains. She has a fever now, and the wound is swollen. It's a mess. A potentially fatal mess. We cannot stop this ship, not for a moment. How long do you predict it will be until we arrive in Illyria?"

"Excuse me, *what*?! Did you say fatal?!" Holt's increasingly panicked voice cuts into their conversation, his anxiety spiking with each word he cries. "Has she been suffering *that much* in silence this entire journey and not told us?! Why would she do something so unbelievably foolish?!"

Astrid shakes her head, groaning. "I don't know. But what matters now is that we get her antibiotics, and quickly. We need to go back to Illyria where we know she will definitely get care. It's the best chance."

"I hear ye, lass," Caspian cuts in, face contorted in worry, "we be on our way, don't ye worry yerself. I won't stop this ship for nothin', savvy?'"

"Good."

Holt almost screams in panic.

"I'm going back to her side now. Make haste," the

mermaid tells Caspian, and with that, she's gone.

Caspian insists on steering the boat for the remainder of the day. It's only when the shimmering imprint of stars are welcomed by the darkening sky that he allows Holt to take over. His hands, calloused and sore from overuse, pat Holt on the back in thanks as he steps to the side. "Ye be a mighty fine sailor," he notes, watching the boy, "I 'ave faith in yer."

Holt grunts. "I shan't fail you."

"Good, matey. That be good. Ye be me fam'ly, yer know. An' I don't want me fam'ly in peril. The quicker we save the lass, the better. Savvy?"

Caspian loves his crew. He loves his *family*. Everybody has been extremely close since the death of what the crew have now nicknamed the 'mutiny trio', and he can't bear the thought of losing anybody else. Of course, Piper hasn't been on the ship for *that* long, but time means nothing when family is involved. He loves her as he loves all of his crew. They would do anything for him, and he would do anything for them, and that's what family is about. At least, the version of family that he's built for himself over the years.

His first family, his birth parents who he still doesn't know the name of and doesn't really *want* to know the name of, abandoned him when he was a child in some shoddy, run-down orphanage in the mountainous region of Araslan. What a miserable place that was; perpetually cold and entirely shrouded in darkness and melancholy. And every night - gasps, whimpers, muffled crying and wretched wails from lonely, despairing children desperate to see their parents again or get a loving family. He was one of them, crying into the twilight. It was every child for themself, and nobody really formed friendships despite secretly wanting to.

He's thankful for the night that Cecily Tyrian and her little crew docked on the shores of that frostbitten land. He's thankful that he strayed from the orphanage when he did and didn't stay tucked up in his metal-frame bed. He's thankful that she found him on the streets and took him in. Most of all, he is thankful that he got a family that evening, a family that loved him and looked after him.

He is not thankful for the day those pirates attacked his new family's boat, *her* boat.

She fought brilliantly. For a long time, he believed she had the upper hand. But when the enemies took hold of him and threatened to slice his little body to pieces, she let her guard down for just a moment.

A moment was all it took.

Her life was snuffed out like a candle in front of his eyes, her black coffee curls covering her face as she fell to the decking in a pool of crimson. "Don't hurt him!" were her last words, he recalls. "I love him! I love you, Caspian. Oh darling, I love you."

She was gone before he could respond, before he could tell her he loved her too. He refuses to lose anybody else now.

CHAPTER FIFTY-FIVE

Mayor Jasper Vanguard of Illyria:
Thank you for your letter regarding our son, Prince Holt Davori of Caldisa. We apologise profusely for any trouble caused.
Sincerely,
King Nicolai and Queen Delilah Davori of Caldisa

"What does that even *mean*? They barely wrote anything. They know, don't they? They know everything. They know about Calawi, and the mermaids, and the experiments, and my God, Scarlett! This is all your fault for letting that stupid little child wander around our house without supervision. Look what you've done! Now Caldisa is going to blow this nation to smithereens and it's all because you were so unbelievably careless!"

Jasper throws the letter down and slams his fists against Scarlett's dressing table, a mismatched mix of beauty products, makeup, and medical tools scattering in all directions. Some fine, pressed powder from the kingdom of Paliron (known very well for its cosmetics) in the shade 'babydoll' tumbles onto the floor and cracks, ruined. Its soft, pastel pink pigment dusts both the ground and Jasper's leather shoes, but he seems far too incensed to notice.

"I can't believe I was foolish enough to think this problem would go away," he storms, starting to pace the room. "And that Piper Tourneau would keep her lips sealed. But no! Not at all! She told that bloody prince everything, and he told his parents, and now look where we are!"

A stray tube of lipstick that had fallen off the dressing table rolls beneath his left foot as he walks. He very nearly trips over it, finally looking down to notice the pink footprints, and yells, ever so dramatically, "Why are my shoes pink?!"

Scarlett, kneeling on the bed, jerks reflexively in surprise when he shouts. It's not hard to tell that he's in a bad mood, and nine out of ten times when he's in a bad mood, somebody gets hurt. That somebody, of course, tends to be her. "Perhaps because…you stepped in blush, Jasper."

"Well then, why is it on the floor? I told you to keep things tidy around here."

"Tidy," she echoes without thinking. "Yes, sorry. I didn't mean to mess anything up."

Of course, she's well aware that she shouldn't really be apologising. It's not her fault that Jasper stepped in makeup that he had caused to fall, and that he was the one that bought it for her in the first place. She's not even a fan of blush because it tends to make her look *too* flushed most of the time. Still, he likes it and says it makes her look pretty. It's the only reason she bothers applying it. For him. Everything for him.

She sits up straight. "I…don't think Piper heard anything," she confesses softly. "And even if she did, she obviously didn't tell the prince…he can't have told his parents anything because they're still looking, right? If he went home, he would be marrying that princess, and Valentina Victory would have written about it in the papers. I think the king and queen were just responding out of politeness."

He steps up to her bedside, pink makeup forgotten, and grabs a fistful of her hair. Yanking her head back, he narrows his silvery eyes and glowers at her as she screeches in shock and pain. "Why must you act like you're smarter than me?" he demands, incredulous.

"I'm just saying what I thin -"

Smack.

The blow to Scarlett's cheek sounds like the snap of a whip, a noise that Jasper finds intensely satisfying. But the cry she makes as a result of it is even better. It's melodious, like a mermaid's cry perhaps, and he makes an effort to keep its sweet sound ringing through the air. Her skin is still as soft and thin as ever. Every injury he inflicts upon her blossoms in colour, causing an almost permanent mark. And she feels *everything*.

He smirks. Humans are feeble and pathetic, but there is something undoubtedly beautiful in how easily they are marked. Hurting mermaids is much harder, requires significant effort. But this, this is easy. This is fun.

Suddenly, the dissonant little tune caused by the timbre of Scarlett's wails stop. Instead, she takes a deep breath in and howls, "You're hurting me!"

"Good."

The wretched complaint does little more than feed his malicious streak. He pushes her down, pinning her to the bed and lets loose another volley of slaps.

Eventually however, she relents and he stops.

"Jasper! Stop, please!" she begs, "I'm sorry. I'm sorry. I don't mean to act like I'm smarter. Of course I don't. I care about you, I've always cared about you."

He pauses, tapping his chin thoughtfully. "Is that so, my dear, sweet Scarlett?"

It feels like some sort of victory when she reaches up towards him, begging to be comforted, or held, or *taken*. "Yes. Jasper, please."

He savours the look on her face. Stands and gazes down upon her magnum opus for a short while. And then, once her sad little face and soft snivelling begin to bore him, he leans back over her. Pulling the blankets from her body, he runs his hands fervently down her torso and sighs quite theatrically. "You know I have work to do, pet," he grunts, his fingers caressing her stomach, "you are being a terrible distraction at the moment. I hope you know that."

She nods slowly, draws breath from her nose, and leans up to meet his lips. He kisses her hard in response - so hard, in fact, that the action pushes her head right back down onto the pillow.

"Jasper."

"Don't speak."

"Okay."

His fingers card through her hair, his tongue sweeps against her lower lip. It lasts for only a few seconds before he drags himself away though, looking somewhat frustrated.

"Your kisses bore me," he grumbles, and proceeds to stand and move away. She reaches out to him in desperation. "Wait-! Jasper, I want you. Please."

With a look devoid of care, he turns from her and

begins towards the door. "Well, I don't want you, not if you aren't going to put more effort in. Have an early night and get some rest, that's an order."

She knows better than to argue with him when he's annoyed with her, so pushes her nightdress down slowly and looks away. "Y-yes…alright…"

"I will be downstairs overnight."

"Okay."

"Don't disturb me unless it's something absolutely vital. Even then, try and figure it out yourself. If you can't, get Wren to sort it out for all I care. I am the last resort, understand?"

"Yes."

"And if there any other letters from Caldisa, I want them sent down to me."

"Yes. But Jasper?"

He groans, frustrated. "What?"

"Forgive me for asking, but what are you actually…doing down there? Just you never tell me anything and I feel I *should* know, really. Maybe I can help you or something? I find myself wondering every day."

"Never ask me this again."

She glances to the side. "But I just…I wonder what she – what Piper – read. What she saw that is so private. What is so important that you are stressed always with the knowledge that she too knows. Can I not help at all? Do you not trust me with this information, as your partner? Jasper?"

"No. Shut up."

He leaves the room.

After a moment, tense and unhappy, Scarlett turns on her side and settles back in the bed with her lips pressed tightly together to hide her pain. Her face is sore. She exhales slowly and stares at the wall, listening to the sounds of this great household as she gently presses against her cheeks. Her cold hands soothe the sore sensitivity. For a long time, she grieves over the absence of his touch. But then, all of a sudden, a revelation hits. A flicker of despair sinks into her expression and she says aloud, so very softly, "He doesn't love me."

The weight of the words makes her feel sicker than she already is, and she forces herself to stand and make her way to the window for some fresh air. It's closed; she pushes it open and looks out at the sea. It shifts foam to water around the jut of several rocks, simultaneously beautiful and menacing. In the distance, the smaller houses of Illyria stand, bland and dull.

She entertains the thought of returning to them and leaving this place, leaving Jasper, for just a few seconds. But then, "I can't," she whispers aloud, her voice breaking. "I can't...I just can't."

This is her *home*. Even when it wasn't her home, it was. She just didn't know it yet. How could she possibly leave it – and Jasper – now, when he's clearly going through such a rough time? And maybe, just maybe when he manages to do what he wants, whatever the plan with Calawi and the mermaids is, he will be content and love her for real.

A dart of green flashes out of the corner of her eye.

She turns her head quickly to follow it, distracted from her thoughts. And then: a ragged, bloody tail flares out of the waves, gleaming as if it is made of glass. A face emerges, mint coloured and shimmering, surrounded by a mass of pale hair scattered through with small starfish and shells. It's a mermaid, and she's injured.

Scarlett steps back from the window in surprise. This isn't the first time she's seen one of these creatures wounded, and under normal conditions, she wouldn't care too much. But something within her wants to help. *Needs* to help. Before she realises it, she's sneaking out of her room and down the stairs.

It doesn't hit her how cold it really is until she's outside and heading to the manor house's private dock. Chill licks at her face, creeps under her silk nightdress and spreads across her skin like ice water. Still, she continues onwards, descending the steps and rushing onto the decking below. Jasper's private boat bobs up and down on the water.

"Mermaid?" she calls weakly, "Mermaid, are you there? What happened to you? Can I help you?"

Tentatively, she crouches down and dips her hand into the water, recoiling in shock at the bitter temperature. *Mermaids are strong creatures,* she thinks, *to be able to withstand such freezing water.* After a moment's silence, she rises back to her feet and repeats herself: "Can I help you?"

Nothing.

Suddenly, a hand emerges from the water and grips her ankle roughly, pulling her down in one swift motion. Combined with the nausea she feels, the force at which she hits the decking causes her to gag and retch between coughs. "W-wait!" she chokes out, "I don't want to hurt you, I"

She cuts herself short when she notices the mermaid is now centimetres from her, staring, its lips parted in shock. "You want to help me," it says slowly in disbelief, "you truly want to help me."

"Yes," she breathes, nodding. "Will you attack me? Please don't. I'll help you, I promise."

The creature doesn't answer her question. Instead, it puts its head in its hands, body shuddering, and whispers, "She's gone. I killed her. She's gone. And I feel no better for it – I thought it would help, but it didn't. He's not coming back, even if she's dead. Even if I made things right."

"Who is dead?"

"His mother."

"You killed 'his' mother?"

"Yes…she's dead. She's gone."

Scarlett sits up slowly, fearing that any sudden movements may provoke an attack. "I'm sorry," she murmurs, teeth chattering violently, "I don't really understand. Who is the 'he' you speak of?"

"My connector. He's dead. She killed him, so I killed her. Now I'm alone. Now I have nobody to love. He's gone…he's not coming back…he can't love me anymore."

"Your connector…okay. I see. What's your name?

"Esther."

Slowly, after a moment's hesitation, Scarlett reaches out and presses a gentle hand to the mermaid's face. Her thumb strokes along a brow, the groove above her nose, and her smooth forehead with a careful, tender deliberation. She cups Esther's cheek in her warm palm, and sighs. "I'm sorry. I wish I could help you, but I cannot bring your 'connector' back. I can help treat your wounds, however. How did you get hurt?"

The mermaid grits her teeth as she forces herself up onto the decking. It's obviously difficult for her, so Scarlett grabs her arms and pulls with as much strength as she can muster in her current state. It works, and within a few seconds, they are side by side.

Esther groans in pain. Her tail, bleeding onto the wood, curves like a perfectly fitted dress. It's torn in numerous places and the fins are tattered as if they've been shredded by knives. "I jumped through glass," she explains. "The sanatorium. I went there to kill his mother, and they sent security after me so I jumped through a large glass window to escape, and flung myself into the sea."

Feeling awash with empathy, Scarlett places a hand on her shoulder. "Let me help you," she suggests gently, "can you shift forms? Or would it be too painful?"

"I will try."

Scarlett can do little to withhold her gasp when she sees the state of Esther's newly formed legs. The skin is streaked with blood, damaged, and grazed. She stands and helps the young mermaid up, a hand clasped around her waist, and guides her into the manor house in silence.

CHAPTER FIFTY-SIX

"Are we nearly there?"

Astrid dips her head in response to Piper's query. She is holding a golden chalice, no doubt part of Caspian's generous goblet collection. It's clasped between her slender, cold hands like a wedding bouquet. "Not quite. Drink this."

Piper groans as the cup is held to her lips. Her body aches as though it has been bludgeoned with hammers, and as she takes a shallow, desperate little breath, a band of burning iron seems to constrict around her throat. Trying to drink is no easier; her insides wrench the moment the liquid moves through her and almost immediately she finds herself gagging. Luckily, she's able to keep the water down without throwing it all up this time.

"Am I really that sick because of such a small cut?" she croaks out as Astrid withdraws the chalice and sets it down, "It hurts…"

She raises her fingers sluggishly to feel at the wound on her knee and flinches. It's tender to the touch, and burns with an icy hotness despite having been cleaned several times and wrapped in a bandage.

Her body in general cannot seem to decide which temperature it is either, and despite being naked under several furs and blankets from Caspian she's both hot and cold. Tossing and turning does little to help; no matter what position she lies in her flesh feels like either glowing-hot steel wire or shards of ice.

"Try not to move," Astrid says from her side.

"Okay…" Piper glances up at her with wide, sad eyes and winds her arms around herself in a hug. Pressing her arms against her stomach, she tries to dislodge the nauseous feeling that has collected there. The air comes out of her lungs in ragged spurts. "I'm trying…"

"Do you want me to sing to you? I can sing you to sleep."

Piper nods almost imperceptibly. She feels like bread dipped in water. Unloosening, falling apart. "Yes. Yes, Astrid. Please."

"Alright, but Piper?"

"Yes?"

The mermaid frowns. "I hope you know I am entirely intoxicated with emotion," she says quietly. "The guilt I feel is unfathomable. I should have noticed it sooner."

"It was my fault. I didn't tell you it was hurting. I thought it would be okay."

They fall silent and the sound of the ship moving quickly through the water overtakes the room. The rigging is humming. The sails are taut, causing the masts to creak and moan. Water roars as it pushes past the hull. Slowly, ever so slowly, there is a new addition to this symphony though – Astrid's song begins to float through the air, a tragic and beautiful melody that caresses Piper's very soul. She realises then why her aunt has always insulted the mermaids' singing; it may not be the reason for their supposed 'mind control' but it surely is the most beautiful sound in the world and Elvira seems to hate beauty. She welcomes the relief the words offer her, the opportunity they give her to fall into unconsciousness. Soon enough she is becoming quite drowsy.

"Oh…Astrid…that's – that's beautiful…"

The jagged shadows cast upon the wall from the lantern on her 'nightstand' – a crate of some unidentified alcohol – become no longer threatening, but rather pretty. Astrid's shadow is especially delightful. She almost wants to reach out and grasp for it, but her limbs feel heavy the moment she tries to do so, as do her eyes.

"Goodnight…Astrid…" she manages to mumble, and drifts into a deep and restful slumber.

Astrid finishes her song and is silent for several moments, simply staring at her sleeping connector. After a few minutes, she climbs into the hammock too. She lays behind Piper, pushing her forehead in-between her shoulder blades and sighs. Her breath runs cold down the small of Piper's back but the girl doesn't visibly react. Thankfully, she stays sleeping and Astrid allows her hands to creep over her stomach for a short while, eventually finding their way to her chest and over her heart.

There they stay for the rest of the night.

Prince Holt stands outside the door, his hand resting against the cold wood. Piper and Astrid are just beyond it. With just one knock he could wake them, perhaps get them to let him in. But…no.

I shouldn't disturb them, he tells himself, *I shouldn't act so needy*.

Pressing his palms against his eyes, he turns away and almost shrieks in surprise as he comes face to face with Caspian. The captain looks tired, exhausted even. He's carrying Vivo in his arms, the little feline's eyes are closed and ears are twitching.

"Princey." His tone comes tired, calm. "What yer doin' wanderin' about this time o' nigh'? I thought ye be goin' to bed after yer shift sailin' fer us."

Suddenly ashamed of himself, Holt flounders for a moment and looks down at the floor. "Yes, it is I. Prince Holt Davori of Caldisa," he says, not at all answering the question. When he looks up again, he meets Caspian's gaze with a suspicious squint, feigning great apprehension and adds, "And what are *you* doing 'wandering about', Caspian?"

"I be mighty tired," the captain responds, petting the cat gently. She purrs lovingly as his fingers disappear into her soft, thin fur. "Another member of me crew had to take control o' the ship, 'cus I was ready to scuttle the thing in exhaustion, harhar. Came to say g'night to the lasses before I go to sleep meself."

The prince raises his brows. "I have no idea what that means. Scuttle a ship?"

"Sinkin' it, lad."

"Well, for the love of Caldisa do *not* do that! I for one enjoy not having to stay afloat in cold water in the middle of nowhere because the captain of the boat I'm on decided to fall asleep at the helm! You should have called for me, I know what I'm doing!"

"Yar. Well, it won't 'appen now. An' ye be needin' yer sleep too. Yer goin' to move aside, so I can get in there?"

Holt coughs awkwardly and wrings his hands, unsure of how to tell Caspian that disturbing the pair inside probably isn't a good idea. "Honestly, Caspian," he begins, "I believe both of them have fallen asleep. There is no sound coming from their cabin door anymore, and I would know for I was…listening and such…"

His voice trails off.

Silence falls upon them, and Caspian takes it as a cue to speak again. "Ye be wastin' yer time goin' after the lass. She be deep in love with that mermai' and there be nothin' yer can do to pull her outta that. Sirens be powerful beings matey. Once ye be findin' yerself fallin' fer one, ye be done fer. There's no escapin' a mermaid's connection. Only death."

Holt's reaction to this comment is dramatic and visceral. As he moves away from Caspian, stepping to the side, he brings his hands over his mouth as if he is about to heave. The boastful, pompous, and downright bull-headed conviction he usually adopts has all but dissolved, and instead he looks on the verge of an emotional meltdown. "I am *not* 'going after' her, and never was! It is *strictly* platonic, Caspian! I have no interest in the ladies, I shall have you know and I -"

He freezes. He's never told anyone such things about himself before. Clearing his throat, he looks to the side and forces himself to continue, "It is the fact that Astrid is – she is – gah! She is so dangerous. Only death?! I worry for Piper. I worry for her, for she is my *friend*. And then there is the matter of having to return to my kingdom and – never mind. I am going to bed," he mumbles, "goodnight Caspian."

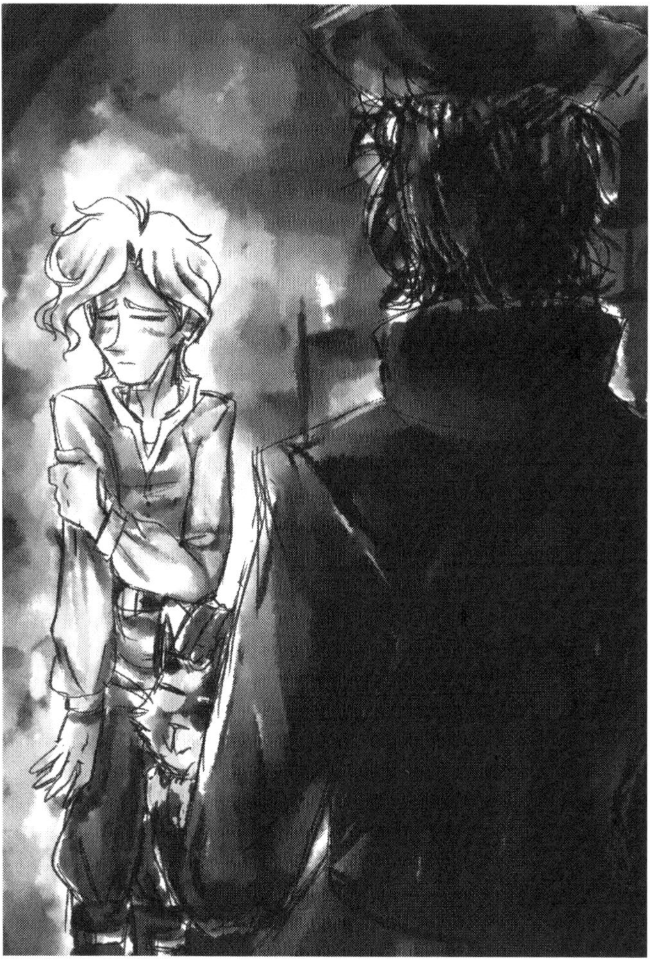

Normally, the smuggler would find this sort of response laughable. But, now, he would rather not see Holt suffer, and instead tilts his head to the side and frowns. He puts Vivo down on the deck gently.

"Holt." He reaches for the young man's shoulder and squeezes it lightly, wearing a look of determination. Holt seems shocked by this gesture and the fact that Caspian didn't use the teasing nickname 'princey' for once, and swats at his arm gently.

"Yes? What is it?"

"I know ye be findin' this all mighty difficult, and, well, yer see, I be too. Yer, Piper, and Astrid, even Lenka and Cadmus – ye be me' fam'ly, as I told yer."

Eyes downcast, Holt laughs weakly and shakes his head. "Why, what a ridiculous statement. If I didn't know any better, I would say you despised me, Caspian!"

"I don't, meartie."

"Honestly?"

"Honestly. Ye be a fantastic sailor, matey."

"Hm. Well…I still despise you, and your entire crew."

"I know yer don't."

Caspian pauses. After a moment's hesitation and a quick survey of his surroundings to ensure the coast is clear, he moves forwards and pulls Holt into a hug. Cradling the back of his head he notes, "yer know…yer don't 'ave to go straight home after we get things sorted in Illyria."

Holt groans softly in what Caspian assumes is embarrassment, but chooses to ignore. "I do. It is my duty, and I cannot keep Lenka and Cadmus from their homes. They want to be home; I know this for certain. I do."

"Yer don't. Yer can stay 'ere, yer know. On me ship, as part of me crew. Ye be good at sailin' so yer would be valuable to 'ave 'ere. I know ye be, I saw yer sailin' earlier. We can take Lenka an' Cadmus home…an' you can stay."

"I cannot. I have yet to talk about this with you, Caspian, but I am engaged to be married to the princess of the kingdom closest to my own. Isadora Petrova. I may not love her romantically, but she is a friend of mine. There is nothing wrong with marrying out of friendship, surely? Isadora will understand. It is my *responsibility* to marry her."

"Alrigh' then, aye, and she be a nice lass?"

"She is kind. A good friend."

"Better than me and me crew?"

Holt glances to the side. The smuggler offers a playful smile, pulling away and placing both of his hands on Holt's shoulders. "Think 'bout it, aye?"

Holt rolls his eyes, forcing a small smile in response. "…Aye. Goodnight, captain," he says, waving his hand, "sleep well, when you finally do."

CHAPTER FIFTY-SEVEN

"Is that alright?"
"Yes."
"It doesn't hurt too much, does it?"
"No."

Scarlett treats and bandages Esther's wounds with careful hands, marvelling at how different her skin is to that of a human's. It's not like the delicate petals of a rose, easily broken, but comparable to smooth and cold stone instead. Then again, there isn't much mermaids have in common with humans really – their forms, for one, are always long and slender. They don't have rounded hips or ample cleavage. Their faces are sharp-featured, cheeks never chubby, eyes always black. They all look the same save for their colourings and hair lengths. But humans…humans hardly ever look the same.

"It was dangerous, what you did," she states abruptly, rubbing a salve over one of the many gashes on Esther's right leg. "Jumping through glass like that. But…I admire your courage."

The mermaid winces in pain. Her eyes are scrunched closed, but Scarlett can easily tell that they are filled with tears. She finishes applying the salve, wraps a bandage around the wound she's tending to and sighs quietly. "You're a strong one, Esther."

"Thank you," comes the mermaid's tearful reply. She opens her eyes slowly, meeting Scarlett's own. "What's your name?"

"Ah, sorry. You told me your name but I didn't tell you mine…it's Scarlett."

"Because you have red hair."

"Yes."

"Will you…touch my cheek again…like you did earlier? Outside?"

A strange request, Scarlett thinks, but one she accepts anyway. She reaches out, her hand coming to rest upon Esther's face, and the mermaid sits up and leans into the touch. She curls close, craving the warmth Falké can no longer provide for her and sighs softly with a sincere and quiet, "Thank you for bringing me here, and helping me – I would have surely died otherwise. And thank you for this, right now. I can…seek comfort in companionship.

With an aching heart, Scarlett nods. "I know. I knew I had to help you when I saw you out there in the water, bleeding. I felt like it was my duty, if that makes sense. But listen – the mayor cannot know you are here."

"Why?"

"I think he's doing something…bad. I've seen things. Heard things. I…I shouldn't have done it, but I saw he got a letter from the Health Centre a while ago and of course I opened it, as I open all the letters unless they are very directly addressed to him, and well…it was strange. I Just, I didn't think it was *important*, just a letter. Perhaps just confirmation of an appointment, or something."

Esther picks at one of her bandages, her eyes downcast to it. "And? What about it? What did it *actually* say?"

"Oh. Well, it just -"

The sharp crack of thunder echoing causes the woman to divert her attention to the window. She stands quickly and hurries over to it, shutting it only seconds before a deluge follows and grey clouds deposit their load. She pauses for a moment, her hands trembling with shame, and slowly approaches a cabinet to her left.

The top drawer is filled with all sorts of things; she rummages through it for a few seconds until she finds what she is looking for: a long, ornate letter opener and a white envelope with the Illyrian Health Centre's stamp on the back. Her stomach cramps suddenly and she leans forward dropping the items, her arms outstretched to grasp onto the cabinet for support.

"Are you alright?" Esther queries. She watches as Scarlett regains her composure, pressing a hand against her abdomen.

"I'm fine. I'm just…I'm a little sick at the moment."

"Sick? Why?"

"I don't know. It hasn't gone away…I thought it would but it hasn't."

"How long have you had it?"

"Quite some time. But – but never mind. Look. Look at this."

She clasps for the letter and opener once again. "I kept it." She turns to Esther slowly, clutching the two items as if her life depends on it. "I kept the letter. I should have given it to him, but then…then he would know I opened it, and I feared he would hurt me so badly for invading his privacy. So I kept it. And the longer I have kept it the worse I have felt."

Once it's been handed to her, Esther removes the contents of the envelope.

Mayor Vanguard,

As it stands, the patients currently being treated at the Health Centre are in only temporary states of physical and/or mental distress, and thus we expect them to make a full recovery. Their deaths would be unwarranted and cause Illyrians to lose faith in the health system. We apologise profusely. If you wish to discuss this further, however, we are more than happy to do so.

Sincerely,

Jonathan Hemsworth.

"I don't understand," she admits. "What deaths are they talking about?"

Scarlett swallows hard. She turns the letter opener in her hands out of nervousness. "I think he's doing something with the patients, Esther. Taking them. Hurting them. Maybe falsifying their deaths or something, I don't know. Just please stay away from him. But he's busy tonight and he will be busy tomorrow, too. I am sure of that. So hopefully you won't need to engage with him whatsoever. As soon as your wounds have healed enough, you should leave."

"I don't want to leave."

Scarlett's eyes widen in shock. She drops the opener on the sheets. "Wh-what?"

"I am a young mermaid - I am barely twenty-four. I don't want to live the rest of my existence without him. Without Falké…"

"You want to…spend it with me instead? But I'm

not him, I don't even know your partner…"

"Please."

"N-no. No, you can't stay here. Jasper can be…rough sometimes. And dangerous. I don't want him to hurt you, if that's what he's doing down there –"

"Like you?" Esther interrupts sharply, passing the letter back and folding her battered, bandaged arms. "Like how he hurt you?"

This question seems to provoke Scarlett a little. She stands, uncomfortable, and runs a hand through her hair in stress before stuffing the letter back into the drawer from which it came. "No, no…he doesn't hurt me! Why would you say that?"

"You have bruises, and marks. Like somebody has been hitting you. And you're also sick right now, no doubt because of him."

"He just…you know, he can be a little rough, but he cares really. And I love him and – no. No, not that. I *loved* him. And I'm not sick right now because of him! I'm sick because I'm careless."

"I don't understand. You can't start loving somebody and then just stop. You can't break a connection like that, an eternal bond between two souls."

Scarlett silences herself for a moment. She slowly closes the drawer and looks over her shoulder at a confused looking Esther. "It may work like that for mermaids, Esther," she whispers, "but for humans you can just…move on if you want to. Sometimes even if you don't want to? Love is strange, I suppose. Nobody truly understands it. And Jasper, he, well, I don't think he understands it *at all*. He doesn't seem to care about anything but his job, really. And about

Illyria and Calawi and how he's going to fix this place."

Esther takes a deep breath, pressing her hands together and bringing them up to her face so her index fingers rest against her lips. "So," she starts simply, "why do you stay with him then? If he doesn't care about you, and he's taking people and hurting them, and you are clearly scared of him, why stay?"

For a long moment, Scarlett is unsure of what to do or say. She stands frozen, sucking on the inside of her cheeks while hot tears burn her eyes. She pushes them away with the palm of her hand and moves over to her closet.

"I-I need to change my clothes. I have your blood on them."

"Why?"

"If one of the servants sees, they might tell Jasper. He could get suspicious or something."

"No, that's not what I'm asking about. Why *stay*?"

Scarlett's body shudders as she sorts through the clothes. Finally, she can take no more; she grabs one of the outfits hanging in the closet, turns around, and flings it onto the chair to her right. "This is my *home*! Okay?! This is my home! Jasper is part of that and – and – it's my home. That's why!"

A beat passes. Suddenly, Scarlett turns on her heel and practically throws herself into the bathroom. As she is sick once again, Esther calls, "Do you need help?"

"I'm fine," comes the woman's weary response.

When she returns, the mermaid clears her throat and repeats, ever so softly, "You're sick because of him."

The realisation hits stronger than any force Scarlett has ever been subjected to. She rests her palm against her stomach, another wave of sickness moving through her, and wails softly. An intense mixture of both joy and disgust overcomes her so strongly that, without warning, she falls to her knees and breaks into a fit of sobs.

CHAPTER FIFTY-EIGHT

*T*wenty-nine. Thirty. Thirty-one.

The number of barnacles that have attached themselves to the underside of Caspian's boat is unbelievable. Of course, it's not too difficult for Astrid to remove them, though – she's strong, and above that she has somewhat of a bond with the arthropods. They *listen* to her. At least, most of them do. Some, like the one she has her fingers clenched around now, refuse to move.

"Hm. You're not going to cooperate, are you?"

Speaking to them is pointless, Astrid knows that. They aren't intelligent creatures, and can't understand a word of what she's saying, whether it's in mermish or human. Nevertheless, that doesn't stop her. It makes her feel like she has some control of the situation, or something – if she anthropomorphizes them, makes them seem conversational, it doesn't feel as mean to forcibly pull them from their home.

She *would* give them a place on her wrists. There are far too many of them, though, and introducing them all to her body would be overkill. She has enough of them on her as it is and she's grown fond of those little creatures over time. So much so that replacing them is out of the question. She drops the new barnacles into the water, assuming that they will sort themselves out eventually. Perhaps they may even latch onto another person's vessel in the future.

It's nice having these little chores to do. The crew can clean the boat from above, by all means, but have no way to mess with it from under the water. In that respect, she's entirely useful. And what's more, doing such things serves as an excellent distraction from the severity of the situation on board.

When she makes her way back onto the boat (it is moving very fast, but she's an extremely fast swimmer so that's not much of a problem) and walks down to the storerooms, the sound of voices captures her attention. There's no mystery as to who they belong to – the low, rumbling one is Caspian's, without a doubt, and the sharp, pedantic one is Holt's. They both come from Piper's room.

She opens the door.

"And that be the story of I how I lost me left eye," Caspian is saying as she enters. When he notices her, he forces a grin and adds, "Ahoy, Astrid! Come to join us, have ye? I be just talkin' 'bout me eye and how I lost it to th' blade of a ghost pirate! What 'ave ye been doin'?"

"Is that so? I have been removing the barnacles from the underside of your ship. I missed your story, and for that I apologise. Perhaps you can tell it to me another time, Caspian?"

The smuggler waves his hands. "Avest ye, Lassie! I be ready to tell yer it now! This lot can 'ear it again!"

"You can't be serious," Holt complains, groaning

loudly. "I'm not listening to another moment of your tall tales, Caspian! We all know you have both of your eyes, and there's no such thing as phantoms! Poppycock, I say!"

Caspian breathes in deeply, noticeably frustrated, and adjusts his hat. What nerve this prince has. Just the other night he was a quivering mess, lonely and desperate for affection. It's as if that never happened. As usual, he's being an argumentative little annoyance, like some sort of unswattable fly. "Right, listen 'ere, yer son of a biscuit eater," he snaps, "I 'ave the scars to prove it!"

"Pfft. You do not. Not *once* have I seen a scar upon your face."

"Yer can't even *see* me eye, yer landlubber! Shark bait, ye be!"

"I don't need to see your eye to know you are making up stories, and that is that!"

Holt's accusations earn him a *look* from Caspian, a look which tells the prince that despite how silly this argument appears to be, it shouldn't be taken lightly. He folds his arms across his chest and huffs. "Fine then, *smuggler*. If you lost your eye in some ghost fight, prove it."

"Aye, that I'll do!" comes Caspian, raising his hand to his face. He pauses for dramatic effect, and then brushes back a mass of dark hair to reveal a very stereotypical eyepatch. Upon seeing this, Holt is shocked into silence. The smuggler laughs at his reaction, and then proceeds to stand and dance about in a circle. There yer 'ave it, princey!" he sings, "bet ye be feelin' like a right fool now! Harharhar!"

Piper piques a bit, sitting up in her bed. "Woah what? You genuinely lost an eye?"

Caspian pauses for a moment. "Narrrr," he admits softly, "I be right as rain, lassie. Just think it looks mighty fine on me, yer know?" He removes the accessory and gestures to his perfectly fine pair of eyes.

Holt sighs in relief over the fact that he was wholly correct about the entire situation and comments, rather pretentiously, "How ludicrously dense. Trust *you* to wear an eyepatch just because it looks cool; you smugglers are utterly ridiculous. It's almost like you *want* to be pirates. And Piper, my dear, please don't strain yourself."

Reluctantly, the girl lies back down.

"Well, I can understand perfectly why Caspian wears the eyepatch," Astrid notes, tucking a strand of Piper's hair behind her ear, "I wear these fish bones in my ears because they look 'cool'. I wear the barnacles on my wrists because they look 'cool'. You wear your fancy royal clothing because it looks 'cool', do you not?"

The prince's cheeks redden in annoyance. "And for comfort reasons! I am not entirely obsessed with how I look you know! I have attributes other than my appearance!"

"Course yer do," Caspian agrees sarcastically, holding the eyepatch out to the mermaid. "Yer can 'ave this, lass. Since ye be so fond of decorating yerself. Think of it as a present, from me to yer."

Astrid cracks a grin, accepting the gift. She turns it in her hands for a moment, examining it, and then puts it over her right eye and turns her head to face Piper. "A present," she echoes, "how do I look?"

Piper tries to give her a small smile, but her brow is furrowed and her eyes filled with a pitiful distress.

"I love it," she says weakly, pain and weakness causing her to tremble under the sheets, "you look awesome. Super awesome. You're a proper smuggler now, huh?"

Caspian nods in agreement. "Yar! Ye be proper smuggler now!"

The room falls silent, and both Caspian and Holt busy themselves with unimportant things. Caspian messes with the cuffs of his jacket, adjusting them, and Holt rubs at the shiny buttons on his own with his sleeve as if to shine them. Neither speak, acting incredibly awkward, but Astrid doesn't seem to notice the uncomfortable tension. She leans forward, brushing a kiss against her connector's forehead.

"How long?" Piper asks meekly as she does so. "How long until we're there? Illyria. How long? And…will I survive it, Astrid? Please…tell me the truth."

The smuggler clears his throat and responds for Astrid, "We be arrivin' tomorrow, lassie. Ye be a strong lass. Yer gonna survive it."

"Yes. You will survive it," the mermaid agrees, "we will get you antibiotics the moment we arrive, I can assure you. And everything will be alright. And in the future, you tell me when something is hurting. Even if you feel embarrassed about it."

Piper nods her head slowly, but the action is painful enough to make her moan; she stops and curls in on herself instead. "Of course, Astrid. I'm sorry. I - I'm going to sleep now. Thank you, Holt, Caspian. For sitting with me and talking to me. And your story was cool, Cass. I liked it."

Caspian digs into the pockets of his jacket, picking at the fringes of lint inside as if doing so will help him cope better with the situation. "Ye be most welcome, lass."

There's a pause. An uncomfortably long pause. So uncomfortable, and so long, that both Caspian and Holt stand at the same time, step to the side, and walk into each other.

"Ah! Sorry. Yes. Aha. Yes. This way. Apologies, Caspian." The prince stumbles, quickly moving around his comrade Caspian and exiting the room with a simple, "have a pleasant evening, everybody. I must leave for my 'bedroom' now, for I am most certainly exhausted."

"Aye, I be headin' to me cabin," Caspian comments, clearing his throat. "Goodnigh' all of yers. Sleep well."

Out of exhaustion, Piper doesn't open her eyes. Instead, she makes a small noise of sorrowful acknowledgement. It's enough; Caspian and Holt leave, and she's left alone with Astrid once again.

CHAPTER FIFTY-NINE

*F*ear is an amorphous concept. Attempting to throw something at it is like trying to stab smoke – it'll do nothing but pass right through. Jasper, on the other hand ... Jasper is a physical entity. He has a soul. A body. A mind. He has a face that Scarlett sees through the smoke of his anger as he heads up the stairs, his feet banging out a quick and exasperated beat. "Scarlett!" he shouts, flinging open the door, "Did I not tell you to refrain from going inside my study? I *specifically* told you that and yet everything has been moved out of place! Now I can't find anything and I can't get my work done! Do you not care about my mental health whatsoever?!"

Jasper isn't 'fear', but he certainly represents it as much as he physically can. When he rushes over to her, fists clenched and eyes narrowed behind the – what is that? A gas mask? – in pure *hatred,* she feels nothing but frightened. "I – I just – well I didn't mean to, it just slipped my mind! I just went in to tidy a bit. I'm so sorry, I'll never do that again -"

His quick glance to the bed where Esther lies solidifies her fear further. He moves his head ever so slightly, not quite a nod but the merest tilt, and his eyes make an urgent, angry gesture all on their own. Her lungs suck greedily for air when she sees it.

Instantly she finds the need to stammer out an explanation. Something. Anything. "I just –"

"What the *hell* are you doing up here?"

"Nothing."

"Nothing?! This is *nothing* to you, is it?!"

"I'm not – I'm not sleeping with a mermaid, if that's what you think!"

"Then care to explain why the mermaid is *in our bed?*"

"I just – she was injured, I had to help."

He steps forwards and she moves hurriedly back.

"Why is it that every time I leave you alone you manage to cause some kind of disaster in this household?! What the hell are you wearing then, if this is *nothing?*"

She looks down at herself and clears her throat. She had just begun changing into some clean clothes and still has some of her undergarments showing; only a navy coloured blouse, unbuttoned, acts as a shield on her torso from being almost entirely exposed. Her legs are bare. On the floor at her feet is a matching bustled skirt. This outfit, this *particular* outfit, was the first one Jasper bought for her when she came to live here. She wore it to dinner on their first night together. Grilled calamari with capers and anchovy. A side of rosemary-infused chickpeas. Pinot grigio wine. For dessert, meringues. She can remember the night perfectly, and highly doubts he can remember when this even happened, let alone the intricate details involved like food and dresses and wine.

"It's nothing – I just was changing because – I went outside and my clothes got wet and she's – well look, she's injured, she's bleeding. I got blood on my outfit so I was changing."

"Injured."

"Yes, she's injured."

Esther nods slowly in confirmation of Scarlett's statement, her lips pressed tightly together. She looks around at the door uneasily, wondering just how capable she is of escaping if need be. She's in no state to fight, that's for sure. Especially not on land.

Jasper watches her judgingly. "And did it not cross your mind that you shouldn't be undressing in front of anybody but me, Scarlett? No matter the reason?"

"Jasper! Bloodstains! And it was so uncomfortable with my clothes wet."

He moves closer and closer. Scarlett cowers, raising her arms above her head protectively. "Please," she whispers pathetically, tears beginning to stream down her cheeks. "Please don't hurt her. She can't fight you, she's been injured. She lost her partner, Jasper! She lost her partner."

"I wouldn't worry so much about the mermaid, Scarlett," he warns. "I'd worry about yourself. You never shut up. You never behave. Why do I put up with you?! By God, I love you but you bring out the worst in me -"

"I'm pregnant, Jasper!" she interrupts him quickly. "I have a baby growing inside me! Please don't hurt me. You'll hurt them, you'll hurt them, you'll hurt them."

Silence.

The man presses his tongue against his teeth. His

eyes wander down to Scarlett's stomach and then back up again. *That's why she's been sick,* he tells himself, cursing his foolish mind for not coming to this conclusion sooner. *I should have known.*

For a fleeting few seconds, he looks…calm. Relaxed. But then, coolly, he states, "Get rid of it."

"What?"

"Get rid of it."

"I – no please. Please. Jasper! You know how much we wanted this!"

"You. How much *you* wanted this. Get rid of it, or I'll get rid of it for you."

"Jasper!"

"Fine. Seems you've picked the latter -"

The next thing Jasper feels is an awful lot of discomfort in his chest. His head pounds to the beat of his now racing heart, his moon-like eyes burn and his vision becomes somewhat fuzzed around the edges. His tongue feels very much like sandpaper all of a sudden, as if he has woken from a terrible hangover. What concerns him the most, however, is the blood blooming from his torso.

A cry threatens to spill from his lips, his smug demeanour stuttering and jaw slackening. "You bloody - bitch," he hisses, struggling to speak, "what - have you - done?"

He staggers backwards and leans weakly against the wall, mind reeling and breath shallow. Her eyes, wide and anguished, meet his as she steps back. The golden letter opener in her shaking hand has been stained with blood.

"*You liar!*" she screams suddenly, and without warning, drives the object into his chest again. And again. And again. His legs buckle and without

Scarlett's support he falls to the ground with a loud moan of pain. She kneels beside him, her weapon lifted, and he strains to escape as the blood spills out of him and onto the carpet.

"You liar! You don't love me, not at all! You liar! You liar! I loved you! I loved you and you hurt me! You lied to me! Go to hell! *Go straight to hell!*"

Any attempts to shout for assistance fail. There's too much blood in his mouth, so much that he can't keep it behind his lips. It's trickling down his chin, into the gas mask. Even if he managed to cry out clear enough, he knows very well that nobody would come to his aid. His staff ignore the screams and yells when he's with Scarlett; he instructed them to do so.

Scarlett pulls off his mask in anger, and her nearly concrete resolve fractures at the sight of him trying to speak, her disloyalty evident in his eyes. She finds herself choking sobs, letting go of him and reeling back with the bloody weapon in her hands. When she reaches the bed, still facing him, he lurches forward on the floor with an agonising moan as if he's trying to call her back. His normally silvery eyes now look a washed-out grey in contrast to his pale skin. His lips seem thin and colourless, unkissable, untouchable. She turns her back to him and throws the mask on the floor, crying.

No more.

His lips move soundlessly, and then close permanently.

Esther blinks twice in shock. "You killed him," she breathes.

Scarlett swallows thickly, her lips quivering. She stares down at the body and says, ever so softly, "I – I – know. I know. I know."

CHAPTER SIXTY

The remainder of the journey back to Illyria is hazy to Piper. The world revolves around the wretched pain in her body. The pounding headache. The fact she can barely keep anything down; even drinking water has become difficult, so much so that Astrid has had to help her swallow. The silk nightdress from Caspian's "clothing loot" that she's been dressed in has quickly become damp with sweat. Her fever is high, and she's become light-headed.

The shutter of her mind opens only on occasion; when Lenka brings her food, when Caspian or Holt – in some instances, both of them - check on her, when Astrid sings to her or slips into the hammock beside her.

This time, when she opens her eyes, something is *different*. She's still wrapped in a blanket, but she isn't in her hammock. Instead, she's being carried, pressed against Astrid's chest, and cold air is whipping her face. She's not in the storeroom anymore. Astrid is speaking and she barely catches a sentence of it before mumbling, "Astrid…? Am I dead?"

The mermaid looks down at her. "Not dead," she

confirms.

Blinking several times as she attempts to make sense of herself and her surroundings, Piper groans softly in pain. "Where are we?"

"We just docked - we're back in Illyria. The vessel has been cleverly disguised as a simple trading ship by Caspian's crew. The work on it is impeccable and very little effort was required to bypass the Illyrian security. We're heading away from the dock now, and taking you to the Health Centre for antibiotics. Holt is coming with us, as is Cadmus for protection's sake, but Caspian is staying aboard ship – ready to sail us back out when we need to leave. It's night-time, we should be quiet."

The girl nods wearily. "Okay…and by the way, you look like an angel or something."

"Angels have wings and belong in the sky. I have a tail and belong in the sea. We are drastically different."

"Astrid…"

"I know, I apologise. You were complimenting me – thank you."

Back in Illyria.

Piper shuffles uncomfortably in Astrid's arms. It's strange to be back here. Back to the place she has called home for her entire life. It doesn't feel like home now. It's just a decaying nation of misery that wants her seized and most likely killed. There's nothing here for her anymore, save from Elvira and Falké, her only blood relatives. She wonders how they are and if they'd be particularly upset to discover she'd died thanks to an infection. Falké would, maybe. He wouldn't admit it outright of course, but he *would* feel a little sad at least. She's not so sure about Elvira, though.

She leans forwards until her head fits in the crook of Astrid's neck. It's no warmer than having her face exposed to the wind but it's certainly more comforting. With her ear pressed to the smooth skin she attempts to detect a heartbeat. Quiet. She falls into temptation and basks into the blissful darkness behind her eyelids for a short while.

They arrive at the Illyrian Health Centre quickly. According to the big clock above its main doors, it's exactly 10:30 pm. The building is, as expected, quiet due to the time. That's good.

"Okay, listen," Astrid speaks up. "From the moment we step through these doors, we're on a time limit. Piper is going to be reported to be back in Illyria and the mayor *will* send people to come and get her and bring her to him. Of course, the doctors will still treat her but they're obligated to report her. We should consider it inevitable. The moment she's in a stable condition – and I mean it – we have to get back out of here."

Holt nods.

The inside of the Health Centre smells strongly of disinfectant. It's not a nice, clean smell, but more an overpowering stench that drives Holt and Cadmus to scrunch up their faces the moment they walk through the doors. "Disgusting," Holt mumbles, and his guard nods. Disgusting indeed. He much prefers the delicate, floral notes of Holt's perfumes, or the warm vanilla and strawberry found when Lenka bakes her favourite cakes. And Lenka in general, actually. He instantly regrets coming on this journey at the thought of her; staying on the ship with Caspian, she assured him she would be fine and that he ought to carry out his duty and guard the prince. Still, he is unsettled, contemplating what is more important to him as of late: duty, or her. He clears his throat and continues onwards.

"It smells quite strongly in here, doesn't it?" Astrid asks as they approach reception, "I wonder how Elvira – Piper's aunt, in case you were unaware, Cadmus –stands this every day. Perhaps the people working and staying here are just so accustomed to it that they don't notice."

"That's what I was just commenting on, Astrid," Holt tells her, rolling his eyes. "When I said disgusting it was in regards to the *stench*."

"Oh, I assumed it was about the surroundings in general."

"It was not. But you make a valid point, for that too makes me uncomfortable. I'll have you know in Caldisa -"

"Now is not the time to speak of our great kingdom, your highness." Cadmus glances across at Holt with raised eyebrows. "As wonderful as it is, we have other things to concern ourselves over."

Holt presses his lips together, turning his head away. "Fine," he grumbles. And after a moment, adds a reluctant and quiet, "I know. You're right."

The receptionist looks unfriendly. She has raven coloured hair, like Caspian, but it's shoulder length and extremely curly. Her sharp blue eyes skim over the group, judging, and then she leans forwards and asks calmly, "Can I help you?"

"She has an infection," Astrid explains, "needs antibiotics. She cut her knee on some coral and it's now serious."

"Alright." The woman presses two buttons on her

desk, one of which seems to be calling for a doctor. The other is red, and Astrid assumes *that* one is calling for security. "Room thirteen. We'd rather *you* stay outside. We don't host mermaids in here."

Astrid narrows her eyes. "You do now."

She turns, carrying Piper down the hall and towards room thirteen. Holt offers an apologetic shrug to the receptionist, who stares daggers, and then hurries after the two girls.

The doctor that greets them seems to be practically swamped in paperwork. There are sheets and notes everywhere. As they walk through the door a quick, "Wait just a minute there!" comes from the corner of the room and a short, thin-chested man with thick, dusty blond hair desperately tries to organise himself. A bunch of folders propped up beside his desk have tumbled to the ground; he's crouched down and shoving them all into his arms. When he glances up to see Piper, he has to blink twice.

"You're the girl -"

Astrid interrupts, laying Piper onto the empty bed in the room. "Yes, and security have already been informed. But before she goes anywhere, you're going to do your job and treat her. She needs antibiotics and she needs them immediately."

He clears his throat and nods, adjusting his glasses and moving over to her. He checks her wound with careful fingers, mumbling things to himself. "Yes. Yes. I see. And what did she cut it on? Rock?"

"Reef. Coral."

"I see. She needs antibiotics."

"I said that already."

"Ah…yes…yes you did. Sorry."

The man lifts his chin, running his tongue over his top lip. He proceeds to clean the wound, apply some kind of salve, and then administers antibiotics. The process doesn't take particularly long but feels like an eternity to Piper. She tries not to squirm despite her discomfort and when the two Health Centre security personnel show up, acts as calm as she can. Their disturbingly serene expressions are enough to make her lose face, though. A high whine escapes her throat like the sound of a wounded dog and her whole body begins to shake as she cries, "I didn't hear anything! Don't take me away!"

She's trying and failing to choke the sobs with her fingers.

Holt casts a sympathetic glance at her and then reaches out and moves her hands from her face, gently holding one. Quivering, she grips his hand tightly as he starts stroking hers. "You are going to be fine," he assures her softly.

He doesn't know if that's true, but he wants to believe it.

Chapter Sixty-One

*J*asper Vanguard's manor house functions perfectly for the remainder of the day. The chefs prepare lunch and dinner; slicing, dicing, baking and boiling. The maids continue cleaning, folding laundry and dusting the windowsills. The advisors plan and schedule the coming days, shifting meetings and adjusting events. All remain oblivious to their employer's death.

It's only when Tobias, having been notified of the Health Centre's discovery, finds Jasper that everything changes. Suddenly, nothing is perfect. He's not even entirely sure the corpse he finds *is* Jasper due to its blood-covered state, but after closer inspection he recognises the clothes. The hair. Those silvery eyes, now dulled grey.

The news spreads quickly through the manor house. By the time the military leaders and authorities discover who is to blame, Esther and Scarlett are gone.

CHAPTER SIXTY-TWO

ccording to authorities, the murder occurred at exactly nine forty pm on Tuesday night. The murder weapon, a golden, ornate letter opener, was plunged into his chest a total of thirteen times. It's speculated that the kill was a crime of passion committed by Jasper Vanguard's long-term partner, Scarlett Vanguard. Sources say that upon discovery, blood from both Mayor Vanguard and an unidentified mermaid were found at the scene, but there is no decisive evidence to confirm this yet."

Piper stares down at the newspaper she's been given. It all makes sense now – earlier in the week, when she first arrived at the Health Centre, security had descended upon her room in minutes. She sobbed and begged for them to leave…and they did. At first, she thought it was a miracle; that they felt sorry for her and genuinely wanted to help. They informed her that there had been a change of plans and she is to continue living normally and that was that. No wonder they abandoned their mission quickly – there was nobody in charge of it anymore.

"There have been many rumours and speculations regarding who will step up – or who has already stepped up – as mayor, but I can provide no solid information as of now. Stay tuned,

dear readers, for the dawn of a new Illyria."

"Huh."

Astrid raises her eyebrows as she reads over her connector's shoulder. "Well, it looks like Jasper Vanguard won't be much of a problem for us anymore, Piper."

"...So...I guess I can go home if I wanted to."

"I guess you can."

The doctor – they've learnt his name is Dr Frederik Arwing now – takes a deep breath, folds his hands together in front of him, and looks down. "Listen," he starts, "Piper Tourneau. Before you leave the Health Centre, you ought to know about your family. Well, how do I start...your aunt – Elvira – she doesn't work here anymore."

"She doesn't?"

He rummages through one of his many folders then, proceeding to take out two more newspapers. He runs a hand over his hair to push it off of his forehead, and slowly hands them to her. The first, an article on her cousin's murder. The second, an article on her aunt's.

"I'll...give you a moment," he says quietly, and scurries out of the room.

Piper stares down at the articles. If the words she's reading aren't bad enough, the pictures make it worse; in both of them, her relatives are smiling. They look happy. Anguish swallows her whole, and soon enough she can no longer see the paper in front of her. All she can see is grief. Grief, thick and black unfurling in front of her like a runway to despair. The weight of her guilt settles with the force of a galaxy colliding upon her and she chokes sobs as she runs her trembling fingers over the photographs. She shouldn't have left. She shouldn't have gone. She shouldn't have abandoned them. With a shaky, frail little voice, she whimpers, "Both of them are dead. Both of them. My whole *family* is dead."

"Oh heavens…" Holt mutters almost imperceptibly, taking one of the newspapers and reading the print with a frown. "I am…so sorry, Piper."

Piper shakes her head, reaching up to the mermaid. It's easy to see she wants to be held, so that's what Astrid does; she climbs onto the bed beside her, taking her in her arms. Piper leans forwards until the crown of her head presses against Astrid's chest, and starts weeping openly. Thinking of the abuse she received from Elvira is comforting in regards to *her* death, but there's nothing to stop her heart from falling heavy over Falké's. They were so close in the past, and she'd always secretly hoped that one day they'd be close again. That maybe he'd stop drinking and start bettering himself.

He'll never have the opportunity now, she thinks. *He'll never be able to change because he's gone. He's gone forever. Like everybody else.*

"My whole family," she says through her tears, her breathing ragged and fast, "all of them, they're all gone. All of them. My mother, my father, my aunt and cousin -"

"Not all of your family, Piper," Holt interrupts, forcing a smile. "You are my family too. Me and Caspian, and his crew, and Lenka and Cadmus."

He looks over at Cadmus for confirmation, and is met with a nod.

"And of course we mustn't forget Astrid, your partner."

"Ah…yeah…yeah. You're right. I just…wish I had the others too."

"Of course you do. I'm sorry," Astrid whispers, stroking the girl's soft brown hair.

I'm not sorry.

Piper shakes her head. "It's not your fault any of them are gone, Astrid."

It is.

And then, unexpectedly, she kisses Astrid. She kisses her while in tears with enough passion to press *her* back against the pillows, to steal the breath from *her* lungs. It shocks the mermaid. She's so unprepared that, for once, she doesn't have an appropriate reaction. Instead, she just stares forwards, black eyes wide and gleaming. And unbeknownst to Piper, Cadmus, *or* Holt, she thinks of how utterly disappointed she is that pretty much the entirety of the Tourneau family is dead. Well, all good things have to come to an end eventually.

"I love you," Piper whispers, and she is telling the truth.

"I love you too," Astrid responds, and she isn't.

CHAPTER SIXTY-THREE

The morning sun streams brightly through the kitchen window of Mahina House and onto the floor, which is newly washed. Piper stands motionless at the doorway with the mop in her hands, watching it shine in the light with all the brilliance of a polished antique. It's as if nothing bad has happened here, as if nobody died.

She wept in mourning all night until she had no more tears left. If her heart was not already broken a dozen times over, it would have broken again at the sight of this kitchen. That and the knowledge that no matter how many times she cleans it the death will continue to cling to every tile, every wall. At least, for a long time. It will leave eventually, as it did after her parents died.

"Astrid," comes her voice, hoarsely. "Has Caspian already left?"

"No. He's waiting for us."

Astrid joins her at the doorway with various possessions of Piper's in her arms, ready to be taken to the ship. "Are you ready to go?" she adds after a pause and Piper shakes her head.

"I don't want to go."

"What?"

"I don't want to go. I want to stay here, at home. I want this house to be good again. Happy again."

The mermaid raises her eyebrows, watching as Piper places the mop to the side and picks up a rag, dampening it in the sink before wiping at the windows. Cleaning and washing and tidying their little world. "You want to stay in Illyria? You know Holt, Cadmus, and Lenka are going with Caspian though, right? Holt wants to go back to Caldisa, get married like he was supposed to. Cadmus and Lenka want to go home. We can go with them and visit their kingdom. You'd like it there, it's got much nicer weather."

"No."

"No?"

"Let's stay here, Astrid," Piper implores, "let's stay here, and if we want to go to Caldisa then… then nothing is stopping us in the future, right? Nothing is stopping us. And Caspian will surely dock in Illyria again, we will see him again. Won't we?"

"We can ask."

"Can we? Can we ask now?"

Astrid nods, putting down Piper's things. "Fine. I'm not *adverse* to staying here, anyway. I have some things that are particularly…precious to me underwater; it would be irritating if someone were to take them for themselves while I was absent. If I stay here, I can defend such things shall the need arise. Although I'm not sure why any of the other mermaids would want those things but you never know. The young ones tend to like shiny things especially. Let's make haste then, we don't want to keep him waiting too long."

The journey to Caspian's ship is quick and hurried. Despite having been on the (rather rocky) road to recovery for the past three days, Piper's body protests to such fast-paced activity and it's not long before Astrid picks her up and carries her. They are happy to see that the vessel is indeed still docked, still masquerading as a merchant's ship, and the crew wave to them as they approach.

"Oh! Piper, Astrid!" Lenka calls once they are on board, rushing over with Cadmus in tow. She is carrying a variety of ingredients in a cloth bundle and looks terribly excited, much to Cadmus' amusement.

"We got a few things from the market," Cadmus tells Piper and Astrid, gesturing to the excited handmaiden. "She's excited to make some new dishes for you."

Lenka nods eagerly. "I'm going to start with some biscuits, but they shall have *ginger* inside and pack quite a punch!" Upon noticing Piper's expression, she quickly adds, "A good punch though, I promise! You like ginger, don't you? I know it is quite a bold taste, so it's not for everyone."

"I er – I mean, I'm sure they'll be lovely, Lenka. But," Piper shuffles her feet. "But I won't be here to taste them. I mean, here on this ship. I er – no, *we* – we came to say goodbye. We're going to stay here in Illyria."

"Oh." Lenka pauses for a moment, processing this information. "I – well, I can understand that perfectly. Prince Holt informed us of the situation, of how you aren't on the run any more. Of course you want to just…stay here if you can. We want to go home too. Don't we Cadmus?"

Cadmus nods.

She continues. "Will we be seeing you again?"

"Oh of course! I want to come visit Caldisa."

"We shall see you there then," Cadmus says. He offers a smile and shakes Astrid's hand, followed by Piper's. "Farewell, both of you. We ought to go put these ingredients away in the galley, Lenka."

"Ah, yes!" she bows to Piper and Astrid. "We will do so now. Oh, and his highness is in our storeroom for the time being, if you are wanting to say goodbye to him too?"

Piper nods, and with one last string of goodbyes Holt's handmaiden and guard have left her side.

As said, Holt is in his storeroom; crouched down and mumbling quietly to himself as he organises his clothes into neat piles. He is very much absorbed in his task, so much so that Piper not only has to clear her throat quite loudly, but also has to speak his name to get his attention.

"Holt?"

He sways back in theatrical alarm, clutching at his chest. "Piper! Astrid!" he announces, "goodness me! You scared the life out of me. Don't creep up on me like that, it's quite nasty." He purses his lips. "But I am glad you're here. Let's get this blasted ship back on the ocean, I say. You *are* feeling better, yes? Your leg isn't hurting anymore? I trust Astrid is making sure you take your antibiotics." He looks accusingly at the mermaid, who stares back for a moment before rolling her dark eyes. "I am not her mother," she reminds him, "she can handle taking medication on her own, Holt."

"Well you never know; she may forget to take a dose or something. Can't be too careful. A reminder doesn't hurt." He brushes some hair out of his face and tucks it behind his ear before sighing dramatically. "Well, shall we go then? Get back to the endless blue?" And with a rather unenthusiastic tone adds, "Caldisa here we come."

"Actually, Holt." Piper hesitates, drawing her lower lip between her teeth as she contemplates how to approach such a confession. "We want to stay here. In Illyria. Just…I don't want to leave my house again. I – I have so many memories there and…I want to recover here. I'm not – well, I'm not ready to go sailing again, honestly."

Holt blinks twice. He is about to protest, about to make a fuss. But she looks so sorrowful, so sincere. He just can't.

"Right," he murmurs, clearing his throat. "Right, okay. Yes, I – well yes, I can understand that. Just I'm getting married soon. Well, by soon I mean instantly; I wouldn't be surprised if my parents dragged me into the ceremony the moment my feet touch Caldisian soil. Just, you are invited. So I suppose you will miss the event…" He pauses. "But, that's alright. Of course that's alright."

"I'm sorry," Piper supplies. "I would come but I just…I really need to stay here, you know? So much has happened. I need to recover from it all, I think. I'm sorry."

He waves his hand dismissively. "Oh! Piper, don't be. Honestly, I doubt the event will be that exciting, anyway. Royal weddings aren't *that* big of a deal."

Astrid raises an eyebrow. She highly doubts royal weddings aren't 'that big of a deal' but is in no way compelled argue against his claim. He's clearly trying to make Piper feel better, after all. She has no qualms with that. "It would probably look strange for an Illyrian 'commoner' to attend a Caldisian royal wedding anyway," she notes, shrugging her sharp shoulders. "We wouldn't want to damage your sterling reputation, Holt."

"My sterling reputation," he parrots, looking to the side with an embarrassed, quiet laugh. "I think at the moment it is closer to scrap metal, Astrid. Especially after my running away, and such. Well, you will both come to visit after at some point, then?"

"Yes, of course we'll come visit you in your kingdom!" Piper exclaims, "as soon as I'm ready for more adventures I promise you I will be there."

He smiles weakly, nodding. "Alright. Have you told Caspian the news?"

"Not yet," Astrid cuts in, "where is he? We only just got onto the ship. We've spoken to Cadmus and Lenka, since they were on deck. You were the next person we came across – aside from the general crew, of course."

"Told me what, mateys?" The smuggler echoes from the doorway, emerging from the doorway and walking in with a grin. Today he has decorated his eyes with some kind of makeup, one that Piper recognises as most definitely Illyrian. They are shadowed with charcoal and purple on both the upper lids and underneath the eyes, redolent of two spreading bruises. Still, it's not *ugly* or displeasing to look at it, even. Piper quite likes it.

"Hello Caspian," she states. "I like your eyeshadow."

"Aye, me crew found it fer me at yer market. Ye be makin' plans in 'ere without me?"

"They want to stay in Illyria." Holt can't help but

spill the information before the girls have the chance. "Piper isn't ready to leave again just yet. Also, I think the eye makeup looks much too...exaggerated, but far be it from me suggest anything to you, Caspian. You practically never take my wonderful advice. Gold and black would have looked *much* better. *And* it would match your outfit."

Caspian ignores Holt's comments on his new 'look', instead opting to focus on Piper's imminent absence from his crew. "Not ready to leave just yet, aye?" he echoes, wondering if he *should* acquire some golden eyeshadow at some point. It wouldn't hurt, and it would shut Holt up. He also admits (to himself only) that it would look very dashing indeed. Much more so than purple.

Piper looks to the side, shameful of her decision. Perhaps it is the wrong one? She doesn't want to disappoint Holt, nor Caspian, but…

A soft pressure against her ankles causes her to look down. She peers at the ground and finds herself staring into the gaze of Vivo, who pushes her head against Piper's leg, purring thunderously. Piper smiles softly before kneeling to pet her properly. "Sorry," she says to both the feline and her friends, "I would like to see you all soon though. Maybe you can dock in Illyria again before long, Caspian? In a few months, perhaps?" And then quietly she adds, "Please?"

Caspian adjusts his hat with an affirmative, "Alrigh' lassie. 'Course I'll come an' dock in yer fine little Illyria. Ye be welcome on me ship any time, yer hear?"

When Piper stands she finds herself being pulled into a warm, tight hug. "Here ya go," says Caspian, and he pushes something cold and hard into her hand. For a moment she is confused, but when she looks down to see a small hand-held mirror she can't help but smile. "A mirror," she notes, "like Sullivan Sands?"

"Like Sullivan Sands," he echoes. "Keep it with yer 'til we meet again."

He looks over at Astrid and nods. "I trust I'll be seein' ya again too, lass."

"Perhaps. I will think about it. You didn't give me a present like *that*. Only a simple eyepatch."

This prompts a laugh from Caspian, a harsh booming sound that fills the whole cabin. "Ye be the funniest mermaid I know!"

"I am the only mermaid you know."

"Alrigh' alrigh'…yer 'ave a point."

Holt clears his throat. "We ought to get going then," he mutters, "shouldn't stay around here any longer than we need to, really. I…well, goodbye, Astrid."

Astrid curls her hands around her hips. "Goodbye, Prince Holt Davori of Caldisa."

He shakes his head with a smile. "Just Holt is more than fine. And…goodbye, Piper. I must admit I have gotten so very fond of you, it is hard to say goodbye."

Piper sighs softly and puts her arms around him, still clutching the mirror. He is so warm. "It's hard to say goodbye to you too. But we will see each other again soon, I promise. I want to come and see your kingdom, you've made it sound so grand and brilliant."

"It is."

She pulls away and steps back to stand with Astrid.

"I hope you have a good journey to Caldisa, and I hope your wedding goes well. Perhaps you can write to me and tell me of it all?"

"I hope so too, and I shall."

When Astrid and Piper descend from the ship and onto the Decks, there is a loud call of "Goodbye, lassies!" from the crew, which makes Piper's heart lurch. She raises her hand in a wave, a sad smile on her face, and responds, "Goodbye!"

Eventually, Caspian's ship becomes nothing more than a dot on the horizon. Piper looks around at Astrid, clutching her hand. Quietly she whispers, "You won't leave me, will you?"

The mermaid moves back slightly and tilts her head to the side.

She still loves me so much despite what I have done to her, to her family, she thinks. *That's funny.*

"I won't leave you," she confirms. "At least, not yet." She takes the mirror from her connector's hand and glances into it, at her cold black eyes and sharp, defined jaw. "But mermaids don't live forever, you know, and I am quite old."

"How many years do you think you have left? I know you told me you stopped counting your age a long time ago, but…"

Astrid lowers the mirror and looks into the distance for a moment, watching the waves. "If I live the average length of time for a mermaid, then perhaps…

thirteen?"

ABOUT THE AUTHOR

Mina Rose lives just outside of London in a small town whose only claim to fame is that some of the local wild rabbits are black – a somewhat fortunate fact since it aligns beautifully with her personality and *aesthetic*.

Mermicide

Printed in Great Britain
by Amazon